EMPIRE
OF
DUST

✦ ✦ ✦

DAW Books proudly presents
the novels of Jacey Bedford:

The Psi-Tech Novels

EMPIRE OF DUST
*CROSSWAYS**

*Coming soon from DAW Books

EMPIRE
OF
DUST

♦ ♦ ♦

A PSI-TECH NOVEL

JACEY BEDFORD

DAW BOOKS, INC.
DONALD A. WOLLHEIM, FOUNDER
375 Hudson Street, New York, NY 10014

ELIZABETH R. WOLLHEIM
SHEILA E. GILBERT
PUBLISHERS
http://www.dawbooks.com

First Printing, November 2014
1   2   3   4   5   6   7   8   9

Acknowledgments

I wish I could say that this book sprang from my pen fully formed, but it didn't. Like any book it's a team effort, though any and all mistakes are mine.

My thanks to all at DAW and especially to my editor, Sheila Gilbert, for ideas, patience, gentle guidance, and for commissioning Stephan Martiniere to do the cover. Thanks also to my agent Amy Boggs, and all at Donald Maass Literary Agency, for enthusiasm and expertise.

Without a series of serendipitous connections from the folk music community (via Felicia Dale) to writer Elizabeth Ann Scarborough, who gave me my first encouragement and short story sale, I might never have got this far.

Many people, possibly too many to mention individually, have contributed information, ideas, and encouragement. They include writers from the annual Milford UK Writers' Conferences, the Recog email crit group, and from the r.a.sf.c. and r.a.sf.w usenet newsgroups for SF writers and readers. You know who you are.

Special thanks for connections and corrections above and beyond the call of duty to: Liz Williams, N. M. Browne, Tina Anghelatos, Carl Allery, Helen Hall, John Moran, Sue Thomason, Jaine Fenn, Kari Sperring, and Hilary Spencer.

Technical thanks to knife-throwing expert John Taylor, to Mike O'Connor OBE for small aircraft design, to Rory Newman for medical advice, and to Alastair Reynolds for invoking Einstein at Milford back in 1998 when I would happily have fallen into the trap of FTL travel.

Last but never least, an extra-special thank-you and much love to my husband, Brian, and offspring, Ghillan and Joe, for their forbearance and for getting their own dinner more times than I care to admit, and to my mum, Joan Lockyer, whose encouragement unleashed my writing demon at the tender age of five.

Chapter One

FLIGHT

I'M DEAD IF I DON'T GET OUT OF HERE.

Cara Carlinni stared at the display on the public terminal. She gripped the edge of the console, feeling dizzy and sick. Too many cups of caff, not enough food.

Her fellow workers erupted from Devantec's packing plant, one or two trying the other terminals in the bay just off the main walkway, and discovering, as she had when she first took the dead-end job, that this was the only functioning link.

She'd scooted out ahead of the crowd to grab it.

Good that she had. At least she was forewarned. What the hell was an Alphacorp ship doing here if not looking for something, or someone? What were the odds *that* someone was her?

She'd been barely one jump ahead of them on El Arish, and on Shalla colony she'd spotted wanted posters and moved on quickly, thankful that she'd ducked port immigration by hitching a flight with a smuggler.

She'd spoken to a man on Shalla who'd once been a low-grade Psi-Mech for the Rowan Corporation, and who was now living off the grid, with a new identity furnished by an organization that was definitely not the right side of legal. On his advice she'd come all the way out to Station Mirrimar-14 chasing rumors of a breakaway group of psi-techs, but she hadn't found them. If they were here, they were well-hidden and well-shielded.

She swallowed bile and checked the screen again, focusing on the immediate problem—a light passenger transport—a ship design she recognized as an unmarked Alphacorp Scout. It threaded along the flight corridor toward the passenger terminal, past the heavy freighters lined up for docking in the space station's commercial bays.

"Hey, Carlinni, you coming to Sam's with the rest of us?" Jussaro, her packing line partner, broke his stride.

He was always friendly, but she kept her distance outside of working hours. A purple-black-skinned, genetically engineered exotic from the Hollands System, he'd once been a high-grade Telepath until being busted for some misdemeanor he wouldn't admit to.

They'd killed his implant. He was *alone* and *silent*.

Permanently.

He was the thing she most dreaded becoming.

She'd stepped out of line, bigtime, but they hadn't caught her yet. If they did, she'd be damn lucky to end up like Jussaro. More than likely they'd just fry her brain from the inside out and have done with it.

"Not tonight." She forced a smile and edged in front of the screen so Jussaro couldn't see what she was checking.

"Why not? Got a hot date?"

"Maybe."

"Ha!" His laugh was more like a bark. Then he frowned, the hooded ridges above his eyes drawing together in a serious case of monobrow. "You in trouble, Carlinni?" He stepped closer and lowered his voice. "You are!"

Your average decommissioned psi-tech went nuts, but Jussaro was a rare survivor. Had he managed to retain his underlying telepathy? If so, that was a minor miracle in itself. Tonight he was entirely too quick on the uptake.

She curbed the need to switch on her implant. They could trace her as soon as she used it. Keep it powered down. She was so integrated with her tech that whatever natural talent she'd started out with had been subsumed. It might still be there, but she hoped she'd never have to find out the hard way.

"Quit my case, Jussaro. You're not my dad."

"Maybe I should have been, and then you wouldn't be in trouble in the first place."

"I told you, I'm not . . . I . . . Look, I can handle it. All right?"

"All right. All right. I get it. Keep my nose out." He stepped away, both hands up in a gesture of surrender.

She shrugged. "Look, Jussaro, if ever I need a dad, I'll adopt you, okay?"

"It's a deal. Don't forget." He waved at her as he rejoined the flow of workers.

She returned her attention to the screen. The Scout had joined the docking tailback. That gave her a couple of hours at most. The temptation to pop a tranq prickled her scalp while she waited for the passenger manifest to load into the system. It flashed, and she pulled up the information. Rosen, Forrest, and Byrne—three names she didn't recognize, listed as businessmen. She checked the crew. The pilot was Robert Craike.

Shit!

Her heart began to race, and her skin turned clammy. To hell with it! She popped a tranq anyway, and felt it buffer the hunger to connect with her implant.

Shit! Shit! Shit!

She fought down panic. Avoiding Alphacorp's regular security was one thing, but Craike was a psi-tech Finder.

There had to be a way out. *Think!*

"You finished with that terminal or do you want to marry it?" A dumpy woman in a red coverall had come up behind her.

"Finished. It's yours." Cara eased up on her death grip, blanked the screen, and turned toward the go-flow station, her thoughts firing in several different directions at once.

Craike was the brawn to Ari van Blaiden's brain. Going up against him would be almost as bad as facing Ari himself. What were his orders? Would he be trying to kill her on-station, or would he be trying to take her back?

She had history with Craike—bad history. Torrence had called him a dangerous crazy, but that wasn't the half of it. He might well be psychotic, but he certainly wasn't stupid. If Ari had sent Robert Craike, she'd never get a fair trial.

Craike was bad news.

Had always been bad news.

She got his attraction to Ari. The emotions he thought he hid so carefully behind a tough scowl and a clenched jaw might fool most deadheads, but even though she barely scored on the empathy scale, she could read Craike. Most times she wished she couldn't.

His jealousy had piled a personal grudge on top of everything else when she'd challenged his authority on Felcon.

If she closed her eyes, she could still smell the hot sand, taste the planet's salt-caked air, feel its oven-intense heat through the sunblock on her face. Her rebellion had killed five people as surely as if she'd put a bolt gun to their heads herself, but she hadn't known, then, how far Craike would go. The memory came back, vivid and painful. Torrence choking his life out, lungs all shot to hell.

Her fault. Her fault!

Craike pulled the trigger, but if it hadn't been for her . . .

Don't go there.

Was it the memory of Felcon that made her blood pound in her ears, or the thought of what was to come? The last time she'd seen Craike was down the barrel of a bolt gun. Now he was here on-station.

As she waited in line for the go-flow behind an elderly man in a technician's coverall, her right hand closed involuntarily over the handpad on her left. If she wasn't careful, the small, flexible sheet of film held her life—and possibly her death—within its memory. Ari's files were as dangerous as a bomb on a short fuse. She'd had the opportunity and had grabbed them without thinking it through. If it had just been her, he might have let her slip away, but he'd never let her keep the files.

She rubbed her forehead to ease the headache and breathed away the faint feeling of dizziness. She'd rather not think about the files right now. She had them; she daren't use them. Part of her didn't even want to.

When she'd started to try and make sense of them, she'd realized that Ari was into all kinds of nastiness, but collating the data would be a massive undertaking. She had, however, found her own name on a red file. That had shocked her beyond measure. She'd seen that he'd personally scheduled her for Neural Readjustment on Sentier-4. She was lucky she got out before they'd taken her mind to pieces.

The man in front of her reached the head of the lineup, and with grace that showed he'd not slowed down with age, he hopped onto the last individual transfer raft. That left her no option but to climb into a transit pod with seven strangers. She eyed them suspiciously, but they all had the pale skin of long-term space-station residents, and the jaded air of tired workers heading home. As the pod carried them all toward the residential sector, she took a deep breath and considered her options. Going up against Craike, one on one, was suicide. She'd have to run, abandon the search for renegade psi-techs like herself, and find a flight. Any flight.

Destination? Away from here.

It should be possible. Security was patchy. Mirrimar-14 was big enough to have cracks that a desperate person could slip through, at least as far as the docks.

Space stations came in all shapes and sizes. Mirrimar-14, run by Eastin-Heigle, serviced only three jump gates and was happy to embrace any traffic that could pay the docking fees. That meant there would be independent captains she might bribe. Time to go to the transients' quarter and see if she could find someone who was ready to ship out, someone who might take an unlisted passenger in exchange for credits or—she gritted her teeth—sex.

◆ ◆ ◆

Ben Benjamin let the comm-link drop. Crowder was pissed with him again, but there wasn't much either of them could do about the delay. Ben hadn't been expecting to be recalled to take over the Olyanda mission. It would take at least four days to get back to Chenon, even presuming he could negotiate the inner system gates without getting stuck in a tailback. You'd think the vast deeps of space would be big enough to avoid traffic jams, but since everything funneled through jump gates, they were still inevitable.

It was a babysitting job for a new colony of back-to-basics Ecolibrians—hard-core separatists. Mixing psi-techs and fundies was a disaster waiting to happen. It had taken long enough for Ben to regain his commander's pin. Refusing this job would sideline him, and failing would finish his career completely.

Rock, meet hard place. Hard place, meet rock. Was someone on the Board setting him up to fail? Could be. Better not fail, then.

The comm booth felt stuffy. He needed air, even spacestation recycled would do. He leaned forward and swiped his handpad through the reader to register the transaction.

He'd trampled on some sensitive toes after Hera-3, probably enough to get himself retconned, or just plain killed, except for the fact he'd let it be known that he'd filed all his evidence with a certain body on Crossways which was virtually untouchable by any legitimate government or megacorp—at least not without a full-scale war. That evidence, mostly hearsay, might not be sufficient for a court of law, but it would be enough to spark inconvenient questions of people with reputations to protect.

For the past two years he'd lived with the possibility of someone high up in the Trust deciding he was too much of a liability. He could have walked away at any time, of course, but if he did that, he'd never find the bastards responsible. Crowder had stood by him, kept him on payroll. Without Crowder, he'd have been on the outside looking in. With so many of his regular crew dead and the survivors scattered to other teams, Crowder was the only constant in his life: boss, best friend, and sometimes stand-in for the father he'd lost so many years ago.

Musing on the value of friendship, Ben stepped out of the booth into the bland foyer of the visitor center and nodded to the desk clerk. Nice to see a real person in the job, not just a machine. He collected a hotchoc from the barista-bot and sipped it. It was thin and weak, almost tasteless except for the sugar, but at least it was warm and wet. He clipped a lid on the drink, grasped a handloop, and pushed off into the rising stream of the antigrav tube, balancing the cup expertly. He exited at the right floor, gaining weight again as his feet hit the hallway ceramic. He popped the top and sipped the hot liquid again as he walked along to the dining hall.

It was early. The room was a sea of emptiness with only two tables occupied. A group of four earnest young men sat at one and the other held the redhead who'd brought her courier vessel into port just after him, and had pushed in between him and the port controller as he tried to secure a next-day systems check. He'd been left fuming as she played the old buddies card and waltzed through the formalities, leaving him standing. She looked up, smiled broadly, and indicated the empty place by her side. No way. He retreated. Maybe he'd have a snack in Gordano's. His belly rumbled. Two snacks.

◆ ◆ ◆

Back in her cramped quarters Cara made another caff for herself, extra strong so she could almost pretend it was made with real coffee beans. Her hands shook as they clasped the mug. Of all the bloody stupid things, heading for the transients' quarter desperate enough to latch onto the first captain of the worst bucket-of-bolts mining barge was barely one step up from suicide.

But staying was suicide.

Sex with a stranger might be the fastest way to get a favor, but she couldn't stop her thoughts from turning in circles. There hadn't been anyone since Ari.

It had been good once.

She'd met him just after she'd been promoted to Special Ops and recalled to Earth, to Alphacorp's facility outside the ancient city of York. Now second in command of a Spearhead Team, she was so proud that she'd broken her self-imposed silence and called her mom, only to be rewarded by nothing more than a vague that's-nice-dear reaction. So much for trying to rebuild bridges. Dammit, it was a big deal for a twenty-three-year-old. Spearhead Teams were the first into a potential colony world and, when necessary, Alphacorp's troubleshooters.

She'd gone out and celebrated alone, but hadn't stayed alone for long. She couldn't even remember his name, now. He'd been keen, but she'd crept out of his apartment early in the morning without waking him. Relationships didn't usually last beyond the next job, and she'd be leaving soon for Eritropea. Two months away for her, biological time, would be eight months for anyone left behind since this trip involved three months each way in cryo with the lumbering colony convoy taking forever to reach the outer system gates that handled the mass of an ark vessel.

She'd not been intending to hook up with anyone else, least of all her boss. . . .

Cara took a shuddering breath and tried to relax away the adrenaline spike. She closed her mind to the past and concentrated on trying to make herself look good; bait the hook to catch a big fish. If she didn't find a ride out of here tonight, she was dead or worse.

She swallowed hard and tried to ignore the churning in her gut, but it was no good . . . Halfway through applying blusher to her cheekbones she dashed to the sluice, hurling bile into the can and ruining her makeup.

She rinsed her mouth, cleaned her teeth and started again.

Despite everything, she didn't want anyone except Ari. Been there, tried that, still hurt. She knew now why he had a neural blocker. He might look like an angel, but Ari scared her spitless. Even so, she couldn't deny that she still felt . . . something. She couldn't even name the emotion.

◆ ◆ ◆

Crews couldn't drink during flights and tended to let rip once they hit a station on shore leave. They wanted intoxication, entertainment, and sex, and Gordano's catered to all three in equal measure.

Ben leaned against the bar in the time-honored way of travelers, squashed between a woman with Militaire veteran's tattoos and a young man with the scaly skin of an exotic from the water world of Aqua Neriffe. His high-neck buddysuit almost, but not quite, covered his gill slits.

Wayside inn on a colony planet, or staging post at the arse-end of the galaxy, the routine was always the same. Gordano's menu offered whatever could be imported cheaply or grown in hydroponics or a vat—standard space station fare.

The smoky blue walls, subtle lighting, and the mist effect made the perfectly clean atmosphere in the crowded bar look thick enough for privacy. They'd tried to make it seem like a dirtside roadhouse, but they couldn't hide what it was.

A honey blonde in a blue dress that clung from throat to hip and then swung to mid-calf eyed him. She wasn't showing everything that was on offer, so she was probably not one of Gordano's girls. He nodded politely and turned back to the bar. Out of the corner of his eye he saw her slide into a booth and begin to check the screen built into the table. She drew his gaze. He took another sideways look and saw that she was just looking away. Pity he was only passing through.

He turned to the bar and ordered the house gold, expecting it would be as tasteless as speed-ale usually was. When it came, it was better than he'd been expecting and he took a second pull.

An argument was brewing at one of the tables. Angry voices cut through the general hubbub, but Ben couldn't make out the words. Maybe some long-term shipboard resentment fueled by a fresh infusion of alcohol. He didn't worry about it. Places like this always had their own security to damp down arguments before they got out of hand.

Or maybe not.

The row erupted. Chairs crashed backward. Two men, one at least a decade younger than the other, launched into each other across a table and crashed to the floor, kicking and punching. A space grew around them, penning them inside a ring of onlookers. Though the older guy had at least ten kilos on the younger one, the fight looked about even, one with a split lip, the other with a bloody nose. Two of Gordano's bouncers closed in on the wrestling pair.

The situation nose-dived when the younger of the two brawlers, Split Lip, flashed a knife. How the hell had he managed to get that onto the station? Only licensed enforcers carried weapons legally, and security was tight. From this distance Ben couldn't tell whether it was a handspan of carbon-steel or a power-enhanced parrimer blade, but it took less than half a second to become obvious. The man took a wide swing at his opponent, missed, and instead sliced across the belly of the nearest bouncer who went down in a spray of blood and a whiff of burned meat.

The second bouncer pulled a sidearm and the onlookers,

intensely aware that they'd turned from voyeurs into potential victims, began to scatter. Ben found himself in the front row and noticed the blonde in the blue dress hadn't moved away either. She was now standing, half-hidden from the combatants, by the booth back.

Briefly surprised that his weapon had connected, Split Lip hesitated for long enough to give Bloody Nose the opportunity to grab the blade and they rolled together, leaving the bouncer no clear target.

Ben curled his fingers to stop them twitching toward where his own sidearm wasn't. He would have taken out Bloody Nose, the man currently with the knife, not Split Lip, but the bouncer was indecisive. The two scrappers broke apart. Bloody Nose staggered to his feet barely an arm's length in front of Ben. Seeing the bouncer take aim and not wanting to get caught by a wide shot, Ben stepped in close, grabbed Bloody Nose's knife hand, twisted hard, and immobilized him, making sure he kept the man between himself and the bouncer.

It was over in a moment.

The bouncer grabbed Split Lip, slapped ferraflex restraints on him, and then came to relieve Ben of his prisoner.

"Thanks."

"You're welcome."

Ben turned to the fallen man, but the woman in the blue dress was already down on her knees beside him. She had the man's own emergency pack from his belt and was holding the wound closed with a clean dressing.

"Your crew?" Ben asked, peering at what she was doing and noting that she was following battle-wound procedure like a veteran.

She shook her head and looked up. "Yours?" She had stunning gray-blue eyes fringed with long dark lashes despite the blonde hair.

"If I had crew, they wouldn't be so stupid."

A siren outside announced the imminent arrival of medics and the law. She glanced around as if sizing up the exits.

"Looking for a back way out?" he asked.

"Imagine the hours of interviews and incident sheets to write up," she said.

"Civic duty?" He wondered just how badly she needed to get out before the law arrived.

"I doubt they'll lay on a decent meal, and I haven't eaten yet."

"Point taken. We can always volunteer our services to-morrow."

"Of course," she said, her voice completely lacking sincerity.

"Come on, then, I'll buy you dinner."

As the crash team hustled a gurney through the front door of Gordano's, Ben exited the back with the honey blonde.

Chapter Two

OPPORTUNITY

DAMN. CARA HAD SPOILED THE EFFECT OF HER best dress—her only dress—with blood. Good job she'd paid a bit more for self-cleaning fabric. It was a good dress, an investment, not overtly showy or loud, but subtly sensual, elegant without being an obvious come-on. She didn't want to get too deep into anything she couldn't get out of.

They took a couple of turns through service corridors. Good, a staff washroom.

"This'll only take a minute," she said, pushing open the door. "Will you wait?"

The man nodded, and she noted with approval that he stepped back into a doorway, out of range of the surveillance eye on the wall.

In the washroom she checked that the cleaning cycle had activated itself. While the fabric digested the blood, she washed her hands clean and checked there were no more obvious stains. She didn't want to attract the wrong kind of attention.

She took several deep breaths to steady herself. If she'd been wearing a buddysuit, it would probably have told her that she still had elevated levels of adrenaline. She hadn't expected that kind of trouble while cruising the bars for a likely captain or cargomeister.

She'd had her eye on the tall, lean man in the bar even before the fight—first his Trust uniform and then the Colony Survey pin on his collar. His dark hair, high at the temples, was long and tied back into a tight braid at the back of his neck. He might be in his mid-thirties, with warm brown skin and strong, even features.

She'd looked for him on the immigration list, skimming the photo IDs.

His name had jumped out at her, Benjamin. How common was the name? There was a Benjamin in Ari's red file. Anyone who could piss off Ari as much as *that* Benjamin had was all right by her. He might be a good bet.

Even that brief thought of Ari's files started a stabbing pain somewhere behind her eyes. Forget about Ari. Concentrate on the business at hand. Even if he wasn't the same Benjamin, he worked for the Trust, so he was a natural rival of all things Alphacorp. She checked his details. He was flying solo in a ship big enough to take a passenger. Yes!

So now she was leaving Gordano's with him, but not in any circumstances that she might have expected. When the fight had broken out, he'd handled himself well. The very fact that he'd skipped the scene without offering witness testimony was a hopeful sign that he wasn't a by-the-book man. She needed someone with a little flexibility when it came to rules.

He was waiting for her outside the washroom. Good, he hadn't changed his mind.

She led the way, and they emerged on the public thoroughfare just as the medics hustled the gurney into an antigrav transport.

"How badly was he injured?" Benjamin asked as the transport began to move through the curious crowd.

"From the smell they'll be doing a bowel resection, but I guess he'll survive if they can get him stabilized quickly."

He nodded. "You handled yourself well in there."

She shrugged, not wanting to give anything away. "Cara Carlinni." She held out her hand.

"Benjamin." He took it, but didn't hold onto it for long.

"Just Benjamin?"

"Reska Benjamin." He smiled. "Ben will do. Only my grandmother calls me Reska."

"All right." She nodded. "Dinner. Where do you want to go?"

"I'm sick of the transients' places. Take me somewhere local." He raised one eyebrow, and she let herself smile.

"Sam's Bar, then." She checked the time. Jussaro and her fellow packers would be long gone by now. "Yeah, I know, there's a Sam's on every station from Earth to the Rim, but this one's not bad. The guy who runs it really is a Sam." She kept her voice light. It was a long time since she'd flirted with anyone, but Benjamin didn't seem so bad. At least he wasn't repulsive or leery.

They crossed the wide, straight arcade that bisected the space station's downtown pedestrian plaza and stepped over the threshold of Sam's. She checked out the diners already seated. No obvious threat. For the hundredth time that day she flicked her tongue over her implant controls. Yes, it was still powered down. Craike was a psi-tech Finder, so she mustn't give him anything to latch on to.

She headed for a table in the far corner, edging Ben out so she could sit facing the door. The other chair had its back to the open floor of the diner, but she noticed that Ben angled it slightly so that he could see the room reflected in the decorative mirror on the wall behind Cara's left shoulder. Was he always this careful? Was it many years of habit, or was he expecting trouble tonight? He handled himself like someone who'd dealt with his fair share of trouble.

Having thrown up earlier she wasn't really hungry, so she barely glanced at the menu on the table screen, selecting almost at random. She needed time to work out whether she'd hooked the right fish. If not, she could still throw him back and return to Gordano's or maybe try Jimmy's.

They made small talk, waiting for the food to arrive on the conveyor, establishing the where-are-you-froms and the-what-do-you-dos. There wasn't much point in lying when her whole life was mapped out on her handpad, so she told him she was from Earth, though he raised one eyebrow when she said she worked on a packing line.

"I didn't say I'd always worked on packing lines," she said. "I said that's what I do now. It's convenient and it keeps me fed." She didn't elaborate. "What about you?"

"Brought up on a farm on Chenon, and I run surveys for the Trust."

"Chenon's the main headquarters of the Trust's Colony Division."

"That's where I'm based, but I don't get to spend much time there."

The food arrived, and they lapsed into silence while they took the first few bites. Cara watched Benjamin guardedly across her steaming bowl of razorfin. It was succulent, but she could have been chewing sawdust for all the notice she took of it.

Benjamin worked for the Trust, so it was likely he had an implant, but she couldn't pin him down without activating her own. She rested her fork in her dish and tapped her fingers on the table.

"All right, Ben, I give up. I know you're a psi-tech, but what are you? What's your specialty? Mechanics?"

He shook his head.

She could sense that she'd kindled his interest. "You're a Finder? A Dowser?" She guessed again. "A Healer?"

"No. You're way off the mark." He pushed his plate away.

"You're not a Clairvoyant, are you?"

"A spook? No. Do you really believe they exist?" He grinned, his eyes crinkling in genuine amusement.

She shrugged. "I never met one. I'm glad you're not the first. I have enough trouble with the past without worrying about the future."

She wondered whether to try and finish the fish. No, she'd only throw it up. She smiled, trying to make the expression reach her eyes. "It's no good, you'll have to tell me. You're not a Telepath, are you?"

"I have difficulty throwing a thought from here to the table. I'm a Navigator, Psi-1."

She was impressed. That meant he could align his implant with the tides of the universe and at any time know where he was and what direction he was going in. She'd tested almost zilch for navigation.

"Flyboy or dirtsider?"

"I've done both. Prefer new colony work."

"But you're not doing that now, are you? You said you

were running surveys." His mouth compressed into a tight line. "Long story."

And he obviously didn't want to tell it.

"You didn't get that faded tan on a way station like this. Or on a packing line," he said. "Psi-tech, yes?"

She was taking a risk. This close up he had to feel the pull of her implant, even powered down. If she'd been good at flirting, she could have distracted him with a pout and a come-hither look. She wasn't good at flirting. When she realized she'd focused on her half-eaten meal, she forced herself to look back at Benjamin's eyes.

"You slapped on that field bandage like a pro," he said.

Cara had a brief moment of panic. She wanted to gabble an apology and run out of the diner, but instead she forced herself to smile, trying not to give too much away, hoping it looked enigmatic rather than vapid. She didn't want to tell him too much.

"How old are you?" he asked.

"That's no question to ask a lady."

"I'm curious. I've got a hunch you've done regular cryo."

"Very astute, Mr. Benjamin. I've notched up eight years in the freezer, mostly in smallish chunks." She held out her hand, wondering how much to tell. In its default state, her handpad recorded three timelines, biological, Earth standard, and local.

"Is that an Alphacorp issue pad?"

Shit! She'd had it for so long she'd forgotten how recognizable it was.

"So why are you here? This isn't an Alphacorp station." He suddenly looked wary. "You've not done NR, have you?"

"Neural Readjustment? Me? No. No way." The edge of her vision clouded. She rocked back in her chair. Her throat clenched. "And I don't like it when you talk dirty."

"Relax. You're attracting attention." He looked at her as if trying to read her.

She pushed her hair back behind one ear.

Was he leading her on? Playing with her? She took a deep breath. "I made a wrong career move."

"Hmm. Bad deal. I know how that goes."

I bet you don't. She suddenly checked herself, hoping she

hadn't broadcast that thought. No; all right, then. So far, so good. Breathe.

He took the hint and changed the subject. "Mirrimar-14 seems a little limited, culturally speaking. What do you do for fun?"

"Watch my fingernails grow."

He inclined his head, inviting more.

"All right, let's see, if you want a tourist guide answer, there's the dome—that's the usual sort of entertainment complex—and various gyms with tax bonuses for working out. They like to keep their workers healthy."

"And you work out?" he asked.

"I'm not going to arm wrestle you to prove it."

"It might be worth it." He smiled and glanced around the bar. "Where to now?" Sam's wasn't a place where they liked you to linger all night and there was already a line at the door for tables.

She thought he might make assumptions, but he didn't. Maybe she hadn't worn the right dress. Maybe he wasn't the kind of man who made assumptions. She found herself liking him for that.

He paid the bill, and she led the way to the go-flow tunnel, checking casually behind to make sure they weren't being followed. Soon they were strap-hanging in the evening crowds, while their antigrav raft hit the accelerator lane and matched speed with the swift-moving continuous loop transporter. She leaned close to Ben on the pretext of maintaining balance above the trolley's center of gravity. Her fingers twined with his as she reached up for the dismount button on the hanging strap and the raft neatly flipped across and slowed to a smooth stop on the platform by the leisure dome.

She led him toward the main courtyard where all the different areas converged. "How about the forest bubble?" she asked.

"It's not like the real thing, is it?"

They passed the entrance, but then Ben hovered by the elevator to the theater. Cara grabbed his arm to guide him past. As she did so, something prickled at the back of her neck.

She glanced sideways. Shit! One of the businessmen—if that's what they were—from Craike's ship was walking down the concourse toward her. She didn't think he'd seen her yet. She hurriedly double-checked her implant and imagined a blank wall of psi-tech nothing around herself. Blend in with the background. Blend. Blend. She pressed closer to Ben, turning her face into his shoulder, trying to slow her racing heart by willpower alone, imagining herself to be no different from anyone else in the plaza.

The man moved like a dancer, free and light, almost as if he could walk on dust without leaving footprints. She turned her face completely away from him, excising him from her mind to sever any lingering mental connections, though she could almost taste his presence as he got closer.

Closer.

And finally past.

Ben had stiffened and didn't relax until she breathed out again. She wondered if he was going to ask any questions, but he didn't. Once the man was safely out of sight, she tugged at Ben's arm and dragged him in the opposite direction.

"Snow slopes?" Ben asked, walking past without slowing.

"Yeah, sorry, I wasn't thinking. That's not very date-like, is it?"

Ben laughed. "Are we on a date? Well, in that case, maybe we could try a little home entertainment."

About time. She'd given him enough opportunities. It was such a cliché, but attempting to keep her voice smooth, she said, "My place or yours?"

"Mine."

She'd hoped he'd say that. Hers was hardly big enough, and anyway, she wasn't altogether sure it was safe anymore. She shivered involuntarily and pushed that thought away. Concentrate on one thing at a time.

"Come on, then, back to the go-flow."

He took her cold hand in his warm, dry one and they headed back to the tunnels.

✦ ✦ ✦

Ben swiped his handpad across the door lock and moved aside to let Cara enter first.

"You keep your place tidier than I do." She examined the room carefully before stepping over the threshold.

"It's easy when you live out of a mission pack. I could spread all my belongings over the floor, and it would still look tidy."

"Washroom?" she asked, and headed for the door he pointed to.

Once the washroom door had closed behind her, Ben pulled a chair up to the station's matrix terminal and swiped his clearance chip. "Access station staff files," he said. "Cara Carlinni."

The files lined up neatly on his screen. A quick glance was enough to tell him her bio was a fake. He'd seen enough of them to know one when he saw one. Usually, second-raters fudged their employment history to get a better job, but in this case her résumé was bland and she was drawing minimum wage on an assembly line. There was no mention of her being a psi-tech at all, yet he was sure she was even though she hadn't admitted it in so many words. Her reaction to his mention of Neural Readjustment had been pretty typical of any psi-tech. Neural was the end of the line for the rebels, the careless, the criminal, and the unlucky.

They certainly weren't paying her psi-tech rates. Maybe she'd been through Neural or—he thought with distaste— had had her implant decommissioned altogether. She was either mentally unstable, which she didn't seem to be; so-cially inept, which she certainly wasn't despite being a little awkward at times; or she was hiding from someone or something.

Or she'd been sent by certain members of the Trust's Board of Directors. All of the possibilities were bad news.

He should kick her out and take himself straight to bed, but she looked stunning in that dress, and he had a mind to see what she looked like out of it. He was pretty sure that was what she had in mind, but not at all sure of the reason.

✦ ✦ ✦

Cara flicked her fingers over her dress where the bloodstain had been. The last traces had gone. Good. She splashed water on her face, checked her breath after eating fish, and emerged from the washroom with a bright smile. Ben had ordered Muscat brandy from room service. It arrived within seconds, and he took it from the hatch along with a couple of glasses.

In another life Cara might have found Ben Benjamin attractive, but she wasn't ready to look at men again yet. He mustn't know that.

She couldn't think of anyone but Ari.

Why now?

Maybe she could close her eyes and make believe Ben was Ari.

No, Ben was unlikely to be anything like Ari in bed.

Sometimes, especially toward the end, their bouts of sex had been gladiatorial, often fierce, always draining. Her feelings for Ari were unlike anything she'd ever had for anyone before. He was manipulative and devious, and—she felt a soft adrenaline bump in the pit of her stomach—she was still tied to him, even though he'd doubtless sent Craike after her. Was it love? Had it ever been love? Whatever it was, it was dangerous.

Ben. Concentrate on Ben.

She hoped she'd judged this right. She wondered whether she was that good an actress, but it was probably too late for doubts. She smiled and whirled around so that her skirt flared out. Ben watched her appreciatively.

Who are you? What do you want?

She wasn't sure whether he'd spoken that aloud or whether she'd picked it up out of his head. A sudden rush of heat to her cheeks threatened to give her away. She didn't answer.

He poured her a generous drink and himself a small one. She downed hers in one, but didn't touch the glass again when he refilled it. A shy teenager on her first date couldn't have been more nervous. Her heart was pounding, but the drink scoured the back of her throat and steadied her. *Get a grip, Carlinni.*

Ben invited her up close, and she didn't resist. She had a vague sense of detachment, a brief moment of awkwardness, then she slid her arms around his neck and pressed against him, raising her face, finding his lips with hers. Ari never kissed her on the mouth, so this was different. It was a good first kiss, not too hard, not too wet, gentle but warm. He was testing to see whether she really meant it. She was grateful for that.

The drink blunted the edge of her inhibitions. She opened her lips to his and the kiss deepened. She could feel the warmth of his hand against the small of her back pulling her close. A heady wave of anticipation combined with nervousness started somewhere in the pit of her belly and washed through her, leaving her dizzy and breathless. She let it take over, hoping she could use it to replace passion. Too late to turn back now.

✦ ✦ ✦

Whore!

The word formed a cold, stony knot in the center of her body, and she felt chilled, even lying in the shadow of Ben's warm body. Ben had been skilled and generous and she'd been . . . uninvolved. Pliant, but disconnected. Whore wasn't the right word. A whore would have given much better value. She closed her eyes tight to lock in the tears and took slow, even breaths.

Ari was still in her head.

She'd tried to leave him when she'd found out what he was up to, but he wasn't ready to let her go. He'd threatened her, obliquely but undeniably, if she tried to back out. *Craike handles severances*, he'd said.

She tried to block out the rest of that painful memory.

She shivered.

Ben pulled the sheet up over her, his hand brushing against her breast in the shroud-darkness of the room. It cut into her thoughts, and before she could stop herself, she flinched. Damn, she shouldn't have done that.

"Did I hurt you?" He hitched himself up on one elbow, voice full of concern.

"No. You were wonderful."

"Cut the crap. I don't need it." He reached over and turned the lamp up to a dim glimmer. "Did I hurt you?"

"No. Truly."

She turned her head toward him, saw the look on his face,

and half-smiled what she hoped was reassurance. She couldn't read his expression.

"Why?" he asked.

"Why what?"

"The playacting, the sex. Why me? Did the Board send you? What do you want?"

"Board? What board? Who says I want anything?" She rolled to get up. "This was a bad idea."

He didn't try to stop her. Instead he followed her and draped the fallen sheet over her shoulders.

"Sorry if I seem to be paranoid," he said. "It's been a strange day. I almost got bounced into infinity crossing the Folds and had to argue with a petty official to get a next-day systems check that's costing me double rate. I was figuring on nothing more than eating some real food and sleeping in a real bed." He breathed out sharply. "Then I hook up with a gorgeous woman!" He sat on the edge of the bed and pulled on his pants. "A man doesn't generally get that lucky without a good reason. I might not even score on the empathy scale, but I know you want something."

"Then why did you go along with me?" She twined the sheet around herself.

He raised one eyebrow. "Have you taken a look in the mirror lately?"

"Just sex?"

"Were you offering anything else?"

"Maybe." She pulled the sheet a little closer.

"You're good. You make all the right moves, but your body's too honest. You don't do this very often, do you? What do you want?" he asked.

There was an uncomfortable pause. "I need to get out of here," she said.

"There's the door." There was a new wariness in his voice.

"I mean off Mirrimar-14. I need to get away quickly and quietly."

"Why?"

"Before I came here, I made an enemy. I had to drop everything and run. This is as far as I got before my credits and my luck ran out. I hoped I'd be safe here. I'd heard about people who help people like me. I thought if I could make the right connection, I could stop for a while."

"Who are you running from?"

Cara rubbed her temples to ease the incipient headache. "You'll probably be safer if I don't tell you. Let's just say I didn't realize what I was getting into. He's a dangerous man to cross and he's got a lot of connections. A ship arrived earlier today and, well, I've got to get out or I'm a sitting target."

"The man near the snow slopes?"

"One of . . . his." She closed her mouth on Ari's name.

"Are you saying he'd kill you?"

"Yes, or hurt me a lot, or probably both, but not in that order. I told you. He's got influence and he's really pissed with me."

"Has he got a right to be?"

"He thinks so. It's complicated. Look, I haven't done anything bad. In fact . . . Oh, please just take my word . . . It's more than complicated."

She'd made a complete mess of that! She wondered whether to tell Ben everything. Her temples pounded and she wasn't even sure she could face going through the whole story. Besides, knowing how dangerous Ari was might frighten Ben off, even though he didn't look like he'd scare easily.

Ben stared at her as if he was weighing her on some internal balance. "What do you know about Olyanda?"

"It doesn't ring any bells. Person or place?"

"Planet in the Taloga System."

She shrugged. "Not one I've been to."

"No one has. It's a new colony. My next assignment. Babysitting a fundamentalist sect setting up their utopia. I thought . . . oh, never mind." Ben frowned. "Don't you need an exit permit to get out of here?"

"I can't leave openly. You're flying private. I can get on board without going through official channels."

"Too risky. First, you'll never make it through the port, and second, I'll be up to my armpits in shit when you don't. It's too much of a risk."

Earlier that evening she'd seen him step in range of a parrimer blade with a dithering enforcer pointing a shaky sidearm in his direction, and now he thought she was too much of a risk. "It's not impossible," she said. "Devantec, that's the firm I work for, runs a courier service. I've been checking their schedules, waiting for the right opportunity."

"Is that all I am, an opportunity?"

"You're probably an expensive opportunity. I can pay—something—not much, but . . ."

Or was he going to want payment in kind? She swallowed hard, activated her handpad and pulled up her credit rating.

"I've saved every spare credit I've earned since I got here. That's what I've got. I'll pay—do—whatever it takes."

"I'm not for sale."

Cara suddenly saw Ari's fair features overlaid on Ben's dark ones and had a momentary panic. If Ben was Ari's agent, she'd played right into his hands. There was no way she could tell unless he'd let her do a mind-scan. Without that, she'd have to trust to her instincts and—hell—they'd been wrong before. She was running out of options.

"How about Olyanda? Every expedition needs more long-range Telepaths. I'm a Psi-1."

"And you're on the packing line at Devantec on minimum wage? Right."

"I've . . . I've been powered down for . . . months. They can find me by . . ."

"You've been completely powered down?" He cursed under his breath, and she could have sworn that was concern in his voice. "How long?"

She swallowed and glanced at the timeline on her handpad. "Eleven months and thirteen days."

The look in his eyes said he didn't believe her, so she pulled out a tranq, held it up for him to see, and popped it. "With a little help." She swallowed the capsule and let her desperation show in her voice. "Look, I'm way out on a limb and someone's sawing down my tree. Will you help or not?"

She watched for Ben's reaction. There was an undercurrent of something she didn't quite follow, something he was preoccupied with. She was so full of her own troubles that she hadn't stopped to think he might have some of his own.

"You know, if you're putting all that on just to spin me a line," he said, "you're very good at it. I think I believe you, but I don't know if I'm thinking with my brain or my balls. I must be slipping." He held her by the shoulders and looked into her eyes, then shook his head. "It's too risky. I'm on the emergency overhaul pad in the Aloha dock. It's the busiest part of the whole port and I won't be cleared to leave until 1500. You'll never make it through the security checks. If I get one more black mark on my record, I lose my job, and I can't risk that. Do you understand me?"

"Yes," she said.

"There's more at stake than just a job. Other things . . . going on."

"I get it. You can't take me." She bit down on her back teeth to stop herself from saying more.

"I'm leaving." She stood up.

"You're welcome to stay until morning."

"What's the point?"

As she dropped into the antigrav shaft, she realized that despite his refusal she now knew the location of his ship and his time of departure. Had he meant to tell her that?

Oh . . .

She began to grin.

Chapter Three

EGRESS

CARA DIDN'T DARE GO BACK TO HER OWN apartment, but there was nothing there that she couldn't walk away from. She'd lost all those little keepsakes of her childhood when she'd escaped from Sentier-4 with only her prison gown under a stolen buddysuit.

Where to go until it was time to make her move?

Jussaro's.

He'd always said if she needed a friend she could call, but she'd backed off as soon as she realized what he was—what he'd been.

No time to get squeamish now.

She hopped the go-flow and dismounted at Accommodation Section Four. Once away from the platform the corridors looked identical to her own neighborhood, numbered medonite doors set in gray walls, most decorated with individual designs showing the personality of their owner. She'd never touched hers, but the previous resident had seared it with the orange hues of an Earth sunset, just a little off-kilter in its colors, as if he longed for something he'd heard about but never seen firsthand.

Jussaro's door, however, was resolutely gray like the walls, decorated only by an apartment number.

It was late. She glanced at her handpad, hoping he was a

light sleeper, and pressed the buzzer. He answered almost immediately, still fully dressed.

"Carlinni!" His purple-black face creased along laugh lines, his eyes almost disappearing entirely behind his nictating inner eyelid and prominent brow ridges.

"You know you said if I ever needed a friend ... ?"

Unquestioning, he stepped back to let her in. His slightly lopsided grin chilled her. She could have been like him if she hadn't got out when she did. Half his memories had been destroyed, and he claimed the other half were unreliable. Neural Readjustment could do that to a person. Routine work was all he was considered fit for. It was a wonder he wasn't insane—or maybe he was, but he hid it well.

Squat and muscular, Jussaro was an exotic, genetically engineered to withstand the heavy gravity and high levels of radiation dousing the second planet of the Hollands System. Altered humans had settled there three hundred years ago to mine the rich deposits of platinum vital to the jump gates. Even though the mines had given up the best of their resources many years ago, seeing Hollanders off-world was rare.

Jussaro kept very close-mouthed about what he'd done to earn his trip to Neural. Whatever it was, it didn't necessarily make him a bad person. She didn't consider herself a bad person. Yet for what she'd done, she'd end up in Neural, too, presuming Craike didn't kill her first. She felt her jaw clench and the back of her neck prickle. Knowing Ari's propensity for revenge, he'd have her implant decommissioned without an anesthetic, wait until she'd gone screaming nuts, and then let Craike kill her.

Slowly.

She shuddered.

"What do you want, Carlinni? If it's my body, you're out of luck." Jussaro pointed her to the single soft chair in his tiny apartment and dragged the blanket from the arm before she sat in it. The cushions were still warm. He must have been sleeping there.

"A million credits, a fast cruiser, and a pony."

"Yeah, right. Let's start again. What do you want to drink?" He turned to his countertop and waved at the hot- and cold-water spigots.

"Spoilsport."

His face lit up, crow's feet crinkling. "I'm having caff."

She spotted three empty caff cartons on the table.

"No wonder you never sleep properly."

He wrenched the top off a carton and shoved it under the hot spigot, but then reached for a glass, filled it from the cold and handed it to her.

She sipped cautiously. "Water?"

"I saw you pop a tranq earlier today. Figured that might be safest."

She colored.

"Thought you could fool me, huh?"

Maybe Jussaro wasn't that far gone.

"Just 'cause I'm . . ." He circled his index finger to his temple. "It doesn't mean to say I don't see things. See things and know things."

She gaped at him now, wondering just how insane he might be.

"Oh, I know, anyone who's been through Neural isn't supposed to recall much. When the shrinks ask—and they do ask—I can't remember a fucking thing about life before being a half-wit, but let me tell you there's only so much they can do if you're determined not to lose it all. There's your underlying ability. They can't take that away."

"Why are you telling me this?"

"You're a psi-tech. You're out on your own . . . and you've got problems."

"Me? No."

He snorted. "It's the middle of the night, Carlinni, and you're on my doorstep looking like you've had sex. You're either on a deep-cover job, or you're on the run. You're popping tranqs because your implant is powered down. That means someone is looking for you."

She gaped at him.

"Yeah, I'm not as fried as they think I am."

For a second she wondered if she'd been transmitting and him receiving, but that was impossible. Doubly impossible.

He sipped the carton of caff. "Well, maybe I am . . . fried, I mean, but I had an implant for twenty-four years before I . . . well, let's not go there. Short of taking my brain apart, synapse by synapse, they can't cut me off from it completely."

He leaned back against the countertop. "Ever wonder what life would have been like if you hadn't tested positive for psi-skills?"

Sometimes she wished she'd never been tested, but it was a fast track to a fully funded education and offered an irresistible opportunity to be completely independent of her mother and to see the galaxy. At the age of fourteen she hadn't appreciated that the guaranteed job for life was part of the deal whether you wanted it or not. If the company paid for your implant and trained you, then the company owned you. Sure, the leash was diamond-studded, but it was still a leash. Step out of line, and they could choke you with it.

When she didn't answer, Jussaro went on. "When I was a kid, I always wanted to be a veterinarian, then I got tested and it turned out I was too valuable a resource to let me have my own way. It's supposed to be a grand thing. Free education, dream job, but look what we lose. What price freedom, Carlinni?"

"I knew, even before they tested me. I wanted it. Seemed so much better than the alternative. My mom was . . . well, let's just say we didn't get on."

"I knew, too. I tried to hide it, but they got me anyway. And look what trouble it brought. I never wanted it and now I can't live without it. And you . . . you got big trouble."

"Who says I'm in trouble?" She took a pull at her water, hoping it would hide the fact that she wanted to heave at the notion of anyone playing with her brain.

"You've been in trouble since the day you arrived."

"How do you know?"

He laughed, a strange barking sound. "We know our own, don't we?"

She had a sudden urge to 'fess up. It would be a relief. Troubles shared, troubles halved. Ha! If only. Anyone she talked to would end up on Ari's hit list, too.

"You ever been in NR?" Jussaro asked.

"Neural Readjustment? Me? No. No way." The edge of her vision clouded. She stood up so fast the glass bounced across the tiles and the armchair skidded backward. Her heart pounded. Her pulse thudded in her ears. She felt her throat constrict and heard her voice rise in pitch. "And I don't like it when you talk dirty."

"Sit down, Carlinni. There's only me here. No one to impress." He picked up the glass and looked at her from under his heavy brows as if trying to read her. "Believe me, I'm no one."

She dropped back into the chair, palms flat on the arms for stability, eyes down. Eventually, she dragged her gaze away from the floor and stared at him, still trying to get her breathing under control. Like all psi-techs, Neural Readjustment was her most deep-seated dread. She'd escaped it so narrowly. . . .

❖ ❖ ❖

She's waking from cryo. It's that moment of seeing everything in a kaleidoscope of scents, hearing everything in color, smelling sounds, and tasting the feel of the restraints. The medic's light is blinding and smells like lemon. As they pull out the catheter and unplumb her, there's salt on her tongue. Even experienced travelers panic. Some go mad, start screaming and never stop; others just die. Once her brain starts working again, she realizes that it's not her screaming. She's not one of the acceptable 0.3% of losses, three in a thousand. This time, anyway.

Then she wants to scream because she realizes that she's not back home on Earth. This isn't Alphacorp's resuscitation wing. Alarms sound in her head. The Felcon mission has been a fucking fiasco. It should be over.

But it isn't.

This is the aftermath.

She reads the label on the med-tech's coverall and adrenaline surges, but she's strapped down and can't go anywhere. She's in Facility 197, Alphacorp's Neural Readjustment Center on Sentier-4. The fear factor kicks in, right as it's meant to do. 'Course it does. Donida McLellan and Facility 197 are notorious among psi-techs.

❖ ❖ ❖

Jussaro was still talking. He didn't seem to notice she'd been elsewhere for a moment. "You really can tell me, Carlinni.

I've been there. I know what it's like. The first time they figured they'd fixed me, brought me back into the fold. The second time . . . that's when they killed the implant. Permanently."

Shit! That was heavy. Bearing in mind how many times decommissioning resulted in suicide or, at best, a lifetime in an institution, Jussaro must have been—and probably still was—heroically determined not to lose himself.

"But they didn't factor in my natural psi talent. I don't know how much others have retained, but I can still receive." He raised one eyebrow and gave her a lopsided grin. "It's not easy, but I can. So, come on, tell me. Have you ever done Neural?"

"Quit pushing, Jussaro, I've never done Neural, right? Never. Ever. Do I seem like a nut?" Her mouth seemed to say the words of its own accord. That wasn't very tactful. She saw the look on his face. She scrubbed at her eyes with her hand to cover her confusion. "Sorry. I really am sorry. I didn't mean to . . ."

"No, that's all right. I just thought—you know—maybe you had and you needed to talk. Why else come here at this hour?"

Cara found herself shaking. She'd powered down her implant because she was scared that they'd use it to track her down. She was like Jussaro—a psi-tech disconnected from that enormous sense of belonging—of family. But it had been her choice. Her choice! It was only temporary, dammit. Temporary!

She took a deep breath. "You're way off target, Jussaro, but thanks anyway."

"So how do you need my help?"

"I need a place to stay for a few hours, and a red company coverall. And if anyone comes sniffing around, you haven't seen me, right?"

"Right. You're getting out?"

"I didn't say that."

"You didn't have to. Have you got somewhere to go?"

"Maybe."

"Time was I could have helped with that." He shrugged and touched his forehead.

"I came to Mirrimar looking for help."

"Ah." He nodded. "Time was I could have helped with that, too."

"You could? All this time and it was right under my nose?"

"Was." Jussaro shrugged again. "Whatever we had is long gone. What do you think got me busted?"

"I hoped . . ."

"What? That there was a place where the corporations couldn't get you? Ha! Nice thought, but no. There were a few small cells hiding in plain sight, not even connected. If one cell was taken, they couldn't betray anyone beyond their own small group. That was the theory anyway. The day they came for us, they took out a dozen groups like ours—or maybe that's what they wanted us to believe. Anyhow, my contacts all disappeared at the same time."

"What were you doing to attract so much attention?"

"Just being. No one likes the idea of rogue psi-techs."

"Oh, I so needed that place to be real."

"Your head's your own, Carlinni. The megacorps may try, but they don't have the power to control you unless you let them. There are plenty of places a psi-tech can find to call home. All you have to do is look. There are more than you think living off the grid."

She resisted the temptation to get up and drop a kiss on top of his bald head.

✦ ✦ ✦

Once away from Jussaro's place, Cara changed in the washroom on the edge of the go-flow concourse and with a sigh of regret dropped her dress into the recycler. Then she excised the station tracer chip from her handpad and stuck it to a tiny piece of tape from her carryall, now strapped round her middle.

That done, she stepped out into the throng of busy people.

They stank of stress. It wasn't an aroma, it was a state of being. Shift change on Mirrimar-14 was always the worst; bodies crammed together in featureless gray walkways not designed to cope with a rush hour. This time, though, the chaos should prove useful.

The go-flow buzzed like a hive with the noise of conversation, the accumulated whirr of flow-ways, and the whine of antigravs. Too many bodies and not enough air. Cara was surprised no one choked.

People shouldered her out of the way for seats on the trolleys, and eager hands snatched up the one-man rafts as soon as they became vacant. In the crush to get one, Cara stumbled against a blonde woman, close to her own build and age. She apologized, putting out her hands to prevent the woman from falling and, as she did so, stuck the tracer chip neatly to the sleeve of the woman's standard-issue red coverall. That should keep security occupied for a while if anyone put out a call on her.

Mumbled apologies over, they separated again. Cara's look-alike claimed a raft and flipped neatly into the stream of traffic, leaving her behind. By edging out a young Monitor cadet, Cara grabbed a ride and made for the fast lane, heartbeat thumping in her ears. So far, so good.

Without the tracer chip, she couldn't pass through any regular checkpoints, but she wouldn't need to if everything went according to plan. She'd face getting through the last security gate when she came to it.

The distinctive rhythm of the go-flow etched itself in Cara's brain, as she dipped into a series of underpasses close to the interchange for the port. The acoustic baffles sliced through the noise as she passed through compartments of sound. Whoosh. Shift. Whoosh. Shift. She wove between lanes, keeping her head down. This was her best chance, before anyone realized that her tracer chip was tagged to a decoy.

She turned onto the slipway for the port, irritated by the traffic delays through the go-flow that connected the two halves of the dumbbell-shaped way station. At the other end she emerged briefly into the open again, this time into an area of warehousing and commerce, its uniform gray broken only by garish logos. She avoided the heavily guarded access road to the platinum vaults and took the throughway. When the next tunnel swallowed her, she dropped her raft down, almost to dismounting speed. Better not break an ankle. She breathed deeply, checked the position of the traffic eyes, punched the auto, and leaped off, letting the raft go on by itself. Her legs impacted on the floor with jarring suddenness. Fuck! That hurt! She straightened both legs and tested her full weight on each in turn, but there was no damage done.

So far, so good. She had to keep going.

Away from the traffic, the sounds receded eerily. Ducking into a maintenance refuge, she retrieved a small multipurpose tool from her belt pouch and forced the catch on the door leading to an access corridor. A broad-shouldered man would have to walk sideways, but she was able to walk forward, taking care not to catch her head on the conduit that ran above. Third right, second left, through the access hatch, down the ladder. She'd checked the schematics, knew where she was going, followed the cryptic guides that prevented the maintenance crew from losing themselves in the maze. The wall itself sensed her presence and glowed as she passed, giving her a working light.

But the heavy silence ate at her nerves.

Did Ari already have operatives on Mirrimar-14? Maybe Craike's passengers had connected with someone local. She was pretty sure Alphacorp had operatives, sleepers mostly, spread all over the galaxy—as fast as colonies sprang up and hub stations deployed, they sent in fact finders—but she didn't know to what extent Ari could call on the whole of Alphacorp's network. How complicit was the Alphacorp hierarchy in Ari's unsavory activity?

Something snatched at her sleeve and she half-turned, ready to lash out, but it was only a loose cable-tie. She hissed a curse under her breath. She had the jitters. Confined spaces could play nasty tricks on otherwise perfectly normal minds. . . .

Confinement.

The memory of the abortive final mission on Felcon flooded back: waking from cryo in Facility 197, Alphacorp's Neural Readjustment Center, knowing it would be her word against Craike's.

She tasted the terror once again.

But despite her fears, they'd left her alone—completely alone—for weeks, her brain so fogged with Reisercaine that she couldn't access her implant. They did her one favor, though; they taught her that it was possible to exist cut off from the thought buzz of everyday living.

She mustn't let herself think about that now.

She stopped. Was that a sound behind? She listened hard, butterflies in her stomach.

Nothing. It was just her overwrought imagination. Breathe. Keep going.

She counted the hatches as she passed. Eight; this was it. It swung open silently, and she stepped through into a broad cargo tunnel. There was the usual security camera system with an eye directly above this door and she needed to put it out of action before she could move out of its blind spot. She'd requisitioned a reel of thin trilene line from stores and had picked up a pebble from one of the precious plant tubs in the concourse. The pebble's weight was enough to give the end of the line some stability. She threw it above the eye-mounting and the line snaked over the top of the flexible stalk. Then holding both ends of the line, she swung on it and bent the stalk so that the lens pointed at the wall. An eye out of place was less noticeable than one malfunctioning.

She freed it with a shake, coiled the line and pebble and pushed it into her pocket, then turned and padded off in the direction of the port, surrounded by silence. Far ahead, she could hear the dull noise of the cargo go-flow, but behind, it was as quiet as a tomb. She could hear nothing . . . or could she?

She turned at the sound of metal scraping behind her. Light as a cat, a gray-suited figure emerged from the hatch. His mouth was smiling, but his eyes were cold. He was the one from the concourse. Oh, shit. The butterflies turned into snakes roiling in her belly.

He stepped forward, menace in every line of his body, eyes narrowed.

"Thought you'd fooled me, huh?"

"Obviously not."

He was a talker. Keep him talking.

"You're worth a lot of credits."

"Sharing them with Craike and your friends?"

The flicker in his eyes told her he wasn't. Hopefully that meant he was working alone.

"Craike, pah!" He made a spitting gesture. "Amateur."

Fucketty fuck!

"I can pay more." Lie. Say anything.

This guy had a fighter's stance, and he thought Craike was an amateur. She'd never been able to beat Craike in a training session and had carried the bruises to prove it.

The man didn't waste any more time. He came in hard and fast.

Adrenaline surged. She dropped, pushed sideways and slid, lashing out toward him in a move that should break his kneecap, except he wasn't there. He was a pace away, coming in on her blind spot. He struck like a snake. She rolled to her feet and skipped out of reach, barely avoiding contact. They circled. The bare corridor offered nothing she could use as a weapon and no getaway route. If she ran, she'd be betting she was faster than him. Plus, it would put them both into the camera zone, and security would be here to grab the winner. That was no consolation either way.

Breathe. Think!

He was taller and heavier than she was, but she was light, fast, and supple.

At least he hadn't pulled a weapon. Maybe he was confident that he wouldn't need one. *Think again, bastard!* A surge of anger subdued the snakes a little.

"Craike's an amateur, is he?" She tried to distract him. "He's the best I've ever seen."

His mouth twitched in disdain, but he didn't waste words.

"Better than you," she said.

No reaction. A pro. She was in real trouble.

Who was she kidding? She was in real trouble anyway.

They circled, each waiting for an opening. She watched closely for a flicker of intent. There! They both moved at the same time. She darted in, twisting away from a disabling kick and striking toward the exposed area of his crotch. Her stiff fingers connected with a light box protector and jarred her knuckles. She whirled away and took half the force of the blow intended for her throat on her left shoulder before they spun apart again.

That was going to hurt—but not for a while. If she couldn't finish this fast, he would. She flexed her arm to test for damage, finding nothing torn or broken. For a split-second they stood motionless, facing each other, breathing hard, assessing, adjusting, reasoning. She didn't let her eyes be drawn to the man's wickedly fast feet, instead she watched his face, but he wasn't giving much away.

She needed an advantage. *Think, woman!* Her brain sorted through ideas, rejected even as they were being formed. She wasn't carrying a weapon . . . or was she?

He came in fast, but in her mind the scene played in slowmo. This wouldn't be a long encounter; he couldn't afford the luxury of playing cat and mouse. He'd already discovered that weaponless didn't mean she was unarmed.

He feinted right and turned impossibly at the last nano-second. She flung herself left. His right foot lashed out again, double-time. *Fuck!* Already unbalanced, she curved away from it, but couldn't avoid it completely.

At the end of its arc, where the energy had almost dissipated, his toe caught the side of her head, just above her ear, with a crunch that she heard as well as felt. Starbursts danced on the edge of her vision. She was in big trouble. Her red cap flew off, but she didn't let it distract her. A quick jab with her left. She caught his extended leg a glancing blow, elbow to knee. It wasn't enough to permanently disable him, but it gave her a breathing space. It was now or never.

Willing herself to keep gray nausea at bay, she ran backward, trusting that the corridor floor was flat and empty. Her hand went to her pocket and her fingers found the pebble and the trilene line. She didn't even have time to unravel them, she just hurled the lot, hard, from the shoulder, putting all her strength behind the throw. And then she followed it. She wouldn't get a second chance.

The line began to unravel as it flew. Damn! She'd be lucky if it even hit him.

He saw it coming and instinct snapped his head back. His eyes widened. Maybe the tail of the trilene line confused his perception for a moment. Whatever. It was enough. She had her opening. She smacked the heel of her right hand into his nose with all the force of her shoulder behind it.

His gargled yelp ended in the middle as the impact broke his nose and dropped him at her feet. It had taken less than a minute.

"Bastard!"

She kicked him in the ribs to be sure, but he didn't move.

Fear clamped, and running purely on automatic, she knelt beside him. He was still breathing. Was she pleased about that or not? How long did she have before he came to? She didn't need long to get far enough ahead of him, and she didn't think he'd admit to Craike that he'd tried to take the reward for himself, though his broken nose would take some explaining.

The nausea that had threatened before rolled over her now and she heaved up Jussaro's idea of breakfast over the unconscious man's left sleeve, fighting off the urge to lie down next to him and close her eyes. Her ears rang with the weird-shit sound of church bells underwater.

Concentrating hard on every movement, she picked up his limp left hand and excised the chip from his handpad, taking both his ident and his security chip. A businessman wouldn't be entitled to security clearance, but Ari's operative might.

She looked at the man's face and shuddered.

There was no time for pondering. He might come round at any moment. Quickly, she ripped off his handpad, leaving blood oozing from severed connections, and ground it under the heel of her boot. Then she dragged him to the service door and dumped him inside, using up almost all her reserves of strength. Bending to pick up her cap sent her to her knees under a wave of dizziness. She staggered upright and stood very still, breathing steadily, eyes closed, trying to find her center. Carefully, she jammed the cap over her bunched-up hair, avoiding the tender swelling above her ear, and walked slowly in the direction of the cargo go-flow, trailing the fingers of her right hand across the wall to keep contact with reality and remind herself which way was up.

Smooth-sided containers trundled by slowly, defying gravity on the moving lanes. Going through the cargo area would be the trickiest part, but the red coverall was standard-issue for all Devantec personnel, from engineers to package couriers, and perhaps these would help. She fingered the stolen chips, hoping that they'd get her through the checkpoint that she'd planned to bluff her way through as a Devantec employee.

Her head pounded like a pile driver. She tucked a stray strand of hair under her red cap, pulled the peak well down over her forehead, and eyed the moving trucks.

There. That was what she had been waiting for! An open mail truck of smaller packages trundled slowly by. She swallowed hard, bit down on her teeth, and took three quick strides to match speed. She grabbed the rim and stepped on to the casing, causing it to sway wildly on its antigravs before stabilizing and letting her find a safe riding position. Nausea threatened. She breathed it away. It was illegal, of course, for employees to ride the bucket, but everyone did it, and no one would haul her off unless she got a real stickler on the checkpoint.

She didn't. The checker even waved as she went through. Approaching the cargo area, she hopped off again, but this time with a random package held in front of her. It was heavier than she'd expected it to be for its size. She stumbled as she landed, feeling her balance falter, but sidestepped and found her feet again without going all the way down.

At the automatic security gate she popped the graysuit's access chip under the scanner and waited. The barrier opened, and it wasn't until she sucked in a lungful of air that she realized she'd been holding her breath.

Once through, she headed for the docking bays, finding it hard to read the signs through blurred vision. She screwed up her face, squinted at the numbers, and found the Aloha dock. She'd checked. Number seven was the emergency overhaul pad. The gate guard gave her a searching look, but she clutched the package to her chest to mask both her gender and the missing insignia on her suit, and muttered, "Delivery for bay seven."

She held her breath, waiting for him to say that the bay had cleared and gone, but he just grunted.

"Is that what the holdup's about?" he said. "The bay's been tied up all afternoon, and I've got eight craft piling up in dispatch. Get in there quick."

She started to reach for the stolen ident, but the guard was building up a head of steam. "Fuck that, just get on with it!" He waved her through.

She got on with it.

Rehearsing what she was going to say, she was surprised to find the wing-step still down. Ben offered her his hand as she climbed onboard the Dixie Flyer. He took the package and dropped it to one side of the cabin, its useful purpose ended.

"You made it."

"You were expecting me?"

"Figured you were the type who wouldn't take no for an answer."

"But you had yourself covered just in case I got caught."

"They might have caught you. Under interrogation, you could only tell the truth—that I refused you passage. Any trouble?" he asked.

"Tell you later."

He nodded. "Take that couch."

She slid into the copilot's couch and adjusted her harness. Even through her fogged brain she could tell that the Dixie didn't shine anymore, but it was well-maintained. It felt right, like a good working flyer should.

The couch molded to her body shape and the five-point restraints snaked over her shoulders, round her waist, and between her legs to meet in the middle and lock with a satisfying click.

Ben sat in the pilot's seat beside her and clipped on the lightweight headset that connected him to the ship's systems and left both hands free. The computer handled the donkeywork, but there was still a considerable amount of individual skill involved.

"Benjamin 4468, pad seven. Ready for air lock procedure," he said.

"Pad seven, running your clearance again," the speaker announced.

"Damn! I thought they'd be so glad to see me gone they'd release straight away," he said under his breath.

"Pad seven, you're overweight."

"Just taken a new systems unit on board."

"That's a heavy unit."

"Yes. Taking the old one back for refurb as well."

"Okay, pad seven. You're cleared."

Cara felt the hum of the boosters rise to a throb of energy as Ben ran final checks and completed his log.

"Delay, pad seven." The harsh voice of the controller cut in. Ben flicked the controls to manual.

"Pad seven, delay. Your delivery boy hasn't cleared the inward gate yet."

Cara held her breath.

Ben made no answer, but he released the lock on the mooring gear. His jaw was set tight and there was a little pulse beating at his temple.

"Pad seven, stand down. Terminate exit procedure."

For a moment Cara thought he was going to risk running the bay air lock without clearance.

"The guard didn't check me in properly—he might not know whether he's checked me out."

"4468 to Control. Check your access files in and out please."

There was a pause. "Control to 4468. We've no records in or out for your delivery boy."

"Well, I certainly got my spares. Suggest you check the efficiency of your gate security. Damn sloppy system, Mirrimar-14. Can you tighten it up, or shall I have a word on your behalf when I get back to civilization?"

"Thank you, Commander Benjamin, we can handle it. Instigating air lock procedure now."

"Thank you, Control."

Chapter Four

BETRAYAL

CARA GRIPPED THE ARMS OF HER SEAT AS the Dixie Flyer rose on antigravs into the air lock, and the double doors slid shut behind them. The outer doors opened. Ben engaged the drive and eased out into the stark beauty of space. Cara's weight fell away. She bounced gently against her restraints. Stars glinted brightly through the radiation-proof forward bubble. On the rear viewscreen the dumbbell-shaped way station rotated gently against pinpricks of light.

Tears prickled behind her eyelids, and she blinked them away. It was over. She was leaving Craike and his crew behind. They hadn't got her yet.

Feeling slightly disconnected from reality, she watched the incoming and outgoing traffic from the station. Mirrimar-14 sat at the confluence of three jump gates, two taking traffic to and from colonies on the rim and one leading toward Earth and the inner systems. At that moment she had the Rimward-B jump gate on her screen in the far distance. The gate itself was nothing, a disk of pure black emptiness, a hole where stars should be and weren't. On either side of that were two modules: the larger unit combined crew quarters and control functions, while the smaller one housed the gate impeller.

As she watched, the black disk winked out and the stars behind it sprang into being.

"No!" She gasped. "The gate . . ." Could Craike order them to shut down the gates? Heart pounding, she looked for the other gates on the viewscreen.

"Relax. It's off line for maintenance. It'll be active by the time we get there."

Relief flooded through her.

They must be relining the rods. Ah, yes. There it was, the platinum fleet, one drone and its escorts, all armed to the teeth. Once the platinum was installed in the rods, it couldn't be reclaimed, but it was vulnerable in transit. They had five runs every thirty days, too many chances to lose several million credits' worth of the precious metal that leeched out into the Folds with every jump made. No wonder they were twitchy.

She concentrated on the platinum convoy, using it to hold onto her senses until it slid off the edge of the screen. For fully thirty minutes they seemed to drift steadily, though Cara knew they were gradually picking up speed.

Ben removed his headset. "Two hours to our time slot for the gate. You look like a corpse. Are you all right?"

"A bit nauseous. May just be the null-G."

"I can give us quarter-grav. It should help."

She felt a slight shudder and gradually she regained weight. She unclipped her harness and winced as she tried to move her left arm.

"You did run into trouble."

"A heavy. I managed to leave him out cold, but he caught me with a couple of smart smacks before I found a way to distract him."

"Are you always this calm when you've just dealt with a hit man?"

"It's not as if I make a habit of it."

Ben left the Dixie on automatic. He crossed to a locker in the aft bulkhead, pulled out a sliding table, and opened up a comprehensive med kit.

"Here."

He gave her a cool gel compress to hold to the soft swelling on her temple. She wanted to close her eyes and sleep, but he shone a light in them and wouldn't let her. Mean bastard.

"Talk to me," he said.

"What about?"

"Anything. Everything. Keep talking. I want to know if you're about to go into a coma."

"Such optimism. Should I be reassured?" She slurred the words slightly, like a drunk and had to repeat "reassured" twice before she was satisfied with her pronunciation.

He helped her to peel the red suit from her left shoulder. Her skin was already turning a deep shade of midnight and burgundy.

"It looked prettier last night," he said, as he packed a fresh gel compress on the bruise.

"Don't remind me. I'm sorry about last night."

"Whatever you say." He turned back to the med kit.

She wished she could wipe the memory of sex with Ben Benjamin from both their minds. He touched her arm again, and she almost leaped out of her skin, but he was only slapping on a blast pack of painkiller.

"Relax. I'm not going to jump on you without an invitation. How's that?"

"Easier, thanks."

"Don't worry."

"What?"

"That was a good act you put on last night, but I know it wasn't for real."

She blushed. "I'm sorry."

"Don't be. At least you had the grace not to fake an orgasm."

"I'm really sorry."

"Ah, now that sounds like the truth. That works for me."

"Me, too." She tried to smile, but her head was pounding and it turned into a grimace. "Thanks."

"You're welcome." He nodded. "I need to talk to Crowder on Chenon. I may have to pull in a few favors to get clearance for you to land."

"Wait. I'm dead meat if my name goes on the port immigration list."

"That's why we need Crowder."

"Crowder works for the Trust, right? He's a company man?"

"But he's also a friend. If anyone can find a back door for you, he can." Ben swapped the gel compress for a fresh one and put the first to cool again. "As soon as we clear Mirrimar-14, I'll send a message via the gate Telepath. We'll have to wait for the reply before we can jump the Homeward Gate."

"I can sustain a triad."

"Not with a roaring concussion. Besides, you've powered down your implant."

"No reason to keep it powered down. We'll be in the Folds soon, and they can't track it then."

She tongued the tiny control built into her jawbone.

Her mind exploded with pleasure. The blank emptiness opened up, and she could hear the background hum that meant she was no longer alone and silent. She even got a buzz from Jussaro back on station as he started his shift and wondered where she was.

But standing way out in front of the background hum was Ben. Not a Telepath, he'd said, but a Psi-1 Navigator able to receive.

Benjamin!

She connected, maybe a little too enthusiastically, like a junkie taking the first hit for months.

He jerked. *Whoa.*

Sorry. Just so glad to be connected again.

So I see. You really are a Psi-1 Telepath?

I really am.

She didn't mention her minimal ability as an Empath. She barely registered on the scale and, anyway, some people, even other psi-techs, got twitchy around Empaths. Besides, she didn't want to know what Benjamin's feelings toward her were. She hadn't let herself become emotionally entangled last night. If Ben had, she was sorry.

So you need Psi-1s on this Olyanda mission?

We'll talk about that later.

She sighed. "Implant's all better now."

"Yes, but you took a ferocious knock."

He cradled her head with both hands and let his fingers gently probe her skull.

"Owww!"

"See what I mean?"

She couldn't keep her voice steady. "Are you a trained medic?"

"No, but I've done my fair share of fixing up."

"Where did you learn that?" she asked.

"I grew up on a farm on Chenon. It was pretty remote. We had to fend for ourselves most of the time. I can shoe a horse, too, and strip and assemble a K46 drive for a tractor."

"How long have you been in the Trust?"

He looked at her with raised eyebrows. "Curious, aren't you?"

"No more than you are. I'm just trying to make conversation. You said I should talk to you."

"So I did. All right. Six years active, eight including cryo. And before you ask, I was brought up by my grandmother; I have one older brother called Rion; I have no allergies. I eat meat, and I'm divorced. I don't suppose there's the remotest chance that you would answer some of my questions?"

"Probably not. I was born on Earth. I still think of it as home, but before my first birthday I was hauled off to the arse-end of the galaxy. My parents worked the frontier planets. Mom was—still is—a marine biologist and Dad was a hydro-engineer, but we traveled a lot. I have no brothers or sisters. My folks split up, and I shuttled between them, racked up some cryo." She sighed. "Dad died, but I couldn't go back to Mom. We never really . . . Oh, that hardly matters, now. She's halfway across the galaxy with her latest lover. I went back to Earth, spent almost a year with my grandfather in Cornwall before going to school. He was an old, old man, but he'd been a professor. His house was full of books, real books, old ones, too."

She could have lost herself in her grandfather's library. Perhaps she should have.

"And your enemy is?"

Her head began to ache even more and she frowned.

"Someone you'd better not tangle with."

She was thankful he left it at that.

◆ ◆ ◆

Cara insisted she could hold a triad with Crowder, so Ben figured the fastest way to get her to give in and rest was to let her try. If she couldn't hack it as a Psi-1, it was better to find out now rather than later. Of course, he didn't really know her, so if she was a crank, then letting her inside his head was going to be a big mistake, but even though he might be on the very low end of the telepathic scale, he had a strong grasp of mental shielding, and he was fairly sure he could shut her out if he needed to.

He sat in the pilot's seat again and let down his shields, then nodded. He felt her flow into his mind with no hint of the trauma she must be feeling. Her gentle self-assurance took him by surprise. Their touch, mind to mind, rocked him to his core. He connected with her in a way that he hadn't before, even when they'd made love—had sex. He corrected his opinion of their coupling. She'd been lovely, but her heart hadn't been in it. He felt her mind float through his. It wasn't that she was rifling through memories; those things he wanted to keep private were still behind barriers, but the connection stripped away a layer of reserve, and there was only painful honesty between them.

He suddenly knew her without knowing anything about her, and by the look in her eyes that knowing had surprised her, too. Maybe it was the developing concussion that had caused the deeper contact, but this was way more of an exchange than professional comm demanded.

Whatever she was running from, she was honest—he was suddenly sure of that. He recognized integrity when he felt it.

All right? he asked.

She nodded.

Then connect me to Gabrius Crowder, on Chenon.

He felt her lift Crowder's contact ID delicately from his mind and hold onto it until it became part of her. Brain and implant meshed. The boundary blurred. She aimed her thought into the blackness of space, across vast distances, through the weirdness of the Folds and into the atmosphere of an inhabited planet, mingling with the backwash transmissions of hundreds of psi-techs. She sought just one specific implant and he followed her, mind to mind. It was like riding the wind.

Most execs had implants as an expensive courtesy. They came with the job along with health and dental plans and— for the lucky—a pension, but there was as much difference between a *passive* and a real psi-tech as there was between a deadhead and a *passive*. *Passives* were basic receivers without any of the true psi-tech skills. Money could buy an implant for receiving communications, but it couldn't give the skills to use it actively.

The skill to use an implant to transmit at Cara's level was rare; more art than science, more aptitude than training. Ben knew instantly that she was a Psi-1.

Her thought found its mark. Ben felt the slight hesitation as her implant offered Crowder's a virtual handshake, and then he was in Crowder's head with Cara holding the triad steady. Words and meanings flowed through her neural pathways.

Benjamin? Crowder sounded exasperated. *Are you on your way back yet?*

Yes. Take it easy. Just hit a minor problem. Ben flashed his location. *I need a favor. I need to bring in someone without going through official channels.*

If I asked why, would you tell me? It's not one of your waifs and strays again, is it?

She's a Psi-1. Aren't we short of Psi-1s for the Olyanda mission?

We might be. Crowder continued, *But I can't circumvent Immigration, even for a Psi-1, even for the Olyanda mission. You've got all your old team, like I promised.*

What's left of them.

There was a moment of uncomfortable silence, and Ben felt Cara's half-question. A comm Telepath wasn't supposed to listen to the conversation she facilitated, but the no eavesdropping rule had been made up by deadheads. It wasn't that Telepaths couldn't hear, it was mostly that they chose not to listen.

He felt her pull back from interrupting, and the silence dropped between the two men like there was an elephant in the room. He suppressed a flare of bitterness.

Do your settlers know about Hera-3? he asked.

Let's not drag out all that again, Ben, not now. The investigation's been shelved. Let it lie until a better time. Meanwhile I've got the Five Power Alliance screaming at me for a status report on Olyanda, and we need ... you need ... to move forward. You need to stay in the system because it's the only way you'll get to those responsible for Hera-3.

Am I that transparent?

Only to me. You know I'll back you if you can find any more hard evidence. Trust me.

Appreciated.

I'll see you here in four days.

Four days, with or without a Psi-1 for the team.

Don't do anything stupid, Ben.

As if ...

"You heard all of that, I guess." Ben turned to Cara, noting her eyes were slightly glassy.

"You expected me not to listen?"

"Of course not. How are you feeling?"

"Like shit. I just want to go to sleep."

"I know you do. Try and stay awake for a bit longer. I want to be sure that when you sleep you are sleeping, not unconscious."

"Tell me about Hera-3."

"A straightforward colony setup mission, but we were hit by raiders. I lost a colony."

"Why?"

"We had something they wanted."

. He suspected that his regular reports to HQ had been leaked. The planet was lousy with platinum. Maybe it was his fault, maybe not. It made little difference to the weight of the dead he carried. He'd only brought home fifty-seven of his two-hundred-strong crew. The rest had either died in the first wave of airborne attacks or been killed trying to protect the surviving settlers. In the end he'd managed to lift fifteen hundred settlers off planet to safety—just fifteen hundred out of six thousand.

"The Trust closed the case. I lost my rank, but Crowder kept me on in Special Ops, running surveys, checking on colonies."

"Crowder—do you trust him?"

Ben didn't even need to think about it. "Of course. He brought me into the Trust. He kept me in when things got rough. I've worked my way through the shit. Olyanda's my first colony command since Hera-3."

"You've not closed the case, have you?"

He shook his head. "Too many lives lost on my watch."

She subsided into silence. What was she thinking?

At length she said, "Does it make you feel better?"

"What?"

"Hoarding all that guilt for yourself."

He was about to deny it, but then he just shrugged. "It reminds me that it's not over yet."

"Fair enough." She nodded. "Tell me about Olyanda."

"It's an Earth-type exoplanet orbiting a Population 1 star—an active star, subject to unpredictable electromagnetic storms, so poor-to-zilch reliable radio communication, hence a full psi-tech crew for the setup."

"So, it's cheap real estate, marginal subsistence possibilities with little chance of future tech development beyond, say, late industrial revolution level. Great! With a little luck the poor sods can reinvent the steam engine within just a few centuries."

"That's about it. Let's not forget they chose it. The settlers are Ecolibrian. They're looking for a back-to-basics lifestyle. Horse-drawn vehicles and everything made by hand."

"Aren't the Ecolibrians politically active, too?"

He nodded. "The FPA wants them out of the political arena before the next election—at any price—and as for them, they're eager to be gone to a world of their own."

"I get the idea."

"You want in or out?"

"I thought Crowder said there was no way into Chenon without going through official channels."

He raised one eyebrow. "I'm not out of ideas yet. There's always Crossways."

◆ ◆ ◆

Gabrius Crowder sat up in bed and pinched the bridge of his nose between thumb and forefinger. He hated telepathic communications. They could—and often did—catch him at inconvenient times. This one had left him with a lingering headache, though he didn't know whether that was a direct result of his implant or from trying to keep secrets. Even though he'd been assured that his receiving implant couldn't breach his privacy, he always worried about letting something slip.

Gods, he wished he didn't have so much to hide.

But he did—and having Ben Benjamin around was proving to be a liability. He'd kept him working away from Chenon, given him every long-distance survey job that came up, minimized his time at HQ, but whenever he came back, Ben was digging into files, checking suspects. Damn! He'd thought the man's persistence would fade with time when he failed to find anything, but he was relentless in his determination to discover who'd been behind the Hera-3 attack. It was unfortunate that Ben's goals and Crowder's had set them on an inevitable collision course.

It was time to find a permanent solution.

The Olyanda mission would take two and a half years: nine months' journey time each way, in cryo, and a year on the planet. He could arrange to waylay the cryo pods of the Hera-3 survivors on the return journey. There was a warehouse facility where such things could be stored long-term. Fifty years would do the trick, or maybe a hundred. Ben would be somebody else's problem then.

Hera-3 had been a bloody disaster. Ben and his team were supposed to be off planet long before the black-ops fleet moved in, but Ari van Blaiden's man, Craike, had mistimed the attack. Ben had not only managed to get himself and fifty-seven of his team off planet, under fire, but he'd brought all fifteen hundred surviving settlers home, too—witnesses who had needed relocating at the far end of nowhere, with a handsome payoff, to make the rest of their lives too easy for recriminations.

Crowder had split up Ben's team, but with the chance to deal with them all in one go he'd managed to gather them together again—no small achievement in itself.

Luckily, none of them had close family. Crowder would have been surprised if they had. Psi-techs tended to work in pairs if they were inclined to have lovers, but those they left behind, families and old friends, became separated by time and a growing age differential. And, deep down, deadheads tended to distrust them. Dammit, Crowder distrusted them, too, and he *had* an implant, though there was a world of difference between having a simple receiving implant and being a true psi-tech. Crowder had once been bitterly disappointed when he'd tested negative for psi abilities, but psi-techs, for all their apparent glamour and want-for-nothing salaries, were used by the megacorps; they rarely ran them.

Crowder sighed and swung his legs out of bed. It was no good. He wasn't going to get back to sleep again, so he might as well go into the office. No one would be surprised to see him so early. He often spent the whole night there. The Trust was his life. He was a whisker away from a seat on the board, presuming Ben didn't spoil everything.

He'd been putting off dealing with Ben. Dammit, Ben had saved his life at Londrissi, and he genuinely liked the man. Even on Hera-3, Ben had only done what he did best— risen to the occasion. It hardly seemed fair that he should end up as collateral damage. Crowder shied away from the obvious solution. He owed the man something for saving his life—even if it was only a one-way trip to the future. Long-term storage was a humane option.

Crowder recognized the irony of the situation. He hadn't hesitated to encourage Ari van Blaiden to attack a whole colony though, in truth, he had been surprised by the ferocity of the attack and the subsequent loss of life. Ari had scooped up millions of credits in loose platinum, and the Trust, according to plan, had swept in afterward and taken over the administration of the remaining resources. It was almost fair. The Trust needed the platinum, and the colonists were being obstinate. He could almost classify it as an expedient political takeover. Disposing of Ben, however, would be murder and despite everything, Crowder had to draw the line somewhere. He'd never met the colonists, but Ben was his friend.

Was it all worth it?

Yes, it was. In Hera-3 he'd gained a huge platinum resource for the Trust, a big deal even after all the payoffs and Ari's personal take. He'd do it again in a heartbeat because the Trust needed the platinum to feed its growing network of productive colonies.

Once he got his seat on the board . . .

He thought about the current board. No imagination. No willingness to take risks. Moribund. They needed him if the Trust was to keep its lead over Alphacorp. Anne di Doren, who had reinvented the Trust in the aftermath of the meteor strike on Earth in the twenty-fourth century, was his many times great-grandmother. He had di Doren blood in his veins; he could lead the Trust to even greater heights, leave Alphacorp eating dust.

Yes, he could.

✦ ✦ ✦

Victor Lorient closed his personal flight case and set it down on the floor. Even as director of their new colony, his luggage allowance was no bigger than anyone else's. He wondered whether he could sneak anything into the admin crate, but that didn't seem fair. Besides, Jack Mario would notice. Jack noticed everything. That's what made him such a great administrator.

"It's done. How about you?" Victor looked across the bed to his wife, Rena.

She smiled ruefully. "My office has been reduced to one small box, but the personal stuff is difficult. I thought I'd already done the hard part when I threw practically all my old clothes and possessions into the recycler, but this is hard, too. I can't take what I'd planned. I saved three good dresses for the time on Chenon, but I guess I've only got room for two." She looked wistfully at the purple fabric lying in a crumpled heap on the pillow. "And leaving behind all the everyday trappings of life here is so . . . well . . . so . . . Oh, I don't know. We wanted to make a clean break, but now the moment is here I realize just how much we're leaving behind. Do you know, I still have Danny's baby shawl?"

"You said you wouldn't go all sentimental on me."

Rena sniffed and wiped away a tear. "I promised that I

wouldn't let my sentimentality get in the way. I didn't say that I could just snap my fingers and turn it off."

"Mom, Dad, I'm all packed now; do you want me to take the archive box down?" Danny stood in the doorway. He was small for his nineteen years, delicately built and dark-haired, with a pleasant moon-round face and heavy epicanthic folds masking the inner corner of each eye. It gave his face a permanent vacant expression, except when he smiled, which he did often. Then his eyes sparkled with good humor.

Danny was special to Victor and Rena and very special to the Ecolibrian movement. When they'd refused to let the medics intervene, Danny had been born, naturally, with Down syndrome, a condition that had been overcome centuries ago by gene therapy. Loved and loving in return, Danny had become a symbol that perfect life did not require technically induced perfection in order to live.

Because of his condition, Victor had been able to keep Danny out of the automatic testing for latent psi-abilities. Victor loved his son far too much to let him be sucked into that trap.

"I haven't finished packing the archive box yet, Danny," Victor said.

"I finished it for you."

Victor frowned, but he didn't let the irritation reach his voice. "I'd better check it again. It's very important that the archives are in order, so that in years to come people will remember us for our beliefs, and they'll know why we chose to leave Earth and resettle on Olyanda."

"I didn't leave anything behind, Dad, honest. Are you mad with me?"

"Of course not. You can come and help me check it while your mother finishes her packing."

Victor put his arm around Danny's shoulders and guided him gently to the study.

"See." Danny opened the crate and lifted out the contents. Most of the permanent records were on crystal dataslides and there were four identical boxes.

"Which was the one from the desk, Dan, and which from the shelves? I meant to label them before they were packed."

"That was from the desk." Danny pointed. "Or was it that one?"

Victor sighed. "Bring me the reader. I'll have to check."

Danny unrolled a slim screen and handed it over. Victor checked the first crystal and slipped it into the base unit. A date, three years earlier, showed on the header. He was going to flip the crystal straight out, but a holographic image flashed upward from the screen and he was drawn to the meeting room where, if he really thought about it, the turning point had come. What they had agreed on that day had led to their current preparations for departure. In years to come this would be the only record, but he remembered it all so clearly: the emotion, the tension, even the smell of Rena's perfume as she leaned against him for reassurance. They'd got what they wanted, but at a price. In order to found a new colony on Ecolibrian principles, they had to agree to work with the psi-techs for the first year.

Just the thought made Victor break out in a cold sweat. Psi-tech abominations were one of the main reasons he wanted to leave Earth. He had firsthand experience. He knew how dangerous they could be.

Chapter Five

CROSSWAYS

*F*ROM: *ROBERT CRAIKE, MIRRIMAR-14 HUB.*
To: Ari van Blaiden: Alphacorp HQ, Earth.
Recipient's eyes only.
Message:
Subject on station but not reported for work today. Apartment checked. Not occupied since yesterday. Berenger and Hoffstead have drawn a blank. Checking departures from shuttleport. Negative so far.
Rosen not reported in yet. Overdue.

Ari van Blaiden sat erect and very still in his office while he absorbed the contents of the message from Robert. Dammit, Cara was resourceful. She could easily have gone to ground and it would take a station-wide lockdown and search to locate her, especially since the Finder on the team seemed to have gone missing.

He didn't want this on record. He deactivated audio and scribbled on his sensapad:

Find her, Robert. I want the whole station turned upside down until you have her safely contained. I won't accept failure. Understand? Is Rosen on the trail? Can he be trusted not to damage her? No mistakes. I want her back alive.

Ari's balled fist showed white knuckles as he hit send.

"Damn," he said softly to himself. "Damn."

Robert had wanted to finish her on Felcon, but Ari had been reluctant to let her go. He was still a little surprised at himself, though he could deal with any lingering feelings he had for Cara if he had to. Besides, she not only knew too much, she had the evidence to back it up. McLellan's conditioning wasn't complete. He didn't know how long the neural block would hold, or even if it would, but the fact that he was still sitting here instead of in a top-security holding cell was practically proof itself that whatever McLellan had done to Cara's mind was still effective.

He couldn't rely on it, though. He needed to find out what she'd done with his files, then neutralize Cara fast. Then, maybe, he'd let Robert have her. It was always good to throw your dog a bone now and then. He trod a fine line, giving him just enough affection to keep him faithful, but not enough to allow him to get too cocky. Robert was too useful to waste. Ari knew exactly what Robert wanted and was playing him like a fish on a line, stretching out the sexual tension, anticipating the moment.

He couldn't pretend he wasn't enjoying it.

It was a game Ari always enjoyed. While Robert Craike simmered, he had Res Darlan at boiling point and was gently warming up Ensign Kitty Keely, a pilot newly seconded to OpCon for his own personal use. He had plans to use her, but not necessarily for her flying skills.

He'd enjoyed Cara, too. He tried to think of her in the past tense. She'd been remarkable. He was even still a little in love with her. He sighed. He was always a little in love with all of his conquests. He was a man who liked to indulge his sentimentality, morbidly fascinated by the highs and lows of his own relationships. It was a pity Cara hadn't worked out. He'd wallowed in the heartbreak of her defection. It had finished too early. He'd had a fancy to try her in a threesome with Robert. Knowing that they hated each other would add a certain piquancy. He smiled to himself. If Robert could take her alive, there might still be the opportunity, and afterward Ari could revel in grief when Robert ended her.

He was conscious of a tightness in his pants. He sent a message to Res Darlan, Be home at six, then called in his secretary. "I need to speak with Donida McLellan. Put in a secure channel call to Sentier-4 and then take a break."

◆ ◆ ◆

Cara's pounding headache proved too much. She felt like shit. Definitely a concussion and nothing to do but take another shot of painkiller and wait it out. She thought she remembered Ben saying he wasn't out of ideas, and when he smiled, the contrast of white teeth against brown skin focused her attention. He had a kind of wolfish grin that she'd not noticed before. She'd thought him a bit of a stuffed shirt at first, but now she was beginning to wonder.

She wasn't sure she'd quite lost consciousness, but there was a gap in her awareness of the last—how long? She was tucked carefully into a light survival blanket and stretched out to full recline in the copilot's couch. Ben was concentrating on the control panel, making minute adjustments to their course.

"Did you say Crossways?"

He turned his head and half-smiled. "Awake, are you? Yes, I said Crossways. Get you a new ident on the black market."

"Is that possible?"

"Well, it's a bit of a detour, but if I can make the right connection at the next jump gate hub, we could just about do it without Crowder's blood pressure soaring too high. There's this little matter of the Olyanda expedition."

"Of course." She eased her couch into a more upright position and winced. "I've never been to Crossways. Only heard about it."

"Whatever you've heard, it's probably not far from the truth. Some parts look civilized on the surface, but there's an undertow. You need good friends or the ability to sleep with your eyes open to survive it. But with enough credits you can get passage to anywhere and no questions asked. You could forget Olyanda and jump ship there. The megacorps don't have the monopoly on transport that they think they have."

"Have I got enough credits?"

"Barely."

"Have I got enough credits for a new ident?"

"No, but Crowder needs Psi-1s. You can get an advance to cover it."

"You sound as though you know your way around pretty well."

"I've passed through once or twice."

"Not on Trust business."

"Not strictly."

He didn't elaborate.

Cara dozed for a short while, aware that Ben was constantly nudging her awake to make sure she wasn't lapsing into unconsciousness. At some point he must have decided she needed to sleep and was reasonably safe to do so because she came round with a muzzy headache. By her handpad, four hours had passed. They were through the Homeward Gate and out the other side. She hadn't even noticed the Folds; her head must be worse than she thought.

"You're awake."

Ben handed her a steaming hot drink, fruit caff by the smell. Normally, she would have sipped cautiously, but she took a gulp, scalded her mouth, and slopped it over her front.

"Fuck!"

Sipping slowly this time, she checked the flight display. The figures on the screen seemed to pulse and glare wickedly, and she was only able to read them by screwing her eyes up to keep them still. They were in a holding pattern.

"Crossways?" she asked.

"Yes."

"Will Crowder take me if I get into Chenon with a forged ident?"

"He can't afford not to. The Olyanda mission is already under strength, and he'll have difficulty attracting Psi-1s to it. Most Psi-1s have got more brains than to sign on for a year of grief. He's got my old team together, but—well—we lost Psi-1s on Hera-3 as well. There are only two left. He'll take you."

Ben made another course adjustment. "Besides, I asked him to and he owes me."

"Why have your old crewmembers signed on?"

"Damned if I know." He leaned across and checked her temperature. His hand on her forehead rasped her skin like sandpaper.

"Here." Ben offered a blast pack of analgesic and she cradled it to the side of her neck, feeling the slight sting as the propellant drove it into her system. The relief was almost instantaneous. It didn't take away the pain completely, but it dulled it to a bearable level.

She dozed. When she woke up again, the viewscreen was filled completely by a close-up of the exterior of a wide-mouthed docking bay.

Her voice sounded quiet, even to her own ears. "Are we there?"

"On final approach now. It's early morning, station time."

There was a peculiar time glitch, and she realized it was caused by her losing concentration halfway through the conversation. How long had she been out?

"You know where I can get a forged ID?"

"I know a woman who does."

Cara desperately wanted to sleep again. Just talking was exhausting her. She drifted and roused to Ben saying, "We'll see what Mother Ramona can do."

✦ ✦ ✦

Ben looked at Cara sleeping fitfully. He wasn't a loner. Like all psi-techs he was used to that feeling of *belonging*. He missed his team. He'd left too many dead on Hera-3. The mission was doomed as soon as the platinum was discovered. The raiders arrived before the Trust's Militaire, so they must have had someone on the inside, someone at Board level possibly. He'd followed the trail higher and higher until he'd hit his head on the ceiling.

The psi-tech survivors had been scattered to other teams when Ben had been stripped of command status. Assembling what was left of his old team was good. And Cara . . . maybe Cara would work out okay. He'd seen a glimpse of her on that first night that intrigued him; it was nothing to do with sex. Well, not completely, anyway. He'd be crazy if he didn't recognize chemistry at work, but he doubted the attraction went both ways. He didn't need to know her life story to recognize that she carried significant damage in the relationship department. And that wasn't all. He glanced over to where she slept. A bruise darkened her hairline, but he thought she'd probably been lucky. It wasn't the worst concussion he'd seen.

Ben meshed his implant with the nav-system as he settled down in his couch. He locked onto the local navigation beacon and swiped his hand across the touch pad to retract the forward shield, giving him a clear view of Crossways, a huge dark wheel turning in space. Even from this distance he could see the segment that had been blown away in its war for independence. The generations who followed had sealed it. Newer sections encrusted the hull like a fungal infection. The visible array of pulse-cannon and the knowledge that the station was equipped with hidden weapons of even greater destruction warned off any force that might try to bring it back under outside rule.

Originally built over four hundred years ago as a transport and trading hub at the confluence of seven gates, Crossways had long since mutated into a miniature artificial world of over a million people. It had its own unorthodox economy and a government based on a surprisingly stable coalition of the heads of the largest organized crime networks and independent trading barons. They imposed order on the disorderly and ensured that nothing interfered with commerce. In a way it was more moral than any of the big corporations. At least Crossways' villains were honest about what they were. Chaliss was the head, or at least he had been last time Ben had come through. Things at the top tended to be a little fluid.

Ben broadcast the identification code he'd secured for himself on a previous visit. He'd had to falsify his credentials, of course. His position in the Trust and his history in the Monitors was something better hidden from the dueling paranoias that ruled this place.

He let the Dixie Flyer glide into the air lock on automatic and settle on to the pad, drive idling. He felt, rather than heard, the clank of metal on metal as the gravity field cut in and the craft's weight regained meaning. The lock cycled and the bay floor descended through two levels and deposited them in a functional hangar, which looked as business-like and as utilitarian as any Trust station.

He changed out of his uniform into a generic buddysuit—no sense in attracting unwelcome attention—and touched Cara's arm lightly, feeling her jump as though she'd been stung.

"Time to go."

Her harness retreated and she swung her legs over the side of the contour couch, a little unsteady on her feet. He watched her begin to move stiffly.

"You okay?" he asked.

She nodded, but didn't speak, and avoided meeting his eyes.

"They use a low pressure, thin-air system, here, to prevent trouble," he said. "It's the equivalent of suddenly being deposited on the top of a mountain without your body having a steady climb to get used to it. We'll get through the port area as quickly as we can, but it's going to be uncomfortable, especially with you like that."

He handed her a finger-sized alloy canister.

"I don't want you collapsing with altitude sickness. If you can't breathe, draw the tube up from the end and hold it close up to one nostril. It delivers enough oxygen to stave off the worst effects. Don't use it unless you have to. They assume anyone with breathing gear is a potential threat." She looked so defenseless that he wanted to be kind, but he needed her on her guard, so he opted for tougher tactics. "But use it if you must. Having you pass out would be highly inconvenient."

"Got it." Her jaw muscles clenched, and Ben reminded himself that looks could be deceptive. She might be sick, but underneath it all she was tough. Just getting through the port had already proved that.

They crowded together to cycle through the tiny air lock and stepped out onto the dockside. Cara's red coverall was bright against the grays of the utilitarian dock and the soberly dressed officials. The conditions weren't conducive to causing trouble. The oxygen-depleted atmosphere made breathing a priority. Ben avoided activating the breathing tube on his suit, but found himself panting slightly just from the exertion of walking across the hangar. He took Cara's arm to steady her and she leaned into him.

As long as you had a good credit balance on your chip, there were no spaceport formalities on Crossways. A professionally neutral clerk greeted them at the gate. He had a fine tube bio-grafted onto his face, which ran from a slim pack worn like a pancake hat on the crown of his head to his left nostril. It supplied extra oxygen, allowing him to function normally, giving him a distinct edge over any visitors making trouble.

"How long are you staying?" the clerk asked.

"As long as it takes." Ben fought to keep distress out of his voice.

He put his hand into the reader, made brief eye contact, then stared, unsmiling, somewhere toward the far side of the cavernous hall, taking care to put over the right persona for the situation, neither intimidating nor intimidated.

"You want the insurance?" the man asked.

Ben nodded. It was no use haggling. At least it would ensure the Dixie was still here when they returned. There was a certain amount of honor among thieves. Crossways wanted its visitors to return to do more business, legal or otherwise.

Cara remained quiet. She clutched his arm for support, but he noticed she wasn't over-breathing. Despite the concussion, she'd grasped the concept that the weak didn't last long here; neither did those who looked as though they had something worth stealing—not unless they had connections.

Ben had a few connections.

They passed through an air lock, into a short, low-ceilinged corridor and out into a busy transport interchange. Mercifully, the air was good again, even though it had probably been recycled a million times. Ben breathed steadily until he felt his system return to normal. Cara gulped the air as though she'd found water in a desert. He gave her a few extra minutes.

He found an autobank booth and checked the credit balance on his main account. Despite being run by and for the underworld, Crossways' interstellar banking connection was first rate.

"Keep both eyes open." Ben steered Cara into the little open-topped auto-cab that was next in line at the rank. "Don't speak to anyone and don't look anyone in the eye."

He tapped an address onto the location panel, passed his handpad over the reader, and was thrown back heavily into his seat as the tub-shaped vehicle whirled them into a traffic lane. It looked more like a fairground ride than a transport system, but with only three glancing bumps from other tubs, all occupied, they eventually arrived at a pull-in by a tall plaza. The airy space was lined with private dwellings built as complete houses, a gross waste of space and resources on a space station, so they were only for the rich. Far above them, the ceiling glowed azure with a natural daylight effect.

✦ ✦ ✦

"If this is Crossways, it doesn't look so bad." Cara stared around her, surprised that it was so light and bright when she'd been expecting something in antique shades of movie noir. If only the walls would stop spinning, it would be fine.

"This is one of the good neighborhoods," Ben said. "But don't let it fool you. It's no safer than anywhere else if you're a wide-eyed tourist. Come on."

They emerged into a street with a line of vendors' booths down the center of a wide boulevard lined with narrow houses. A few shoppers clustered around a fresh food stall and a caff stand looked to be doing good trade. At first everything seemed normal then, gradually, it seemed as though people moved away from them. A woman snatched up a small child and retreated through a door.

"Uh-huh. Not sure I like this." Ben glanced behind him. "The citizens of Crossways have a good sense of when to lay low."

"What's happening?"

"I can't spot anything, but that means nothing." He took Cara's arm, pulled her close, as if they were lovers, and put his lips to her ear in case anyone following had audio enhancers. "I'm pretty sure we're being followed."

He steered her away from the exposed area in the middle of the street. Keeping close to the houses, he walked fast, but not fast enough to attract attention.

"You know where we're going?"

"I'm a Navigator, remember? We need to head rimward by two blocks. It's a spiderweb layout. You go rimward and hubward."

At the next corner Ben turned hubward into a narrow alley between two dwellings, then paused to check the street behind.

"Thought so. Can you link with me?"

Cara opened up a channel between them and saw what he saw. A shadow ducked sideways. She felt Ben weigh the odds of waiting round the next corner for the man to catch up, but it was difficult to tell what sidearms a thug would carry on Crossways. All weapons were available here if you had the right contacts. If a thief, or worse, had targeted them, it was likely he'd be carrying a bolt gun or a tangler and maybe even wearing stun bands on his knuckles. One punch from someone wearing a full set of those could disable permanently.

She wasn't sure she needed to know the grisly details.

"This way." Ben took Cara's hand and pulled her along. She stumbled behind him. "Run."

She rallied. Her coordination became steadier, though every footfall pounded in her skull. He kept hold of her hand, and she made an effort to follow his lead through the maze of streets. He dragged her a little faster.

She kept the link light, and he let her into his thoughts. He needed to get to where they were going quickly or to find the right place to stand his ground, preferably somewhere without witnesses. The authorities on Crossways always took the side of their own citizens against visitors, no matter what the charge. He didn't seem to be scared. That was all right. She was scared enough for both of them. In her condition, she wasn't fit to be much more than a bystander.

They turned two sharp corners and came out into an open square of condos built right up to the blue-sky-roof. There was no shelter anywhere, but there were several alleys leading off.

Not far now. Ben took the one on the left, close to the point they'd entered. They walked quickly, going rimward, parallel to the first alley, and came out into an area of houses surrounded by high walls with gardens. A willow drooped over mock brickwork and a brightly colored bird fluttered in its branches.

Cara's breath rasped in her throat. She was almost at the end of her strength.

There should be an opening somewhere ahead. Yes, there it is. Ben didn't waste time looking behind. If their pursuer had a good sight line, they'd probably be dead already. Two more turns and Cara felt a wave of satisfaction from him as he found what he was looking for, the entrance to a narrow passage and, partway down it, a solid, unmarked door.

Here. He jerked Cara to a standstill.

She sagged against the high wall, her knees trembling.

The door had a metal grille at head height. Ben tapped on it and it slid open immediately.

"Speak." A voice came out of the grille.

"Thornhill renaissance," Ben said and glanced over his shoulder. *I hope that code's still good.*

Cara hoped so, too. She couldn't go on much further. If he had to carry her, he couldn't deal with whoever was following. She suddenly realized that she never for one minute thought he'd leave her behind to save himself. The thought warmed her.

The door slid aside to reveal a tall man in a buddysuit, a professional enforcer.

Ben nodded a silent greeting and motioned sideways with his head to indicate they were being followed. He pushed Cara through the gate and into the safety of an enclosed patio garden, lush with tropical ferns and palms.

"One moment," he said softly.

Cara grabbed the arm of the stranger to steady herself, then bent over, hands on knees, concentrating on not passing out. She heard the soft click of the gate as Ben launched himself into the alleyway, but by the time she looked up, he'd gone.

Had he been armed? She couldn't remember. With heart pounding, she lurched forward and wrenched open the gate, but she was too late to help. It was all over.

Chapter Six

DISGUISE

ALL PACKED. VICTOR LORIENT WAITED FOR the transport to take them to the final press conference, Rena and Danny at his side, smart in clothes they would abandon after today.

"All right?" he asked.

In answer, Rena grasped his hand and squeezed. "This is the last hurdle."

The door screen announced the arrival of the VIP auto, complete with a uniformed steward. Jack Mario was already inside the copious rear of the luxury vehicle, his stocky figure occupying a back corner.

Danny bounced in and flopped down next to Jack with a broad grin. "Hello, Mr. Mario. How are you today?"

"I'm fine, Danny." Jack had a soft spot for the boy and went through Danny's exaggerated handshaking routine as if it was normal. Shake, shake, fistbump, shake, shake.

Victor and Rena stepped into the auto and settled themselves opposite Jack and Danny. The steward held the door politely, poured them champagne, and then retired to the front compartment.

Danny sniffed his, jerked his head back in surprise at the bubbles up his nose, and looked to Rena for permission.

She nodded and sipped her own glass slowly. Danny copied her movements, but screwed his face up at the taste.

"Director Lorient." Jack downed his own champagne in one gulp as though it was water, coughed, and started again. "I've been checking figures with Mr. Crowder on Chenon. The uplink they've provided has been excellent. He'll be at the press conference via a holo-link and wanted to know if you needed to speak to him privately before it all kicked off."

Victor shook his head, wondering whether psi-techs could sense anything over a holo-link.

"Mr. Crowder promised me I could go flying!" Danny shoved his still-full glass into Jack's hand and bounced up and down in excitement, interrupting their low-voiced conversation. "On Olyanda."

"What? Oh, yes, flying," Victor said. "I'd forgotten."

Jack smiled at Danny and continued, "Everything's A-okay for departure tomorrow. I know how you feel about psi-techs, Director, but I've done all I can to minimize contact for you."

"Thank you, Jack. What would we do without you?"

"Will there be psi-techs at the press conference?" Rena asked.

"Gunther Paxton has flown in from Berlin to sign the Olyanda contract on behalf of the Five Power Alliance. I believe he has a receiving implant."

"Oh, that's all right, Victor, isn't it?" Rena's doe eyes were pleading with him. God, she was still beautiful, even with the pressure of caring for Danny these last eighteen years.

"A receiver? You're sure that's all he is?" Victor couldn't stand to see Rena upset, not when they were balancing on the threshold of the future. "Then I'll be fine." He turned back to Jack. "You take the first part of the conference; handle all the administrative details. Let Rena talk about her work with the families, and I'll finish it off from the Ecolibrian angle."

"All right." Jack sounded almost surprised.

Victor laughed. "Sorry, I know we have to work with the psi-techs. I wanted this to be a hundred percent perfect and we've reached ninety-nine. Under the circumstances, we could have done a lot worse. You're much more of an optimist than I am, Jack. You can present this in a much better way than I can, and you worked just as hard for it as I did."

They arrived at the Trust's office on the north shore of the Thames and were ushered through the impressive double doors to the press suite with its crystal clear window overlooking the kilometer-wide river spanned by the hundred-year-old glass bridge, which looked like something from a child's fairy tale.

Victor did a double take because Gabrius Crowder was sitting on the podium already. Then he realized it was only a hologram. Even so, he could see every detail of Crowder's bulky body, with its folds of ill-fitting skin showing above the neck of his formal suit.

Danny bounced forward. "Hi, Mr. Crowder."

"Hello, Danny." Crowder smiled.

There was barely a hesitation despite the distance between Chenon and Earth. The holo-link must be being beamed via an open jump gate.

"Gunther Paxton will present you with a parchment copy of the contract and the transfer of ownership for Olyanda so that the journalists can see you sign it publicly." Crowder waved his own copy. "They like capturing real historic moments, so I don't think there's any need to tell them that the original was signed and ratified yesterday, do you?"

"Not at all." Victor already had his copy of the document filed safely in Geneva. Nothing could break that contract. He felt safe enough to smile back at Crowder while mentally counting, as he always did in the presence of psi-techs: two hundred and sixty-five; thirty-three; six hundred and seventy.

"Thanks for letting me sit in," Crowder said. "The press always gets technical details wrong, so I'm really only here to field those sort of questions, though feel free to throw anything over to me that you don't want to handle."

"It's time." Jack checked the antique-style timepiece on his wrist that had replaced his handpad when they'd all had the little devices surgically removed.

They took their place on one side of a long table facing down the length of the room. Victor was in the center with Danny on his right and Rena beyond Danny. On his left were Jack and Gunther Paxton with Crowder to the far left looking almost as real as the rest of them.

"Ready," Jack said, and the doors swung open to admit the world's press.

They rushed in, jostling for the front rows of chairs.

The contract was signed and handed over with due ceremony and the journalists allowed their questions.

"Director Lorient, tell us about the new colony. What will it be called?" one woman in the front row asked.

"It's called Olyanda," Danny, sitting between his parents, shouted out before Victor had time to answer. Victor saw Rena's hand twitch at Danny's sleeve almost imperceptibly and Danny sat back, but not before there was a ripple of approval round the room. The reporters all liked Danny. His guileless personality seemed to bring out the best in people.

"Danny's right." Victor smiled his Sunday-best smile. "Olyanda is the name of the planet. Jack Mario, our chief administrator, will tell you more about it."

Jack stood up and assembled his notes. "Olyanda was first designated as a potential colony planet three hundred years ago when the gate technology opened up that sector of the galaxy. It's a little cooler than Earth, but temperate around the equatorial band. We're not going to have much technology to start off with, so everything will be based on a sustainable agricultural lifestyle."

"How are your people going to cope with living agricultural lives in a pre-industrial civilization?"

Jack answered again. "We've never made any pretense that life on Olyanda will be easy, but all our colonists know what they're letting themselves in for and they've been training for the last year. Ecolibrians are pro-ecology, so our machines will be human muscles, spades, plows, and the wheel. In preparation, our people have already begun to wean themselves off their handpads." He held up his own hand to show off his timepiece. "This is my tech now. It's called a wristwatch and it's a mechanical timepiece. All it does is tell the time of day. We've even got a couple of our colonists who have learned to be clockmakers. We have revived a lot of old skills set aside half a millennium ago. Even our medics have had to retrain in the use of old techniques. Many of our people are already living in our Readiness Communes located all around the world. I believe some of you have visited our camp on the Isle of Arran. All our colonists have undergone physical and mental fitness tests before being allowed to buy into the expedition. Of course, for the first year we'll have the benefit of some technology because our psi-tech setup crew will help us to get established."

"Isn't the use of psi-techs against your beliefs?" The question from the back hit home.

Everyone in the room looked toward Victor for the answer. He pressed his lips together and tried not to give his feelings away. Empaths often made great reporters. They asked leading questions and then sucked your own emotions out of you until they dried you out from the inside.

He cleared his throat. "We do, of course, look to a bright future with no psi-techs; however, futures have to be built, and we will build ours carefully. We've tried to balance creed against need. Right now, here on Earth, we live and work among psi-techs every day of the week. You might be psi-tech yourself. I could have a conversation with you and never know it. I don't think we're asking too much of our people to live and work with psi-techs. It's only for one short year. After that they'll leave and take their technology with them, and then we'll have the rest of our lives to live and grow as our conscience demands. Next question."

"Why did you choose to go with the Trust's tender, rather than Alphacorp?"

"We believe the Trust offers excellent value for money and that they will do a good job on our behalf."

"Have you made any special provision for children?" one woman asked.

Rena leaned forward. "We're taking complete family groups. No one under six, of course, because of the age restrictions inherent in the cryogenic process. And though we fully recognize the value of our most senior citizens, the settler life is physically tough, so we capped the upper age limit at sixty. I've been working with families to prepare them for what's to come."

"Are there any dangerous animals on Olyanda?"

Thank goodness it wasn't a question that Victor needed to worry about. Crowder stepped in to answer it.

Victor felt sweat prickling on his brow. Balancing need against creed would be the biggest trial of his life. Rena leaned across and briefly touched the back of his hand in a much needed gesture of support.

It was easy to preach against technology, but another thing altogether to abandon the safety of it. At what point did technology become unacceptable? Where, in the long history of mankind, had they stepped over the boundary of good technology: the invention of the wheel; the splitting of the atom; the blast-off into outer space; the unlocking of the genetic code; a cure for cancer; the use of antigravity technology; the discovery of foldspace?

Crowder was still talking: ". . . So there are very few creatures on Olyanda that would threaten a human, though, of course, there can always be surprises. Our surveys have been broad sweeps so far. More detailed work will be done during the settlement year. We're sending an experienced team of professionals, led by Commander Reska Benjamin."

"Would that be Ben Benjamin?" the woman in the front row called out. "The guy who lost the Hera-3 colony?"

"And the one who got hauled up before a tribunal for running the Daystar blockade with some Burnish refugees?" the man behind her asked.

Crowder leaned forward. "There were no grounds in law for the Daystar charges and Commander Benjamin was exonerated of all blame in the Hera-3 investigation. His record is exemplary. You're trying to dredge up a sensation where there isn't one."

"Yeah, that's old news," one of the pressmen shouted from the back.

"Do you envisage any problems between the settlers and the psi-techs?" A young man with an earnest haircut took the opportunity to fire a question at the panel.

"None." Jack fielded the question.

Crowder nodded in agreement. "The psi-techs are there in a professional capacity. There won't be any social interaction between the settlers and their tech crews."

"You mean no half-breed psi-techs left behind at the end of the year to muck up the gene pool?" A sharp-featured man spelled it out.

"Something like that." Crowder smiled and his dewlaps rippled.

Victor heard one or two uncouth comments and tried to fight a rising urge to scream.

Jack stood and faced the crowd. "I think that's all we have time for today on the Q and A. I'm going to hand it over to Director Lorient to say a few final words."

He held out one hand to indicate that the floor was Victor's.

Victor stood up and took a deep breath. He hadn't prepared this speech. Things often went better if he didn't.

"Friends, the Ecolibrian philosophy is about respect. Respect for each other and respect for the world we live in. Centuries ago, when our founders first formalized the tide of feeling that we were damaging not only our environment, but our souls, with our carelessness of the world around us, we gathered together. The media laughed at us and called us tree huggers, but in spite of everything the Ecolibrians gained strength.

"On Olyanda we will no longer be Ecolibrians, we will be Olyandans."

He cleared his throat. "Ladies and gentlemen, please wish us well in our new life."

◆ ◆ ◆

Ben let the door slide almost closed. Their stalker had made a big mistake. He gave in to a surge of anger, let it bump up his adrenaline levels, then pushed it back. Anger was useful, but it could also make you stupid, and leaving a trail of bodies behind, even on Crossways, wasn't a good idea. He reached into a concealed thigh pocket and drew out a slim parrimer blade, activated it, and felt the hilt mold to the natural shape of his hand. The razor-sharp blade glowed and the end of the hilt mushroomed out slightly into a dome which emerged from the outside edge of his curled fist like the end of a miniature dumbbell. It was a small weapon, but dangerous at both ends. He waited silently, content that Mother Ramona's enforcer was letting him play it his own way. He concentrated, listening for the slightest disturbance outside. There! He heard a soft footfall, and a shadow flickered across the gap.

Ben reached inside himself and found the anger again.

He opened the door quickly and stepped through into the alleyway. His opponent, a thickset man with mousy hair, had a bolt gun held ready, but pointing forward in his right hand. His mistake.

Coming from the left, Ben delivered one blow just below Mousy Hair's ear with the parrimer hilt and, with the other hand, twisted his arm until the gun fell from nerveless fingers. Then he backed him up against the alley wall, stamped down hard on the man's left foot with his right, and kept all his weight on it. He thrust the parrimer blade to the man's throat, the tip already glowing with enough energy to slice through his windpipe and cook his jugular into a blood sausage before the wound stained his suit.

The gate opened, but Ben didn't let it distract him.

The enforcer picked up the fallen bolt gun and clicked on the safety. A bolt gun was powerful, but lacking in finesse at close quarters, so the man was probably a thief and not a professional assassin.

"I don't like being followed," Ben said, holding the parrimer blade close enough so that Mousy Hair could feel the heat. "Who sent you?"

"No one. I work solo."

"Then no one will miss you." The blade edged closer.

"Wait." Mousy Hair burned his own chin as he spoke and his head jerked back, eyes wide. Ben eased the blade away slightly, but held it ready.

"Conroy. I work for Conroy," Mousy Hair said.

Ben looked at Cara, who had grabbed hold of the gatepost to stay upright. "Conroy? Mean anything?"

She shook her head.

He looked at the enforcer. "Conroy?"

"Small-time."

Ben nodded, adrenaline evaporating. "He's just an opportunist, then. I'll let you deal with him."

He stepped back and the enforcer grabbed the man as Ben let go.

"Mother Ramona doesn't like her customers interfered with." The enforcer growled at his prisoner and dragged him into the shadows of the yard.

Ben winced at the dull sound of stun bands hitting flesh, but considered it wise to let the enforcer do his job. He shepherded Cara beneath overhanging vines and gaudy jungle flowers, past a white-coated houseboy who nodded them through an open door.

✦ ✦ ✦

Ben and Cara stepped over the threshold into a cool, inviting interior.

"*Thornhill renaissance*," said a low, female voice from the shadows. "It's two years at least since I've used that code."

"That's the last time we spoke. You gave me a good contact in a very efficient law firm. It's even longer since I've been here in person." Ben turned. "Just after the Burnish rebellion."

Mother Ramona stepped forward into the light. She was small and delicate with white skin marbled in blues and grays; pretty in her strangeness. Her hair was a deep cerulean blue with silver and black highlights. An exotic from the planet Eldibane where body mods were commonplace, especially among those in the sex trade. If Mother Ramona had begun life as a sex worker, she must quickly have bought out the whole whorehouse. Her business acumen was legendary on Crossways.

"Benjamin. I remember. We made love on the couch, and I sold you illegal idents for some Burnish refugees."

"I'm flattered after all this time." He hadn't forgotten their last encounter, either.

"Will we seal bargains on the couch this time, hey?" She turned, looked at Cara, and made the obvious but incorrect assumption. "Your woman looks as though you should take better care of her."

Mother Ramona had a cackly old-woman laugh, though her body still held the promise of youth.

"Are you still working for the Trust?" she asked.

"Yes. This is a private matter, though. I need a new ident for Cara."

"Fast and no trace-route, I presume. Come into my den."

It was a den rather than an office. The couch was covered in furs and sagged from overuse. The walls were lined with glaring bad-taste trophies: animal, mineral, and possibly vegetable as well. Mother Ramona took Cara's hand and lowered her onto the couch. Then she swept aside a pile of plasfilms to clear a spot on the overcrowded table opposite and perched on it.

Ben looked across at Cara, tight-lipped and silent. Scared, he thought, even if she was trying not to show it. His heart did a backflip.

Stop it, Benjamin, don't get involved. But it was already too late for that.

Mother Ramona reached out and held Cara's chin, turning her head this way and that, noting the bruise, studying the planes of her face. "How much time have you got?"

Ben shook his head. "Very little."

"Four thousand." Mother Ramona leaned forward.

"Three and a half."

Mother Ramona put her head on one side. "Three eight, that's my bottom line. Take it or leave it . . . and I'll throw in the new haircut for free."

"We'll take it."

"Can we trust you?" Cara said from the couch. Her voice sounded weak.

"As much as I can trust you." Mother Ramona paused, then smiled. "Benjamin knows me. Give me your hand, child, and let's get started."

"I excised the tracer chip."

"You did? Oh, well, not much use anyway. I only need the bio one."

Cara held out her left hand and Mother Ramona scanned it into her pad. She swore under her breath. "There's a search out on this one."

"Who's looking?"

"Can't tell without pinging it right back to its source. I'm guessing you don't want me to do that?"

Cara shook her head mutely.

"It's going to take too long to alter it. I'll have to do a complete new build."

"What does that involve?" Ben asked.

"Time."

"How much time?"

"Three, maybe four days."

"Too long."

"Of course, it would save time if I could use a real ident," Mother Ramona said. "Have to buy one in. Only cost you an extra three thousand."

Ben shrugged. "Haven't got that."

"Then it's going to take at least three days to build a new ident from scratch."

He couldn't wait that long, but he didn't want to leave Cara behind. He took a deep breath. "How about this?" He held his own handpad forward and transferred information into the port on Mother Ramona's machine.

"This looks good. Complete, too. These babies are hard to get hold of. How did you manage it?"

"She disappeared. It took me some time to find her, and I cracked the central records to get her full download to make it easier. Might as well make use of it; she's not coming back."

"Serena Benjamin. Your sister?"

"Wife. Ex-wife to be more precise. Like I said, she's not coming anywhere close to where I am. She's out on Romanov, with a baby and an alpaca farmer, and that's where she intends to stay. Had enough of following a Monitor around from posting to posting, and she hated it out on the Rim. Can you use it?"

"I'll have to make Cara look more like her, but that's not impossible. They're about the same build, and I can do something about the face shape temporarily."

"Wife?" Cara came round from her daze. "If you think ..."

"Would you rather stay here?"

She shook her head.

"Then go with Mother Ramona."

Mother Ramona took Cara's arm. "Wait here, Benjamin. The physical alterations will be temporary, so better get her through Immigration on Chenon within the next seven days. Give me about two hours. You'll not recognize her when I've finished."

Ben watched her lead a slightly dazed Cara away.

◆ ◆ ◆

Maybe the concussion had eliminated all her natural inhibitions, but Cara wasn't scared of this strange exotic woman at all. Ben seemed to trust her and that was good enough.

So when did she start trusting Ben?

"Just a hypospray. It'll feel cold." Mother Ramona pressed something to the corner of her jaw, first the left and then the right. "Sit. While that's taking effect, I'll see to your hair. I'd normally have one of my boys do this. Not everyone gets personal attention." She painted something that stank of chemicals onto the shorter strands and tousled it all together with gloved fingers.

She stripped off the gloves, felt along Cara's jaw, and grunted in satisfaction. "It's working. Your jawline's heavier now, but it still looks natural. Changing your skin color will be the hardest, and I need to add six or seven kilos to your weight. I can probably make your breasts look a lot heavier with the right underwear.

"Here, strip and lie on the bench."

Cara complied and Mother Ramona draped a lightweight blanket over her, adjusted the angle of the head, and raised the section beneath Cara's knees so that she was comfortably supported. She checked the bruising on Cara's shoulder and went to the other side instead, fixing a drip. Then she rolled back the blanket and used the hypospray again around Cara's waist and across her belly.

"This will add some fluid and bodyweight. Don't worry, it's temporary. I need you to keep still for an hour now while the drip does its job. Can you do that?"

"No problem. Do you mind if I snore?"

Mother Ramona laughed. "Go ahead."

Cara dreamed of Donida McLellan saying something about Mr. van Blaiden wanting to know that his secrets were safe.

McLellan turned into Ari van Blaiden, but the question was still the same. *Are you looking after my secrets, Cara, my love?*

Of course. Why wouldn't she?

She surfaced from the dream and wrenched her mind

into the present, but there was a lingering desire to drop everything and run to Ari's embrace.

She jerked awake. That was one step too far. These memories weren't natural.

Eyes. She could just remember eyes boring into her own. Not Ari's eyes. Cold eyes.

Donida McLellan. The Telepath from hell.

The dream sucked her back into its depths.

A mind bored into hers. She had no defenses.

Mr. van Blaiden wants to know that his secrets are safe.

What have you done to me?

Keep his secrets safe. Bring them home.

The words echoed. Secrets. Safe. Home.

Never tell what you know.

It was like stepping off a cliff.

*Never . . . *

She was falling.

*tell . . . *

Still falling.

*what . . . *

The ground rose toward her.

*you . . . *

She put out both arms and arched her back, tilting her head up and up like a diver bottoming out in deep water and reaching for the surface.

know.

She reached up to the air and . . .

Now forget.

forgot. . . .

Cara came to in a daze and felt a tug on her arm. Oh, that's right, the drip.

"Sorry, was I snoring?"

"No, you were sleeping like a baby." Mother Ramona checked the drip. "Nearly ready. Ben will hardly recognize you."

"If I look like his ex-wife, he may recognize me too well."

Chapter Seven

CHENON

BEN GUIDED CARA BACK TO THE PORT AND onto the Dixie Flyer without incident. She stumbled on the ramp, flopped onto the passenger couch, and fumbled with the harness fastenings. He leaned over her to check it. He'd done some dumb things in his time, but this was probably the dumbest.

"Don't touch me. I can do it. Not helpless, y'know." She pushed his hand away, then changed her mind and held onto it. "Sorry. Not quite myself at the moment. No need to snap, is there? Just feel so . . . so . . ." She searched for a word. "Out of control. Don't like it at all. There are holes in my head, and I keep falling down them. I just climb out of one and—oops—here comes another."

She released his hand. He clicked the fastening and activated the environment unit that provided some cushioning against the effects of the Folds. He did the pre-flight checks as the Dixie Flyer rode the elevator back up to the docking bay.

"Don't think you're claiming matrimonial rights," she said.

He wasn't intending to claim any kind of rights, matrimonial or otherwise. Sex in space sounded exotic, but it was very overrated, especially in the confines of a small flyer, fitted only with narrow contour seats. Besides, Cara had made it very plain that their first night together had been their last. That was a pity, but he didn't have any right to argue with her decision.

He was grateful when she stopped struggling with her demons and drifted into a light sleep. He needed all his concentration for the jump through foldspace. This was where a psi-tech Navigator really won out. You could go through the Folds on automatic, but ships had been lost that way. His own parents had taken a luxury cruise to celebrate their tenth anniversary and had been lost along with three hundred passengers and eighty crew. Every time he crossed into foldspace he imagined their vessel drifting forever, the pilot frozen in the command chair, out of time, out of oxygen, out of luck. It was never entirely clear whether the losses were due to pilots not being able to latch onto the nav beacon, or whether foldspace held unknown terrors. Only the dead knew . . . and they weren't telling.

Sometimes Ben thought he saw the ghosts of lost ships, but nothing was as it seemed in foldspace. Instrumentation went wild for no apparent reason, so if you had the ability, it was better to fly on manual. His psi-nav skills kept him on the right course even when the ship told him lies. Sometimes the boundary between natural instinct and implant blurred into insignificance.

Cara's sleep didn't last. She woke with a jerk and tried to sit up against the harness. Her eyes were glazed over. "Y'know, Benjamin, a peck on the cheek or even a smile wouldn't have gone amiss. After all, it's not every day a girl gets married."

"You're out of your head." He kept his eyes on the console display. The gate was less than two hundred seconds away.

"Maybe, just maybe, I've got under your skin a bit. I'm sorry. Y'know, Benjamin." She slurred it. "I'm truly sorry if I have, because in the emotion stakes, I'd have to fly very high to reach absolute zero."

"Who left you feeling like that?" Maybe in this state she'd let the information slip.

She didn't. "Fucking you proved it once and for all. No

spark. I've got no fucking spark." She giggled. "No spark to fuck. No fucking spark. Get it?"

A hundred and twenty-seven seconds to the gate.

"Clear screen shields," he told the onboard computer. The shields slid back, and the forward bubble looked out onto a portal hanging in space. Two modules, one three times the size of the other orbited gently around each other, crew quarters and gate impeller itself. The gates were a blessing and a curse, allowing humanity to expand throughout the galaxy in an increasingly crazy spiderweb of overlapping and interlocking gates and hubs—hundreds of hubs, thousands of colonies—while creating their own monster in their insatiable hunger for platinum. Amazing to think how much platinum leeched without trace into the Folds every jump. That platinum loss—which no one had yet been able to eliminate from the system—left corporations cutting each other's throats for the next discovery of easily extractable ore.

A technological miracle. An economic curse.

Thirty seconds to the gate.

Between the modules hung an ellipse of pure black. Total absence of light.

The gate.

Ben felt the pull and distortion of foldspace, even from this distance. It absorbed him totally, ate into his brain, and left little room for unrelated thought.

"I said, d'you get it? Answer me, dammit." Cara cut through his concentration.

"You'll get it back. Your spark." He tried to fob her off to shut her up.

"Perhaps I don't want to."

They were on the brink of the ellipse. Ben briefly considered warning Cara that the Folds were coming up, but whatever hell was out there waiting for them, Cara was locked up inside her own personal version. He ignored her and concentrated on the gate.

✦ ✦ ✦

There's a pop and the blackness of space becomes a deeper blackness. At first nothing moves, then something begins to swirl as if it's alive. It's long and narrow, sinuous and serpentine. At first it lacks definition, but as it swims toward the Dixie, one golden eye opens and it stares. Ben stares back. Void dragons are a myth. He's heard theories and dismissed them, but here, up close, it's hard to disbelieve.

"You're not real," he says.

Aren't I?

His imagination provides an answer.

"Not real."

Its lips curl back from crocodilian teeth punctuated by saber-like canines. Teeth that could punch a hole in the Dixie's hull like a hot knife through butter.

Not. Real.

This time he doesn't say the words out loud, but he believes them with all his heart.

The void dragon begins to fade and he hears its sigh. Again. Soon. The words are in the air, floating on an impossible breeze.

It's gone.

The journey to Chenon stretches into weightless infinity, and then it's over.

❖ ❖ ❖

Ben shook his head to clear away the illusions. Void dragons, indeed. For a moment he'd almost believed.

Cara seemed aware that they'd reached their destination.

"How are you doing?" Ben asked her.

"I've been better." Her voice sounded croaky.

"Can you walk?"

"Do I have a choice?"

He put his arm under hers and for the first few steps she leaned heavily on him, but then she straightened. Once through the formalities as Mrs. Benjamin, Ben hustled her into a rented hoverpod and she relaxed in the passenger seat behind darkened plasglass and closed her eyes.

Ben's instincts told him Cara was bad news, but whatever had passed between them during that first mind-contact had jolted him to his core. It wasn't just his White Knight Syndrome; it wasn't even that she now looked like the woman that he'd once thought to spend a lifetime with. His feelings had become much more complicated than that. He should be building a wall between them if he didn't want to get hurt, but walls sometimes kept in the bad and kept out the good. You couldn't live your life behind walls. It wasn't living.

He piloted the little hoverpod quickly to a hospitality complex and booked in.

Once in their room Cara looked nervously at the bed and backed against a wall. "Are you some kind of closet weirdo?"

He sighed. "Would you believe me if I said no?"

There was no strength in her limbs. She staggered forward and perched on the enormous bed, rocking gently from side to side. Then she rolled over and curled into a fetal position. Ben ignored her and used the holo-comm to make a call. "Crowder?"

"Ben. Where are you?"

"Indira Ridge."

"What are you doing there?"

"Sorting out your new Psi-1. Cara's concussed. I'm going to let her sleep it off for a couple of days." It was more than a concussion. He realized that the concussion was compounded by the withdrawal from the tranqs she'd been dosing on for too long.

"Ben, watch yourself. Do you know what you're getting into?"

"You sound like you ought to be my dad, Crowder."

"I feel like it sometimes. Get here as soon as you can."

"I'll be there. And . . ."

"Yes?"

"Thanks, Dad."

Crowder chuckled. His holo image faded, and the line went dead.

Ben checked the bathroom, pulled off his buddysuit, and found a clean shirt and trousers in his bag. He freed his hair from the tight braid, shook it out down to his shoulders, and then tied it in a loose ponytail. That felt better. He turned to Cara. "Do you want a drink?"

"What's your plan?" She didn't move, just mumbled into

her curled-up arms. "You gonna get me drunk and then take advantage?"

"No. I'm just offering you water."

She nodded.

When he put his arm around her to sit her upright and hold the cup of water to her lips she winced at his touch. The cold liquid must have hit all the nerves in her teeth. She flung her head back and sprayed droplets all over the floor. There was a heady cocktail of chemicals in her system—including Mother Ramona's—that she'd be better off without.

He'd been hoping he wouldn't have to resort to the Amfital that Mother Ramona had given him as a precautionary measure. He'd used it himself once, years ago, thinking it was harmless enough, then he'd used it again. After the third time he'd thrown the rest away, but it still brought a shiver to his skin at the thought of it.

He filled the bathtub, took the packet from his pocket, tore open the corner and sprinkled powder in. It fizzed and turned the warm water slightly pink as it dissolved. It smelled of hothouse flowers with a tang of citrus.

He stripped down to the waist, so he didn't get his last shirt soaked and stained, and tried to stand Cara up to undress her. The second time her knees buckled he laid her back on the bed and began to strip off her clothes. She swung her fist at his head, missed, and almost hit herself on the rebound.

"I hope you realize I wouldn't do this for just anybody," he said, more to himself than her. He got down to the last layer, but he needn't have worried; she wasn't much of a turn-on. In this condition she was more like a helpless child.

He finished peeling off her sweat-soaked clothes, then scooped her up, carried her into the bathroom, and lowered her into the bath. She began to panic, splashing and wriggling, arching her back and making it difficult for him to hold onto her. The bath was deep enough to float in, so he daren't let her go. In her state she'd slip under, and it would only take a few drops of this stuff sucked into her lungs to close down her breathing altogether. He felt a blast of raw panic from her, implant to implant, and shut his receptors down.

"It's all right. It'll make you feel much better. Come on, trust me. Relax. Let go. That's it. Good girl."

She began to respond, though whether it was exhaustion or the soporific effect of the warm drug-saturated water was difficult to tell.

"Is that better?"

Her only reply was a vague, "Hmm," but it was a comfortable sound.

The pink water began to turn viscous, and the arm supporting Cara's semiconscious body felt numb. He pulled it out from under her as the gel solidified enough to support her weight and rinsed his skin with the fresher spray in the cubicle, flexing his fingers to restore feeling. He returned to the bath and scooped the warm jelly over the bits of her body that had been uncovered as the water had begun to thicken. He piled it onto her breasts and around her shoulders and throat and then up and over her ears and head, making sure that it was massaged down through her hair to her scalp, especially over the bruise. Finally, he smeared it across her cheeks, chin, and forehead and waited until her eyes closed and all the tension had gone out of her. Then he covered her eyelids. Only her mouth and nostrils were clear.

He had at least twenty-four hours before she came round again. Time to see Crowder, meet with the head of the settlers, and then catch up on some much needed rest. No, make that the other way round. Rest first. He put the do-not-disturb code on the outside door and called reception to reinforce that. Then he dragged the bed over to where he could see Cara through the open door. Satisfied that he'd done all he could for now, he rolled onto the bed and fell deeply asleep.

❖ ❖ ❖

Max Constant's first space flight was a real letdown. He'd wanted to see that iconic view of the Earth as a pale blue orb. Unfortunately all he saw was the inside of a tube, the anxious faces of his neighbors on the seats at either side, and the back of the seat in front of him, barely a handspan from his face. Someone had made a remark about flying cattle class and someone else had come up with: "Quiet in the cheap seats."

That was the truth of it. They were being transferred from Earth to Chenon as cheaply as possible. They'd spend a few months on Chenon in a training camp and then be frozen in cryo for the long journey to Olyanda.

Well, he hadn't paid for first class, so what was he expecting? Director Lorient and his family didn't get to say goodbye to Earth properly, either. Their seats were just a few rows in front of his own. Mrs. Lorient had looked pensive when they'd boarded, but their son, Danny, had been grinning broadly and saying hello to as many people as he could before his mother nudged him into his seat.

Max had grinned back at Danny—the kid was hard to resist—but then as everyone settled, he compressed his lips. Here he was, on the point of no return. Had he made the right decision?

This was a sensible move for him. He'd committed all his savings. Now, if only he could take that final step and commit his heart. He felt as though he'd left unfinished business behind him. Or rather, unfinished business had left him behind. When Leila had walked out of his life, he'd sworn never to fall for another psi-tech. It wasn't as if Leila was his first, either. He should have been more wary, but somehow he always seemed drawn to them. Settling on a colony that had none was perhaps a pretty extreme way of breaking the cycle, but after Leila, he'd just wanted to get away.

He'd admitted to the recent breakup, but not told the Ecolibrians that his ex was a Psi-4 Telepath. His counselor had warned him that in going forward there would be strands of his former life which would anchor him to the past. He must accept them as memories. The only important thing now was his new life on Olyanda.

"Ready for takeoff." The message boomed over the speakers, and there was a general hubbub of trepidation. They'd been warned what to expect, but the pressure from the upward thrust still came as a surprise. It was over quickly, though, and then he got the full effect of the strange weightlessness, which was mitigated by the snug harness.

He needed to pee. No, he didn't. They'd been given suppressant shots since they wouldn't be allowed out of their seats for twenty-three hours until they reached Chenon. It would be over quickly, though. Pretty soon the cabin would be flooded with a gentle sleep gas, a standard tactic when taking space-virgins through the Folds, apparently.

He was still thinking about the sleep gas when he woke up. Now he really did want to pee. How long had it been? He glanced down at his handpad, something he was hanging onto for as long as possible. Twenty-four hours. Oh, they were actually down on the ground. His first space flight and he'd slept through it.

"Ladies and gentlemen, welcome to Chenon. Please exit as directed. There are fresher facilities on the concourse." The announcer cleared her throat. "Lots of fresher facilities."

A small cheer went round the cabin.

✦ ✦ ✦

Cara feels her grip on reality fading in and out. She has a jumbled impression of the last few days, but she doesn't trust her memory. She remembers running from something or somebody. There's a white-faced woman and—is she really married? No, that's ridiculous.

She doesn't even seem to be able to communicate now, either mentally or verbally. Her head is one throbbing ache.

She's felt like this before.

There's a memory hidden below the surface of her mind, but it refuses to reveal itself. She tries to catch it, but it sinks deeper and slips away. She follows it into a dark building. Her heart pounds in its cage of gristle and bone. Maybe around the next corner . . .

She's in a corridor, and there's a door with a small clear panel in it. She doesn't want to look, but she has to.

She peers through and sees a bank of machines; herself in a padded chair, in a movement restraint, and there's someone in the room with her. A woman, thin and dark. The woman has a name.

The woman has a name.

The woman has a name.

Her mind whirls several times around the same thought.

Name: Donida McLellan.

Place: Sentier-4.

There's someone else, too. Someone she knows well, but . . .

The door and window vanish. She's in the room now. She's in the chair, and the machines are alive inside her head, crawling through blood vessels and slithering across synapses. She doesn't want to look at the woman.

Pinprick eyes.

Implants meshing.

Stare.

The woman is confusion. The darkness is inside. She tries to look away, but the walls recede. There's nowhere to hide.

She must get out. Out of the chair. Out of the room.

Out.

She sees her own face at the window. White. Eyes like bruises. Looking in.

Out. That's where she needs to be.

Out.

That's where she needs to be.

That's where she needs . . .

She's outside the room again. She turns and runs toward the light; running blindly, stumbling forward.

Someone catches her.

Ben.

He lays her down gently and she's bathed in warmth and sunlight. Her body floats. Breathe in. Breathe out. The room and the chair fade, getting smaller and smaller until they're barely a memory.

Then no memory at all.

She relaxes.

◆ ◆ ◆

Victor Lorient sat stiffly in the highback chair in the lobby of the Gateway Hotel in Arkhad City, just a few months to go to achieve his life's ambition of setting up an Ecolibrian colony far away from Earth and the genetically engineered psi-techs. He waited for his guest with eyes fixed on the entrance. His dark wavy hair drooped fashionably over his forehead, but he detracted from the effect by running his fingers through it to push it back. He attracted covert atten-

tion from more than one of the women passing. Victor
didn't care; Rena was waiting up in the suite with Danny,
and she was all he'd ever needed. Better get this over with
quickly so he could return to them. He tapped the tip of his
first and second fingers against his thumb in a little two-
time rhythm, then stopped himself, reluctant to show anything that might be classed as a nervous tic.

Apart from the hologram at the press conference, he'd
not seen Gabrius Crowder in person since the initial Olyanda agreement had been finalized. Victor had left Jack
Mario to deal with the psi-techs whenever necessary.

It wouldn't be possible to keep his distance for the next
phase of the project, however. Now that they'd transferred
from Earth to Chenon, he'd be forced to deal with the psi-
techs who'd been assigned to take them to Olyanda. There
was no choice. Space law was complex and, though he'd
studied it for loopholes, there were none. They were stuck
with the psi-techs, like it or not.

After early failures, the Pretoria Convention bound
megacorporations and planetary governments alike. All
new colonies must have a technical setup team for a minimum period of one year. Victor had accepted the condition
initially without realizing that all the setup teams were psi-
techs. Safest, they said. More efficient, they said. Better
communication, they said. Victor privately thought it was
mainly to line the pockets of the corporations providing the
service. They could charge through the nose for psi-tech
personnel on the grounds they cost so much to implant and
train.

He wasn't entirely sure about Ben Benjamin. The journalists at the press conference had said something about
Hera-3, but it had been glossed over in his file, so it probably wasn't important. Some row over platinum. The first
mission commander he'd been offered was a Psi-1 Telepath,
for goodness sake. Benjamin seemed like a more acceptable
replacement. At least the man was a Navigator, which was
marginally more tolerable than someone who could get inside your head.

Victor shuddered. Even so, he must have been crazy to
agree to this meeting so soon after landing. The journey had

been draining, and his body clock was completely out of sync. Chenon's double-length days and slightly higher gravity threw him off balance and made him nauseous. It wasn't the best time to confront the enemy. He'd prefer to feel he was in full control of his senses before facing any psi-techs at close quarters.

He took out a handkerchief and blew his nose. Taken one by one, his features were rather too big for his face, but they gave him presence, made people listen. To anyone else, that nose would have been a disaster, a reason for corrective surgery, but Victor wore it like a badge of office. If nothing else, it seemed to prove to his followers that his genes were natural, unlike psi-techs who represented genetic and micro-cellular engineering at its rampant worst. How could you trust someone who could go searching around in your head?

He, of all people, knew how bad they could be.

His father, a strict Ecolibrian all his life, had taught him to imagine numbers in the presence of a psi-tech; pictures of numbers; sounds of numbers, jumbled and chaotic. That would mean they couldn't get at your innermost secret thoughts.

He'd once thought his father a fundy nutter, had kicked over the traces briefly, gone to the other side for a while, but now he knew. He thought of numbers all the time. The bastards wouldn't ever get inside his head again.

But even he couldn't sense who was psi-tech and who wasn't. That was what made them so damned dangerous.

He'd been one of the campaigners for the tattoo law in his third year at the University of Western Australia. On the night of the vote he'd attended a preemptive victory celebration and had drunk something more than alcohol. Next morning he'd woken with a hangover and found a prominent blue "Psi" drawn on his forehead in indelible marker. The news that the vote had gone against them had sent him to the washroom where he'd frantically scrubbed and scraped at the mark until his skin bled and hot tears of shame had run down his cheeks.

So many psi-techs on Chenon. He hoped his people appreciated the effort he was making on their behalf. Nothing short of freeing the Ecolibrians in the long-term would induce him to work with the abominations now.

A hulk of a man approached and headed straight for Victor's chair. Crowder looked even less appealing now than he had done on Earth or via hologram. Victor tamed a shiver that was threatening to become a visible shake, stood up, and took the proffered hand.

"I am a man of principle, Mr. Crowder. I make no pretense of being comfortable around you psi-techs."

"I'm not psi-tech, Director Lorient." Crowder smiled as though Victor had not insulted him and sat down. "Though, of course, I have a basic implant to enable me to receive."

How could he tell if the man was lying? Numbers. Think of numbers.

Crowder accepted a cup of coffee from a waiter. Victor left his cooling after a sip that confirmed that it wasn't what he was used to at home. He'd been told that CFB was the best he could hope for in the colonies, but this was disgusting. He was glad Crowder was picking up the tab. He lived in hope of being able to grow real coffee beans on Olyanda. Around them, the brightly decorated hotel was beginning to fill with people. It was the long twilight time between day and night, and out in the city the lights were building automatically as dusk deepened.

"Thank you for agreeing to see me," Crowder said. "I know you've only just arrived. You must be tired. Adjusting to Chenon takes some time; our gravity; our long days."

"Unpleasant, but temporary, thank goodness."

"Ah, here's Commander Benjamin." Crowder turned as a tall, dark man, severe in a buddysuit, entered the room.

Victor shivered. He'd been told Benjamin was barely telepathic at all, but how could he be sure? *Eighteen, twenty-four, three, four hundred and ninety-seven.*

"Commander Benjamin." Victor shook Benjamin's offered hand without removing his glove; rude, but he was sure psi-techs were used to it. Not everyone trusted them. He saw Benjamin's mouth twitch up at one corner. He'd noticed the slight and decided to ignore it. All well and good.

"Director Lorient, pleased to meet you. I've only just

been assigned to the Olyanda mission, but let me assure you I'll be doing everything in my power to make your first year as smooth as it can be."

"I'm sure you will, Commander. I have . . . every faith in Mr. Crowder's choice."

"As soon as you're feeling up to it, I'd like to show you and your family around our headquarters and introduce you to some of the people who'll be working for you on Olyanda."

Victor felt a rising tide of panic. "No!" It came out a little stronger than he had expected, so he covered it up by pretending to sip another mouthful of the piss that passed for coffee. "Jack Mario's our chief administrator. He'll do all our liaison work." Another sip. "I'll be at the facility you've provided, working with the settlers. I have . . . organizational matters to attend to."

It was a cop-out. Crowder and Benjamin probably knew it as well as he did, but at least it saved face. *Forty-three, fifty-six, nine hundred and forty-seven.* Numbers, think of numbers, and dream of a new planet on the first day after the psi-techs returned to Chenon. Then it would all be worth it.

Chapter Eight

INTRODUCTIONS

CARA AWOKE. IT WAS QUITE A SURPRISE. Finding she was alive and pain-free brought a surge of joy followed immediately by cold fear. She fought down panic. Numb. Unable to move. Unable to communicate. Total paralysis. What was wrong with her? Ari. Damn him. Had he won after all?

It was dark. Pitch-dark. Darker than the middle of the night. Where was she?

Chenon.

Of course she was.

No, wait a minute, her own brain hadn't supplied the answer to that question.

Ben?

Welcome back.

Can't move. Can't see.

Don't panic. It's the Amfital.

He offered his own vision and she saw herself through his eyes; the distorted shape of a naked woman in a bathtub, submerged in something pink. He began to scrape off the gel, first from her eyes and face, then her ears and hair, throat and shoulders. She could see his hands working over her body, but it wasn't remotely sexual. She couldn't feel anything. Her skin was numb. Weird. Amfital was illegal on most planets except under medical supervision. She could see why.

Instead of the pounding headache, she felt a gentle, soothing warmth all over. As the cool air of the room breathed on her flesh, her skin began to reawaken.

"Come on."

This time she heard Ben's spoken words. Her ears were functioning again. Strong arms lifted her out of the remains of the glutinous mass and into the fresher. Her legs wouldn't work; her brain didn't own them, so Ben held her upright while the mist jets, soap, and clean warm water rinsed off the remains of the slippery Amfital. As feeling began to return, she took her own weight and stood upright by clinging to the handgrip and leaning against the warm massage wall. It responded by vibrating gently and shaping to her back, kneading and rippling across her muscles.

"Bend your head forward," Ben said.

"Yes, Mom." She wasn't normally body-shy, but now she giggled to cover up her sudden embarrassment.

He washed the glop out of her hair, taking extra care with the bruise, though it wasn't nearly so painful now, then steered her back into the center of the jets, the needles of water hammering life back into her.

"End," he said, and the water stopped to be replaced by the warmth from all-round dryers. He slipped a thick hotel robe around her shoulders.

"Better?"

"Hmm. Much." She pulled the belt tight.

He let her stand on her own while he dried himself and drew on loose trousers and a shirt. It was only then that she realized that he'd been naked, too. She almost said something, but he didn't seem to treat it as a big deal, and he certainly hadn't tried to make a move on her, so she ignored it.

"Was that really Amfital?"

"Yes. Good stuff."

"Phew! No wonder it's illegal. You could get lost inside it. I feel as though I've slept for days."

"You have. Nearly two."

"What?"

"Two days."

She caught sight of herself in the mirror and saw a stranger. No long blonde hair; it was now a jaw-length bob and dark. She decided she didn't much like it. Her jawline— hadn't that been changed, too? If so, it was back to normal now. She ran her hands down her waist and across her belly, but found only her own shape beneath the robe.

Ben saw her puzzling over it. "Mother Ramona's Formine injections should have lasted longer, but the Amfital purged it all from your system. I prefer you with your own shape."

"I can't remember much."

She dressed quickly, dumping Mother Ramona's tawny dress in favor of clean clothes that Ben had brought for her.

"You've got good taste." She checked out the outfit in the long mirror. A plain, close-fitting top and pants, with a stylish waist-length jacket, all in black.

"Serena used to say if you can't make up your mind about color, just go for black and expensive."

"How expensive? I seem to recall that I'm short of credits."

"You can pay me back out of your first salary. Crowder's keen. He says if you're still a Psi-1 after all that, you've got the job."

"If I'm still a Psi-1?" The realization hit her like a brick. Was she? Was she still able to broadcast at all? Head injuries could have peculiar effects. Who could she contact to prove she still had what it took to be a Psi-1?

Jussaro?

It was risky, but she had to know. If she could get through to him, she could get through to anyone.

She accessed her implant and aimed a thought at him. It felt as if she was using muscles that had atrophied. Her head began to ache, and she closed her eyes and held onto Ben for stability while she concentrated.

Jussaro, it's me.

She got a flicker of recognition, pleasure, then consternation.

Carlinni! Where are you? Are you in trouble? You are!

Sorry, can't say where. I'm all right. What kind of trouble am I in?

They found a corpse and they're trying to pin it on you.

A businessman called Rosen—from Alphacorp. In an access shaft with his throat cut.

Blood pounded in her ears, and her scalp crawled. A murder charge was the last thing she wanted on top of everything else.

Throat cut? I had a run in with someone. Don't know his name, but I didn't kill him. Do you believe me?

She'd been out of it for too long, but she had quite clear memories of the fight with the graysuit. She'd not killed him. She fought down guilt. It wasn't hers.

I do. The emphasis was on the I, but probably meant that she was number one on the list of suspects.

Look after yourself, Jussaro. Don't get involved in my affairs. Don't even say you've heard from me.

I know when to keep my mouth shut. Good luck, Carlinni.

The whole exchange had taken only a few seconds. Cara found that she was panting and feeling queasy, but at least her Psi-1 status wasn't impaired, even if she needed to rebuild her strength.

She looked up at Ben. "Good news and bad news. I'm still a Psi-1, but they've found the graysuit's body, and I'm the chief suspect."

"You said you left him unconscious."

"I certainly didn't cut his throat."

He looked at her. "You had a concussion. You might have forgotten."

"Forget cutting someone's throat? I don't think so—besides, I wasn't carrying a knife, and I do remember checking his breathing and leaving him alive."

"They're fitting you up, and he was obviously expendable. You're playing a game with a dangerous bunch. They must want you pretty badly. What did you do?"

She shook her head to clear the pounding behind her eyes. If they could kill the graysuit, what could they do to her? Ari hadn't been joking when he told her that Craike handled severances. Head from body, limb from limb; it would be nothing for Craike's twisted little mind. He probably enjoyed it.

She needed to get clear. Briefly, she contemplated telling

Ben. Her head started to ache. How could she keep Ari off her back permanently? Damn, the only way was to keep moving. Try to stay one step ahead.

"You can trust me, you know," Ben said.

She looked at him without saying anything. She thought he was probably right. "What if you can't trust me?" The words were out before she could bite them back.

"I think I can."

She wanted to burst into tears; to run from him screaming, *You can't*, but instead all she did was nod. Was that a promise? "Maybe."

"And now, Mrs. Benjamin, this is yours." He handed her a document.

"What is it?"

"Your payroll registration as Serena Benjamin, but you can use Cara unofficially. I slipped it in as a middle name. Serena's middle name is Catherine."

"It wasn't just a dream, then?" she asked. "I did come in as Mrs. Benjamin."

"It's about time Serena started to earn that divorce settlement."

"I remember the white-faced exotic, what was her name?"

"Mother Ramona."

"She could have had us killed, couldn't she?"

"Her word's good. She stays bought."

Cara's legs still felt like jelly. She sat down on the edge of the bed. "Knowing who to trust is a good gift."

Ben picked up the start-card for the hoverpod. "I've got business. Stay here, rest, watch some holos, take it easy. I'll pick you up at twelve tomorrow. Be ready."

✦ ✦ ✦

Victor Lorient towered over his kneeling wife in the artificial daylight from the overhead in their temporary home on Chenon, a utilitarian box in the center of the settler compound, comfortable enough, but soulless.

"When we get to Olyanda, I want a home made of wood," she said through a mouthful of pins. "One with unnecessary nooks and a real fireplace with a stone hearth."

She pinched in the slack on his trouser seam between thumb and forefinger and pinned it carefully.

Victor smiled at the top of her head. How many times had they had this conversation?

"I hate Chenon," she said. "Pink grass, long days and even longer nights."

"I know. Me, too."

"Nothing they can do in terms of lighting helps my body clock." She sighed and fiddled with the pins jabbed into a pincushion strapped around her wrist. "My circadian rhythms are still tied to Earth."

It was late morning according to the ticking clock on the wall. They'd gone to sleep in bright sunlight and woken to dusk.

"Chenon itself is bad enough, but . . ." Victor shuddered. "Psi-techs, I thought I'd come to terms with the idea of relying on them, but I'm finding it hard."

"Turn around," she said, tapping his buttock. "There, I've taken the pants in a little at the waist as well. How does that feel?"

"Better. You're good at this."

"I can hardly urge everyone to relearn domestic skills if I don't lead by example, though I've got as many men as women in the sewing classes. You should join us sometime. I never get to see enough of you."

She ran her hand down his thigh. Was that just to smooth the seam or was it an invitation? She'd not shown much interest in sex since they arrived. He felt his balls tighten and his groin grow warm.

"Maybe you've got to bend a little," she said and moved her hand away as if she knew his thoughts.

He bent forward to cover the growing tightness.

She laughed. "No, not like that. You know I meant your principles about psi-techs. Stand up straight." She made another adjustment to the outer seam of the trousers. "Some of them seem genuinely keen to help us."

"That's the trouble with psi-techs. Whatever they *seem* to be, they are what they are. Don't be taken in by them. We mustn't waver. We have the opportunity to create a new world. We've come so far. We can't fall at the last hurdle."

"I'm not taken in. You know how I feel, but I just think that this project is important enough to swallow our principles and get through the first year as well as we can. It's difficult here, being in the compound and all, but I'm sure we'll be able to keep physical contact with them to a minimum on Olyanda, and once the year's over, we'll be free of them forever."

She prodded Victor again, and he turned sideways to let her check the fit over his hip. She didn't need to make clothes yet. She could have insisted that he buy standard-issue, but once they were on Olyanda, there would be no handy shops or a community manufactory.

They were all learning skills lost centuries ago: how to spin and weave, to plant and grow and to prepare and cook raw food. How to tend and breed livestock for transport, flesh, hides, and fleece. It would be a whole new way of life on Olyanda, a reawakening.

"Take a look in the mirror. How's the fit?"

"Good. No, it's more than good, it's great. I'm proud of you."

"Glad you said that. Who else is going to make your trousers? You're a visionary, Victor. The stuff great leaders are made of. You tell us how it will be, but it's up to the rest of us to make it happen." She levered herself to her feet, the top of her head barely coming up to his collar bone. "But we need the psi-techs. Without them, we'll never get to Olyanda. We can't cross the Folds alone." She reached up and cradled the side of his face in her hand. "I can accept them if you can. I can swallow my principles if I have to."

Victor looked thoughtful, "Our principles are all we have in this crazy world, but you're right, of course." He brushed his lips against the top of her head. "We should suffer the psi-techs in silence. It's only for a year. Jack Mario told me yesterday that I was letting it get to me. Do you think I am?"

"You are the one, out of all of us, who keeps our belief secure. You should hold firm. Let the rest of us carry the burden."

"You're my rock. Without you, I'd crumble to dust."

"I don't think so." She looked up.

Oh, gods, she could melt him with one of those looks. He

pulled her to him, stroked her mouse-brown hair, and felt himself harden against her belly. After twenty years of marriage, she still had the power to make him want to lay her down and tear off all her clothes.

"You're a wonderful woman, Mrs. Lorient. How could we fail? And I admit that working with psi-techs for a year is a small price to pay for the freedom we'll gain. I know that. I have a hard time dealing with it sometimes, but I do know."

"You'll do the right thing, you always do. Now take off those trousers so I can stitch the seams."

"Is that the only reason?"

She brushed her hand against his cock and he twitched. "Maybe not. We've got an hour before Danny comes back."

He didn't need a second invitation.

She gathered up the discarded trousers and laid them on her sewing table. By the time she turned round again he'd taken off his shorts, too.

"Oh, my, Mr. Lorient!" She laughed softly and dropped to her knees, grasping his hips and taking his erection into her mouth.

"Ahh!" he gasped and pulled back. "Give me strength, woman. You want me to lose it?"

She pulled him down onto the floor, and he slipped his hand under her skirt finding nothing but bare legs and a warm inviting wetness between them.

"You planned this all along." He nuzzled her neck and breathed in the scent of her shampoo.

"How could I waste the opportunity? Oh!"

She stopped trying to speak and writhed against him as his fingers found her bud. She pulled him between her legs, her hands kneading his butt cheeks. Rational thought deserted him as he slid inside her.

By the time they lay spent on the floor, Victor was feeling much more optimistic about the next few weeks on Chenon and the year ahead on Olyanda.

"I love you, Rena Lorient."

She straightened her skirt. "You're not so bad, yourself."

He kissed her on the cheek and stood up, offering her his hand to pull her to her feet.

"Where are my . . . ? Oh, there." He pulled on his shorts

and trousers and tucked himself in again. "And you're right, it's my job to lead the way. I'll be first on the list for medical checks tomorrow. We'll go together, you, me, and Danny."

Rena shivered.

"What's that? Still nervous about cryo?"

"I'm worried for Danny. I know it's supposed to be safer than eating seafood and that there's no alternative, but I don't have to like the idea of being frozen and packed into a tube for nine months."

"Danny will be fine."

"He's not strong."

"You cosset him too much."

"He's my son."

"He's mine, too."

"Did you want me, Mom?" Danny shambled into the room. His moon-round face split into a grin.

Victor looked at Rena and they shared a brief conspiratorial look. Good thing Danny hadn't come back a few minutes earlier.

"No, darling, why?"

"I thought I heard Dad say my name."

"You've got good ears, son," Victor said.

"Can I bake cookies?" Danny made one of his sideways subject leaps.

"If you want to. Can you manage on your own?" Rena asked.

"I wrote all the instructions in my notebook."

"Good boy. Call me if you get stuck with anything."

Weak on measurable intellectual ability, but strong on love and affection, Danny's gentle simplicity touched everyone around him. It was as if he'd been imbued with the light. Anyone he came into contact with felt better for the experience. Neither Victor nor Rena could ever bring themselves to discipline the boy. It would be like kicking a puppy. Luckily, disobedience wasn't in Danny's nature.

"Bake an extra big cookie for me, will you?" Victor asked as Danny headed for the kitchen.

"I'll write Dad on it with frosting."

Rena smiled and sighed as Danny left. "Lord, I do love that boy."

She turned to her treadle-operated sewing machine and picked up the handmade trousers.

Once on Olyanda there would be no power drives for sewing machines. There wouldn't even be primitive electricity. A foot-operated machine like this would be a luxury. Needle and thread might be all that was available, and lamp- or candlelight would have to suffice. And when all the needles were broken, they would have to make more. It was easy to say, but soon they'd have to live by those words.

Victor shoved his feet into his boots and then realized Rena's silence was a little too long for comfort. "Are you worrying again?" He looked up and frowned. "You've got that expression on your face."

"I'm sorry. I didn't mean to ... Only ... sometimes ... I wonder ... how I'll feel when the tech teams leave and we're truly alone? What if we have to sit by and watch Danny die for lack of comprehensive medical facilities?" She shuddered. "What will it be like to see women old at forty from childbearing and hard labor? Are we going back into the dark ages or forward into the light?"

"It's natural. We're all worried about small things, but it's the greatness of the plan that'll carry us through." Victor took the cloth from her grasp and held her hands.

"We've come so far," he said. "Ten thousand of us already here on Chenon. Ten thousand who all believe so strongly that what science has done to the human race is wicked. And thirty thousand more will follow on the second ark. We have a chance now to prove what we know to be true. We can build a new Earth on Olyanda. Grow a new, strong race from the last survivors of the old."

"I know. I do believe. I really do."

"You don't have to prove it to me. I'll speak to the assembly tomorrow. Come down with me. Sit on the podium." He kept his voice gentle and persuasive. "Bring Danny. Let's be there together."

✦ ✦ ✦

As they drove in through the gates into the Trust's massive Colony Operations compound, Cara craned her head to take it all in. Accommodation blocks, warehouses, hangars for shuttles. In the far distance a control tower marked the edge of a landing pad. Dominating the compound was the main HQ building, slab-sided and functional.

Ben punched the autopark, and they left the hoverpod to settle itself down among a host of similar machines. Cara's handpad was already logged on the system, and she had instant access through security on the ground floor. Ben led the way via the maze of corridors and antigrav shafts up to the third floor.

Gabrius Crowder was working in the operations room, leaning over a large table that resembled an antique military maneuvers board, except this one was circular with the spiral arms of the galaxy represented two dimensionally. He moved small exquisitely carved figures from one position to another.

"Ben. About time, too, and this must be the lovely Mrs. Benjamin. Welcome, my dear." Crowder's smile was open and easy, maybe too open and easy. Cara suppressed a shudder and began to say that she was using her own name, but his attention had swung immediately back to the board.

"Engage," he said. The figures leaped upward to hang suspended, and the galaxy became three dimensional.

"There, Ben." Crowder's finger touched a pinpoint in the myriad stars. "Cotille colony. That's the latest. We're beating Alphacorp by more than fifty and the next nearest is Arquavisa, and they've only got three hundred and thirty-six."

Cara studied the two men. Ben, tall and lean; Crowder, wrinkled and shapeless. She hadn't expected him to look like a pachyderm. He was gray and running to fat. Parts of him sagged like old elastic. He stooped slightly and had round shoulders from all the desk-jockeying.

Ben had warned her that Crowder had a needle-sharp mind. On the workaholic scale of one to ten, he'd reached at least nineteen and still had some potential for growth. He made no secret of the fact that he was hungry for a seat on the Board of Trustees. The Olyanda project had been his since he'd won it from Alphacorp for the Trust; if it went well, it would take him one step nearer to his ambition.

Cara's scalp prickled as she was introduced to him. Something at the back of her mind said, *I don't trust you.* Though he had a receiving implant, he also had a damper that effectively blocked her empathy. Well, perhaps she shouldn't be surprised. Ari had one, too, and it was fairly common for people with a lot of important secrets in their head to take precautions. She shrugged it off for now. Perhaps she was looking for reasons not to trust her new boss after making such a stupid mistake with Ari.

She forced her face into a polite smile.

"Mr. Crowder, I prefer to use my own name, if you don't mind."

He flicked his head in her direction as though she was an insect that had annoyed him briefly and then carried on as if he'd not heard her. He handed a plasfilm to Ben. "Staff list."

Ben read down the list and frowned. "You've got Cara listed as Benjamin."

Crowder shrugged. "There's a good reason for that."

Cara went cold all over, then hot.

"You've got to be joking!" Ben said.

"Dear boy . . ."

"You only use *dear boy* when you're trying to lay one on me. What's up?"

Crowder sighed. "Victor Lorient's up. The settlers have insisted on a social segregation clause in the colony contract; no fraternization between psi-techs and settlers. Lorient has said, not in as many words, you understand, that he doesn't want any bastards with psi tendencies left growing in settler bellies after you've left."

"Even if . . ." Cara shook her head. "A basic psi tendency is virtually useless without an implant and training."

"Quite." Crowder turned and smiled directly at her. For some reason she wanted to shudder. "But Lorient really dislikes the idea of psi anything."

"I bet his colonists can't prove they don't have some inherited psi gene somewhere in their family tree."

"But since all our psi-techs obviously carry the gene, there's a perceived greater danger from any genetic input that we leave behind, so they want as many of our psi-techs as possible in settled relationships. You know their stance on traditional marriage, so it panders to their sensibilities if we follow suit where we can. I've had to massage the figures a little to make it look good, but if my mission commander takes his new wife along on the trip, it looks as though we're making an effort."

If Crowder had had just a hint of a smile on his face, she'd have thought he was joking. The idea was just too ridiculous. She suppressed a laugh when she realized Ben was less than amused.

"That's not going to fly. Cara and I barely know each other, and besides, I went through the whole traditional marriage thing once because Serena wanted it, and look how that turned out . . ."

Cara shot a look at Ben. "He's not joking, is he?" She turned to Crowder. "This is not part of the deal."

"If you want to go back to Mirrimar-14 . . ."

She picked up a wave of surprise from Ben at Crowder's threat. He'd been as blind-sided as she'd been.

Although all her instincts told her to turn around and walk out of the office right now, out of the building and out of Benjamin's life, she didn't trust Crowder not to call the Monitors. How far would she get? Besides, if Crowder wanted to get antsy, she'd taken an advance to get the new ID on Crossways. She needed to play along. She didn't have to like it, though.

She bit back a juicy retort involving Crowder doing impossible reproductive things with his own anatomy, looked down so he wouldn't see the resentment in her eyes, and shook her head quickly.

Crowder didn't seem to pick up on her real feelings. "Good. What you two make of it is up to you as long as it looks convincing to the settlers. How you play it with the rest of the crew is also up to you. Probably best to keep it under wraps before lift-off, of course. Don't want any . . . legal complications." He gave Cara a long, level look. "I'm taking a lot on faith. Ben tells me I can trust you, and I trust Ben, but I want you to know that the mission is paramount. If you jeopardize it in any way, the trouble you've had before, whatever it is, will seem insignificant compared to the trouble I can conjure."

Cara nodded again, suddenly dry-mouthed. What a bastard! But at least he was open about it. "My personal troubles can't follow me to Olyanda without going through you, Mr. Crowder, and though Olyanda may be a bolt-hole for me, it doesn't mean I'm a passenger. I'll give the job everything I've got. I'm good at what I do."

Crowder nodded. "There's a lot to learn in a very short time. It may not be entirely pleasant, but it's probably expedient for Cas Ritson to transfer the information directly. It's probably the only way to assimilate it all in time to be useful."

She nodded, groaning inwardly at the thought of an implant-to-implant infodump. It was like being smashed on the head with a hammer.

"Why don't I have someone give you the grand tour while Ben and I ponder the staff lists?" Crowder thumbed the mechanical comm. "Ms. Marling, are you available to escort a new team member around our fine establishment?"

Less than a minute later the outer office door opened, and a young woman walked in, She was petite, with Asiatic coloring, dark-haired and almond-eyed, but there was something about her that lifted the whole package from pretty to beyond beautiful. Cara felt dowdy in comparison even in the tasteful black suit that she knew complimented her figure and paler complexion perfectly.

"Mr. Crowder." The newcomer's face split into a warm smile. "Hey, Ben."

"Gen." Ben nodded, not quite smiling. Cara suddenly got the feeling that he was embarrassed.

Crowder looked from Gen to Ben and back again. "Ms. Marling, would you show Mrs. Benjamin around the facility? She's joining the team for the Olyanda mission."

The smile froze on Gen Marling's face, but she made a good recovery. Ben gave her the faintest suggestion of a shrug.

Cara felt entirely stuck with something she didn't want but didn't know how to get out of without chewing it over with Ben first.

Is there something I should know? she asked Ben on a tight thought. *You and Miss Marling?*

Something casual. No commitment. I've been away for months. And when I was here, she was away.

Cara decided to see how it all played out. If all else failed, she could cut and run and be no worse off than she had been on Mirrimar-14. She stood up and smiled brightly at Gen. "I'd love to see everything."

Chapter Nine

GRAPPLING

GEN WALKED WITH CARA RATHER THAN LEADing her. She smiled and said, "Mrs. Benjamin, eh?"

"Please, call me Cara. Or is everyone formal here?"

"Only Mr. Crowder. You and Ben got properly married? That's a smart move to get on the Eco's good side." Gen's voice was just a little too bright. "Mr. Crowder has been pushing everyone to partner with someone for the duration of this mission."

"Are you?"

"What?"

"Partnered."

"Not anymore." Gen shook her head and looked at the floor.

Cara began to get an inkling of the problem.

She followed Gen down a couple of pale, marbled corridors into a large open office. There were no privacy screens, but she could hear the faint not-quite-noise hum of sound baffles surrounding each desk in its own silence.

Half a dozen people worked at a variety of desks and stations. All wore the standard blue-and-black Trust uniforms with psi-tech insignias. Gen didn't need to raise her voice round the sound baffles. She slipped straight into broadcast.

This is Cara Benjamin—Ben's wife, she announced. *Come and say hello.*

Cara felt all their eyes turn toward her at once. Some looks were surprised, others just curious. An attractive gray-haired woman was first up out of her seat.

"Hi. I'm Anna Govan, Chief Medic on this trip, both before and after takeoff. Come to me if you need any bodily functions or mental traumas sorted out." She reached out and touched Cara's bruised head gently.

"Thanks. I'm over the worst now," Cara said.

A fresh-faced strawberry blonde, possibly fortyish, looked surprised, then gathered herself and smiled. "I'm Morwenna Phipps, Exploration and Mapping. I'll be Ben's Second on this trip. Please call me Wenna." She held her left hand out to shake. "Sorry for being lopsided," she said. "That's the one that feels. The other one's biosynthetic, and they haven't got the nerve grafts operational yet. I'm living in hopes. Works well enough, but it's not very personal, if you know what I mean."

Cara nodded and took her hand.

"What's your designation, Cara?" Wenna asked.

"Psi-1, Telepath." Again, she didn't mention the empathy.

"Nice. Welcome aboard," Wenna said. "Crowder must be especially pleased to see you. We're desperately short of long-range comm-techs."

"Yes, indeed. Marta Mansoro." A dark-haired woman with glistening, scaly silver-black skin and gills on the side of her neck introduced herself. The way it came out was more like Mansssoro with super-sibilant esses. "Head of Ss-storesss and Sssupply." She raised one eyebrow and half-smiled. "An unfortunate desssignation for sssomeone of my sssubsssspeciesss." Cara smiled in return. Mansoro looked and sounded like an adapted colonist from the water world of Aqua Neriffe. She gave the palms-together greeting that her mother had taught her and was rewarded with Marta's delighted laugh and the return gesture.

"Me next." A tall brown man with iron-gray hair stepped forward. "Gupta, not-security. Name's Vijay, but no one ever calls me anything but Gupta." With his upright bearing, he looked every inch an old soldier.

"Not-security?" Cara asked.

"Not officially." He grinned. "We don't have a security team on this run. The settlers are supposed to police themselves. I think my team's official designation is Maintenance. What we maintain is entirely up to the mission commander."

Cas Ritson. The psi-tech whammy that surrounded the dark, dumpy woman was undeniable. She was definitely a Psi-1 and staking her claim to seniority with the strength of her broadcast, just like someone shaking hands with a bone-crushing grip.

Pleased to meet you. Cara deliberately didn't try to match her, though she was sure she could if that was all Cas had. It wasn't a contest. She wouldn't be part of the team for more than one mission. *I believe I need to talk to you about an infodump.*

Whenever you're ready.

"Serafin West, Engineering and Construction." An older man grinned at her and spoke out loud. "Sonovabitch, you're a surprise! A pretty one, though. Ben's a lucky dog."

Cara tried to keep all the names in her brain at once. It was a useful party trick. Tag each name with some minor fact as an aid to memory. Anna Govan. Gray hair. G for Govan; G for gray. Serafin West. Serafin. Sounds like seraph. Angel. Anything less angelic would be hard to imagine. Serafin was pure gargoyle, crinkled like a walnut and weathered like sandstone. Wenna. She'd remember Wenna's prosthetic arm and she'd heard Ben's conversation with Crowder. She gathered Wenna had been injured on Hera-3. She made a mental note to try and ask for details sometime. Marta Mansoro. With gills for survival on her home world giving her strange throat architecture and three esses for every one unless she was talking telepathically. Shoulders like a man. Man; Mansoro.

For each person she built a little pictorial connection in her mind. She was sure that once she got past the first day, she'd be fine, but it was good to remember names right from the beginning.

"Here's a workstation," Gen said. "Things are pretty hectic. You'll be lucky if you see much of Ben between now and takeoff. Crowder will be on his case bigtime."

"They don't get on?"

"Oh, they get on just fine, but sometimes they don't agree about how to do things."

✦ ✦ ✦

Cara got a lightning-fast tour around the offices, the ops room, and the training gym from Gupta, while Gen went to sort out her accommodation. Then Marta took over as her guide to the prep area, a long, low building across the compound where small stores and personal tools and equipment were being crated ready for shipment up to the ark, currently loading in orbit around Chenon. Cara had to listen hard to pick up what she was saying because of the sibilance.

"Have you worked with Ben for a long time?" Cara asked. She knew Hera-3 was a touchy subject.

"I knew him from before the Trust, when he was with the Monitors."

"Monitors?"

She'd registered the brief reference in the earlier conversation, but not had the opportunity to ask about it. Ben didn't look like an ex-cop—whatever an ex-cop was supposed to look like. Cara didn't seem to know as much about Ben as everyone else did.

"Didn't you know him then?" Marta asked.

Not wanting to lie, Cara just shook her head.

"He had a tough time on the Rim. You ever hear of the Londrissi hijack?"

It had been big news, galaxy-wide. A big Trust liner, held to ransom in an unpressurized docking bay of the Londrissi Leisure Station. The hijackers had started to jettison victims into the vacuum. The team that went in to end it took heavy losses.

"I saw Ben soon after. I knew he'd had it up to here with the Monitors. Did you know he pulled Crowder out of there? Saved his hide for sure. Crowder got the Trust to buy him out of his Monitor contract. Ben has worked for Crowder ever since. That's why they're pretty good friends, even if Crowder pretends to pull rank every now and then. Crowder kept Ben working for the department after Hera-3. It might even have been Crowder who talked him into staying."

"Should I avoid asking about Hera-3?"

"It was a big, ssstinking conssspiracy. The colony we were setting up was wiped out. No one knows who attacked, but we all know it had something to do with newly discovered platinum deposits." Her voice shook, but whether with anger or sorrow was hard to tell, maybe both. Whichever it was, it heightened the sibilance.

"It all happened very fassst. We lossst too many—colonistsss and team alike."

"Pirates?"

Marta took a deep breath and got the sibilance under control again. "If it was pirates, it was the best equipped bunch I've ever heard of. Had the kind of resources only a megacorp could come up with on short notice. And it was short notice. The news had barely broken before they were on us."

"You think it was a megacorp?"

"Could even have been the Trust itself. They had as much reason as any, since the colonists were planning to sell the platinum on the open market."

"Crowder?" Cara asked, wondering what she'd walked into.

"No, Crowder's straight, but the Trust is so big it could have been any one of a hundred other departments or regions. Ben was ordered to evacuate the team and leave the colony before the strike. Of course, now no one can find a trace of that order, but we were there when it came through. We know."

"He just left civilians under fire?"

"'Course not. Not Ben. Ben held them off while we pulled fifteen hundred settlers off the planet with almost no resources. It was a miracle, but we still lost too many civilians and all but fifty-seven psi-techs. How we got out is a longer story than I've got time for now. You'll have to ask Ben sometime. When we got home, Ben went head-to-head with the men upstairs. I heard he took his suspicions as high as the Board, but I don't know for sure. Ben's not talking.

"Anyhow, the next thing we heard Ben had been disciplined and demoted.

"We were all, Ben included, offered the option to leave the Trust, free and clear, all debts suspended. How often do you hear of that? Once any megacorp has its claws into you, you never pay off the cost of your implant and your training, so you're stuck on contract for life, building up debts for your professional indemnity insurance and maintenance of your implant. We represent millions of dollars' worth of investment, yet the Trust offered the opportunity for fifty-seven of us to walk away free and clear on condition we signed confidentiality agreements."

"You're still here."

Marta shrugged. "I like my job and I had nowhere else to go. No family. No dreams to chase. A lot chose to cut and run, and I don't blame them, but twenty-three of us stayed on. We all thought Ben would quit, but he stuck it out." Marta shook her head as if still slightly puzzled. "He saved fifteen hundred colonists and they knocked him back to stinking survey work as a reward! The rest of us were split up, but we kept in touch. You don't go through something like that without bonding. They've finally brought us together again. All twenty-three Hera-3 survivors are on the Olyanda mission."

"Thanks, Marta. I tried to look up Hera-3, but the records lack detail."

"Yeah, I'm sure—little details about being bombed to hell by a black-ops fleet coming out of nowhere. Ben wanted the Board to authorize a full investigation via the Monitors, but they said it wasn't cost-effective." She pursed her lips and shook her head. "But my bet is that Ben's still working on it."

"I see." Cara suppressed a shudder, hoping whatever Ben was investigating wouldn't turn and bite him while she was around. She had troubles enough of her own.

They crossed back to the admin building, arriving just as Ben emerged from Crowder's office. He smiled at Cara and headed in her direction, but got waylaid by Serafin. "If I was the lady, I'd divorce you. You might have invited us all to the wedding."

Ben had the grace to look suitably abashed. Cara caught

his furtive glance in Gen's direction, and Cara's suspicions were reinforced.

She focused a tight communication to Ben. *I don't care what Crowder says, I'm not lying to these people. They know you too well. Marta's just had to fill me in on your life story. Do you trust them?*

He nodded to her and held his hands up to quiet the congratulations of his team. "Sorry, guys, this isn't quite what it seems, and Crowder's being a manipulative bastard again." He silenced their reactions with another hand wave. "Marta, can you activate the sound baffles in this room? Serafin, can you take care of the eyes temporarily?"

Marta hit a control close to her desk and Serafin selected a small black pyramid from his desktop and activated it.

"Secure, Boss."

"Good. This is strictly need-to-know. Okay?"

They all nodded or murmured agreement.

"Thanks. Crowder's doing it for all the right reasons, but this is a sham. Yes, I am married—or I was. My wife divorced me years ago."

Cara breathed again.

"Cara had a bit of trouble. You don't need to know the details. I brought her in on my ex-wife's ID, courtesy of a friend on Crossways."

"Mother Ramona?" Wenna asked.

"The very same." Ben smiled.

"Then you're not married," Gen glared at Cara.

Cara wondered whether she should tell Gen that the coast was clear as far as she was concerned. She decided to default to saying nothing.

"Crowder wants me to set a good example by having my wife along on the journey," Ben said. "For now, it seems that it helps with the settlers. We should keep the truth within this very select group, but I won't lie to you all."

"And I don't want to be here under false pretenses," Cara said. "Ben told you I'd had some trouble, but I sure as hell don't intend to let it get in the way of doing a good job as part of this team."

"You're welcome, Cara, and thanks for being straight with us, Boss," Wenna said.

"It's not a habit I intend to break." Ben nodded in acknowledgment.

◆ ◆ ◆

With Ben away working on the logistics of loading the ark vessel so that last in was first out, Cara spent the next few days getting to know her new workmates.

Wenna, the office matriarch, held everything together. She'd wangled her way back to active duty again for the Olyanda mission, having been purely administrative since she'd lost her arm.

Cara wasn't the only new girl. Anna Govan had only arrived a few weeks earlier to take over medical after some kerfuffle with the previous head, Ronan Wolfe, who had suddenly been dropped back to number two. Cara had not met Ronan yet as he'd been out at the settler compound since she arrived. Wenna had been oddly reserved when Cara had asked why the change, but Gen had just tapped the side of her nose and said quietly, "Tell you later."

The opportunity came on Cara's third day.

Gen pointed out of the window to a spherical building across the pink-turfed lawn. It was right on the edge of the Trust compound.

"There's a grapple arena. Do you play? The Trust built it here as a sop to the city when they wanted to expand the compound. It's a public building, but we have use of it when there are no official matches on."

"I've played, but never in a full-size arena."

"Tonight, then, straight after work. We're playing trios, come and join us."

"You probably have your teams all worked out."

"No, we never play in the same formation twice. It's a great icebreaker for newcomers."

"All right, then, I'll come."

"Good." Gen smiled. "I hope you're good, I've arranged a needle match against Serafin, and he's got Yan Gwenn and Suzi Ruka on his team. You've not met either of them yet. Yan's in charge of transport, so he spends most of his time in flight control. Suzi's our agriculture specialist. She's been setting up extra training programs at the transit camp, but she's due back later today with Ronan. She's one tough woman, a real ball-breaker type, built like a battleship. Even her muscles have muscles."

"Sounds charming."

"Actually, she is."

That afternoon, Cara sat at a workstation on the perimeter of the main office and began to familiarize herself with the systems. A couple of times she noticed Crowder walk through. Her skin prickled when she caught him looking at her. Looking wasn't a crime, but she picked up the weirdest sensation from those looks. She didn't think he trusted her. Well, that was all right because she didn't trust him, either. Maybe she should give him a chance, but she didn't really want to trust anybody at the moment.

She had trusted Ari and look how that had worked out.

At shift end Gen looked up and stretched. "Come on, I'll take you to get a grapple suit and a pair of mag boots."

As they walked over to the arena, Gen said, "You'll enjoy this. Winning's good, but it's the loafing around in free fall that's the best fun. I love it. On my last mission we ended up partying in a grapple arena after we got home. What a blast. Have you ever tried sex in free fall?"

Cara stopped as if she'd run into a wall. Sex in free fall. Ari had once hired a local arena just for that purpose. Equal and opposite reactions made intimate movement rather strange. Whatever force you exerted, it rebounded in the opposite direction, so you really had to grab hold and . . .

She went cold all over and couldn't speak.

". . . plays havoc with your bodily fluids."

She caught the last little bit of what Gen was saying, but suddenly she couldn't open her mouth to reply.

"Are you all right?" Gen asked. "Only you've gone gray. I know the story was a bit off-color, but I didn't think it was that bad."

Cara forced herself to breathe.

"I'm fine. I may be a bit out of practice, though — at grapple I mean."

"Hey, it's only a game."

"Serafin's needle match?"

"Oh, yeah, but I can cream him any time."

"You're sure?"

"Of course. Besides, Serafin doesn't know it, but I have Ronan Wolfe as third man. It's fun, and we usually end up in the bar afterward."

"Sounds good. You were going to tell me about Ronan—why he's been busted down to second when he was heading up the medical team. What's wrong with him?"

"Nothing. Great doctor, nice guy."

"So what's the story?"

"It all goes back to Hera-3."

"Seems like everything around here does."

"Yeah, you had to be there to understand . . . We got hit hard from the air, lots of casualties. We didn't have any fire-power to retaliate. We regrouped in the mountains, but it's hard to hide a couple of thousand settlers from heat-seeking ordnance. We had to clear out pretty damn quick, and some of the injuries were . . . grim." She sucked in a breath through half-closed lips and then blew it out slowly. "We didn't have enough transport for all the injured, and we knew everyone we left behind was going to be blown to bits. Ronan was the one making the tough decisions on who to save and who to leave. Triage, you know. Save the ones with the best chance of surviving. Wenna had been hit. Her arm was pretty much a mangled stump, and she'd lost so much blood . . ."

"Ronan decided to leave her behind."

Gen nodded.

"What happened?"

"Ben happened. He wouldn't leave Wenna. Said not on his watch. He brought out Wenna and three others in a groundcar so badly damaged it scraped a furrow out of the rock. The others didn't make it. Wenna lost the arm, but she survived—just barely."

"And she blames Ronan."

"Worse. He blames himself. Says he made the wrong de-cision. This is the first time they've been assigned together since then, and it was a big shock for Ronan when she ar-rived. Wenna's been stuck with admin since she got back to active duty, but Crowder brought the old team back to-gether partway through the Olyanda project—as many of them as he could, anyway. Ronan tried to transfer out, but

Crowder wouldn't let him. Ronan refused to be responsible for triage again. In the end they compromised and Crowder brought in Anna as chief medic over Ronan's head."

Cara wondered how Wenna felt about working with someone who'd wanted to leave her for dead.

✦ ✦ ✦

When they arrived at the arena, it was all laid out for a game of trio. Cara took the one-piece cream softsuit and the pair of mag boots that Gen had requisitioned for her and followed Gen into the communal changing room. Serafin was already there with Cas Ritson, tonight's referee, and Yan Gwenn, the pilot in charge of all the tech crew's transportation on the new colony. They all stripped off their clothes and ziplocked themselves into the suits and boots.

Cara was just straightening up from putting her boots on when a tall woman with a slab-sided face came in.

"Hi, I'm Suzi." She spoke Basic with a pronounced American accent.

"I'd have recognized you from Gen's description," Cara said, while Gen signaled behind Suzi's back for Cara not to repeat her exact words.

"Let's see, Gen's description. That would be something like, built like a bull, bends iron between her buttocks."

"She told me you were charming."

"Yeah, I bet." She looked across to Gen, much smaller and softer. "We're gonna cream you tonight, Genevieve. Don't think we won't."

"You and whose army?"

"We got an army. There's me, Serafin, and Yan. You've only got the new girl, so far. Who's your third?"

"Me." Mr. Dark-and-Dashing walked in to the changing room. Cara took one look, then another. Ronan, obviously. In other circumstances she might have found him extremely attractive. Dammit, she did find him extremely attractive. He didn't look like the sort of man to duck out on his responsibilities.

"My secret weapon," Gen said. "Cara, meet Ronan Wolfe."

"Hi." Ronan flashed her an easy grin as he dropped his bag on the floor and kicked off his shoes.

"He played grapple for Magna colony while he was still at school," Suzi said. "And he's been the Trust's interdepartmental grapple champion for the last three years in a row. You pulled a fast one, Genevieve."

"Now let's see who gets creamed," Gen said, with obvious delight.

They finished getting ready and walked out into the arena, a fifty-meter sphere with a seemingly random assortment of poles and ledges jutting inward from every angle. Once the game was in progress every way was up.

"Gravity off." Serafin gave the instruction to the arena's AI and they all clamped on with their mag boots.

Cara wasn't quick enough and she began to float.

She reached for the switch on her cuff and activated it.

With a resounding thump her boot soles dragged her the meter and a half to the floor where she wobbled and threw out her arms to balance.

"You all right?" Ronan called.

"Is that a professional inquiry, Dr. Wolfe?"

"Does it need to be?"

"No, I'm fine, just missed my timing. It's a while since I've played. Maybe I'll stay safely on the floor and let you do all the daring stuff."

Ronan switched off his mag boots and pushed off hard with both feet, somersaulting in midair.

"From where I am, you're hanging upside down from the ceiling."

"Hoop," Cas commanded from the referee box, and a ring made of resilient medonite shot from one of the vents into the center of the sphere. Ronan, already in position on one of the sidebars, propelled himself toward it, snatching it just before Suzi could. His glide took him to the far side where he ricocheted, connected with a ledge, and pushed off toward Serafin's goal, dropping the hoop neatly through the loop.

"Ten points to us." Gen pushed off from the wall and did a victory roll down the center of the arena.

"Twenty-nine minutes to go yet; don't get cocky," Suzi called out.

With Ronan on the team, they didn't really need Cara, but she enjoyed watching the slow-mo cut and thrust of grapple played not only for sport, but for fun. The players soared and dived in and around each other in a graceful ballet of form and figure.

After a few minutes to get her stomach under control, she launched into the fray, reveling in the graceful flight from ledge to pole and back again. Ronan passed the hoop to her as both Suzi and Serafin targeted him for some minor mayhem, and she dropped it neatly through the loop.

"Three to Gen's team," Cas announced. "One to Serafin's."

The hoop went through the loop seventeen times altogether, nine of them through Serafin's goal, making Gen's team the winners by one goal and ten points.

"Whirly bath," Suzi yelled. "And then the bar. Winners buy the drinks."

Serafin yelled, "Gravity on."

They all drifted to the floor as gravity increased slowly. Cara felt heavy and stiff.

"That bath sounds like a good idea."

"It's wonderful." Gen put her arm around Cara's shoulders. "Come on."

"Next time, Genevieve. Next time we'll paste you to the walls." Suzi grinned, pulled off her softsuit, and threw it in the disposal bin. Heavy-breasted and stately, she waded into the large, circular communal bath and took up a position on one of the benches. Ronan followed her; Cara couldn't help but admire his body. Gen jumped in next. The water was almost deep enough to swim, so she floated for a few seconds before finding her feet.

Cas nudged her sideways to get a place at the far side of the tub.

Cara threw her suit into the bin, too, and splashed into the water. It was pleasantly warm and the gentle bubbles soothed her skin.

"Hey, Ronan, would you do my neck?" Gen asked.

"Come over here, sweetie. Anything else you want doing?"

"If you weren't gay, I might take you up on that offer."

"If I weren't gay, you'd have to fight me off." He turned to Cara. "How about you?"

"I'm not gay, and I'm still deciding whether you might have to fight me off. Do you fight hard?"

Ronan made light banter easy.

"For my honor? Always." He laughed. "Do you want me to do your neck or any other bits of your anatomy that ache?"

"Another time."

"Every bit of my anatomy aches." Serafin slid into the water delicately. "I'm getting too old for grapple. But I'm not gay, and I'm wondering whether Suzi would oblige." He winked.

"Where do you want me to rub?" Suzi laced her knuckles together and cracked them, then grinned wickedly.

"Be gentle with me." Serafin sighed and sank into the water. Suzi settled next to him.

"Gentle? Pah! I need practice. I've a score to settle with Boy Wonder over there."

"Who's settling scores?" Yan was the last man into the tub.

"Suzi's going to take me apart with her bare hands next time we meet in the grapple arena. At least I think she was only talking sport-type vengeance," Ronan said.

"Yeah, you're safe from me, body and soul." Suzi laughed. "But Serafin might not be."

She grabbed hold of Serafin from the back and pulled him into her lap. Then she wrapped her legs around his waist and began to knead the back of his shoulders. Her hands worked downward under the water and Serafin's grin deepened.

"Hey, you're pretty good for an old guy, Serafin. You wanna come and play out at my place tonight?"

Suzi leaned forward and whispered into Serafin's ear. Cara heard him say "What?" and then grin.

Gen leaned over and said, "Increase," into the command grill.

The bath began to bubble more fiercely. Cara lay back and let it froth and foam around her.

She must have closed her eyes only for a moment because she felt as though she was still in touch with what was going on in the tub, but an awful aching emptiness came over her, as if she'd forgotten something that she desperately needed to remember.

She blinked and opened her eyes again. Good, no one seemed to have noticed.

Then she looked again. Ronan, still massaging Gen's shoulders and neck, glanced in her direction with a puzzled look in his eyes. Of course, he must be an Empath. He'd sensed her momentary confusion.

If you need me for anything, just call.

She nodded.

What a shame he was gay.

She sighed. Who was she kidding? She might sail the ocean, but she'd never go fishing, not while Ari van Blaiden was a shark in her waters.

Chapter Ten

ARI

ARI VAN BLAIDEN LOUNGED CASUALLY against a desk in a dull green room. The furniture was sparse, one desk, two chairs. In front of him, bolt upright, sat a squat man with a scaly black head.

"Jussaro, isn't it?"

The man nodded. He was sweating slightly. Ari intended that he should sweat a lot more yet. Jussaro was frightened, and with just cause.

Ari had tried being nice; it was, after all the cheapest way to get information, but the man was quite resistant to it. Ari sighed. That was Jussaro's problem. Now he would have to get tough and information obtained under duress was less reliable.

Jussaro had had plenty of time to wonder why he'd been grabbed and shipped to Sentier-4. The reputation of the place had the desired effect.

Ari glanced back at Robert Craike, who loomed, quiet but menacing, by the door. That drew Jussaro's attention first to Robert and then back to Ari.

"How long did you work with Carlinni, Mr. Jussaro?"

"I told you. Only about two months."

"And in that time she never said anything about her past?"

"She made a joke of it." He looked at Ari's face. "Er . . . a sort of joke. She just said that we wouldn't want to know."

"But you've been a Telepath. You worked together. It's hard to keep secrets, isn't it?"

"I don't know anything about that."

"And she hasn't been in touch since she disappeared."

"No."

"We'll see. I presume you don't mind taking a little test."

"What kind of . . ." Jussaro's question was stilled as the office door opened and a small woman entered. Jussaro looked up. There was no recognition on his face.

"Mr. Jussaro, this is Donida McLellan."

Jussaro's eyes said he'd heard of her. There was a new fear there.

"Look, maybe Cara did get in touch, but it was only brief and she didn't say where she was."

Ari van Blaiden nodded and McLellan turned to Jussaro, her face an absolute blank. A look of pure panic crossed Jussaro's face, and then he stiffened as he was caught in her mental grip.

Ari watched McLellan work. He could trust her. He had enough dirt on her to keep her on a penal planet for more years than she had left to live; besides, she wasn't immune to his charms, though a little mild flirtation was as far as he'd gone. She really wasn't his type.

She was a pleasure to watch, though, a real specialist, with telepathic skills better than any battering ram or truth drug. Of course, she didn't always leave the subject completely undamaged, but she could be guaranteed to get good results. If Jussaro had learned anything about Ari's affairs from Cara, Donida McLellan would find out. If he knew where Cara was now, she would strip that information from his brain.

It seemed like hours. In reality it was perhaps less than a minute. McLellan suddenly relaxed and Jussaro toppled forward from his chair.

"Sorry. I had to go much deeper than I expected. He's got a lot left even without his implant. Interesting subject. I don't suppose you'd let me have him when you're sure you don't need him anymore?"

"Maybe. Eventually. But not yet. What did you find?" Ari asked.

"Nothing. He was telling the truth more or less. She has been in touch, but he doesn't know where she is now."

"Thank you, Mrs. McLellan."

"Do you want my opinion?"

"Did I ask for it?"

"No, sir."

"But you're going to give it to me anyway."

"I was just going to say that I did the prep work on Car-linni. She may not have had a full Neural, but I went in pretty deep. She might be unstable or irrational, but one thing I'm sure of is that she's going to be pretty well fixated on you. The first thing I started to reinforce was her loyalty, and that could surface at any time. You might be able to use that against her."

Pity that loyalty didn't prevent her from turning on him and stealing his private files. "Mrs. McLellan, do you still have enough of a link to be able to get through to her wherever she is?"

"I might. I'd probably need to use a Psi-1 to boost my range. Distance isn't my specialty."

"Then I'll take that into consideration. Thank you for your input."

He tossed a credit chip to her and toed Jussaro's semiconscious body on the floor.

"Can you erase his memory of this little chat?"

She nodded.

"Good. Do it. Keep him isolated for a while. I might need him again."

Ari beckoned Robert and they left the room together.

In the corridor, away from Donida McLellan, Ari kept his eyes fixed dead ahead, conscious of Robert's warmth by his side. "It seems as though Cara has kept her mouth shut, so far. Are we any closer to tracking down all the ships that left Mirrimar-14?"

"Not all of them, but our shortlist is getting shorter."

"Good. Put more people on it, and come to me when you've got something useful."

Robert hesitated and turned, putting one hand on Ari's

arm. "Do you really think she's so dangerous, or is it because you want her back?" he asked. "This is about Cara, isn't it? The information is just an excuse. You have feelings for her, even now, even after she betrayed you."

Ari smiled. "Put your mind at rest, Robert. She's a loose cannon. I can't trust that she'll disappear and not use the information, either to blackmail me or to implicate me in something I can't shake off."

"Is that all? I've never seen you so personally . . ." Robert seemed to search for a word carefully. "So personally bothered by anything before."

"She escaped from me, Robert. Left me bound and gagged and naked. Downloaded the contents of my handpad. Of course it's personal. No one does that to me and gets away with it."

"As long as we both know why we're doing this."

Ari smiled. "When we find her, we can find a suitable way to make her pay, both of us together. How fitting."

◆　◆　◆

Cara got up a couple of hours early so she could ride a monopod to a shopateria on the outskirts of Arkhad. She'd drawn enough credits to buy a few personal items to replace those she'd had to leave behind. It was early in the daily cycle, but the city never closed. Chenon's long day meant that human body clocks had people sleeping through half the daylight hours and working through half the night, so Cara's morning was barely midafternoon in Chenon's long cycle. On a whim she walked into a hair parlor and came out with her hair cut elfin-short and dyed back to its own natural honey color. She ran her fingers through it, feeling it already beginning to curl with the unaccustomed lightness. She'd worn her hair long all her life, so to suddenly find that it was short enough to wash and dry in five minutes was a novelty. Maybe she should have cut it years ago.

She steeled herself for the infodump from Cas—implant to implant—all the background and data she needed to get up to speed on this mission delivered mind to mind. She knew she'd be fine once she'd assimilated it, but the actual dump was a strange and often disconcerting procedure that she'd never liked. Despite all the training, infodumps were still briefings from hell as far as she was concerned. Anticipation made her feel nauseous. She knew she couldn't refuse it if she wanted to join the team, but by the time she'd walked across the grounds and floated up to the office in the antigrav shaft she was shaking.

Cas wasn't playing one-upmanship today. The older woman took one look at Cara, practically dragged her up to the med station and shoved her into a side room containing nothing but a chair and a narrow bed with a light cover. "I've seen happier looking corpses. Relax, girl, I'm good at this."

Cara started to mumble some excuse about being tired and just getting over the concussion.

Cas pushed her down to sit on the bed and pulled up the chair. "Yeah, you're right. No sense in taking chances." She leaned her head out of the door and bellowed, "Doc . . . you got a minute?"

Ronan appeared in the doorway and leaned against the doorframe, looking workmanlike in antibacs.

"Did you want Anna, or will I do?"

"Ronan, honey, you'll always do for me."

He squeezed Cas' hand and returned the peck on the cheek she gave him. "I have to go out again this afternoon. Another batch of settlers is scheduled for cryo, but I'm yours until then." He turned and smiled at Cara. "Nice grapple game last night. You play well."

"Not as well as the rest of you. It's a while since I played."

"I've been hearing more about you from Ben."

"About me?"

"Well, Ben told me the important bits, though I suspect he left a lot out."

"She's recovering from a concussion, and I need to do an infodump this morning. I was going to ask Anna to check her over before we start, but I'm sure you can do better than that," Cas said.

"She looked fine at the grapple game, but you're right, no point in taking a risk. Want me to put in a fix?" He took Cara's hand. "Lie back on the exam couch."

She was immediately fortified by his warm, steady grip. She had to make herself let go of his fingers.

"If you're not too tired," Cas said.

"Oh, you're a psi-tech Healer." Cara suddenly caught on. No wonder she hadn't wanted to give the poor man his hand back; he'd been giving out since they first touched.

"Right," Ronan said. "I'm a real doctor as well, but I've got some small talent for channeling energy."

"He's a Psi-3," Cas said proudly. "Any higher than that and he'd be a miracle worker."

"Psi-3 Healer? I'm impressed, Dr. Wolfe." Cara smiled.

"Save that for after we see whether I can do anything for the remains of your concussion . . . and please call me Ronan. You'll have realized we're not very formal around here. Just put your feet up on the bed, lie back, and relax."

Cara let Ronan cover her with the sheet and take her hand again. He sat on the edge of the bed and immediately she got an all-will-be-well feeling. She opened her eyes wide. "Are you a broadcasting Empath?"

He shook his head. "Nah. Think they'd let me loose on the frontier planets if I was? Especially on this trip with a bunch of superstitious settlers, probably half of whom already think that we can take over their minds with or without our implants?" He grinned. "But I'm Empathic and, unless I'm very much mistaken, so are you . . ."

It wasn't quite a question, but she nodded anyway. "Barely a Psi-5."

"That's still good enough to grease the communications slope between us in both directions. Shut up, now, and let me work."

Cara closed her eyes and relaxed—not a difficult thing to do when her hand was being held by someone who seemed to be pouring warmth and affection in her direction, willing her to be cured of all ills. Ah, if only life could be so simple.

"You'll do."

"What?"

"The concussion's not going to be a problem. There's no intracerebral hemorrhage, no long-term damage—just a diffuse injury that's well on the way to repairing itself. I'd say you're fine for the infodump."

"Thanks, Doc," Cas said.

"Yes, thanks," Cara echoed.

"You're welcome—anytime." He squeezed her hand gently and let it go.

"Bye, honey." Cas sighed as Ronan left them, and Cara saw the look on her face.

"He's gorgeous, isn't he?" she said. "Pity he's gay."

Cas laughed. "Everyone falls for him, but he's in a relationship with Jon Moon, one of Wenna's cartographers from Mapping and Exploration. It's all a bit new, but they seem very suited. Lie still now."

Cara cleared her mind and activated her implant to receive. Cas fired packets of information directly into her mind. Over the next two hours it would be dispersed into physical memory while she slept. When she awoke, she'd know everything she needed to know about Olyanda and the upcoming mission.

"All right?" Cas asked.

Cara nodded, unable to speak.

"Sleep now. I'll wake you with a hot drink in a couple of hours. Better service than the best hotel, eh?"

Cara did sleep, but the infodump manifested in a dreamlike parade of facts. As she digested it all, she began to appreciate just how tricky the year on Olyanda was going to be.

It would be a physically difficult place, temperate around the equatorial band and three quarters of the single land mass covered by a retreating ice sheet. Prone to sudden violent storms, but little seismic activity. Part of the available land was rendered barren by mountains and yet another part by a dust desert. Still, the habitable area would ultimately support an agrarian population of maybe fifty million. The colonists had a long way to go before they ran out of space and at the rate the ice was receding, they'd reclaim more land each year.

The big problem was going to be the electromagnetic activity. Even if the back-to-basics settlers had wanted to take technology with them, they'd have been disappointed. Olyanda orbited a very active star with visible sunspots and dramatic solar storms occurring irregularly. Anything reliant upon radio waves was a nonstarter, and without heavyweight shielding all the computer systems and even sophisticated AIs would fry.

The population would be protected from the worst of the radiation by the atmosphere, though they'd have to learn to wear thick sunblock and protective clothing when the sun was acting up or suffer a cancer epidemic. But with the resulting spectacular aurora, they'd certainly get fair warning.

Adapting to the land was a long-term problem, but possibly the bigger question in the short-term was how were the ten thousand Ecolibrians going to rationalize their fear and loathing of the psi-tech team during the first year? That thought was still in Cara's head when Cas touched her arm gently.

"Tea?"

Cara forced her mouth to work. "Uhh. Thanks." She sat up and swung her legs over the side of the bed.

"Everything all right?"

"I think so. It's going to be a hell of a year." She took the mug of tea from Cas.

"Well, you wouldn't want to have it easy, would you? Where's the fun in that?"

Cara sighed. *Yes, just for once I would like it to be easy, please. I'd like a mission where no one comes home in a body bag; where the crops don't fail; where the provisional government isn't overthrown by the loony faction; where platinum mining doesn't bleed the heart of the planet dry and ruin the farmland; where the sun shines gently and the wind doesn't blow the roofs off the temporary shelters; where a quarter of the plows aren't lost in a shuttle accident; where the original bio survey isn't so snafued that none of the native botany matches up with the imported biology . . .*

"I don't need to be a Clairvoyant to see that we're sitting on top of a short-fused bomb with the Ecolibrians hating everything we stand for."

Cas grinned without humor. "It's ironic, isn't it, that the FPA would probably like nothing better than to stick all the fundy Ecolibrians in a rocket ship and send them off to the far side of the galaxy to sink or swim on their own, but with the political situation on Earth, they daren't. The Ecos applied for a waiver on the setup team legislation, you, know, but it was turned down."

"Yeah, I got that." She rubbed her temple. "I guess they were as pissed as all hell."

"Still are from what I can make out."

"Great."

✦ ✦ ✦

Ben was waiting for Cara at the office door when her shift ended. "I thought I'd walk you home," he said. "You're looking better."

"I'm feeling better." She told him about the grapple match.

"Sorry I missed it."

"Cas did a direct infodump for me today. I hate that kind of thing, but I guess I needed it."

"Me, too. I get mine tomorrow."

They left the building by the antigrav shaft and headed across the open lawns outside, their boots crushing the dewy deep-pink growth of Chenon's native grasses and sending up bursts of a faintly sage-like scent given off by the bruised leaves. It was dusk, but with Chenon's long day, dusk could last for four or five hours depending on the cloud cover.

Cara stared at the ground. "Gen got us a double apartment in the staff hall. Said we don't both have to use it, but that it looks better if anyone asks."

It didn't sound like an invitation. He cleared his throat. "I've still got a small place in Arkhad. I'm staying there for now."

They walked side by side, not touching.

"Are you sure?"

He glanced across.

"Not that I'm offering or anything." She looked down again.

"I doubt that anyone will notice unless we draw attention to it." He turned sideways to look at her. "Of course, any time you change your mind, just let me know."

Cara cleared her throat, shook her head, and continued walking.

"I know it's awkward," he said. "But at least this way we don't risk back-checks via immigration."

"I suppose so." She hesitated "What about Gen?"

"What about Gen?"

"She seemed awfully upset when she thought our marriage was real."

He shrugged. "I've been away for months. Gen was on assignment before that. We've been apart for almost a year. We don't have exclusive rights on each other. It was more a bedfriends thing. No commitment. It pretty much fizzled out."

"Did it fizzle out for Gen, too?"

He supposed that it had. Was there any suggestion that Gen didn't think so? He'd have to straighten that out with her.

"Awkward question. Sorry. I wanted to know the score. Didn't mean to play the jealous wife, especially when I'm not."

Would he like it if she was? Ben found himself dwelling on the stupid question. He barely knew the woman. With an inward groan he admitted to himself that he'd like to remedy that, but rushing her was the last thing she'd respond to. He kept his voice neutral. "I'm sorry about all this. Do you mind keeping up appearances? Or is this thing too stupid? I can tell Crowder to forget it."

"Is it just keeping up appearances?"

"That's up to you." Ben stopped and took her hand, pulling her around to face him. "I won't pretend that I don't find you attractive, but there are still no strings attached."

"I suppose we can work it out together."

"But not bedfriends." He knew the answer to that one even before she shook her head.

She changed the subject. "You really like Crowder, don't you? Is that why you stick around here, working for the Trust when you could get a transfer and be earning more from the independents on the Rim?"

He did like Crowder; the man had always been straight with him, but that wasn't all of it. "I've got my reasons. Besides, I've been on the Rim. There are credits to be made if you don't mind breaking heads."

"But you mind."

He shrugged and turned to continue walking.

"Marta told me you were out on the Rim with the Monitors."

"For a while. I learned the hard way that the bad guys don't always wear black hats."

"I can sympathize with that. The Trust is . . ."

"The Trust is like a Swiss cheese." Ben dropped his voice low and glanced over his shoulder. No one around to overhear. "So is Alphacorp. And all the big corporations. So full of holes you can't help but fall into some of them occasionally. They're too big and they've been around for too long." He shrugged. "I'm not enough of an idealist to think I can do much about it in a big way. They're stronger than the government of any one planet, even Earth itself. Cut off one head and they grow another."

"But you still work for the Trust."

"Sometimes it's more effective to work on things from the inside. Besides, I work for Crowder. That's different. He's never let me down."

"If you say so. I trusted my boss once . . ." She put her fingers to her forehead and screwed up her eyes.

"Still got a headache?"

"It's nothing." She shook her head as if to clear it. "Call me paranoid if you like, but if Crowder's on the level and playing by the Trust's book of rules, why has he hired an unproven rogue psi-tech with no résumé, no references, and no history? If I were him, I wouldn't have hired me."

Ben had to admit to himself that it was out of character for Crowder.

"I told you. He owes me."

Chapter Eleven

FAMILIES

VICTOR WALKED OUT ONTO THE PLATFORM and seated Rena and Danny to one side. They were a perfect family group. Lit by the brilliant overheads, their holographic image projected into the air, larger than life, for the crowd in the outdoor arena. Here were those who looked to him for a better future.

He knew Rena didn't enjoy the limelight, but she was an important part of all this. Her tireless work with families, making sure everyone went through basic skills training, had been invaluable. Sometimes both she and dear Danny were necessary window dressing. He hadn't planned what to say to the assembled crowd. He rarely did. He waited for the moment to take him and somehow it never let him down. In front of a huge crowd a light switched on in his head, and he became perfectly focused.

"My friends. Thank you for coming." Victor held his hands in the air, palms out, and there was a warm cheer from the people. He spoke into a tiny filament microphone hovering at chin height. "Not just here, this afternoon to this place, but thank you for coming on this great adventure. Our success will pave the way for other dissidents to follow. They'll all have their own worlds if we are successful on ours."

He felt the swell of support from the crowd. There was something visceral about these moments. They were with him. He was the reason they were here. And it was all due to him, not due to some implant enhancement which enabled him to control the masses. This was his own talent, what he was born for.

"Friends, I must ask your patience," he continued. "In order to achieve our freedom, there is one last barrier to overcome. We have to work with those very creatures which we are seeking to leave behind—psi-techs."

There was a disapproving rumble from the crowd.

"I know. I know." He held up both hands. "You all know my feelings on this matter. Think of this as testing our resolve. If we can bear this for only one year, then we'll be free."

He stretched his arms to embrace the whole meeting, his face lit with passion. "Free!"

"Free! Free! Free!" his followers chanted back.

"I have searched my heart and found a place in it for our psi-tech associates. So, my friends, I ask you for my sake, for your own sake and for the sake of our children." He turned to Danny and the boy's pleasant face beamed back at him in a broad smile.

There were a few cries of "Danny, we love you,"

"For the sake of all our children." Victor dropped his voice to a sincere low rumble. "Accept this temporary imposition. Work with the psi-techs. Accept their help, and then you can wave them farewell forever."

There was a huge cheer.

❖ ❖ ❖

Ben called for Cara early so that they could walk to work together. It was fully dark. Cara wondered if she'd ever get used to Chenon's double-length days and double-length nights. Every second working day was dark. This hardly felt like morning, though she'd just woken after seven solid hours of sleep.

"We get a couple of leave days before departure," Ben said. "I'm going to fly out to the farm to see family tomorrow. If you don't have any other plans, would you like to come?"

"Sure." Her mouth answered before her brain thought it through.

"It's a five-hour run. Meet me on landing pad B at six so we can make the most of the light."

◆ ◆ ◆

She was ready and waiting for him, a small bag packed, by a quarter before six, and at five-fifty a compact copter settled down before her. Ben waved through the bubble top.

They made the journey halfway round the planet in just a little over five hours, following the dawn.

"There it is."

Ben hovered the copter high above the farm, a patchwork of bioformed green grass and native pink vegetation. It was a large spread by Earth standards, but, he said, small for Chenon. Honey-colored cattle dotted the pasture near the low pink turf of the barnyard roofs. The house, set a little apart, was mostly underground: circular with a ring-shaped turf roof angled down to the outer wall and a central atrium to let light in to all the floors.

Ben landed on the pad outside the yard. The copter doors slid backward with a hiss. Cara felt the fresh cool breeze on her face and tasted the countryside on the air, a mixture of newly mown grass and paruna with a sweet hint of aurelia blossom and the warmth of animal dung.

Their descent from the neat little bubble-shaped machine was greeted by the noisy barking of a pair of cattle dogs, black and white with intelligent eyes and, by canine standards, smiling faces. Ben called them by name, touched each one on the head in recognition, then laughed as they leaped and bounced around him.

"Tam, Lol, heel." The command was sharp as the crack of a dry twig, and the dogs shot back toward the long-coated woman striding purposefully toward them.

"Reska. Good to see you, boy."

Cara's brain stumbled over the use of Ben's given name.

Ben's mother, thought Cara. Even though she had a wind-weathered Caucasian complexion instead of brown skin, she looked so much like him, the straight nose, the high cheekbones. She was tall for a woman, and strong looking. Ben hadn't told her that his mother was here as well.

"Nan."

"Come inside. The kettle's hot."

"Nan, this is Cara. Cara, this is my grandmother."

Grandmother! Cara tried to work out this woman's age. She didn't look a day over sixty. She must have lost a lot of years in cryo.

"I prefer to count my age in local time, rather than Earth years. It sounds better." She looked at Cara and laughed. Cara hastily revised her opinions and checked her shields. She didn't think she'd been broadcasting.

"Call me Nan. Everyone else does. And in case you're wondering, I'm a Psi-2 Empath, Psi-4 Telepath, and class one farmer."

"Pleased to meet you." Cara took the proffered hand.

"How long can you stay?"

"Only until tomorrow, Nan," Ben said, "or we'll both be busted to brush-pusher when Crowder catches up with us."

"Your timing's bad. Rion's taken Ricky to Foster Bailey's place to negotiate for a new bull calf. They won't be back until late tomorrow."

"He knew we were coming."

Nan sighed. "You know your brother. He hates good-byes." *Seems like he's not too fond of hellos, either,* Cara thought. Nan glanced at her and she was reminded to keep her thoughts to herself. The old woman was fiercely perceptive.

"I should go over to the Bailey place," Ben said.

The slight rise and fall of Nan's shoulders said he could please himself. "Bring Ricky back. I'm sure he'd like to meet Cara."

"Will do." He kissed Nan on the cheek. "Entertain Cara while I'm gone."

"Of course. I'll give her a tour of the place." Nan looked sideways. "If she'd like one."

"I'd love it." Cara said.

"Coffee first?"

"Nan's brew. Dangerous stuff," Ben said over his shoulder as he turned for the copter.

"Mmm, thanks. Coffee would be lovely."

Nan led the way down the steps into the kitchen, which was on the upper floor of the house. A large curved window looked down over the plant-filled central atrium. She held up the pot.

"How do you take it?"

"Cream if you have it."

"This is a farm." Nan's eyes twinkled.

Cara laughed. "I never thought of that." She accepted the mug gratefully and inhaled the wonderful aroma. Real caffeine-laced coffee. She tasted it and smiled. "I thought Ben must have grown up on tea, or really bad caff, but this coffee's wonderful."

Nan smiled. The clear blue morning light flooded in from the atrium and rearranged the small wrinkles on her leathery face into laughter-lines. "I always wanted a daughter-in-law who could drink my coffee without flinching. Sorry, I should say granddaughter-in-law, but it's such a mouthful, and I think of Reska and Rion as my sons, though sometimes they hardly seem to be related to each other."

"Ben . . . Reska . . . and I . . . We're not really married . . ." Cara began, but Nan waved her hand dismissively.

"Oh, I'm only kidding. Reska told me."

"I don't want to be here under false pretenses."

"You're welcome here on whatever pretenses. Reska doesn't often bring friends home. He says you're in trouble, but he won't tell me any details."

"I didn't give him any."

"You must have convinced him somehow; otherwise you wouldn't be here."

"I guess he took me on trust."

"Trust's a good thing. You don't trust him enough to give him the full story?"

She didn't answer. Just thinking about giving anyone the full story made her mouth dry out and her flesh go clammy. She had the whole dirt on Ari van Blaiden and for some reason she didn't want to use it, even though he was a complete bastard.

"No matter. Just think on it." Nan's chair scraped on the floor as she stood up. "I've got a crazy amount to do today, but I can spare an hour. Do you want to see the farm?"

Cara nodded. "Yes, please."

"Here, take one of my spare jackets from the hallway. It's chilly at this time of year."

Cara slipped her arms inside a quilted jacket and felt its heater circuits kick in to make it snug and warm. She followed Nan up the stairs to the outside, where all that could be seen of the house above ground level was the head of the stairs, a series of solar cells and dense pink thatch, netted with trilene mesh to prevent the weather and the birds from denuding it.

The wind blew her hair, and she ran her hands through it, trying to get used to the new short cut. It was certainly easier on a blustery day like today.

"Do you ride?" Nan led the way down a wide ramp into a dugout barn. "I keep horses here, just for the pleasure of it."

She hit a switch on the side wall and the soft lights began to rise slowly, like day breaking. A warm animal smell, sweet and clean, met Cara on the threshold. As her eyes adjusted to the gloom, she could just make out four heads hanging over loose-box gates. A couple of the horses whickered a greeting. Nan went to them first, slipped something out of her pocket, and fed them treats.

"Brigand and Blossom, my two favorites. You didn't answer me. I asked if you rode."

The last time she'd been near any riding animal was on Felcon. They'd escaped from Craike's men and made a run for it on crestedinas, great saurian riding beasts. Torrence was so badly injured she didn't know how he kept in the saddle. Eventually his strength had failed. His crestie had raised its head and called. Funny how they seemed to know. She could still hear its cry reverberating. Still remember how it felt . . .

She pulled herself out of the memory. What had Nan asked?

"Yes, I ride." She tried to keep her voice even.

"Brigand's stronger; he'll pull your arms out of their sockets if you let him, but Blossom is devious. Which do you fancy your chances with?"

"Either."

"Take Brig, then. He's Reska's favorite."

Cara patted the big horse's neck and let him nuzzle her hand. The lights were full on now, and she could tell he was all-over nut-brown with a long, coarse mane and tail. He lipped the edge of her hand to check her out for treats.

His tack hung on pegs on the far wall, neatly labeled, so Cara saddled and bridled him, and led him up the ramp into the yard. Nan was already mounted on Blossom, a strawberry-roan mare with fine-boned legs. Cara tightened the girth, swung herself into Brig's saddle, and shortened the stirrup leathers a notch to fit her leg length.

Nan watched and nodded in approval. "I was afraid you'd only said you could ride to humor me. Did you grow up on an agricultural planet?"

Cara held Brig back to Blossom's pace along the frost-hardened earth track. Nan was right, he did pull against her hands in an effort to get ahead. She used her legs and seat to drive him right up into the bit and then relaxed her hands, so he dropped his nose and stopped fighting her.

"I was born on Earth, but I grew up all over the galaxy. My parents traveled a lot. They took postings wherever the jobs were, sometimes on planets where the only transportation was animal-based. I learned to ride almost anything you can slap a saddle on, but horses are my favorite."

"Mine, too. They're so elegant. Reska rides well."

Somehow that didn't surprise her. Ben seemed to do everything well. He was one of those irritating people who didn't appear to have any flaws. She suspected there was a flaw and when she found it, it would be so massive that it would shatter all her illusions.

Nan gave a running commentary as they rode. "All the buildings here are turf- or thatch-roofed dugouts with solar cells; environmentally friendly, sustainable, and energy efficient. There used to be a crystal dome covering the house, but I had a battle with one of the big landowners in the neighborhood when the boys were young. After it had been mysteriously blown for the third time, I couldn't afford to replace it. That's when I went native and had the thatch done. The atrium has been open to the elements ever since, and I think I like it better that way."

"A battle?"

"In a manner of speaking. This farm is small by Chenon standards, and a big landowner tried to buy us and our neighbors out. When we wouldn't agree, he tried to squeeze us out."

"What happened?"

"We're still here." Nan's face crinkled up into a grin. Cara wouldn't like to be on the wrong side of Nan in a battle of wills. No wonder Ben was as tough as he was.

Cara warmed to this obstinate old woman.

"I can see where Ben gets his stubbornness from."

Nan laughed. "He's always been a determined one. Never gone any way but his own. You make a good pair."

Cara was about to protest the pairing thing again, but Nan gave Blossom her head and set off at a smart canter across the pasture. Brigand chomped at his bit and threw up his head, eager to be off. Cara touched her heels lightly to his sides and he shot forward, hooves pounding, easily catching Blossom, but then being content to keep pace to the top of the incline.

"There, that's taken the tickle out of their toes," Nan said. "What do you think of Crowder?"

The sudden change of subject caught Cara unawares.

"I hardly know him. Ben trusts him."

"But you don't."

Cara didn't commit herself.

Nan's eyes narrowed. "Reska's going to need someone to guard his back on this mission. It's going to be a stinker of a job. I could have wished for a more straightforward assignment, especially for his first colony command since Hera-3. You know about that, of course."

"Some of it."

"Crowder's either showing great trust in Reska's abilities, or he's setting him up to fail by giving him an impossible task."

"Which do you think?"

Nan pushed back an unruly curl that had escaped from her iron-gray bun. "I'm hoping it's the former, but I worry that it's not. Reska's smart, though. If anyone can pull this off, it's him. Crowder may have underestimated him."

Cara reined in Brigand, who obviously wanted to be off again. "I'll do all I can to help."

"I do believe you will."

◆ ◆ ◆

The sun was blazing down by the time Cara heard Ben's copter on the landing pad. She was chopping onions in the kitchen while Nan seared meat and spices in a pan. Soon after the drive noise faded, there were voices on the stair, Ben's warm tones and youthful, excited chatter.

The door burst open and a light brown boy, all elbows and smiles, ran over and hugged Nan from behind.

"Careful, Ricky, or your dinner will be all over the floor." Nan chastised him with a smile on her face. "How was Rion?" she asked Ben.

"He was Rion." Ben said it as if that was enough. "He sends his apologies, Cara, but he's traveling back slowly with a new bull calf and won't be here before we leave. Mmm, that smells good. What's for dinner? Can I help?"

"It's almost ready," Nan said. "By the time Ricky sets the table, it will be done. You could open some wine. Last year's elderflower is very good."

"Rion's?" Ben asked.

"Kai made it when he was home from university last summer." Nan turned to Cara. "I'm sorry you won't get to meet Kai. He's in Arkhad City doing an agricultural course, but right now he's on a placement on Sansoom studying hydrotropic food production."

"Kai's gone to the moon," Ricky said to Cara with a mixture of pride and envy. "And he's not even got a psi-tech implant. I want to go to the moon one day. To the moon and beyond like Uncle Ben."

"Well, if you work hard at school . . ." Cara began, only to notice Ben give a slight shake of his head.

Why not? she asked. *The kid's got psi potential. Anyone can see that.*

Rion can't, and he's dead set against it. Won't have him encouraged.

So the kid's going to hit puberty and then what? He'll get tested, right?

Oh, sure, Nan will see to that, but Rion doesn't want him influenced before then. He hopes the kid will choose to turn down an implant despite psi potential, like Rion himself did. Like Kai did.

They turned it down?

Ben gave the equivalent of a mental sigh. *Rion's been terrified of the idea of crossing the Folds ever since our parents were lost. It's colored his whole life. It was the root of all our disagreements. He wanted me to stay on the farm as well. When I didn't, he—well—he wrote me off as already gone from his life.*

Your brother sounds like an ass.

Sometimes. Anyhow, I agreed not to wind Ricky up about space travel, but the more Rion plays it down, the more fascinated Ricky becomes.

We always seem to want what we can't have. How true that was, Cara thought. Right now she might be tempted to settle for a quiet life on the farm if she could be sure Ari wouldn't catch up with her, but that was impossible.

"I've learned a lot about the Trust because of Uncle Ben," Ricky said over dinner. "I know how it's organized, with regional headquarters in different sectors of space and I studied which ships they have in the Colony fleet and in the Militaire fleet and the Transport fleet, cargo and personnel carriers. And I know which ones are explorers and which are survey vessels. Is Alphacorp the same? Uncle Ben says you worked for Alphacorp."

"I did." She supposed that was an open secret, but she really didn't want to go over everything again. Ricky was a hard kid to refuse, though. His enthusiasm was catching, and, for a nine-year-old, he asked intelligent questions. "Alphacorp has all its departmental headquarters on Earth. The main one is right in the middle of the Saharan rainforest."

"Oh, I'd like to see that. Did Alphacorp do the terraforming?"

"Some of it. It was a joint project, back before there were so many colony planets."

"Is that where you worked?"

"No, I went there a few times, though, and I went to an

Alphacorp school in New Tamanrasset. That's in the Sahara, too, a bubble town with climate control because it's so hot and humid. After the Academy, I was stationed on Lukeman's World in the Perseus Arm. There are a lot of new colonies opening up out there."

She didn't mention being recalled to Earth. That's when she'd met Ari and things had started to go wrong. She'd made two bad decisions, first to get involved with Ari at all, and second to stand up to Craike on Felcon. No, that second one hadn't been bad. It had been the only choice. Craike was out of control. Pity it turned out to have such bad consequences for both her and her team. She couldn't tell Ricky about that.

✦ ✦ ✦

They left the farm early the following morning with promises to keep in touch and to return after the Olyanda mission. With cryo time, it would be two and a half years for Nan and Ricky, though only a year for Cara and Ben.

"Look after each other," Ben said. He hugged Nan and solemnly shook Ricky's hand "I'll be back before your twelfth birthday."

Just as they were turning to the copter Ricky raced up, flung his arms around Ben's chest and gave him a desperate hug, then, wordless, but with shining eyes, ran back to Nan.

"The boy loves you," Cara said as they rose into the air, still waving through the copter's bubble.

"That's only because I'm the exciting one who arrives for short visits with a few tall tales. He thinks it's all excitement out there. His dad has a point about staying on the farm."

"You don't really mean that."

He grinned. "No way! Rion's welcome to it."

✦ ✦ ✦

Max Constant stood behind his fellow settlers, on the edge of the crowd, taking in, but not taken in by, Director Lorient's performance.

The director was a charismatic speaker. His resonant voice held the promise of a better life to come. He had inspired a generation of Ecolibrians through his massively popular telecasts, and now his followers, those who had believed enough to give up everything and exchange all their savings for the promise of a new world, were with him in body as well as spirit.

Max just didn't get their rapture. The faces of those around him shone with some kind of inner light. He wished he had that light. It would make being here so much easier.

He could watch the performance quite objectively while appreciating the quality of the rhetoric. He'd studied Victor Lorient's way of winning over the crowd many times, but still he couldn't pin it down. What made him so loved? Why him and not any one of a dozen Ecolibrian politicians?

A young Asiatic woman in the crowd turned to leave as the light on the podium faded. She bumped into his chest and smiled at him. "Sorry," she said. "My fault." She was startlingly beautiful. He was sure he'd not seen her in the settler compound before—he'd certainly have remembered.

"It's these double-length days on Chenon," Max said. "Having darkness throughout every other day-cycle takes a bit of getting used to, and the humidity . . . Whew! Makes me misstep all the time. Olyanda will be better, though. Twenty-six-hour days and a cool temperate climate. We can handle that."

"There's a lot to think about, isn't there?"

Max nodded as he picked his way down the grassy bank and offered the woman his hand, which she ignored.

"I'm going down to the lake," she said. "Do you want to come?"

Did he? He didn't have anything better to do. He fell into step beside her.

They walked without speaking, through the compound, between dormer blocks and the dining hall where they all ate in shifts. The lake, one of the saving graces of this place, was barely a hundred meters from the nearest bunkhouse, but it was like another world. As they left the crowd behind, Max broke the silence. "I'm Max. Max Constant."

"Pleased to meet you, Max. Genevieve." She didn't offer her surname.

"Do you think everyone's ready for the trip?" she asked.

Max shrugged. "Those who aren't are mostly keeping it to

themselves, though someone in my bunkhouse was talking about having his parents buy him out of the expedition."

"I guess it's better to change your mind now rather than wish you had later."

Had he made the right decision? "Do you ever look back at what you've left behind?" Max asked.

She shook her head. That was either a no or she didn't want to talk about it.

He wondered how many people were running away, rather than toward something.

"How about you?" she asked.

"I used to be an accountant. I know, boring, right?"

Most people saw it as boring, but Max had ambitions to end up in colony administration. Once they got to Olyanda, he'd try to make the move to admin. Until then he had to play the dedicated settler. "I've done a course in woodworking."

"You'll be an independent artisan."

"Something like that." Woodworking was a very satisfying hobby, but he couldn't see himself making furniture for the rest of his life.

"How do you feel about psi-techs?" she asked.

"Oh, they're just people. They don't frighten me. I used to work with them." He didn't mention Leila. "You're not worried about them, are you?"

She shook her head, but he took her silence for nervousness.

"They never let new colonies loose without backup." He tried to sound reassuring. "There were too many disasters in the early days. Too many lives lost. Using psi-techs cut down on the colony failures."

She stepped away from him slightly. "You know a lot about psi-techs."

"I've done my research. Did you know they originally developed psi-tech implants for Navigators, to make flying through the Folds safer?"

She shrugged as if she didn't really care.

He'd better watch what he said. Obviously a liberal attitude wouldn't win him any friends. He wondered whether there were other people who felt like him. Judging by all the whooping and hollering over the director's speech, not a lot did. The settlers were basically a nice bunch of folks until someone mentioned psi-techs, and then they got all sancti-monious.

"You want to go get a drink?" he asked. "Caff or some-thing stronger?"

"They said no alcohol for twenty-four hours before cryo. Isn't everyone in this sector scheduled for tomorrow?"

"They're still serving it in the refec."

"Take my advice, don't."

"You sound as though you know what you're talking about. Have you done cryo before?"

She shook her head. "Just heard about it. Go get a good night's sleep."

He watched her walk down the hill alone, then turned back toward the bunkhouse he'd been sharing with a bunch of other single men. He sighed. There was nothing left at home that he wanted to go back to and no parents to buy out his contract.

"Olyanda, here I come."

Chapter Twelve

DEPARTURE

THE LAST LEAVES CLINGING TO AN ORNAMENtal tree rustled in the cold, crisp breeze. Ben fancied he could feel a touch of frost. It was the middle of the long night on Chenon, but there was so much artificial light in the city that it was almost like day. Only the drop in temperature and the faint scent of the pink turf outside the compound, sharper at night, really made it feel different. He shivered and wished he was wearing his buddysuit.

He walked briskly round the grounds twice and then took a deep breath and went back inside the building. Marta was still at her desk. He didn't draw attention to himself, but sat down quietly next to her and activated the sound baffles.

"I need to talk to you in private."

She was a short-range Telepath.

This is private, she said.

I want you to do me a favor, a quiet one. I know that it's not on the manifest, but I want you to find room for my Dixie Flyer in the hold. Exchange it for a flitter if you have to, but get it in there somehow, and don't clear it with anyone, even Crowder. Understand?

Okay, Boss, you've got it.

You're not going to ask me why?

No. I trust your hunches. You wouldn't ask if it wasn't important.

He felt much better.

✦ ✦ ✦

With the information assimilated, Cara settled down to do her share of the prep work, supervising, packing and loading, checking inventories, and taking her turn on long-range comms. It seemed as though there was so much to do that they'd never get through it all, and then, suddenly, it was done. The shuttles with the essential equipment and supplies to see them through the first few weeks after landing were the last to depart on the principle of last in, first out.

All that remained was to celebrate the end of the first phase and then to take their final day of personal leave before being frozen and racked alongside the settlers for the journey.

The team from HQ ate together that night in a private room at one of the city's more exclusive restaurants.

Sitting next to Serafin, Cara noticed Ronan come in a little later than everyone else and avoid the empty place next to Wenna in favor of squeezing in between Gen and Yan Gwenn. If she hadn't been watching closely, she might have missed Wenna's slight headshake as he failed to make eye contact with her.

Cara bent over a plate of steamed zamberries and mopped the sweet juice with crusty bread, then licked her fingers clean.

"I can't believe we're so close to departure," she said to Serafin.

"Believe it." Serafin brushed crumbs from his chest. "Anna froze a hundred of ours in body pods today and that's the last—apart from us. Two days from now we'll be shipped off to the arse-end of nowhere."

"You're looking forward to it, Serafin, admit it," Marta said across the table. "Me, I hate cryo."

"What's not to like about cryo?" Serafin said. "You go under, you come out again. Subjectively, it's over in minutes, it saves months of talking to the inside of a cabin the size of a coffin, and you don't even age. Besides, I love new planet work. You have a fresh page to draw on and you can make the picture exactly what you want it to be."

"Yes, but these settlers are going to be breathing down our necks all the time." Gen cupped both hands around a glass of spiced juice. "I slipped into one of their meetings to try and get a feel for their attitude. It was like a religious rally—all that anti-psi feeling."

"Even with straightforward colonists there's always that danger," Ben said. "Always some loudmouth who thinks he, or she, knows best in a tricky situation. Sometimes, of course, they do."

Gen leaned forward, across her plate. "I did speak to one guy after the rally who didn't seem to buy into the hype, but I think he was the exception rather than the rule. The rest of them . . ."

Ben nodded. "Lorient's got some hard-liners, prejudiced against us before they start. And Lorient himself is bordering on psi-phobic. We're sullying their promised land with our implant technology. We're not real humans to them."

"Puh-lease," Marta said. "You think you've got problems. I'm the one with gills. If anyone calls me a fissssh-woman, I ssswear I'll get physsssical." She emphasized the esses deliberately. There was a momentary silence, and then she grinned and they all cracked up laughing.

"They're especially wary because most of us don't have gills. We don't look any different on the outside," Ben said. "There isn't even a scar from the implant." He looked around the table. "It's bad for us, but healthy for them. They have to be in the right frame of mind to see us leave at the end of the year without panicking about being cut off from help. During that year we tread a fine line between being acceptably supportive or unacceptably overwhelming."

Suzi Ruka arrived late, and they moved up to make room for her. She squeezed in next to Serafin, and he patted her thigh almost absentmindedly. "Anyone want my salad?" she asked. "I see so much of the damned stuff growing that sometimes I can't face it."

"I'll take it." Serafin took the proffered bowl and started to pick at greens with his fingers.

Ben reached over, picked out an olive, and ate it. "There

was never any question that Lorient would lead the settlers, but I could have wished that Jack Mario had been given overall charge. Lorient's a charismatic figurehead, but Jack's a real solid administrator and he's a genuinely nice guy."

"Hello, boys and girls, just popped in to make sure you were all enjoying yourselves." Crowder appeared in the doorway and they all turned toward him. "Don't stop eating. I just wanted to wish you luck, not that you'll need it with all that talent."

"Grab a plate, come and join us." Ben moved over.

"Yeah, we were just talking about the mission anyway," Suzi said. "Saying Lorient's hard-liners might be a problem."

"Well, you know you have my backing whatever happens. Mixing psi-techs with fundies is bound to cause a few awkward moments, but nothing you can't handle." He looked at Ben and inclined his head. "As far as I'm concerned you play it strictly by the book. If they give you too much trouble, you simply pull out ahead of time. I can send a couple of light personnel carriers through the Exan Gate within seventeen days to lift off the tech teams."

He said all the right words, but Cara was still wary of Crowder. She turned to look at Ronan, but the young doctor, the only other Empath, was staring at the wall, lost in thought.

"I'm not planning on failure," Ben said.

"Of course not," Crowder said. "So I'll leave you to it. I still have some numbers to crunch back at the office. You all enjoy yourselves this evening, and your day off tomorrow, and I'll see you the day after for loading."

Serafin watched Crowder leave. "He's a good boss, Boss."

"Yes, he is." Ben nodded.

Cara kept her doubts to herself. The ark would take nine months to reach its destination, but though transporting passengers in cryo on an ark ship was the most economical, it wasn't the only way to travel. Vessels pulling less mass could still make a safe journey through the much smaller Exan Gate in a matter of two to three weeks, no cryo required, but the expense was enormous, and rising all the time as platinum reserves dwindled and base rate prices increased. Crowder's willingness to sanction that expense as an emergency backup measure made everyone feel more comfortable.

If he means it. That thought nagged at Cara.

◆ ◆ ◆

Neither Cara nor Ben took their day's leave and, unsurprisingly, most of the others came into the office at some point, though they didn't spend the whole day there. Ronan came in early and left as Wenna arrived. Suzi only dropped by to persuade Serafin to take a break and that was the last anyone saw of either of them for the rest of the day. The time flew by in a blur of desk-clearing and checking. Cara had packed everything that she wouldn't be needing into storage. All that remained now was to turn up at the med-center for cryo processing in the morning.

After the last box had been safely stowed, Cara walked with Ben along the level path from the office building to the dormer block. To keep up appearances, he'd taken to going home with her for an hour and then leaving quietly and heading for his own apartment in the city. She'd begun to look forward to that part of the day.

"Want a coffee before you go home?" She stepped over the threshold of her apartment and invited him in. The ritual as before. She always asked and he never presumed.

"As long as you still have some CFB left."

"I've got both. I bought another packet of the insipid stuff especially for you."

"Excellent." He watched her spoon powder into his mug and then took the cup she offered and sniffed it appreciatively. "I'll take you out to dinner if you've no plans for this evening."

"I'm not sure I could eat. My insides are all churned up. Wise to have the get-together yesterday."

"Did you enjoy it?"

"I did." She thought about it. Except for Crowder's brief appearance she'd enjoyed it very much, especially as the evening wore on and the spiced wine started to go to their heads.

"Do you have eggs? I'll make us omelets," Ben offered. "You need to eat something."

"You cook?"

"I cook." He grinned. "I'm a frontier specialist. Give me anything, meat, vegetables, whatever, and I'll just apply heat and eat it off a burned twig or else I'll stew it all up in a single pot until it tastes like . . ."

"Maybe I should make the omelets."

"No, it's okay. Omelet is my other specialty."

She sat with her elbows on the table and watched him beat the eggs in a bowl with herbs and salt while butter heated in a shallow pan on the hotspot.

"Are you worried about cryo?" she asked.

"Not about the process, but I don't like to be out of control and there's nothing more out of control than being frozen, cocooned, and stored on a rack for nine months."

He poured the eggs into the pan and began to draw the mixture from the rim to the center as it sizzled in the butter.

She nodded. "I never used to think about it, but I do now. It does make you very vulnerable. I guess I'm obviously more twitchy about that than I used to be."

She took a deep breath. She'd been thinking about it a lot. She owed Ben an explanation. She should tell him about Ari.

As soon as that thought came into her head, she began to feel slightly dizzy. Whenever she thought about telling anyone about Ari, she always ended up deciding against it. A number of times she'd been on the point of telling Ben, but the old prickly sweats and shakes had started. Ari must still have some kind of a hold over her. Her feelings for him ran very deep.

This time she acted almost on instinct and tried to get it over with quickly. "I want to tell you about A . . ."

That was as far as she got.

A wave of nausea swept over her and her body locked rigidly, hands half stretched out and fingers splayed. Part of her brain registered her coffee mug falling in slow motion. The contents splashed across the tabletop and the ceramic mug bounced once on the wood and then crashed to the floor and shattered into a hundred pieces.

She saw Ben turn from the stove and felt him grab both her hands. She pitched forward and he steadied her, gently rubbing her shoulders until the sickness began to subside and her cramped muscles released.

"Don't move. Don't speak. I've got you."

He didn't let go until she started to breathe normally again and said, in a weak voice, "I'm all right now."

"You're sure?"

"Sure."

"What happened?"

"I don't know. Nausea. It just came on and now it's gone. I've never felt anything like it before. Sorry, Ben, I don't think it was the smell of your cooking."

"We need to get you to a medic," Ben said.

"No. So soon before takeoff, they'll ground me for tests. I've not come so far to be stopped at the last minute by a bad bout of indigestion and a mammoth case of nerves."

"Just talk to Anna."

"Not now. If it happens again, I'll talk to her or Ronan after we get there."

She seriously doubted whether he'd let it go if she showed any signs of a relapse, so she ate her omelet as though nothing was wrong and chatted cheerfully through a pounding headache. Only after Ben had left did she let herself sink into a chair and stare at her handpad. There was something she needed to remember . . .

What was it?

❖ ❖ ❖

Cara quelled her feelings of alarm as she went through the pre-flight medical checks and took the shots to begin the hibernation process. She'd done this many times before, but it still gave her the creeps. She knew that she'd wake on a new world, and her belly tingled with the same mixture of excitement and trepidation that she always felt at the prospect, but, for now, going into cryo was like dreaming of falling down a deep, dark hole.

Surrounded by other bodies, their nakedness, like hers, covered only by a thin sheet, she lay on the gurney, warm and comfortable, as her life signs began to slow. She trusted that she would go to sleep gently, here on Chenon, and that her body would be encapsulated, loaded onto a transporter, and transferred to the ark. She hoped they'd tied the right luggage tag on her toe.

The drugs helped to keep her natural anxieties submerged as she drifted with the ebb and flow of her mind, but just when she was almost asleep, she pulled back from letting go. In a momentary spasm of panic she reached out with her mind.

It's all right. I'm here, Ben said, relaxed and unafraid, somewhere to her left.

That image of Ben echoed around Cara's head as the cryo drugs opened up a void that swallowed her.

✦ ✦ ✦

Gabrius Crowder straightened the writing tablet on his empty desk. The team for the next colony mission would move in soon, but in the meantime the upper suite of offices echoed with emptiness. It was a relief to know that Ben's Hera-3 survivors were safely chilled and racked, heading for where they couldn't cause him any trouble. It would be two and a half years before he needed to worry about them again. Arranging to have their cryo pods buried in long-term storage on their return would not be a problem.

He lowered himself carefully into the float chair behind his desk and pressed the comm-link on his handpad.

"Sir?" It was his secretary's day off, so the AI answered.

"I'll take that call from Ari van Blaiden now." He'd kept Ari waiting for long enough to make a statement.

It took a few minutes before the holographic image of Crowder's former protégé appeared suspended before him. He certainly looked as though he took care of himself. Crowder had engineered van Blaiden's move from the Trust to Alphacorp with certain understandings in place. The young man was ambitious beyond belief, motivated by a healthy desire for personal wealth. He'd watched his meteoric rise through the ranks with ambivalence and feared the distinct possibility of the student overtaking the master. Which side was Ari on now? His own, Crowder suspected.

He was a devious bastard and might eventually become more trouble than he was worth.

Whatever Crowder did, he did for the sake of the Trust and not for his own gain. Ari skimmed personal profit from their joint activities. Greedy men were dangerous. Any understanding he had with Ari might soon have to be terminated, but that would have to be handled very carefully when the time came. It was unlikely he'd get the opportunity to put Ari into long-term storage, especially with Craike around, Ari's junkyard dog. When the time came to do something, he'd have to take care of both of them, and that would be a job for a professional.

"Well, Ari, it's been a while. You wanted to talk to me. Is it a social call? It's not my birthday, is it?"

"Cara Carlinni."

"Who?" Crowder gave nothing away in his voice.

"Carlinni. My people traced her to Mirrimar-14 and lost her on the same day as one of your people, none other than your little pet, Ben Benjamin, flew out of there. The same Benjamin who took out an armed landing vehicle and two of our skiffs on Hera-3."

Crowder noted Ari's use of our and your. Yes, indeed, the time was drawing very close when young Mr. van Blaiden would be more of a hindrance than a help. Crowder kept his voice even. "There must have been a lot of flights out of Mirrimar-14 on that day."

"Thirty-four possibles. Nineteen of them have checked out negative so far. Your man was flying private. That gives him opportunity."

"But not motive. I presume you suspect no prior connection."

"No."

"So you're basing your suspicions on random chance, or picking on Benjamin because he's caused you trouble in the past. Ari, I taught you better than that."

"Don't patronize me, Crowder. Benjamin's leading your Olyanda colony team. His wife's signed on with him even though they apparently divorced years ago and the real Mrs. Benjamin is living with an alpaca farmer completely unaware that she suddenly seems to have been upgraded to a Psi-1 Telepath."

"You've done your homework, but that's more than I knew. Cara Benjamin's ID checks out and, as I'm sure you know, I never met Ben's wife in person."

"I always do my homework, Crowder. So do you."

"Apparently not as well as you, this time, but unfortunately I fail to see what I can do about it now. They're already in transit. Maybe I'd have checked more thoroughly, but I wanted to keep Benjamin happy. You know—happy enough to slow him down in his Hera-3 investigations."

Crowder watched van Blaiden carefully and saw a fleeting look of—what?—surprise, disappointment, or maybe something more feral behind Ari's pale blue eyes.

"You said you'd called Benjamin off."

"As much as I could without arousing his suspicions, but he's an ex-Monitor. He has connections beyond this department, and he doesn't have to answer to me for what he does in his spare time. Sending him to Olyanda has bottled him up for two and a half years. I suggest you call me back in . . ." He checked his handpad. "October, Earth-time, if you still can't find your fugitive. They should be on Olyanda by then."

Van Blaiden's image wavered and vanished without even the simplest courtesy.

Crowder smiled to himself. It was playing out well. Lucky he still had tabs on Ari's team. He'd known who Cara was immediately, but discovering Ben had been enterprising enough to bring her in on his ex-wife's ID had been quite a surprise. He wondered if Benjamin might be emotionally involved. It was difficult to tell; Ben played these things close to his chest.

Ah, what the hell. The problem would be resolved one way or another when Crowder warehoused the Hera-3 survivors. He'd planned to have Cara Carlinni stored away with Ben since it was likely she'd cause a stink if he left her out of it. The last thing he needed was a loose cannon, but maybe van Blaiden would take care of Carlinni. He'd only deliver her to van Blaiden if and when there was some advantage in it for him, though.

Knowing something van Blaiden didn't might end up being an advantage in this game they seemed to be playing. Crowder smiled to himself. He knew Ari well enough to know which buttons to push when the time came.

◆ ◆ ◆

Ari van Blaiden wasn't a patient man, but Crowder had said the Olyanda mission wasn't due to land until October, so he had no choice but to wait. He'd not been idle, though. He'd checked every other lead and drawn a blank. Cara had to be on the Olyanda mission.

With Benjamin. How ironic.

He waited until late September to call in Donida McLellan.

Ari had always found Mrs. McLellan's profession distasteful. Rummaging around in other people's minds would make him feel dirty. She seemed to revel in it, however, and she wasn't averse to stepping over boundaries once he'd agreed to a blanket professional indemnity agreement.

She knew how to keep her mouth shut, too. He appreciated that in an employee.

Seeing Sentier-4 had made him profoundly grateful he'd never opted for a receiving implant. His dirty little secrets were his own and were going to stay that way.

He made sure that whenever he wanted to discuss options with McLellan, he did it face-to-face over a good dinner. McLellan had little enough social life on Sentier-4, so she always appreciated a trip to Earth, a good hotel inside the bubble city of Old York, tickets for the theater, and an escort agency on standby in case she fancied company.

She must have been a good-looking woman once, though she was long past the first flush of youth and either her work or life had soured her. Ari never liked to ask about her personal circumstances. Theirs was an entirely professional relationship.

Tonight he'd booked a table at the Sonata, a cozy restaurant in one of the preserved buildings on Petergate within sight of the magnificent Minster. The city had been encapsulated in the early twenty-second century when the sea level had risen. Rather than lose the city with its Roman and medieval past, the good burghers of the town had raised billions to build the flood defenses and the dome, turning the whole place into little more than a theme park, but eventually recouping their investment ten times over.

It was known, now, as Old York.

The modern city of York lay to the west on higher ground, partly over the ruins of the pre-meteor city of Leeds. They'd managed to avoid calling it New York even though that other city had fallen into the Atlantic when the meteor strike, in reality a multiple strike, had changed the face of the planet, ending America and China as superpowers and elevating Europe and Africa in the aftermath.

Ari arrived first, securing his usual table in an alcove at the back of the restaurant where sound baffles allowed for private conversation. He was perusing the wine list when McLellan arrived, somewhat overdressed for such an intimate venue. He guessed she didn't have much opportunity to wear sparkles in Sentier-4's staff canteen.

"Mrs. McLellan, you look lovely tonight."

"Thank you, Mr. van Blaiden. I try."

She had a wide smile, showing perfect white teeth, but the expression rarely touched her eyes. She accepted a menu from a waiter without even glancing at him, and began to read with the tip of her tongue just peeking between glossy red lips.

"The paté is excellent," Ari ventured.

"Reminds me of ration paste made from vat-meat," she said. "I'll have the Coquille St. Jacques followed by the wild boar."

Ari selected the mushroom paté and a delicate goat-cheese pasta.

"Wine?" He always offered, but she never accepted.

"Thank you, no. It goes straight to my implant."

"That's one advantage to being a deadhead, then." He ordered a simple Zimbabwean dry white for himself.

Ari was running out of pleasantries by the time the main course was over, so he was glad to get down to business when she sat back and said, "You didn't bring me all the way to Earth because you like my dinner conversation, Mr. van Blaiden."

"I didn't. Very perceptive of you. We have unfinished business with Cara Carlinni."

"I tried for a year. She's either dead or completely closed down, which is as good as dead. No one with her talent can survive for that long without using it."

"Try again. I have reason to believe she's been in cryo, but she should be waking any time now. Whether she's entirely sane is anyone's guess, but you won't be guessing, will you? Can you contact her?"

"If her implant is unimpaired, probably." McLellan sat forward over her empty plate. "I do hate to leave a job half-finished."

"I'll leave the details up to you."

"Thank you." She ran her tongue over her teeth. "I believe I'll have a double dessert now."

Chapter Thirteen

OLYANDA

STARSHIPS THE SIZE OF ARKS DON'T LAND. They are built in space and remain there until they are decommissioned and recycled. Ark D, Series 982, named *Maternal*, was scored and pitted, but still many years from being scrapped. She hung in space above Olyanda, potbellied, gravid, ready to spawn a new colony.

Ben stopped pacing along the length of his small cabin and stared at the viewscreen above his workstation. The blue-green planet floating in the dark emptiness of space stared back at him, swirls of cloud showing a storm system moving across the ocean.

He could pinpoint their landing position, some fifty klicks inland between the mountains and the coastal plain, close to a gentle river valley. The first survey team had left a beacon three hundred years ago, and the recent drone survey had confirmed the site unchanged except that the vegetation now included some species successfully seeded from Earth, particularly grasses that would ensure livestock had fodder.

It was hardly a managed environment. Sometimes the best you could do was to randomly introduce staple crops and hope for the best. There was always the ethical argument about the extent to which humans had the right to ride roughshod over a planet's ecosystems, but the introduction of just one human to a planet was a game-changer. So far no recognizably intelligent alien life-forms had been encountered, though they'd found plenty of creatures, not all of them benign.

This planet had few native species that could be classed as truly dangerous to humans, and its vegetation was surprisingly compatible with introduced strains, but it was always a tradeoff. Humdinger storms were the biggest danger. The settlers would have to adapt, learn coping strategies, just as people had always done on Earth.

It was a privilege to be a part of the process and see a new colony growing from nothing.

He smiled slightly to himself, feeling his facial muscles still stiff. He hadn't dared look in a mirror yet. His hands shook, and his normal warm brown skin tone was closer to gray from the cryo. That would pass. He walked some more, stamping his feet to get rid of incipient pins and needles, and swinging his arms to stretch his shoulders and rib cage. His motor function and his brain had been disconnected for nine months.

The buddysuit helped. It automatically monitored his vital signs and gave him whatever he needed. Right now, that was gentle warmth, soothing massage, and light analgesia. He stopped pacing and picked up a cup of chembal, tasting it cautiously. The warm, viscous liquid hit the back of his throat and made him want to hurl, but he needed the balanced intake it provided. Whether to sip slowly and prolong the experience or whether to down it in one was hotly debated. He downed it in one and kept on swallowing until he was sure it was going to stay down.

He shuddered. Despite the drugs fizzing around in his bloodstream, he still didn't feel warm. Psycho-induced, he thought. Nine months in a freezer was bound to play games with anyone's brain. He checked the readings on his buddysuit again. His temperature was normal. He flicked the controller and felt the pulsing tingle of the skin massager start up again. That was better.

"Commander Benjamin, the landing vehicle is ready now." An ensign rapped on the open hatch and waited outside. "Launch in forty-three minutes, sir."

"Is Yan Gwenn out of cryo?"

Ben gestured to invite the young officer into the small space, noting that the boy was showing every sign of recent revival himself. The ark didn't need most of her crew to be awake for the whole journey. The long haul fell to two pilots. Even the captain slept the journey away unless there was an emergency.

"Yes, sir, he's already checking out the flight systems on the LV."

Yan would be in charge of all transport on Olyanda, but his first job was to pilot the primary landing vehicle down to the surface, with Ben as Navigator and copilot.

"And the others?"

"Your medical team is boarding now."

"Good." Ben nodded. That would be Anna, Ronan, and four med-techs.

He picked up his flight bag and followed the ensign to the docking bay.

The landing vehicle crouched in the center of a hangar the size of two football fields, a huge saucer shape, domed on the upper and lower surfaces. A single-use vehicle, unmarked and inscrutable, it held the capability of becoming his technical team's headquarters, but from the outside, none of its potential showed. Even its sensor arrays and propulsion units were masked by the seamless casing.

Ben hit the comm-link on his handpad. "Yan?"

Here. Yan, a short-range Telepath, was inside his head immediately, and the LV's hatch dropped to give Ben access to the familiar interior. He walked through the hold, past the three hundred cryo pods; strange, semitransparent cocoons carrying his sleeping psi-tech team. Cara was in one of them, but in this state they all looked the same. His boot soles clattered on the grating beneath his feet and clunked on the rungs of the ladder to the flight deck. Yan was already sitting at the pilot's console.

"All systems checked, Boss. Launch in thirty-two minutes."

"I hope you didn't wake the sleepers in the hold." Ronan was already strapping into a passenger couch, his hair wet and slick, his face pale.

"No, that's your job."

"Hi, Ben." Anna clunked up the ladder. "Let me check your vital signs."

Anna and a small medical team were the only ones besides himself and Yan to be revived on board the ark. The rest of the three-hundred-strong psi-tech team would be revived planetside. Body pods and cryo revival units were stored side by side in the LV's hold, along with essential supplies for the first landing.

Ben offered her his wrist, and she bent her head to read the display on the cuff of his buddysuit. Her silver-gray hair caught the light from the overhead.

"Still a bit sluggish. Here—this is a bit more powerful than your suit will deliver." She slapped a blast pack to the side of his neck. He felt a cold shock as the mild stimulant hit his bloodstream. Almost immediately his body began to respond.

"Thanks. Is everyone all right?"

"All cryo pods are functioning at one hundred percent. No problems so far."

It wasn't unknown to lose even seasoned crew members in cryo. Every now and then someone had an unpredictable reaction to the stasis drugs and didn't pull through. It was one of the chances they all took each time they made a long journey through space.

Ben took his place on the couch at the navigation array and punched in the coordinates. This was what he was good at. This is why he ranked among the elite, despite his lack of active telepathy.

The medical crew harnessed themselves into the passenger stations, and Yan checked with *Maternal*'s flight controller for clearance. Ben felt a familiar bump of adrenaline as Yan released the docking clamps. The forward monitor showed the bay doors open and the vastness of space beckoning them on. A relay from the ark's monitors showed the LV sliding out of her parent vessel, sleek as a wet fish. He settled back to enjoy the journey. Once they landed on the planet, the medical crew would begin to revive the psi-techs and the real hard work would begin.

"Ten minutes to touchdown," Yan said.

Ben made a quick nav check and nodded. "Right on target. Take her in easy and put her down on the south side of the river."

Yan Gwenn was completely at ease in the pilot's chair. He brought them in, square on, and dropped the LV into the designated spot as if he was landing an airbus on Earth. It was the same location where the original planetary survey team had landed three hundred and six years earlier, but the landing pad was as green as though it had never suffered an alien invasion.

The LV shuddered as its landing gear took the weight. "Down and safe," Yan announced. "Securing anchors and clamps."

For now the LV would sit on short stilts, but once the Psi-Mechs were out of cryo, they would dig it in, so that everything below the ship's copious equator would become, in effect, a basement. The redundant flight deck would be secured until the tech teams were ready to leave. There was just enough power in the LV's drive to lift off, fly to the nearest ocean, and ditch. At the end of the planetary year the colonists would be left, at their own request, with a pre-industrial civilization.

Ben thought their choice of level of technology was harsh. A clean, self-sustaining power plant could provide enough output to keep the settlers warm through the winters and give them light through the night. There was plenty of sustainable power available from the sun and the tides even if they didn't want a fusion plant. Where was the harm in light and heat?

"Harness release," Yan warned the passengers, and the snug straps and fittings that had anchored them during the flight snapped open and slid back.

Ben and Yan locked down the LV's systems while Anna and the med-techs readied the cryo resuscitation chambers in the tiny area next to the main cargo bay. Once the construction teams were thawed out, they'd get a medical center built on the site and have more space to revive the ten thousand settlers still in storage up in the *Maternal*'s cavernous hold.

✦ ✦ ✦

Coming out of cryo was like trying to crawl out of a tar pit. Cara didn't want to leave the no-place where she'd been to struggle up through the sticky blackness. Her head was buzzing with an annoying dream that was fading fast.

"Cara! Cara! Wake up! Cara! What's your name? Come on; make an effort! What's your name?"

She half recognized the voice, but finding a name and face to fit it was too much of an effort.

"Cara Carlinni, SP472."

"Carlinni? Close. Try again." She heard a man's voice as if through water.

"Benjamin. Serena Cara Benjamin." It was Ben's voice, cutting in, "She's still dreaming. Come on, Cara, give us your real name."

"Serena Cara Benjamin." It sounded more like Seena Caa Bemjin. She felt drunk.

"Good girl. Wake up now. Okay. Thanks, Ronan, I'll see to her. She's coming round. I don't think she'll need another shot."

Ronan. She tried hard to remember. Ronan—oh, yes—young doctor with gorgeous eyes. Anna's second. But that wasn't Ronan's voice. The muttering voices moved on, and Cara felt her body manhandled into a sitting position as though it didn't belong to her. She was so cold. She began to shiver.

"Ari?"

"Ben. It's Ben. Who's Harry?"

"My pet rat. He bit me so I ran away." She thought again. Where had that come from? "Sorry. Talking rubbish. Mouth and brain disconnected." She tried to focus, but her head felt like it was lined with lead.

"Come on, Mrs. Bemjin."

She felt herself physically lifted from the gurney and manhandled upright into a fresher cubicle. Her fingers and toes felt swollen to twice their normal size. They were the sort of numb that usually precedes pins and needles. Sharp jets of steaming water stabbed her back and shoulders, made tender by nine months of inactivity. She gasped and then began to enjoy the sensation. The fresher washed the coldness out of her bones and the stasis gel from her skin. She became aware that Ben was holding her upright, and it brought back the time when he'd nursed her through the concussion. She mustn't get to rely on him. She staggered slightly as she took her own weight.

"Come on." He backed off and threw a towel at her. "There's a robe on the rack." She caught the towel and held it away from the jets of water.

"Your buddysuit's wet all down the front," she said. "Sorry. Good thing it's waterproof. I tend not to come around too well after cryo. I should have warned you. Thanks for being there. It seems to be your specialty."

"Let's get you some real clothes and a Chembal ration, then we can pick up your kit. It should be out of cargo by now. I need you to link for me. Set your handpad for a twenty-six-hour day. It should feel almost like Earth standard time after Chenon."

"I should have known you only needed me up and about so I could start work."

"Welcome to Olyanda." His mouth twitched up at the corners, and his eyes crinkled in a genuine smile.

Cara began to take notice of her surroundings. She could hear thumps and bangs in the cargo hold of the landing vehicle; someone else must be awake and working.

While Ben waited outside the door, she dried herself and pulled on her own buddysuit, full of the complex circuitry that monitored her well-being as well as fed information in from numerous sources. Her suit was strong, with built-in body armor, but weighed next to nothing and moved with her like a second skin. She checked her vital signs on the cuff display and found them remarkably stable given that she'd just been frozen for nine months. The suit's heater circuits kicked in. It gave her a mild shot of analgesic, and she began to relax.

Cara and Ben emerged from the dark womb of the LV, reborn into frost-sparkled sunlight shining down from a single yellow-gold sun. The air, so cold it scorched Cara's lungs with every breath, carried a peaty, lemony smell that she could taste at the back of her throat.

It was almost too much to take in through one pair of eyes. Sky, slightly more lilac than azure. Two moons, both faintly visible in daylight; one tiny and distant, the other irregularly shaped like a lump of putty, badly molded. They'd settled in a wide valley. A fat, snake-like silver river meandered through, but there was nothing gentle about the startling rocky outcrops along the valley sides crowned by needle-like pinnacles, jagged teeth of rock jutting skyward. They might be called hoodoos if they'd been on Earth, but Olyanda was nothing like Earth.

Why was it always a temptation to measure every new planet against the one she was born on? Was she such an Earth girl at heart? Perhaps. She wondered if Ben compared every new planet to Chenon. Was that just the way humans reacted to new environments? Compare and contrast with something familiar; assess the immediate area for dangers; catalog potential assets.

All of that, yes. That was her job, but this was more than a job. It was a privilege. She blinked away tears and swallowed a lump in her throat. Olyanda was breathtakingly beautiful.

She hesitated on the ramp of the saucer-shaped landing vehicle and stared out beyond the localized power-burn to an untouched world. "Oh, wow!"

"Just 'wow'?" Ben said. "That's not very articulate for someone of your fine sensibilities, Mrs. Benjin."

She made a face at his teasing, and cleared her throat. "Okay, not quote of the century, but just look at that."

Clumps of something closely akin to trees jostled on the edge of the river; their thick green trunks and dense purple-green, lollipop-shaped canopies made them look more like giant broccoli than any native Earth tree. Low down, the trunks split into tendrils that thrust into the earth and snaked into the water as if drinking. The valley widened to a rolling plain stretching out to infinity, covered with a sea of bleached-blond vegetation, hip-high. In the distance creatures moved slowly through the growth, but with nothing recognizable against which to measure scale, they could have been as small as antelope or as big as a mammoth.

Cara ran down the ramp ahead of Ben, her boot soles crushing the flattened vegetation still further and leaving prints in the dark soil below. Footprints in the soil; that was something you never got on Mirrimar-14.

Beyond the river, maybe thirty or forty klicks away, jagged peaks rose, sparkling snow-capped needles ascending in upthrust alien shapes.

She knelt and examined the soil on the edge of the burn. A shower of semitransparent, insect-like creatures scuttled away, leaving little puffs of dust in their wake. Wisely, she didn't reach out for them. Even the smallest of creatures could be deadly, intentionally or unintentionally.

"This is the bit I always look forward to." She breathed deeply. "That first moment on a new world, that first breath of planetside air." She stood up. "Can we take a look around?"

"Usual warnings apply," Ben said.

"How's the solar flare activity?"

"Quiet today. No need for sunblock."

It didn't matter how many times Cara saw the preparatory holos; the scale of a new planet made her realize how small a human being was in the grand scheme of things. Maybe here she could put Ari into perspective.

In the waving vegetation, something slithered away—no, not slithered, more, twisted or rolled. She looked closely, but it was gone. That was something for the exobiologists to investigate.

"It doesn't look as Earth-like as those promotional holos made it appear." She smiled. "But I've seen worse."

"Smell that?" Ben asked. "Within a few hours that scent will be so firmly fixed in our nostrils that we'll learn to ignore it."

Cara saw movement in her peripheral vision and whirled round. "Whoa! What's that?"

A small blue-green creature cleaved through the waving vegetation, whizzed toward them through the air at about knee height, stopped dead, hesitated for a moment or two, and then whizzed back the way it had come, without turning round. It was hard to tell which was the front and which was the back.

"Trikalla?"

"Almost certainly."

She accessed the memories left by the infodump. "Totally harmless. Live on traces of copper in the soil, hence the verdigris coloring. Weigh next to nothing, float on helium sacs, and propel themselves by farting."

Ben laughed. "Not quite farting, though near enough. Blowing jets of pressurized exhaust through their outlet vents."

"Can't this planet come up with fluffy bunnies?"

"It doesn't look like a fluffy bunny sort of place to me, and even if it did have them, they'd only eat all the settlers' crops."

"Cynic." She looked at him sharply, but his eyes were focused on distant horizons.

✦ ✦ ✦

Four hours later Cara made her way to the hastily rigged kitchen shelter where she joined the lineup for caff, changed her mind at the last minute, and had a peppermint tea. She shivered as she took a cup from Ada Levenson. Smart idea to make sure that someone from the catering staff was in the first batch of psi-techs to be revived.

"You're not one hundred percent yet, are you?" Ben came up behind her.

She shrugged. "I'm always envious of anyone who can hit the ground running after cryo. I inevitably get a hangover, but I'll be all right. I can keep up. What are you doing next?"

"Just checking the perimeter. How easy is that?"

Easy, but not always safe on a new planet. Ben would be setting the perimeter beacons on full alert and with a weapon to hand. In this case, the weapons they could legitimately carry, according to the planetary charter, consisted of smart-dart guns containing a fast-acting anesthetic, but the settlers were still in cryo and what they didn't know wouldn't hurt them. Ben had temporarily issued powerful jet pistols to crew members moving outside the perimeter.

"Have you got a Dee'ell with you?" Cara asked.

"Youen Biggs."

Youen was one of the best field exobiologists they had, a
Dee'ell, short for Dolittle, named for some character in a
book who had talked to animals. They were the oddballs of
the psi-tech crew, but essential on a new planet.

"You need someone to watch your back?"

"Checking up on me?" Ben raised one eyebrow.

"Just making sure." She smiled. "We wouldn't want to
lose you too early. There'd be no one to blame when it all
went wrong."

She wondered if she'd said the wrong thing, but he
grinned.

"Thanks for that vote of confidence."

"You're welcome."

"You mean you want to come for a look around?"

She raised one eyebrow. "Well, Youen's a great Dee'ell,
but he won't be focused on anything other than livestock."
She held out her hands. "Look, the shakes have subsided.
I'm good with a dart gun, better still with a DR-20, it's got
more heft to it. And, besides, you might need your telepath."

He nodded. "Get yourself a weapon. I've got a groundcar
waiting."

She grinned. "Yes, Boss!"

✦ ✦ ✦

Though Cara kept vigilant watch from her station atop the
hood of their groundcar while Ben fixed perimeter beacons,
the afternoon offered nothing more dangerous than a flotilla of trikallas emerging from the hoodoo-like rock forma-
tions and taking an unusual interest in their activity. Youen
Biggs was enraptured and insisted on extra time to observe
them, eventually deciding that what was attracting them
was the metallic content of the beacons themselves.

The three of them arrived back later than anticipated to
find the first long, low tunnel-shaped riser had already been
erected by Serafin and his crew.

As darkness fell, they all gathered to eat rehydrated rations, sitting companionably at the long communal table set
in the gap between two of inflated beds.

Wenna came in, pale from cryo, her hair still wet from the
shower.

"Hey, Wenna, over here," Cara called.

"How are you doing?" Ben asked, shuffling up to make room.

"Why is Chembal the single, most unpleasant-tasting thing in the whole universe?"

"We've got field rations to eat."

"I take it back—the second most unpleasant-tasting thing in the universe." Wenna dropped down into a chair and rubbed her eyes.

The door opened again and Ronan entered. He didn't quite look in their direction, but it was obvious from the stiffness of his back that he was self-consciously avoiding doing so. He grabbed a ration pack and took it outside.

Wenna sighed.

"Is he still avoiding you?" Ben asked quietly.

"Sadly, yes." She massaged her arm. "When we have to communicate, he's so polite it's painful."

"Hang in there, he'll come round."

Serafin got up from the far end of the bench, wandered over to the serving table, and helped himself to caff. He walked past Suzi Ruka and lightly ran his hand across her back. A few minutes later, she got up, nodded to him, and walked out into the compound. He followed her.

Cara watched them leave and smiled to herself.

Wenna chuckled. "Do they think they're being subtle?"

Ben caught on to what she said. "Suzi and Serafin again?"

"Looks like it," Wenna said. "I'm glad. I hope it lasts this time."

Cara spooned down the last of her meal, nutritious but bland. "It'll never replace real food." She pulled a face.

"Come and look at this." Aster, a junior med-tech, hovered in the doorway, half in, half out of the riser. "Best aurora I've seen in a long time. Sunblock tomorrow."

Fastening the neck of her buddysuit, Cara followed Ben outside and then stopped and gaped. Across the whole sky a rainbow of gossamer curtains—green and yellow, blue and subtle violet, row on row, fold on fold—dangled and shifted from a midnight-dark sky.

"Listen!" Cara turned her face up to the shifting pattern of incandescent light. A hush fell on the small knot of people, lonely humans, a pinprick on the surface of the vast cold planet. Above them, like the winds of forever, whistling over an empty plain, the aurora crackled with energy.

No one wanted to break the moment.

Wenna was the first to leave. Gradually people started to drift toward their beds until only Cara, Aster, and Ben remained.

Aster yawned. "I'm dead on my feet, and I've got an early call in the morning. Good night." He turned back into the riser.

Neither of them moved, but with Aster gone, Cara was suddenly aware how close Ben was. It was as if the distance between them held infinite potential. She froze. It would be so easy and so natural to step into his arms.

Ben smiled. "I think he was trying to give us some time alone. Is it going to be hard playing Mr. and Mrs.?"

"Harder here than it was on Chenon. We should make it public."

"The people who need to know, know. If we open it up wider, won't we risk the settlers finding out?"

"I suppose so."

"So should I give you a good night kiss, Mrs. Bemjin?"

She was never going to live down the *Bemjin* thing, but coming from Ben it was as much an endearment as a tease. She rocked toward him, then caught herself and stepped back.

"No need to go too far. Let's be thoroughly professional people who act like good working partners unless the doors are locked."

"There aren't any doors yet."

"There will be, soon."

"And when the doors are locked?"

Yes, what then? She cleared her throat. "Then we can relax without having to pretend. Good night, Ben."

Cara slipped back inside to her bedroll. Cocooned in her airquilt bag, she lay awake for about half an hour, images of Ben and Ari chasing themselves through her mind. All around her were gentle snores and deep breathing, but Ben's bedroll remained stubbornly empty. He still hadn't

come and taken his place next to her by the time she drifted
into sleep.

◆ ◆ ◆

Hey, Nan, just wanted to let you know we arrived safely.
Ben spoke to his grandmother via Cara's link.

*Reska. Always nice to hear from you at . . . uh . . . three in
the morning.*

Ouch, sorry.

*Don't be. I'm having to get up every couple of hours to
check on a milk cow that's got mastitis. She's one of the elderly ones, and we're a bit worried about her. Rion sat up
with her all of last night. Ricky volunteered to sit up with her
tonight and let us know if there was any change, but last time
I checked he was fast asleep in the straw.*

How's he doing?

*Still spaceship mad. I don't think Rion's going to turn that
boy into a farmer. How are you doing, Cara?*

Fine, Nan, thanks. Your grandson's keeping me pretty busy.

How are the settlers taking to it?

They're still in cryo, Ben said. *We've only been here a
few days.*

*Keep 'em in the deep freeze until you're just about to
leave.* Nan's thought rippled with the equivalent of a mental laugh.

You're not the only one to suggest that, Ben said.

*I know this kind of long distance exhausts most Telepaths.
You tired yet, Cara?*

I'm doing all right, Nan.

Well, get some rest now and keep in touch.

We will.

Ben pushed a bottle of water into Cara's hand. "Thanks
for that. Above and beyond the call of duty."

They were on the redundant flight deck of the landing
vehicle. Ben had claimed it as his retreat.

"Happy to oblige. I like your Nan."

"She likes you, too."

◆ ◆ ◆

Cara spent the next three days at Ben's beck and call as his comm-tech, envying Gen who was flying survey. The temperature was up to plus five and it felt quite balmy, though the layer of radskin on her exposed flesh helped to keep her warm as well.

The compound looked like chaos, but Cara knew there was an order to everything. She watched Serafin's team, working in gestalt to excavate the foundations for a med-center. The dig was accomplished using thousands of tiny drill bots controlled in swarms by Psi-Mechs with their implants. The area looked as if a miniature earthquake was turning the soil to the consistency of a dry liquid.

The sky darkened. Rust-streaked clouds roiled in from the west, a solid front looming in a matter of minutes. An icy gust of sub-zero wind hit her in the face. Cara shivered and turned up the thermostat on the cuff of her buddysuit.

"Looks like a storm blowing up," Ben said. "Open a channel for me, please."

She did. *There's a storm coming.* Ben broadcast. *You've had the warnings. Don't leave anything out in the open unless it's tied down.*

Can I have volunteers to help finish this riser? Serafin asked. *Once the ends are in place, it'll withstand almost anything the weather can throw at it, but right now it's as good as a sail.*

I've got five pilots who are grounded, Yan Gwenn offered. *You can borrow them.*

Another icy gust slapped Cara hard, making her ears sing and taking her breath away.

How many survey flitters are in the air? Ben asked.

Three, Wenna replied. *Gen's is the closest to the storm path. She's flying north to try and get out of the way. The other two are farther away. They're in a little turbulence, but nothing that will hurt.*

"Let's see how much Serafin still has to do." Ben sprinted across the compound and Cara followed.

The second riser, in line with the first, was almost completed. Serafin had pulled four Psi-Mechs off digging foundations, and they were all moving the riser sections into place while the five pilots steadied them and bolted them to each other, then sealed the medonite joints with a heat inducer.

The far end of the riser was already in place, meaning that if the wind blew before the other end was built, it would be likely to lift the whole thing from its stout ground moorings. They needed to complete the structure fast to keep the wind out. Both Ben and Cara joined the ground crew, bolting and sealing, bolting and sealing. By the time the last arch section was in place and they were ready to position the curved end, the sky had turned deep green-gray. Huge spots of icy rain splashed down straight and heavy. Then the wind gusted again and lashed the rain sideways.

Cara worked with numb fingers, not daring to stop to pull on her gloves or weather helmet even though her suit beeped to remind her. One gust of wind followed the next until it was nearly continuous. She struggled to draw breath against it. Icy water streamed down her hair and face, dripping off her jawline and running down the shoulders of her buddysuit. Her suit's heater kept her body temperature up, but she felt chilled to the bone.

Last piece, Serafin said.

They'd all given up trying to make their voices heard against the roar of the wind and the creak and crack of the bioplas and medonite panels. Between gusts they worked in a wordless ballet, hive-mind.

The wind snatched the corner of the last panel from Cara's frozen fingers and she felt a nail tear down below the nail bed. That was going to hurt later, but for now she grabbed at the flapping corner with her other hand and held on until another pair of hands reached over to grab the edge.

Got the bastard! Serafin grunted in satisfaction. Ben leaned in to steady it into place. Between them, they held on while three Psi-Mechs fused the final section.

Quick, inside. Serafin ran for cover and they all crowded through the door and slammed it closed.

"Phew!" Archie Tatum grinned. "Just in time."

"Everyone all right?" Ben raised his voice above the din.

"Fine, Boss."

"Yeah, fine. Thanks for the help."

Is everyone under cover? Cara broadcast.

There was a shower of answering affirmatives. She listened for a moment longer, for any weaker distress calls, but there was only a steady mental silence.

She turned to Ben. "No problems. Everyone's found shelter. Gen's way off course, but she's down and safe. The other pilots are clear of the storm's path."

The rain smashed against the side of the riser as the wind built up, howling through the landing site like a banshee.

"Get down, just in case," Ben said and they sat on the floor in a huddle.

If the riser went with the wind, there would be little they could do but cling to each other. Something clanged into the bioplas, overhead, and Cara ducked instinctively, but the wall held.

The storm raged on for over an hour at the landing site and then died as suddenly as it had come, leaving behind a palpable stillness.

Chapter Fourteen

REVIVAL

MARTA MANSORO FOUND BEN IN THE MAP-ping office in the aftermath of the storm as he was checking weather patterns.

"I have your Dixie Flyer, still under wraps. Where do you want me to put it?"

"Did you have any problems getting it on board?"

"Nah!" Marta waved her hand. "Well, a couple, maybe, but nothing I couldn't fix." She grinned. "There have been one or two comments, but no one's questioned it officially."

"Thanks. I owe you."

"You sure do."

"Have Yan Gwenn put it in the Mapping hangar, but ask him to keep the wraps on it, please."

"You're not thinking of leaving us, are you, Boss?"

He pushed his chair back. "I hope not. My sweet little old grandmother taught me never to build a house with only one door."

"Boss, those of us who've worked with you before have learned to go with your feelings. You'll get your flyer delivered and stowed before the first settlers start sniffing around."

✦ ✦ ✦

The new settlement at Landing looked like it had been there for several months instead of just one. Cara worked comms for Ben. She saw everything unfold. This scheme was beautifully put together; a credit to Crowder. Whatever she thought of him personally, he sure knew how to assign the right people to the right jobs.

She said as much to Ben. They were in Riser One, snatching a late lunch and trying to keep out of Ada Levenson's way because she was still trying to get Ben to shuffle the erection of the kitchen to the top of the priority list.

"It's a good team by anyone's standards," Ben said. "Oh, look, rescue me, please. Ada's on her way over."

"Hey, Boss, have you talked to Serafin yet?" Ada asked.

"Excuse me." Cara got up and headed for the washroom, trying not to grin at Ben's *don't leave me alone with this woman* look.

She left him trying to explain to Ada that the most important thing in the early stages of a new settlement was the order in which things got done and that the ark had been packed on a last-in, first-out basis.

"You've done wonders with the camp kitchen, Ada. If you can do so well with next to nothing, I'm looking forward to you getting a kitchen, just as much as you are, but . . ."

Cara counted to ten, then turned and hurried back to Ben. "Wenna needs you in Mapping," she said. "It sounds pretty urgent."

"Coming." Ben stood up. "Sorry, Ada. Got to go."

Cara headed for the LV and Ben caught up with her halfway across the compound.

"You lie like a professional." He grinned at her. "Thanks. I'd better show my face in Mapping or my cover story will be blown."

Cara had tried very hard to remain neutral, but she had to admit, even to herself, that she *liked* Ben Benjamin. He was a good friend to have.

Perhaps it was because their relationship had begun with casual sex that she'd originally had a hard time actually believing that he would not, eventually, make a move in that direction. He was, after all, very masculine.

Cara pulled herself up sharply. She desperately wished she could rewind their first meeting and replay it without the sex. She knew that she'd seriously misjudged Ben at first. Sex wasn't a price she'd needed to pay to get his attention.

She veered away from that embarrassing thought.

✦ ✦ ✦

The shuttles, pot-bellied things with cavernous cargo holds, began the task of ferrying down essential supplies, equipment, and livestock for the new colony. Every piece of cargo, every domestic animal, beast of burden or core breeding stock, cost many times its worth to ship, but its value here was incalculable. Every kilo of medonite, every sack of seed, every ingot of metal, every tray of rations carried a heavy transport penalty, so the inventory had been calculated to the last gram and the stowing order finely tuned so everything was unloaded in the right order for the experienced teams to deal with.

The broccoli trees yielded wood that was close-grained yet easy to work, and it was already being put to good use.

Temporary infrastructure grew out of chaos: the med-center, with its cryo resuscitation units; accommodation risers; storage sheds; and, finally, a food hall with a fully equipped kitchen. Ada Levenson was happy again. As long as it was biologically compatible, had some food value, and wasn't actively poisonous, her team would figure out a way to make it edible.

Eventually, with all the psi-techs awake and working, it was time to begin reviving the settlers, Victor Lorient and Jack Mario first.

Cara was curious about Victor Lorient. She'd seen him on holovids, of course, but he'd avoided visiting HQ on Chenon and she'd never met him in the flesh. His reputation said he was charismatic, and so she was hardly prepared for the hollow-eyed, gray-faced figure sitting wrapped in a foil blanket in the med-center recovery room. His face seemed to be out of proportion to the rest of him, all nose and cheekbones.

"Director Lorient." Ben offered his hand and, after only a slight hesitation, Lorient stood shakily and took it. "My . . . wife, Cara."

"Commander Benjamin, Mrs. Benjamin."

Cara felt Lorient's clasp, cold and flaccid, slither off her own. He barely touched her before snatching his hand away. He was probably still dazed from the cryo, poor man. "Sit down, Director. I always feel disoriented when I come out of cryo. I hate the hardy types who can shrug it off as though they've just been asleep overnight."

Lorient grimaced. "I didn't expect to feel quite so . . . weak."

"Have you had a Chembal ration?" Ben asked.

Lorient's mouth turned down at the mention.

Cara sat down next to him, wondering if she'd done the wrong thing when he stiffened and inched away from her, but she kept her voice light. "That looks like a yes. Just make sure you drink plenty of fluids for the first couple of days. Speaking of which, can we take you across to the food hall and get you a nice cup of tea? Any flavor. It's all powdered, of course, but it's warm. It's two hours to lunch, but if you're hungry, there are ration packs."

Lorient turned slightly paler at the mention of food.

Ben looked around. "I was expecting Jack Mario to be here, too."

"I'm afraid he's one of your hardy types. He's already on his feet and exploring."

As if summoned by his name a compact muscular man appeared in the doorway. His thick physique made him appear almost squat, but he was only a few centimeters shorter than Ben. He wore standard-issue fatigues. His cropped dark hair was still damp and spiky from the shower, but he looked wide awake and full of energy.

"Jack Mario." He held out his right hand.

Cara took the opportunity to move and give Lorient some space. Jack seemed to have no reservations about physical contact. He shook both their hands enthusiastically, Cara first, then Ben. "Nice to see you again, Commander Benjamin. Strange feeling this cryo. Glad it's a once-in-a-lifetime event. Any better, Director Lorient?"

"We've been offered tea, Jack." Lorient sounded doubtful.

"Excellent. Lead me to it."

"Ah, you haven't tasted Ada's tea yet." Cara smiled and turned to Lorient. "Can I trade you a coat for that blanket, Director? There's a chill wind blowing from the north."

Lorient nodded. Cara directed a thought to a passing med-tech and was pointed to a store where she found a selection of basic clothing for the revived settlers. Marrying up people with their luggage boxes couldn't be done in the cryo revival unit, and Serafin's engineers were still building the riser next to the hospital where newly revived settlers would pick up their basic kit. Director Lorient's personal possessions had already been delivered to the riser allocated to the settlers for both accommodation and administration.

She requisitioned two padded jackets and took them back to the recovery room where Anna Govan was completing a final check on Lorient. She gave him a hypospray shot into the inside of his left arm. "That should help a little, Director, but only time will really cure the way you feel. Any better?"

"Still cold."

"Here." Cara handed him a padded jacket, taking care not to invade his personal space. He shrugged into it and tightened the adjuster straps for a better fit. Jack Mario just slung his jacket casually over one shoulder and almost bounded to the door. Lorient walked like a man whose back was made of glass.

They paused on the front doorstep of the hospital building, and Lorient drew a deep breath of planetside air. "What's that smell?"

Cara realized she'd already acclimatized. "Olyanda. The air, the water, the vegetation, the wildlife. It's just the way the planet smells. You won't even notice it by tomorrow."

"It's beautiful," Jack said. "Fresh. New."

Lorient gazed out across the compound while Cara tried to picture it through his eyes: a mishmash of earthworks, low, gray risers that looked like tunnels, some finished and some not; vehicles; crates; people hurrying in all directions;

heavy machinery; bots; and the saucer-shaped landing vehicle. Across the river another building stood alone with only a narrow pontoon bridge linking it to the rest of the compound.

Lorient's voice was polite but cold. "Tell me what I'm seeing here, please."

Ben caught Cara's eye. He didn't even need to say anything. His look said: *watch your step*. He pointed to the saucer and kept his voice perfectly light and friendly. "The LV is our technical headquarters. It contains all the equipment that we'll need to use during the first year, shielded from the electromagnetic surges. It's ATC, Air Traffic Control for all the shuttles to and from the ark as well as for all the planet-based transport. It's also a base for the mapping and exploration teams. All the planetary data is stored in the central matrix."

"This is the one you remove before you leave."

"If that's what you still want at the end of the year. We won't actually take it away because it costs more to transport something like that than the hardware is worth, so we'll recycle the metals for you and bury all that can't be used. You have the whole year to make up your mind about living without the benefits of any kind of technology. We can still set up a basic fiber-optic underground telecom system for you if you decide you want one, and leave all the ground-cars in working order; they're all mechanical, pretty well EM-proof, though they'll have corrosion problems like anything else on a high EM planet."

Lorient shook his head. "We'd spend too much effort trying to maintain technology we couldn't replace. Better to make a clean break and go back to fire and the wheel. Right, Jack?"

Jack barely hesitated. "Yes, of course."

Lorient nodded stiffly. "What are all the other buildings? It looks like a city already."

"It's all temporary. They are either biodegradable or made of material that can be recycled. Some risers are dormitories, others are stores and workspaces. The big one in the middle is the food hall, also a communal meeting hall, and the smaller one next to it is yours. I'm afraid for starters you'll be living and working in the same space. We can put up dividers wherever you need them, though."

Lorient made a noncommittal grunt that might have been approval or not. He set off briskly across the compound, but soon slowed his pace as his physical condition caught up with his intent.

"I'm itching to start work," Jack Mario said. "When does our stuff arrive?"

"Your personal packs are in your quarters already," Cara said. "The colony admin records should be shuttled down within a day or two. Everything is all running more-or-less to schedule."

"The rest of our people?" Lorient asked.

"Your admin team is in resuscitation already, and tomorrow we begin reviving your artisans and specialists," Ben said. "We've already got some preliminary survey results which show ironstone outcrops about thirty klicks away. We can take your smiths there as soon as you are ready to make a start on smelting. There's good clay for building the furnaces and enough wood nearby for charcoal. Yan Gwenn has an airbus standing by to take them out to the ironstone site."

Lorient nodded, but the listlessness in his eyes was fast disappearing. He walked on a few more paces and then turned. "No airbuses. Do we have timber for wagons?"

Ben nodded. "Of sorts." He stopped and pointed to the growths by the river. "Suzi Ruka's got a fine Latin name for them, but for want of something easier those are what we've started to call broccoli trees. The thick trunks yield planks more than a meter wide—a lightweight but close-grained wood. There's a forest of them—that dark line in the distance beyond the bend in the river—about ten klicks away." He started walking again. "We'll take your foresters."

"No." Lorient spoke sharply, and then, as if he'd realized he'd overstepped the mark, he softened his voice. "They have to build this colony themselves. Ten klicks—it's not impossible, is it? They can go there by themselves."

Ben frowned. "But it's chicken and egg. You need wagons to bring the timber and iron down to the manufactory, and to build your wagons you need timber for the carcass and iron for nails and to strengthen the hubs and rims of your wagon wheels and for your couplings. You've got to start somewhere. That's all we're offering, a start. It's what we're here for."

"What about native wildlife?" Jack asked. "Anything we should know about?"

"There's a big predator in the mountains, a quadruped that can walk upright and climb like a cat, but it's solitary and seems relatively shy of us. The lyx is about the size of a wolf, but it has six legs and no tail. It's a hunter, a meat-eater and runs in family packs, but it generally takes the easiest prey, so probably not adult humans, unless they're starving. Don't let your children wander off alone, though." Ben counted them off on his fingers. "There are leapers, only medium-size predators, but they pack a punch. They have colossal hindquarters and enough spring in their back legs to propel them ten meters in one leap, and they have forepaws with talons that inject a soporific, so all they need to do is sink their claws in and wait for the anesthetic to take effect so they can rip their prey apart."

"Sounds dangerous."

"I was with Youen when he found the one in the mountains, Director," Cara said. "It didn't seem to know what to make of us and didn't stay around for long enough to look threatening, but creatures adapt just like we do, so take note of any behavioral changes."

"The Dee'ells attached to Mapping are logging new species all the time," Ben said. "But not too many real native nasties yet. The most dangerous creatures we've found so far are reptans. We don't know much about their habits, but they seem to be restricted to the swampy ground of the delta. They're not very big, but they're venomous and mean."

They walked on in silence for a while. Cara was well aware that they were here because the law said they had to be, not because Lorient wanted them, but she thought that he had accepted Ben's logic. However, he stopped again and waved toward the river.

"We'll cut a few of those trees to make the first wagons. We'll take the smiths to the ironstone site and build the first manufactory right there."

"Director Lorient, can we discuss this?" Jack asked.

"There's nothing to discuss, Jack." Lorient turned to Ben. "When do we have use of the first beasts of burden?"

Cara saw Ben's eyebrows raise slightly, but to his credit he kept his voice even and reasonable. "The first few draft horses and oxen will be revived within the week. Some of the riding horses a little after that. Most of your stock has to be tank-reared, of course."

Cara glanced across the river to the large prefabricated building standing alone.

"Clones." Lorient's mouth set in a hard line.

"Oh, not clones, Director," Cara had to chip in. "Calvin Tanaka is so proud of the bloodlines he's secured for you. Rare breeds that have been preserved in sanctuaries: cattle from Dexters to Charolais, Shire horses and Clydesdales, Saddleback pigs, Merino sheep . . ."

"Grown in vats."

"But from genuine frozen embryos. Truly, they're all individuals, not clones."

She frowned. Did he really think they'd pull a bait-and-switch trick?

Lorient rubbed his eyes and his shoulders sagged. "We'll talk about that later." He took a deep breath. "For now, we have a plan."

Cara tried not to catch Ben's eye again. She could feel what he thought about doing it the hard way. *Standing up in a hammock.* She aimed a thought at him and saw his cheek twitch as he tried not to laugh. It served to defuse his thoughts, though.

Lorient paused to watch construction on a row of four identical dormitory risers. "The panels just slot together?" he asked.

"More or less," Ben said. "They come flat-packed, but each sheet of medonite has a built-in memory which, when activated, changes the sheet to a preprogrammed shape."

"Interesting." Lorient approached the dining hall, the same shape as a dormitory riser, but much larger, with the curve of the roof rising to about seven meters. "And this hall is made in the same way, yes?"

"Yes, medonite and bioplas panels with memory."

"I see." He stepped inside and looked around.

Cara took medonite risers for granted. They were a fact of life on new colony worlds, but she wondered how someone like Lorient felt, seeing a temporary town for the first time. To him, it must look like the vids of disaster rescue operations on Earth—the aftermath of a tsunami, earthquake, or hurricane—with all its associated emotions. Yet inside, the dining hall looked mundane enough; rows of empty tables and benches, only the first few made of imported medonite, the rest made from local broccoli wood.

She waved at Ada Levenson, busy in the kitchen area at one end, and flashed her a message not to disturb them. There was always hot water available from the spigot and a choice of instant powders. "Tea?" she asked Lorient. "Any particular flavor? Or there's caff, but it's not good."

Ben pulled a face. "Cara was raised on Earth. She likes coffee. I've grown up with this stuff. Tastes fine to me. Pick your poison, gentlemen."

Everyone helped themselves to a drink from a selection of powders, filling their mugs with hot water from the spigot, and they sat at the nearest table.

Jack sipped his drink cautiously, then grinned and took another swallow. "That's not bad."

Lorient sat down opposite Ben, looking thoughtful.

"This place . . . all the risers . . . they could be taken down and moved?"

"They could, but at the end of the year we'll recycle them as raw medonite for your artisans. Their value doesn't merit a ticket home."

"You misunderstand me. I mean can they be moved now? I'd like to set up a separate village, close to the trees."

"Two separate camps?" Ben massaged his forehead with fingers and thumb. "We'd still have to revive your settlers here. All the equipment would have to be ferried across from the shuttles. We'd have to have storerooms on both sites . . . two lots of plumbing, double security . . ."

"Director Lorient?" The look on Jack's face told Cara that this had come as a surprise to him, too.

"I've thought about it, Jack, and that's what we'll do. I'd

like us to be separate right from the start." He turned to Ben. "Take it as a nonnegotiable request."

Cara felt that Ben was squashing down if not anger, at least frustration, but he merely half-inclined his head to Lorient. "It's your colony."

"Yes, it is."

No plan survives first contact with the enemy, Cara said, directly to Ben.

You're right there. It's going to be a long year.

◆ ◆ ◆

When Lorient requested they revive his wife and son immediately, Cara was surprised that Ben agreed to shuffle the resuscitation order, but even so it was another three days before they were able to have Rena and Danny Lorient's cryo container shipped down from the ark. Since it wasn't possible to retrieve just two individuals, the whole container of a hundred body pods had to be revived, out of order. By bumping the Lorients up the list, they had to revive another ninety-eight nonessential personnel, families and lower grade administrators, before the blacksmiths and artisans. Cara would have argued, but Ben judged that giving Lorient his family would be a stabilizing influence and therefore worth the time penalty.

Cara was curious about Lorient's family. Rena and Danny had been well in the background on all the holovids of Victor Lorient, despite the fact that Rena had done a lot of good work with families. She knew about Danny, of course, from the files. He could have been perfect, but they'd let him be brought into the world with Down syndrome, something that had been curable for centuries *in utero*. Cara had her own views on that.

We're in the food hall, Anna, Cara said when the doctor announced that she was about to start the revival process and that Lorient was practically breathing down her throat.

Can you come over to the hospital? I've stuck the director in the hallway for now, but I'd sure appreciate it if someone could distract him while I get on with this. Danny Lorient is on our red flag list, and I need all my wits about me. No one has ever put someone like him through cryo before. I don't know what complications might arise.

Ben's talking to Wenna. I'll get him, and we'll come right across.

Cara caught Ben's eye and explained the situation, and they left the food hall together, walking across the compound in the cool spring sunlight. There were four large scars where accommodation risers had been removed for transplantation to the settlers' new village, which Jack Mario had firmly named Timbertown after someone had jokingly called it Broccoliburg. Most of Serafin's engineers were away working on the new site, ferried there daily by Yan Gwenn's drivers in groundcars. The regular route had been pounded into a hard roadway, but they'd need to lay a road surface before wheeled wagons could use it, especially if it rained again.

On the edge of the compound a shuttle, its cargo doors open, sat squat on the landing pad while Marta, bright scarf wrapped around her neck to protect her gills from the chill air, supervised the unloading process, tagging containers for storage, transport to Timbertown, or immediate use in Landing. Cara smiled when Marta's markers on the Timbertown crates turned out to be "BB"—Broccoliburg.

Everything was running, if not according to the original plan, at least smoothly.

Can you connect me with Anna? Ben asked.

There was an answer but it was vague. She tried again. **Anna?** Cara picked up Ben's consciousness and sought Anna's to form a triad.

Not now, Cara. There's a panic on. Danny Lorient has gone into arrest. She caught the echo of Anna's hurried command to her team. **A shot of Concordine on my count of three. One, two, three.** She was still open to them as she transmitted instructions to the emergency staff.

Cara looked at Ben.

"Keep up with what's happening," he said.

She patched him back into Anna's head. **Another shot of Concordine. One, two, three. Come on, Danny, breathe. In, out. In, out. Good boy. Life signs?**

Weak but stabilizing. That was Ronan Wolfe's mental

voice, then . . . *What the hell . . . Who said he could come in here?*

With a jolt, Cara realized that Lorient was in the emergency room.

Ben and Cara began to run in the direction of the stairs. They found the emergency room by the commotion. Two med-techs had manhandled Lorient back out into the corridor. He took a swing at one of the nurses, who retaliated by grabbing his wrist and twisting his arm behind his back until he gasped for her to let go. By that time Ben was there.

"I'll take it from here," he said, putting himself between Lorient and the emergency room door.

"Victor—oh, please don't hurt him." A pale-faced, mousy woman, hair slick from the shower and wearing a hospital gown, stepped forward. Rena, Mrs. Lorient, Cara supposed. "He said he heard Danny calling out."

"I don't think that's possible." Ben shoved Lorient up hard against the corridor wall as he tried to struggle free. "Take it easy, Director, Doctor Govan's doing everything she can."

"I didn't hear anything," Rena babbled. "What's happening? What's the matter with Danny?"

Ben obviously needed no help with Lorient; though he was a big strong man, his movements were unfocused and he didn't use his body well. Cara didn't need to be Empathic to read the fear and anxiety coming from both Lorients. In Victor it had manifested as anger, in Rena as near panic. She took a deep breath and found her own quiet calm and put a comforting arm around Rena Lorient's shoulders and led her to a seat. "Danny's had a bad reaction to cryo, but they've stabilized him. He's going to be all right."

"How do you know?" Lorient called across. "You've not been in there."

"I'm a Psi-1, Director Lorient. Doctor Govan will be out in a minute to confirm what I said."

It was slightly less than a minute before Anna emerged.

"Danny needs a lot of rest, but he's recovering from the reaction now. He's stable and you can go in and see him. After you've visited, we'll transfer him to intensive care and keep an eye on him until he's back to normal."

Anna looked at Ben as the Lorients walked past her. *That was a close call.*

Is he really okay? Ben asked.

As much as he'll ever be. Danny will always be fragile, but we'll do our best for him. He seems like a good kid.

Chapter Fifteen

DISCOVERIES

BEN SAT ALONE AT A TABLE IN THE FOOD HALL and pushed the remains of his rations around the can with a spoon. He'd come in early to avoid the Lorients and any potential social unease. Truth to tell, he didn't feel very sociable tonight. He was dog-tired and more than ready to roll into his bunk. It had been a long day spent mostly in Broccoliburg.

He yawned and then realized he'd done it very visibly. A knot of young med-techs clattered through the door for their evening meal and paused in their chatter as they saw him already seated. Oh, well. He was allowed to be human once in a while, even though he was the commander and therefore as close to omniscient as it was possible for a human to be . . . at least as far as some of the younger members of the crew were concerned.

Ha! Omniscient! That was a laugh. If only they knew. He was barely half a step ahead of them most of the time.

Some of Serafin's engineers joined the med-techs in the lineup and tables began to fill up. Time to go before he got trapped into being polite to some well-meaning rookies on their first mission.

Wenna came in and plowed through the throng of med-techs purposefully, heading straight for him. "Boss, can I have a word with you?"

He wanted to tell her to bug off, that he was going to get eight hours straight sleep, but instead he pushed the ration can away and smiled. "Sure, Wenna, now?"

"Not here. Finish your meal, but soon would be good."

He sighed and got up from the table. "I've had enough." He followed her across the compound and through the cavernous body of the LV where walls had been erected to turn it into a suite of offices, smaller rooms around a duty room where all the teams logged their daily finds into the matrix.

Rather than engaging the main holographic screen, Wenna pointed Ben to her own terminal.

"What's up?"

"I thought you might want to see this." Wenna engaged the main matrix and stepped back.

"What is it?" Ben sat in front of the flexi-screen and started to scroll through.

"I almost missed it. I was just archiving the first month's scans. I crosschecked it with the download from Gen's survey scanner from the day she was blown off course by the storm. Look."

Ben checked the data and checked again. He could feel a cold knot in his belly as the last thoughts of sleep evaporated. He checked again, but there was no doubt.

"Ah, fuck!" He pushed his chair back and looked up. "Platinum."

Wenna nodded. "Significant deposits."

"Has this gone in the upload?"

"The raw data has already been sent to Chenon. It's fairly well buried . . . I doubt anyone will spot it immediately . . . It was pure chance that Gen left her scanner running during the storm."

"But it's on file, sitting there for anyone to stumble across. If this leaks out . . ." He rubbed his forehead. "Who else have you told?"

"No one. What do you take me for?"

"Sorry. I should have known better. This isn't something you're likely to sound off about. What about Gen?"

"Didn't process the information herself. Since she was

busy running ahead of the storm, I doubt she even glanced at her scanner."

"Good."

"There's enough here to make us all rich." Wenna sighed. "Don't worry, Boss. I know that's not going to happen."

"There's enough to get us all killed, settlers included. How long do you think Olyanda's closed-planet status will hold if anyone outside gets wind of this before we can get the settlers some protection?"

"About as long as it takes for a black-ops fleet to mobilize its big guns. It'll be Hera-3 all over again." She shuddered and massaged her shoulder with her good hand. "What are you going to do?"

"I'd like to wave a magic wand and pretend it's not there, but I don't think that's an option. It's the settlers' planet, their decision, which means it's Victor Lorient's decision. This couldn't come at a worse time. Maybe I'll leave it a day or two before telling him—ack, no—best to tell him before we unload any more personnel from the ark. He should seriously consider transferring the whole colony to another planet. That's what I'd do if I were in charge—negotiate a settlement, let the Trust have the platinum, and buy a nice, shiny, new A-list planet with the profits. He's got another thirty thousand settlers in transit on the second ark. We can divert them before they reach Olyanda."

"What about the rest of the settlers? There would be a hell of a stink if they found out they'd been robbed of billions of credits worth of platinum."

"Platinum is just numbers. It's like finding you've won the lottery and then discovering each individual credit chip is impregnated with poison. Finding platinum is everyone's dream and it almost always turns into a nightmare. If you find it, you have to be strong enough to keep it . . . and a bunch of settlers will never be able to stand up against the galaxy's big guns. They might—if Victor Lorient is canny—be able to sell it before someone steals it from them. We should give them that opportunity . . . Keep it under wraps for now. I'll talk to Lorient."

He rubbed his forehead again, aware of an incipient headache. "There's our team to worry about, too. We've got good people, but there are three hundred of them and I can't guarantee every single one, especially the rookies who haven't seen what pirates can do. Make sure you keep this completely under wraps until I've spoken to Lorient. Tell no one."

"Not even Cara?"

"No one."

Ben wanted to say, *especially* Cara. Her shadowed past suddenly seemed far too close. He pushed that thought away. He'd shared minds with her and found no deceit there, but she was an exceptional Psi-1 and his telepathy skills were next to nothing. Even if she hadn't lied directly, Cara could have misled him.

✦ ✦ ✦

Victor Lorient saw Benjamin from a distance across the compound and increased his pace to avoid him, but it was no good. The man was between him and the hospital and bearing down remorselessly in his direction. He felt nothing but embarrassment about yesterday. He'd lost it completely—not something a director should do, though Rena had tried to tell him that he had a good excuse for acting like a parent, not like a director.

Benjamin didn't mention anything, but Lorient knew what he was thinking. *Nine, fifty-seven, four hundred and thirty-three.* After a polite inquiry about Rena—fine, thank you—and Danny—doing much better, thank you— Benjamin finally spat out what he'd come to say.

"Director, I wonder if I can have a private word with you on a matter of extreme importance."

"About Danny?"

"No, not at all."

Lorient let himself breathe again. "That sounds pretty serious."

Ben fell into step with Lorient and turned toward the riverbank. "Let's go this way, where no one can overhear."

Victor nodded. *Two, sixteen, eight hundred and thirty-seven.*

"We've found deposits of platinum in the upland area of Olyanda, large deposits."

Lorient drew his brows together, still counting in his head. "That's serious?"

Ben hesitated. "It's serious enough for me to advise you officially that Olyanda has just become a dangerous place. We've got to get your settlers out of here while we still can."

"You're making no sense." Another cryo journey? Victor thought of Danny's pale face, so near to death. No way would he take his son off this planet. They were here and here they would stay.

Benjamin kept his voice low. "Platinum is currently the single most valuable commodity in the known universe. Without it, the jump gates can't function, but unfortunately they consume it—literally. It's a superconductor, a catalyst. With each jump a small but significant amount of it disappears into the Folds and the scientists have never been able to work out a way of recovering it. One day they will and platinum will go back to being a useful commercial material, but until then we're constantly having to find more in order to keep the whole jump gate system running."

"Tell me something I don't know, Benjamin. Platinum yada yada. Valuable yada yada. Platinum occurs throughout the universe, doesn't it? It's a rare planet that doesn't have platinum."

"Yes, but usually in minute quantities, difficult or expensive to recover. That means any commercially viable platinum find will immediately attract attention. Unless it's well protected, it will attract very unwelcome attention from nasty people with big guns."

"Surely any platinum we find belongs to us, doesn't it? We have a contract for the planet. Filed in Geneva."

"Technically."

"Then what's the problem?"

"How well do you know your history? Do you remember the oil wars on Earth in the late twenty-first century?"

Lorient shrugged. He hadn't been a history major, but the oil wars had been a turning point for Earth. The Middle East in turmoil; Alaska declaring independence; the USA invading Canada and Mexico. Millions dying. Rogue traders getting rich off the profits before the collapse. When it finally ended, mankind had turned itself around, vowing never to repeat the mistakes of the past.

"How is that relevant?"

"Platinum attracts that level of attention, galaxy-wide. You could find Olyanda invaded and your settlers wiped out from the air."

"What? This is a peaceful colony, Commander Benjamin!"

"Just because you designate your colony as peaceful doesn't stop people who aren't peaceful from dropping by unexpectedly." Benjamin raised his voice, then dropped it again. "You know about Hera-3?"

"A failed colony. It was in your files."

"Not a failed colony. It was destroyed. I commanded the psi-tech crew for the Hera-3 colony, an agricultural settlement with a two-year initial setup program. It wasn't designed to be a closed world like this one, but rather a garden satellite for the domed cities on the more industrial Hera-5. They're both moons of a gas giant in the Cronus System. We took ten thousand farmers and heavy machinery to clear wide tracts of land. Three months into our term we found platinum. The colonists were overjoyed. There was huge excitement and much celebrating. The colony's council immediately informed the government on Hera-5 and started planning how to spend the profits.

"The Trust made Hera-5 an offer for the mining concession. Alphacorp came in with a counteroffer and a bidding war started. In the meantime Hera-3's own council started to mine and stockpile ore themselves. The raw ore is harmless even though the strip mines deplete a lot of land, but processing the ore for use in the jump gates is truly toxic. Hera-3 declared independence from Hera-5 and tried to open a bidding war, cutting out both Alphacorp and the Trust.

"About five days later a black-ops fleet hit us from the air. We had no warning at all. It was . . . grim. We saved fifteen hundred out of six thousand settlers, and that was mostly due to luck."

"I see."

"I hope you do see. I have no concrete proof, but that

black-ops fleet was too big and too well-equipped to be rag-tag pirates or mercenaries. It was a solid, precision operation and whoever was in charge was well-informed."

"You think it was one of the megacorps?"

"What I'm saying is, you can't trust anyone once the news gets out."

So the news hadn't got out yet. Victor latched onto that. "And will it?" he asked.

"What?"

"Get out. Who knows about this?"

"So far only you, me, and Wenna Phipps, but the data is in the archive, already on its way back to Chenon, and once it gets there, it's available to anyone who wants to examine it. At any time someone could stumble on it and put two and two together."

"So what do you suggest? You want us to run home with our tails between our legs? We've come too far, worked too hard for that." *And I'm not putting Danny back into cryo for all the platinum in the universe. Thirty, eighteen, five hundred and forty-nine.* "We've all put everything we had into this colony. The planet's not much, but it's the best we could afford."

"If we do this right, you'll be better off. Crowder can negotiate for you. You could trade Olyanda for another planet, one without an electromagnetic problem and with a better climate, and still have some credits left over for creature comforts. We'd need to do it quickly. Most of your settlers are still in cryo, so we could easily move them to a new world."

And Danny would die in transit. Three, forty, one hundred and eleven.

Benjamin sounded too eager. What was in it for him? "You'd get a cut of the settlement figure, no doubt."

"What? No. I hadn't thought . . ." Benjamin sounded surprised. Victor gave him credit for his acting ability. *Fifteen, ninety-seven, four hundred.*

Benjamin frowned. "I'm more concerned with getting everyone clear of Olyanda before something loud and dangerous falls out of the sky. I lost all but fifty-seven of my team on Hera-3, Director Lorient. I don't care about the platinum. I'd rather we hadn't found it at all."

Victor found something to latch onto. "What if we hadn't?"

"We have." Benjamin spread his hands wide.

"Can't we hide it? You said no one knows about it except you, me, and your Ms. Phipps. Can you recall the archive information, or cover it up?"

"Only via Crowder."

"And is that possible?"

Benjamin stopped and took a deep breath. "I'd trust Crowder with my life. He's the one person I know is straight."

"And your Ms. Phipps?"

"Lost an arm at Hera-3. You don't have to worry about Wenna."

"Do I have to worry about you?"

Benjamin shook his head. "If you tell me to sit on this news, I'll sit on it, but I think you're wrong. The platinum find is important. It's vital for the jump gates. Without them, hundreds of colony worlds are cut off."

Victor didn't care about the jump gates. "Once the psi-techs left, they had an agreement that Olyanda would become a closed planet. Once that happened, no one could get at them, platinum or no."

"Let the Trust have it," Benjamin said. "Reap the benefits, eliminate the risk. What's so special about Olyanda? Won't any planet do?"

"No, Commander. We're here and this is where we're staying. I'm not moving my family, my colony. Not for anything."

And that was final!

✦ ✦ ✦

The shuttle settled safely in the ark's number two bay, and Ben waited for the air lock to cycle. For the hundredth time he questioned the sanity of doing what Lorient wanted. He should just start negotiating with Crowder, get a deal for the settlers, and ride roughshod over Lorient, but, dammit, there was no guarantee that would protect the colony either. Better get it over with. With a nod to his pilot, he stepped out of the door to find Captain Grant waiting for him.

"Wenna Phipps said to keep this small, Commander Benjamin, so I've dealt with it myself. Molloy is waiting for you in sick bay with Dr. Golding." He didn't ask Ben for any details and Ben didn't volunteer any.

In sick bay Ben shook hands with the doctor, a fresh-faced young man probably barely out of med school, and with Molloy, the ship's Psi-1.

He drew up a chair. "I'm sorry to have to ask you this, but I need an urgent communication and it must be private—totally private—Mr. Molloy. Please don't take it the wrong way, but even you mustn't know."

Molloy's face was pale, whether from the many years in deep-range space vessels or whether from the prospect of what Ben suggested was difficult to tell. "You want me to get a neural block after the communication?"

"Yes. I'm sorry, I know it's a lot to ask. Dr. Golding, is that something you can do safely?"

"Safely, yes, but it won't be pleasant for Mr. Molloy."

"I know. I wouldn't ask if it wasn't important."

"What about your Telepath down there?" Molloy asked.

"It's got to be more than private."

Molloy nodded. "If it's so important, I'll do it."

"Thank you."

Golding got Molloy to stretch out on an examination table and then strapped him to it with wide, padded restraints.

"Comfortable?"

"What do you think?"

Then he turned Molloy's arm over and inserted a cannula, hooked a drip into it, and inserted a hollow needle into the base of the feed tube. He connected a small vial to the extra needle and held out a controller to Ben. "As soon as you've finished, start the sedative. He'll be out in less than a second, and I'll do the block immediately after that."

"And you're sure he'll remember nothing after that."

"Only that he's lost a very small chunk of memory, but he won't have any recollection of your communication."

"Thanks, Dr. Golding." Ben drew a chair next to Molloy's couch. "Whenever you're ready, Mr. Molloy."

Who to? Molloy's touch was as strong as Cara's, but a little coarser.

Gabrius Crowder on Chenon.

Molloy connected with Ben's implant.

In Ben's mind it was as if he and Crowder were face-to-face. He could almost see the details of the room and the people surrounding Crowder in his office.

As Ben entered Crowder's implant space, Crowder straightened up.

This must be important, Ben. Crowder's thought held puzzlement and curiosity.

It is. Are you sitting down? We've discovered platinum on Olyanda. He paused to give Crowder a moment to take it in and felt Molloy stirring at the news.

Who knows about it?

So far only you, me, Lorient, and Wenna.

I'll need a full survey.

No. You have to help me sit on the information; that's what Lorient wants. There's some raw data in last week's packet. Should be with you already. You have to erase it.

Platinum, Ben.

Yes, but it's not ours.

Ben felt the first stirrings of alarm. Crowder's immediate concern should have been for the colony, not the platinum. He wanted to yell, *Remember Hera-3,* but he knew Crowder wouldn't forget. It had been Crowder who had debriefed him and stood with him at the hearing; defended him for losing one hundred and forty-three of his team in order to bring out fifteen hundred civilians from what had become a war zone.

What an embarrassing mistake to make, Crowder said. *To suddenly find the planet you've contracted out to a farming colony has platinum . . . How did the original survey miss it?*

This planet's coming out of an ice age fast. Vast tracts of land that are now green again were still frozen during the initial survey. You can see how recently the ice has receded, especially in the uplands.

Even so . . .

I'd like to relocate the Olyanda settlers to a new planet, but Lorient won't hear of it, Ben said. *You'd need to send a new fuel cell for the LV and transport for the revived techs, but the settlers are easy; we've barely begun to revive them yet. I could talk to Lorient again, offer him a deal on the Trust's behalf.*

No! Crowder was emphatic. *The contracts have all been signed and ratified at the highest level. If Lorient disposes of the planet or its mineral rights, it has to be offered on the open market. There's nothing we can do without drawing a lot of the wrong kind of attention to it.* Crowder dropped his mental voice as though someone might overhear them, *If it goes public, Alphacorp will try to muscle in. I'd rather lose the platinum altogether than let any other megacorp have it. And I'm not being held to ransom over this by the Ecolibrians; I'll damn well bet that this "cover it up" game of Lorient's is just to soften us up and get a better price.*

Ben shrugged. *I don't think so, somehow. Besides, it's their planet. You've just said so. I don't think they'll try and sell anyone the platinum. They don't want it. It's my guess that they won't mine it, or let anyone else mine it either. They'd be much better off if the platinum didn't exist at all.* Ben leaned forward to emphasize his point, feeling as though he could almost touch Crowder across the void of space.

But it does exist, Crowder said the words softly, almost to himself. *You must have been tempted, yourself.*

How do you know I haven't stashed a few kilos of ore already?

I know you.

I'm just too honest for my own good.

Crowder was silent, obviously deep in thought.

Then he said, *All right. How easy is it to pick up on the platinum? Do you think you can hide it from your psi-techs?*

Possibly. Most of them wouldn't recognize platinum ore if it flew past their noses. The survey team is likely to find it, but I can contain that. Ben ran over the staff lists in his head. *And you're my backup. I need you to plug leaks just in case.*

Crowder still sounded doubtful. *All right.*

*I'm up on the ark, and our psi-tech, Mr. Molloy, has agreed to a wipeout afterward. I even used an excuse to get *up here. I told them that the ark had discovered a grain short-age.*

There was a short pause while Crowder appeared to be thinking it through. *Then I'll back that story up with a sup-plementary grain shipment.*

If the budget stretches to it.

It will. One more thing ... Better not contact me direct through your own psi-techs from now on. I might let the in-formation slip accidentally. Contact Ishmael for all routine items.

Good idea.

Without even indicating that the conversation had fin-ished, Ben set the sedative in motion and slammed his mind closed to Molloy's touch so that he didn't plunge into un-consciousness with him as the drug took effect.

He called Golding into the room. "He's all yours, Doctor. Tell him once again that I'm truly sorry for the trouble, but he's much better off without that information in his head. I hope he feels okay when he wakes."

"He'll have a hell of a headache, Commander Benjamin, but no permanent damage."

Once he was on the shuttle back to the surface, Ben let his head roll back and closed his eyes. He felt nothing but a sense of relief. Crowder was a good man to have at your back.

✦ ✦ ✦

Gabrius Crowder sat back as Ben's mind link faded. Plati-num. The Trust needed platinum, since the reserves on Io-lan Seven only had a projected life of twenty years at best.

He smiled, but the smile didn't reach his eyes. Gods, what was he about to do? Such a small step to take now, but the repercussions could echo across the galaxy for centuries if he got it wrong.

He heard the echoes of Ben's voice, "I know you well enough to trust that you'll do what's best for the settlers."

Under ordinary circumstances, yes, but platinum . . .

Sorry, Ben, I truly am. Maybe you don't know me as well as you think.

Ben was a compulsive White Knight. He believed in doing what was best for people, individuals; he didn't sit back and look at the big picture. And he never could understand that the Trust meant more to Crowder than anything else.

Anything.

There had to be a way to access the platinum. He'd better do some sharp thinking and some solid research. Maybe there was a loophole in the contract. That was the first thing to check. Try and do this without loss of life if he could. Hera-3 had left a bad taste.

And if he couldn't? The question echoed in his brain until he had a cracking headache.

And if he couldn't?

Well, it wouldn't be the first time, would it?

Chapter Sixteen

RESURFACING

CARA DIDN'T HEAR THE FULL STORY UNTIL later, and then only from Marta, who had the next office to Mapping in the LV.

"I'm surprised you didn't hear it from the horse barn," Marta said over lunch, her sibilance barely noticeable today—or maybe Cara was just getting used to it. "Lorient was throwing his weight around as if he wanted everyone within earshot to know this was his colony and not ours. The upshot is that even though he's moving the settlers to Broccoliburg, he's attaching a bunch of his volunteers to work with Mapping. He says he doesn't want anything with potential to be overlooked."

Cara had been helping out in the horse barn all morning. Her eyes widened. "What did Ben say to that?"

"Pointed out that they'd need to be trained and then said okay."

"Hell, the man's got the patience of a saint. If it was me, I'd have decked Lorient right there and told him not to be such a dick. How can untrained volunteers fit in with experienced mapping teams? It's just not going to work."

"You should have heard Wenna offer the same opinion afterward—though not so politely." Marta laughed. "But then Ben said something I didn't catch, and she gave in. Even agreed to train them."

Cara didn't get the chance to talk to Ben about it until the sun dropped behind the horizon and she returned to Riser One. She was starting to think of it as home. She sighed. That was a bad sign. She'd spent the last four hours in the horse yard trying to settle a pair of Clydesdales skittish from cryo. She'd walked them around the yard so many times she'd lost count, and now she was bone-weary.

Marta was already in the lineup for food. "Hey, Marta, did Serafin add to the plumbing today? What would I give for a nice soak in a hot tub."

"No tubs. They've gone to Broc—Timbertown." Marta picked up her tray. "If you want to avoid the walk-through, I've got two double cubicles working. I'll allocate you five minutes after Lee and Serafin."

Ben came in behind Cara and grinned. "Put me on the list, too, Marta, please."

"Unit 2 with Cara."

The long table was loaded with bowls of unidentifiable foodstuffs. Ben picked one up for himself, sniffed at it, and led the way to two places at the long table. Cara poked at the contents of her bowl suspiciously before trying it. Curry of some description—she recognized the spices—but the meat was close-grained and a little bit fishy.

"You look cheerful," she said. "I thought Lorient would have spoiled your day completely. What was that about, wanting to send novices out with the survey teams?"

"It makes him feel that he's in control. The best we can do is work around him. Humor him when we can and let him know when we can't."

"Shower's free," Marta yelled. "Benjamins. Use it or lose it."

Ben stood up. "Coming?" he asked.

Cara still had a quarter of her meal left, but she'd been toying with it and it was almost cold.

"There's an offer you can't refuse," Gen said, grinning from across the other side of the table.

Without losing face, or making a lame excuse, Cara really couldn't just sit there, so she joined Ben in the changing area. Lee Gardham and Serafin moved over to make room for them.

"Hey, I'm done." Lee snatched her shirt and hairbrush, obviously not done, but getting out of the way of Cara and Ben quickly.

Cara watched her go with dismay.

"I don't know what she thinks you might be getting up to in there with a five-minute time limit." Serafin winked at Cara. "You need a chaperone, Miss?"

Cara rolled her eyes. "As if."

Serafin chuckled and left.

"Should we have told Lee?" Cara asked. "She still thinks we're . . ."

"We have to draw the line somewhere. I don't know Lee so well. Let's leave it as it is for now. Hey, it's bound to get a little awkward, but we're grown-ups; we can cope, can't we?" He released the closures which held his buddysuit together at the middle and took off the top half. Cara couldn't help but admire the view.

"You said, no strings."

"Have I attached any strings? Don't make more of this than there is. I'll scrub your back if you'll scrub mine."

"Is that all?"

"Unless you want more." He almost made it a question.

"No."

He finished undressing and set the fresher temperature.

"Ladies first?" she asked.

"I'm not that much of a gentleman." He stepped in and held the door for her.

She hesitated only slightly and then stepped in after him. Steam enveloped them both, and Cara let it swirl around her. The spray, so fine it was more of a mist, warmed her, and she stretched her neck to loosen tension in her shoulders.

"Here, let me." Ben turned her to face the wall and began to massage her shoulders and down her spine. His hands were capable and firm.

"You're good at this."

"Ben Benjamin; dragons slain, damsels rescued, backs massaged. I'd give you my business card, but I seem to have the wrong suit on."

"Never say I don't return a favor." Cara, turned to face him. "Well, turn around, then, and I'll do your back, too. That's what we're here for, isn't it?"

"I suppose so, though if you ever want to make it more, just let me know."

Before Ari, she wouldn't have hesitated. She swayed toward him and then rocked back on her heels.

"I—I can't."

"Is there someone else you haven't told me about?"

"There was." She wanted to tell Ben everything. A whirling sensation shot through the middle of Cara's head. She felt her knees buckle.

She came to leaning against Ben's chest, with a fine mist of water on her face. He'd caught her before she hit the floor.

She raised her left hand to her forehead. "Oh, shit, what was that? How long was I out?"

"Seconds. I'll call a medic."

"No, please, I'm all right. It's gone now, whatever it was."

"It's not the first time; so what if it happens again?"

"It's never happened before."

"Yes, it has. Just before we left Chenon; remember? You passed out in your kitchen while I was making dinner. You said you'd get it checked when we arrived. You should do it."

"I—I'd forgotten, but—how could I have?"

Ben was right. The last time it had happened was when she'd been on the verge of telling him about Ari. A cold shiver ran down her spine despite the warmth of the fresher.

✦ ✦ ✦

Cara awoke the following morning feeling as though there was something she was supposed to be doing, but after breakfast, she got swept up into the grunt work of unloading and unpacking.

Leaving Riser Three after delivering a scanner, she felt the pull of a searching mind from a long distance. A contact from the ark. She opened her mind to take the message and almost staggered under the realization that it wasn't the ark. She cannoned into the side of the riser and looked to see if anyone had noticed her falter. No, she was all right. Straighten up. Keep walking, but slowly.

Ari van Blaiden wants to know that his secrets are safe.

Who are you? What do you want? She sent out a quest-ing thought.

You know who I am. I'm Cara. I'm your conscience, your skin, your brain, your heart, your lungs, your liver. I'm your hopes, your fears. I'm the clothes you wear, the shoes you walk in. I'm the air you breathe. I'm Cara. I love Ari van Blaiden. I owe him all my loyalty. He wants to know that his secrets are safe with me. They are. He wants me home where I belong.

She started to shake.

She reached Riser Two but instead of heading through the door, she walked down the side of it and leaned against the cool, curved wall.

She felt stripped naked from the inside. Memories sur-faced, thumbed their nose at her, and sank again. She tried to grasp one and hang onto it, but it was as slippery as an eel.

I love Ari van Blaiden.

Cara was empty. Bereft. All she could think of was Ari: his arms around her, his face close to hers, his breath on the side of her neck, his hands pulling her close, his body hard and hot.

No. It wasn't right. She didn't believe it.

Who are you?

I am Cara.

No! YOU! Who are you?

This Telepath was a real master. She—yes, it was a she, Cara hadn't been sure at first, but now she was—she was more than a Psi-1, if that was possible. She let the aching emptiness run through her. She daren't let herself believe it was real. Oh, she so wanted to. She tried to step round the feeling and concentrate on the mind trying to intimidate her. That's what this was, intimidation.

There was tremendous pressure to forget.

Cara suddenly knew who it was and what it was.

She sank to the floor, sliding down the smooth wall of the riser until she sat on the ground, hugging her knees. Donida McLellan. The Telepath from hell.

He wants to know that his secrets are safe. I'm Cara. He wants me home where I belong.

Stop it. You're not me. I'm me. What have you done?

I'm Cara. The other Telepath didn't give up. *He loves me. I love him. I can't betray him.*

Cara ran the words again. Secrets are safe. The block, and then the double block. First forget, and then forget you've forgotten.

This was what she'd been dreading all the time she'd been on the run. She'd never dreamed that it had happened already. The psycho mindbending bitch from hell had already messed with her mind and now she was trying to reinforce it.

And as soon as she'd finished, she'd make Cara forget again.

She needed a way to remember.

Never tell what you know. The other voice began.

It was like falling off a cliff edge. Cara sank into the words and lived their meaning.

*Never . . . *

She thrust both hands down into the dry soil and . . .

*tell . . . *

clawed at the ground finding . . .

*what . . . *

small rough pebbles and . . .

*you . . . *

picked one up and . . .

know.

pushed it between her first and second fingers and then . . .

Now forget.

she forgot.

Cara came to in a daze. She must have fallen. What was she doing sitting on the floor between two risers? Feeling very foolish, she bent to push herself up and noticed.

She stared at her right hand. Pushed between her first and second fingers was a stone just too large to be comfortable there. Odd, to get a stone wedged . . .

She stared at it again.

And remembered.

Whether she'd be able to tell anyone was another matter,

but she knew what McLellan and Ari had tried to do and what they were still trying to do to her. They should have left her alone.

Now, if only she could bring herself to hand Ari's information over to Ben. She'd made a copy of Ari's files, but she'd never found the courage to explore it herself or give it to anyone.

Inbound shuttle will be landing in fifteen minutes with medical equipment.

Cas Ritson punched the message through.

Cara staggered to her feet and started to run toward the LV, wobbly on her legs at first and then with increasing strength. A groundcar drew level and Ben leaned over from the controls to lift his lunch from the passenger seat and make room.

"That's the last break any of us will have for a while," Ben said. "Let's get to the landing site. Did you see Ronan?"

Ronan. That's what she was supposed to be doing today, seeing Ronan. Ben had insisted . . . "Not yet, but I will before the day is out."

Cara held her hand up and showed Ben the stone between her fingers.

"Very nice," he said, "Does it have a purpose?"

"Ask me . . ." She started to feel sick. "Later."

She grinned at him triumphantly and dropped the stone into her pocket.

✦ ✦ ✦

Max Constant shivered and downed the last of his cooling coffee to take away the strong taste of the stew. It would take his system some time to adjust to eating dead animals. He glanced to either side of him. Some of the diners were tucking in as if they hadn't eaten for nine months—which they hadn't. Others were pushing lumps of meat around their plates more cautiously.

He'd not seen much of the settlement yet, only as much as was visible on the walk from the resuscitation room to the bunkhouse, yesterday, and this morning, from the bunkhouse to the catering hall that was little better than the gray structures he'd left behind in Europa. The only difference was the smell. They said it was the water and that he'd get so used to it that he'd cease to notice. It wasn't unpleasant, just different.

A gaggle of small children erupted from the far corner of the hall, dodging between benches and tables in that age-old game of tag. Kids were so resilient. Even after cryo, they could still laugh and shout and run about. Some were almost as tall as an adult and others looked tiny, but they had to be at least six years old because of the six-to-sixty age limit set for this expedition. Max wasn't very good with children, but they looked very young to him. Young and noisy.

He winced as they knocked over an empty bench, laughed, and ran out into the crisp morning. Another couple of youngsters from a family near the door followed and were absorbed into the pack.

Max's head felt fragile, a migraine hiding not far behind his eyes. He still had a small pack of painkillers the sweet young doc had given him when she'd checked him over after resuscitation. He fished the pack out of his pocket, burst one of the bubbles, and put the tab under his tongue. It tasted bitter. They could probably have made it taste like anything they wanted to, banana or maybe coffee, but he reckoned they made it bitter deliberately so you knew it was doing you good.

The Ecolibrians all around him were mostly in family groups or pairs, but he was alone. This had been a stupid idea. *Remind me not to be so impulsive next time,* but there would be no next time. Olyanda was a one-way ticket.

He'd been desperate for a complete break from his former life; well, now he'd got what he wanted—in lumps.

He dumped his dirty food bowl in the cleaner and headed for the door. Across the river, by a series of large sheds, the area bustled with activity. He walked across to the perimeter safety fence.

"Hey, what goes on over there?" he asked a psi-tech who was straightening out the load on an antigrav cart.

"The tank farm? It's where they revive and rear the frozen embryos. Cattle, sheep, pigs, horses. All the domestic livestock that you guys are going to need. And before you ask, they're not clones."

"I wasn't going to ask."

The antigrav cart swayed, and the boxes piled on it slipped sideways. Max ducked under the fence and caught one as it slid. The tech hit the control bar, and the cart settled on the ground.

"Thanks. I guess I just overloaded it. There's still so much stuff to haul and more shuttles arriving all the time."

Max gave him a hand to stack the cart.

"There's no need . . . I mean, you're a settler . . . but thanks."

"Does being a settler mean I can't help out?"

"Your kind and our kind don't mix much."

"I'm not psi-phobic. My last girlfriend was psi."

"Really?"

"Is there anything wrong with that?"

"Not from my point of view. I'm just a little surprised, that's all. Some of the settlers who come and collect the supplies for Broccoliburg can barely bring themselves to talk to me without good cause. I have to go now." The tech activated the cart and it lifted clear of the ground.

Max ducked under the fence and walked back to the food hall. A big settler with a slight stoop met him at the doorway. Another, shorter than Max, but thickset, slid up to Max's other side.

"You're just out of cryo, aren't you?" the big man asked.

"Yes."

"We could tell that because you're still acting stupid." The smaller man pressed close to Max's side and put a heavy accent on "stupid."

"What do you mean?" Max started to move away, but the big man put a warning hand on his arm.

"He means, you don't talk to the freaks unless you got absolutely no fucking choice."

"Why?"

"Because you don't want the features on that nice handsome face of yours rearranging on some dark, moonless night. Understand?"

Max understood. These were the sort of men who didn't listen to excuses. He shook them off and sat at a table by himself. He could still feel the touch of the big man's grip on his arm, and their warning stayed with him.

He helped himself to a caff and sat down again.

"Were those guys bothering you?" A sharp-featured man with a long nose and thin, graying hair slid onto the bench opposite. He looked like a professor, but who could tell in the standard-issue coveralls? "They've been hanging around here for days, picking on people. Most of us just try to ignore them."

"They said I shouldn't talk to psi-techs."

"They tried that on me and my family, too. I don't like the idea of someone putting an implant in my brain, but what anyone else wants to do with their brain is their own business. It's not as if it's catching. I heard . . ." He leaned in conspiratorially and glanced sideways toward the two heavies. "I heard that part of the deal for us to come here was that we brought some of the folks that the Five Power Alliance wanted rid of. Those folks who caused trouble back on Earth."

Known Ecolibrian terrorists—Max had heard the rumors, too. "I wonder how many of them there are."

"See, this is the thing. Those two guys, just the same two guys, have been hanging around doing to others just what they tried to do to you. Just two guys, but I've seen them try to intimidate lots of people. Back in school we called it bullying. I didn't like bullies then, and I don't like them now. Our new society is no place for people like that."

Max wasn't sure he was quite ready for politics yet. Give it a year and it wouldn't matter; the psi-techs would be gone. He looked sideways at the men who'd now lost interest in him completely. The psi-techs would leave, but the bullies would remain. He knew which he'd rather have.

A cheer spread around the inside of the canteen.

"It's the director," the anti-bullying man said.

Victor Lorient, followed by his wife, came into the hall, flanked by a couple of thick-necked men. Surely they didn't need minders here.

The minders hung back while the Lorients moved around the hall, talking to small groups with encouraging smiles and handshakes. Rena Lorient split up from her husband and engaged a group of women, her face animated as it hadn't been on the platform when he'd seen her at the last meeting before they'd shipped out of Chenon.

Max noticed that the bullies moved closer to Director Lorient, hanging on his every word.

Victor himself didn't get as far as Max's table before he stopped to address the whole room. It was the usual stuff about pulling together and working hard.

Max tried to concentrate on the content of the speech. The director was a good orator, possibly a great one. The two bullies had gravitated to the pair of minders who'd come in with the director. They seemed to know each other. Did Victor Lorient recommend strong-arm tactics to his followers? He'd always professed to have no connections with the fundy terrorists on Earth, but seeing the way the thugs revered Lorient made Max wonder.

He found himself listening to the way Victor said things, rather than what he said. It was all so sincere. The crowd loved him. Max felt even more isolated. Why couldn't he be part of that crowd? Why did he have to see beyond the obvious and search for hidden meanings in the subtext? Max admitted to himself that it was probably because something deep inside told him not to trust Victor Lorient. Perhaps it was because he'd come to the Ecolibrian cause late.

He recalled one lot of foster parents, from the Ecolibrian Children's Society, trying to fill his head with the ideals. It hadn't seemed so terrible when he was ten; however, the couple who had fostered Max for the last six years of his childhood, the ones who had given him some stability and a sense of self-worth, had been much more lib than Eco. He'd gone to university and taken an admin job with Alphacorp, in accounting.

Since cutting loose on his own, he'd paid lip service to Ecolibrian ideals until his promotion to the accounting office in Special Operations in York had introduced him to Leila. Living with a Telepath, he'd drifted away from Ecolibrianism and had only gone back after the split. They'd welcomed him with open arms, of course. He was their lost sheep returned to the fold.

Stupid, he told himself again. What had he let himself in for? This was crazy. Thirty-nine thousand, nine hundred and ninety-nine rabid Ecolibrians and him, all with more optimism than good sense. It was only Leila's words, "You'll be back," that had driven him on. He would not be back, ever. He'd die here; later rather than sooner, he hoped.

Victor finished the pep talk and handed over to his wife, who addressed the families before handing over again.

"Welcome to Olyanda." Jack Mario, the colony's chief administrator, and one of the few folks Max reckoned had real common sense, raised his voice so it carried out across the benches and tables. "These early days are going to be both taxing and exciting. The system we devised on Chenon is now operating smoothly. Your family groups are as previously posted. In order, beginning with . . ." He glanced down at his notes. "Group one hundred and sixty three, you can make your way to the barns to pick up your horses, then collect your wagons from the compound, hitch up and drive to Stores, where you'll be issued with equipment and rations for your journey."

One six three. Max's number was one seven eight. He had a little time yet. His family group was earnest, but boring. As a single man he'd been allocated a traveling place with the Einbackers, three brothers and their father. They had done the training course and were now hoping to make a life for themselves as sheep farmers, spinners, and weavers. He wasn't obliged to stay with them forever, just to travel as far as the settlement in their wagon, but he got the distinct feeling that Gerta Einbacker, their cousin, traveling in another wagon in the same party, was sizing him up as a prospective mate and that was no joke. She was eighteen, ten years younger than him, with a frame like a lumberjack, a broad, plain face and square, capable hands. Not his type, but she had a sweet smile.

The wagons looked just like the pictures of the old Wild West, except they were built out of different materials. They'd all had to practice driving them on Chenon. Each had a lightweight, foam-metal chassis timbered with panels cut from the weirdly-shaped broccoli trees, and the upper covers were ripstop polytarp, brought in at great expense. Everything had come in at great expense. It had cost Max almost all he had saved to buy into the expedition as an independent craftsman.

The Einbackers had expressed a preference for horses to

pull their wagon, rather than oxen, and they had vouchers for four sturdy Cleveland Bays as well as for a start-up flock of forty sheep, a milk cow in calf, and two pigs. They'd blown their last credits on a store-bought handloom that they'd have to haul overland to their new home, wherever that might be.

They all depended on the wagon-train captain and a psi-tech communicator for the journey. They didn't know where they were going, but they trusted that they would end up in a place suitable for raising sheep, crops, and children. Each of the Einbackers, including Mr. Einbacker senior, had a designated spouse, a mail order bride, who would arrive on the second ark. It seemed archaic, but the colony needed children and strong communities to survive. Max had managed to avoid being paired. He still wasn't sure if he was where he should be, so there was no sense in dragging someone else into his misery.

He'd hoped to worm his way into the admin department, but all the doors he'd tried had been closed to him, so he'd taken the basic carpentry course, fancying the satisfaction of making something honest and solid with his hands, but, now, he stared ahead to the future and admitted, bleakly, that he'd learned to use a saw and chisels, but he wasn't a craftsman at heart. The set of woodworking tools, waiting in stores for him, had already lost its appeal. He'd better find his niche pretty soon; there was no room in this kind of colony for someone who didn't pull his weight.

"We should go." Byram, the youngest Einbacker, had been sent to get him. Max stood up. He wanted to tell Byram and the whole family to go to hell, but he thought they were probably not so far from it already.

He trailed behind Byram down to the horse barns where the rest of the family had gathered in a sandy yard. Inside a barn he could hear voices. Peering round a group of onlookers, he saw a man and woman struggling to hold onto the lead rein of a big brown Shire, as they led it into the light. It was monstrous. It flared its nostrils and rolled its eyes. Its head was way up as it stared around with its ears flicking nervously this way and that.

"Here, like this," Max heard a woman's voice, and seconds

later the Angel of the Stable appeared. At least that's what
he thought she must be. She was willowy, with a halo of fair
hair, a fresh outdoor complexion, and a soft lilting voice.
Quietly she went up to the Shire and took the rein. Speaking softly to it she walked forward and it followed her, doc-
ile as a lapdog.

"There. She'll be okay now. Ease up on the rein a little.
Keep a light contact. Don't swing on her mouth. Imagine
how you'd like it. Right, who's next?"

She brought out two Clevelands for a gaunt outdoor type
who had a young boy firmly by the hand. He thanked her
and swung the boy up on one of them before leading them
away. Next she brought out two riding horses, smaller and
neater than the Clevelands, for a young couple. She adjusted the stirrup leathers and saw them mount safely.

"Take them to the schooling arena behind the stable until
you get used to them. They're a bit frisky; they've been in
cryo, too."

The horses had to use up valuable cryo space; they
weren't ready for work until they were four. You couldn't
tank a horse to maturity in a couple of seasons and train it
as well.

A young man brought out two huge Cleveland Bays for
Byram's father, but when Byram handed over the second
voucher, he looked at it carefully.

"Are these all for the same family?" Byram's father nodded.

"Have you got two wagons or one?"

"One."

"You'll hardly need four Clevelands. You could manage
with two and take a couple of strong ponies, especially if
you're herding sheep. You'll need a good dog, too. Have you
got a requisition for one?"

They hadn't.

"We used our last credits for the loom," Byram said. "We
figured it was more important. We hoped we could trade for
a puppy later."

"Don't leave it too late. Your loom won't do you much
good if you can't get your sheep in from the fields."

While Byram and his family sorted out the change of requisition, Max found the Angel of the Stable down at the schooling arena, helping the young couple with the riding horses.

"Use your legs a bit more positively," she called out to the man. "Firm but gentle. Don't let him think he can get away with anything. Horses aren't stupid; they'll take advantage if they can."

Max leaned on the rail next to her. She turned and looked at him, and her smile was radiant. It touched his soul more than anything else he'd seen since he'd staggered out of the resuscitation room yesterday.

"Marry me," he said. Then he looked over his shoulder to see whether any settlers had heard.

She laughed. "Too late," she said, "Anyway, it's illegal. I'm psi-tech. A Dee'ell."

"So you talk to animals. I'm not prejudiced. Marry me anyway."

She laughed again. "Find yourself a nice settler girl. I have a partner already."

"Your horses are prettier than the girls I've seen so far. Are you sure you won't ditch him and marry me?"

"Won't and can't. But thanks for the compliment, for my horses, I mean."

"Are you ready?" Byram shouted.

Max waved to indicate he was coming and turned back to the Angel.

"Max. Max!" Byram's voice had an edge of panic in it.

Max sighed. "Got to go," he said. "Maybe I'll see you again later."

He went up to the yard where Byram waited, obviously agitated.

"What's the matter?"

"She is." Byram nodded toward the Angel. "She's psi-tech. You shouldn't be talking to her."

Max had felt safe with the Einbackers, but suddenly he felt even more like a real outsider. In the Einbackers' book, psi-techs were deviants and therefore to be avoided. It was a fervor that bordered on religious zeal.

The Einbackers lined up with their horses. They had two Cleveland Bays with hooves as far across as dinner plates and two strong ponies, small in comparison, but still big enough for a man to ride.

"I'll manage one of these; someone else can tame the monsters," Max said and took the rein of one of the ponies, which immediately flattened its ears and tried to nip him. He shortened the loose rein, got his hand under the pony's jaw and held it at arm's length so it couldn't bite him on the way to the wagon compound. All the way there the brothers argued over the apparent disastrous lack of a sheep dog.

All the wagons were the same design, open box-shapes, with the hoops in place but not covered. The idea was to harness the horses and then lead them through the long shed and load their allocated stores before driving down to the collecting field and camping for the night. Their bunks in the utilitarian accommodation block were already occupied by a fresh batch of settlers straight from resuscitation.

Max went through the motions. The horses were in a co-operative mood; perhaps their psi-tech handler had suggested that they make every effort to help the callow newcomers. Max left the harnessing to the brothers.

He screwed his eyes closed, finding his chest heavy and breath in short supply. He had that awful feeling that once he left with the wagon train, he'd be lost. He wasn't cut out for carpentry.

He was slipping into oblivion.

Chapter Seventeen

TRUST

BEN WAS RIGHT. CARA WINCED AT HER ACH-
ing muscles. She'd been everything from site manager to
stevedore, juggling comms while she manhandled cryo units
into place with Gen in the med-center. It didn't matter how
many antigrav grippers you had, there were never enough
to go around. What would she give for a whirly bath—but
at least she'd managed to get a private shower now that
Serafin's crew had installed more plumbing.

"What did you want to tell me, earlier?" Ben asked as
they finished up their evening meal.

"Tell you?"

"You said something about asking you later. Very enigmatic."

"I said that?"

She rubbed her temples. "I don't know. Whatever it was,
it's gone out of my head now." She shrugged. As he went to
take the empty containers to the recycling, she fished the
stone out of her pocket and jammed it between her fingers
again. It was warm now, but still grit-sharp.

"What did Ronan say?"

"Ronan?"

"You were going to see him this afternoon. For goodness

sake, Cara, what's wrong with you? I'm grounding you until you've seen him, and I'll tell him so myself."

◆ ◆ ◆

Max excused himself from the Einbackers' company and walked quickly in the direction of the latrines, then dodged around the corner and away.

Director Lorient had returned to Timbertown, but Jack Mario was still in the compound. Max made his way to the settler admin office and walked in confidently, as if he owned the place. He was in luck. Jack Mario was alone in the office, no secretaries or assistants to get past.

For a moment Max was distracted by a whole wall full of books crammed on tightly packed shelves.

"Can I help you?"

"Mr. Mario."

"Yes." Jack Mario had that do-I-know-you look in his eyes.

"I've come about the job."

"What job?"

"You needed an assistant."

Jack Mario looked puzzled for a moment, then his face creased into a smile.

"Nice try, Mr. . . . . er?"

"Constant. Max Constant."

"Yes, very nice try, Max, but I've got an assistant already."

"Perhaps your assistant needs an assistant?"

"I don't think so."

"Maybe you need a librarian." His eyes strayed to the books again. "I'm happy to do anything. I can push paper, crunch numbers, or punch buttons."

"Sorry. These books are a precious resource. They're going with the colonists, and they're cataloged and indexed already."

"Pity, but I can be very useful. I've got good admin qualifications and I'm a lousy carpenter. You don't want square pegs in round holes. I'll do anything."

"Anything except take a covered wagon across Olyanda, is that it?"

"Something like that."

Mario shook his head.

Max was disappointed, but it had been worth a try. He turned to go.

"Wait. Can you pilot a flitter?"

Max perked up. "A domestic one. Yes."

"Got basic survival training?"

"Did the course like everyone else."

"How do you feel about working with psi-techs?"

"I don't have any problems with it. Worked with a lot back home."

"Got any qualifications in survey work, geology, geomorphology, or associated sciences?"

"Only a degree in economics and administration. Will that do?" Max's voice slumped and then picked up again. "But I'm a fast learner. Have you got something specific in mind?"

"We're looking for volunteers to do temporary duty with the psi-techs, in their mapping section. Interested?"

"Am I just!"

"Go and see Morwenna Phipps. Her office is in the landing vehicle. If she says you're in, you're in."

"Thanks."

"You might not thank me. They aren't looking forward to their settler volunteers. Just remember to stay out of trouble, or I'll have you working on a pig farm for the rest of your life."

"You betcha."

Max felt elated. It was the best he could hope for. He wondered how the psi-phobic thugs would take this. The order had come down from Lorient, so no one could argue. Mapping sounded infinitely more interesting than sitting on a wagon watching the rumps of two Clevelands plodding into the sunset. Then he felt guilty. Byram and his brothers had accepted him into their family.

He almost ran back down to the stables and looked for the Angel. She was in the schooling field, cantering circles on a sturdy pony who tossed his head around and looked ready to rebel until she gently, but firmly, changed his mind.

Max waved.

"You again. More marriage proposals?"

"No, but if you ever change your mind, I'll be in Mapping." Max grinned. "This morning the man who gave us the horses said something about a sheep dog. Where can I get one and how much will it cost?"

"Over the way at the small livestock sheds." She thought for a moment. "You can buy a puppy for about eighty credits."

"Eighty? Just for a puppy?"

"That's cheap. A fully trained dog will cost you nearer two hundred."

She must have seen the disappointment on his face. "Ask for Ryga. Tell him Kattia sent you for the runt he needed a good home for. Offer him sixty. Don't be fooled. The puppy's small now, but with the right care she'll grow just fine."

"You're an angel. Do you know that?" Max heard her laughter on the air as he headed toward the small livestock sheds.

Less than an hour later he found Byram with the horses.

"I'm not coming with you," he said. "Thanks for everything, but I'm joining Mapping."

Byram started to ask a question, but Max stopped him. "Here. A leaving present." He pushed a little bundle of fur into Byram's arms. "Her name's Kattia. You need to be nice to the psi-techs. They're good people."

✦ ✦ ✦

Ronan caught up with Cara the following morning after breakfast. "Ben said you wanted to see me."

"He did?"

"He also said you might act all coy. Come and take a walk with me."

She followed Ronan into the weak winter sunlight. "Let me refresh your memory. From what Ben tells me, on the night before we shipped out, you collapsed and then said you'd forgotten it happened. Day before yesterday in the shower you collapsed again, and promised Ben you'd come and see me. Yesterday you acted as if nothing had happened. So what's up?"

Despite the sun and her buddysuit, Cara felt icy chills in

her spine. She fingered the pebble in her pocket. Her head began to ache.

"I don't know what you're talking about, Ronan, honestly. Is it Ben? Is he . . . all right?"

She perched on a packing crate opposite the med-center.

"Welcome to my consulting room, Cara."

"You're serious? You want to talk to me about my health? Honestly, Ronan. There's nothing wrong with me."

"That's the second time you've said 'honestly' and it doesn't sound convincing."

Ronan put down his bag and sat beside her. "So you've collapsed twice. Anything before or since?"

What was it with Ben and Ronan? She'd know if there was anything wrong. She took the pebble out of her pocket and fiddled with it. Ronan just watched, not hurrying, not commenting. She tossed the pebble in the air and caught it. Did it again, and then once more. On the next flip Ronan's hand shot out and grabbed it. Without thinking, she cried out and clawed at his fist, suddenly desperate to get it back.

He opened his hand and let the pebble drop to the floor. She dropped to her knees and scrabbled about for it frantically, grasping it and pushing it into the gap between her index and second fingers It was just too big to be comfortable. She stared at it. It was supposed to remind her of something, but what?

Oh, fuck!

Her head spun. "I think I . . ."

She began to feel woozy. It was a little like the stage between being dead drunk and passing out. Now that she knew what she was looking for, it was horribly obvious. Shit. What had happened in the weeks that she'd been in the facility on Sentier-4? She tried to recall, but her memories were of nothing but being in her cell, cold, hungry, and lonely.

"I was . . ." The blood pounded through her ears, and she felt as though she'd been spinning round and round to make herself dizzy, and her stomach churned as if she was going to lose her breakfast.

She sucked in air through her teeth and screwed up her eyes.

"Got it again?" Ronan asked.

She sat on the crate again and let her head sag forward.

"Hold on, don't try to talk. I'm going to scan you. Is that all right?" Ronan took hold of her wrist, ignoring the read-out on her suit in favor of feeling for her pulse with his fingertips. The human contact steadied Cara's rising panic.

"Breathe," he said.

She concentrated on breathing, and the nausea began to die away.

"Have you ever had Neural Readjustment?"

"Me? No. No way—and I don't like it when you talk dirty. Why do you ask?"

The words just popped out of her mouth and she remembered both Jussaro and Ben asking the same question and getting exactly the same answer, word for word.

"You can tell me, you know, I won't pass it on."

"Quit pushing. I've never done Neural, right? Never. Ever. Do I seem like a nut?" She heard her own voice, sharp and firm. Again. The same words, but they weren't hers. She wanted to tell Ronan, but her free will had been taken away. She stared at him, unable to believe that she was a Psi-1, a certified and trained Telepath, and she couldn't communicate.

All the time, he never let go of her wrist. His eyes looked steadily into hers and he said quietly, "Breathe."

"Ben. Where's Ben?" She suddenly needed to see Ben very badly. She stared at her hand again. The stone was still there, jammed between her fingers.

"Ask me . . . that . . . again . . . later . . ." Every word was an effort to squeeze out.

"We'll get Ben." Ronan stood up. "Come on. He'll meet us at the LV."

✦ ✦ ✦

Ben arrived first and climbed the ladder to the LV's now-redundant flight deck where he had made himself an unof-ficial getaway. He hadn't been there more than a few minutes when he heard Cara and Ronan below. Ronan had sounded serious, worried even.

Cara climbed in silence, her face pale and strained. What

if she was really sick? What if it was something they couldn't
cope with on Olyanda? She might die because he'd let himself be persuaded that some terrible syndrome was indigestion and . . . what had she called it? A mammoth case of
nerves.

"You wanted to see me."

She nodded and held out her hand with the stone wedged
between her first and second fingers.

"A stone. You wanted to tell me about a stone." He remembered; she'd had it in her hand the other day.

She nodded.

"Are we playing charades?"

"I think we are." Ronan came through the hatch behind
her. "This is something to do with memory, right?"

She nodded.

"So now do we get twenty questions?" Ben asked. He felt
out of his depth.

Ronan brushed his fingers across pursed lips and then
nodded. "She can't tell us anything, but she's trying to tell us
that there's something to tell, only we have to find out what
it is. The stone is a memory trick. She's remembering something that someone wants her to forget."

Ben looked at Cara. A look of panic came over her face.
She took the stone out from between her fingers and
dropped it onto the floor.

"Hey," Ben said.

She stared at him blankly, hardly seeing.

He reached out for her, and she stood passively while he
held her arms.

"There's a war going on inside her head. Sometimes she's
on top and sometimes she's sinking," Ronan said.

"Cara?" Ben shook her gently.

"Ben? I . . . What . . ."

Ben reached down and picked up the stone and put it
between her fingers.

"You wanted to tell us about this?"

She looked at it and shrugged. "Did I? I've never seen it
before."

Damn.

Ben felt something sliding away.

"No, wait," Ronan said and turned to her. "Have you ever had Neural Readjustment."

"Me? No. No way—and I don't like it when you talk dirty."

"It's the same words." Ronan sounded as though he'd proved a point. He turned to Cara. "You can tell me, you know."

"Quit pushing. I've never done Neural, right? Never. Ever. Do I seem like a nut?"

"Yes!" Ronan was excited now. "Sorry, Cara, not yes to your question, but, yes I've just sussed it out."

He looked at Ben. "Cara has had Neural Readjustment, or at least someone started it, but I don't think they ever finished. And I think someone has tried to reinforce a botched job—probably recently—and then tried to make her forget again." He turned to Cara. "That stone was to remind you that you'd forgotten something."

"Ronan, I don't know what you're talking about," Cara said quite calmly and sat down on the edge of one of the passenger couches.

"You don't remember the bouts of sickness, fainting, dizziness?"

She shook her head.

"Or Ben telling you to come and see me about them?"

"No."

"Or coming here to talk about it to Ben?"

Ben sat next to her and touched her hand. The stone was still in place.

"Tell me who's after you."

"You really don't want to know."

"Ah, but I do, and you wanted to tell me, but someone won't let you."

Ben felt her hand tremble beneath his. She pulled it away, looked at the stone, and screwed her eyes up as if to try and prize the memory clear.

"May I?" Ronan asked.

She nodded and he came to stand in front of her.

"Hold her, Ben, she might fall."

Ben moved behind Cara and wrapped his arms about her.

And you, too. He brought Ben into the link he had with Cara.

If a mind was a series of rooms within rooms, there was a door locked. Ben saw it. It wasn't only locked, but it was bright and new, bolted and barred. Then it was as if Cara stood with them, looking at the door from the outside. She acknowledged it, but made no attempt to open it.

"Now we know what the problem is," Ronan said.

Cara slumped against Ben, and then gradually opened her eyes.

"I saw it," she said, her voice cracking. "You were right. I'm sorry."

"And you can't tell us who did this?" Ben asked.

"No. There's a part of me that doesn't even want to anymore."

"Do you remember undergoing Neural?"

She shook her head. "Me? No. No way—and I don't like it when you talk dirty. Why do you ask? Oh, shit! I . . . I . . . I'm sorry."

Ben squeezed her. "Don't be sorry. It's not your fault. We'll get to the bottom of this. Give it time." He took the stone, pushed it into her sleeve pocket, and sealed it.

✦ ✦ ✦

The following day at least Cara remembered she was supposed to be seeing Ronan. They met up by the bridge and picked up where they'd left off the day before. Both Ronan and Ben agreed there was no point in grounding her since she wasn't ill.

"I'll ignore what you say and take your answers in nods and shakes," Ronan said. "Let's walk."

She got up and followed him along the riverbank. He held out his hand and she took it.

"People will talk, Dr. Wolfe."

"As long as it doesn't get back to Jon Moon, I don't mind. I wouldn't want him to get the wrong idea."

"You're a couple? It's official?"

"We're not rushing into things." He smiled. "But we have an understanding."

"Good for you."

They kept the conversation light while they walked past the bulk of the tank farm.

"Now, I'm going to keep hold of you and start asking questions," Ronan said. "If you'd undergone voluntary NR, you'd know about it. If you'd undergone legal treatment, you'd not only know about it, but you'd have a full set of notes on your handpad." Ronan squeezed her fingers reassuringly. "Neural Readjustment is very expensive, not something you can buy on any street corner. Forgive me, but if you'd just crossed some petty crook, you'd be dead, not mindwiped. It's possible you've been involved with something that's either bigtime illegal or covert."

"That's not a fair . . ."

He didn't give her time to protest.

"Have you ever spent any time in a recovery facility, say after a tough mission?"

"My first mission." That had been before Ari. She didn't seem to have any problem with telling it. "Rydal—my lover at the time—was killed in a border dispute. I had reconstructive surgery on my left knee, and post trauma counseling, but nothing more."

And then there was Sentier-4. Her mind slid off Sentier-4. She stiffened and pulled away from Ronan altogether.

"Relax. Take a minute or two."

She nodded and turned toward the slow, silver river, watching its deceptively untroubled progress toward some distant sea. Her mind felt like that, calm on the surface but with a cruel undertow.

"Ready again?" Ronan put down his bag and took her right hand in his. "What is it you're not talking about?"

Her left hand fluttered to the stone in her sleeve pocket, fingers feeling the hard lump beneath the seal. She was sweating slightly now, despite her buddysuit and the coolness of the day.

"Do you want to tell . . ."

He hadn't even completed the question when her head began to shake from side to side, more and more violently. She couldn't stop it. He let go of her hand and held her head, palms warm on her cheeks, until she stopped fighting him.

"I know," she said. "Breathe."

"That's right, you're getting it. Look, I can't just give you a pill and make it better. I can't do anything else right here and now, but I can work with you—maybe deep monitoring sessions. We'll have to work by instinct; there's no easy answer, but we've made a start. At least, now, it's obvious that you have some kind of block in place, probably illegal because you can't remember how it got there. The dizziness and sickness you feel is caused when you try to go against whatever it was designed to do."

"I've been programmed?" She stumbled over the word.

"For what it's worth, I don't think you've undergone complete Neural Readjustment, but I think someone has tried to gag you. Tried to make you forget something."

"I've not forg..." Flashing lights danced through her skull again and she shut up. That was better.

"I see. You know the information, you just can't communicate it to anyone else. Is that it?"

"No." She said the word that jumped into her mouth and her eyes widened.

"I get the picture."

She breathed.

❖   ❖   ❖

"Any luck?" Ben asked as Ronan climbed up to his den.

His teeth started to hurt, and he realized he'd had them clenched while he'd been thinking about what had happened to Cara. Ben had been in her mind. How had he missed it? Surely Ronan was wrong. He'd seen people after Neural Readjustment and Cara didn't seem like any of them. She seemed so... What? Normal?

"Are you all right?" Ronan asked.

His turmoil must have shown in his face, or else Ronan had read him like a book. He pushed away the emotions that threatened to paralyze his reasoning.

Ronan answered his unasked question. "She didn't realize. It didn't affect her until she tried to tell you whatever it is she's been programmed to keep hidden."

"Before we left Chenon, she was trying to tell me something." Ben recalled the dead-end conversations about the identity of Cara's enemy. "So she couldn't tell me who?"

"What?"

Ronan obviously hadn't followed his thoughts; maybe that was all for the best.

"It would help if I knew some of Cara's background," Ronan said.

"You're going to break the block?"

"She has to do that herself, but I'll guide her in the right direction."

Ben nodded. "I can't help you much, but . . ." He wondered how much to say. "Look, Ronan, doctor/patient confidentiality is going to be working overtime here."

"I would never . . ."

"I know, but there are some pretty major things you aren't aware of. I can tell you some of it, but Cara's the only person who can fill in the gaps."

Where to begin. He leaned against one of the passenger couches. "I met her on Mirrimar-14. She needed a way out of there, and I was it. She came on to me one night and—I guess—made a play for my sympathy."

"It worked, then?"

"Hell, no, but that didn't stop her." He grinned. "She said someone was after her, but wouldn't say who. Couldn't, I guess."

"Now you're not telling me everything, but that's okay."

Of course. Ronan was an Empath; he knew Ben was giving him the short version. He drew in a slow, deep breath.

"All right. Whatever it is, it's between the two of you."

"Not just between the two of us. There's someone in her past." Ben swallowed hard to get rid of the lump in his throat. She'd told him she'd have to fly very high to reach absolute zero on the emotional scale. He shoved the rising tide of jealousy and resentment away as far as it would go, but it sat on the edge of his awareness, making him feel dirty. "Can you break the programming?"

"Maybe not—not immediately anyway. I'm going to try a series of deep monitoring sessions; use regression to try and take Cara back to the time it happened. She needs to remember what happened to her. When she's reached that stage, then she can begin to do something about it." He shrugged. "She has to try and edge past it."

"Can I help?"

"Maybe. Once I've shaken it loose and she's smashed it, you can try to pick out the splinters. If she wants to talk, just let her talk. Maybe, piece by piece, we can crack it between us. The alternative is to build a wall around it and forget it."

"But then we'll never know the extent of it, will we?" Ben said the words and then wanted to kick himself. He felt guilty for thinking the worst, but what if she was someone's plant on the Olyanda team? Was she a time bomb waiting to go boom? Would she wake up one morning and do whatever she'd been programmed to do?

"Can I trust her?" he asked.

"Whatever they've done to her, she's still Cara. Do you trust Cara?"

"I trust the person I think is Cara." It was the person or persons unknown who were pulling her strings that he didn't trust. He was suddenly very glad that he'd not told her about the platinum.

✦ ✦ ✦

Gabrius Crowder sat in front of the comm-unit. He couldn't use a psi-tech for this conversation. He was nervous. Since Ben had called him, he'd pulled the platinum data and had been thinking and planning. A planet full of platinum couldn't be ignored, but there would be people on the Board who would block any overt action. That was the trouble with the current Board. He had one ally, but most of them weren't willing to take risks.

He'd deliver the platinum despite them.

He'd examined the Olyanda contract from all angles. He couldn't see a legal or an affordable way of separating the settlers from their planet. Illegal it had to be, then. The end justified the means.

It galled him that he needed van Blaiden now. The feeling was unsettling to say the least, but he'd be making an offer that was too attractive to turn down—at least if you were a greedy grasping son of a one-legged whore, or maybe Ari van Blaiden.

Crowder knew the way van Blaiden thought. Hell, he'd helped shape the man, helped to insinuate him into Alphacorp's hierarchy, helped him toward his first promotion.

He knew which of van Blaiden's strings to pull to make him dance. Yet van Blaiden was a classic example of the student outperforming the master—or striving to. Crowder wasn't ready to roll over and play dead. But Ari was dangerous.

The comm-unit array glowed and a holographic head-and-shoulders image sprang up, full-size.

"Crowder." Ari van Blaiden's voice had knives in it.

"Ari, dear boy." Crowder went for the soft approach.

"Do I understand you are asking for my help?"

"Let's say I'm offering you another business opportunity. This is personal, for you, you understand, not Alphacorp."

"Talk."

"In strictest confidence?" Asking Ari to do anything that he didn't want to do was like spitting into the wind, but it was all part of the foreplay of the deal.

"Of course." Ari sounded sincere, but that was one of his talents. That's probably why he got what he wanted so much of the time, and why Crowder had abandoned any formal understanding they might once have had. If he wanted to work with Ari now, he did it on a strict one-deal-at-a-time basis.

Crowder hesitated only fractionally. "I need somewhere where I can offload thirty thousand settlers. Maybe a planet, but one far from the regular shipping lanes."

"You want to trade? A planet, even a non-bioformed one, is not something you can buy for a few credits. What have you got to offer?"

"Platinum. Interested?"

There was a pause.

"Maybe. Tell me more."

"Not on screen. We'll meet in person. For now, find me somewhere to dump the settlers out of harm's way."

"The Trust has plenty of planets. Why come to me?"

He wanted to say: because I wouldn't be ruthless enough to dump thirty thousand people on a non-bioformed planet without backup, or fire them into the Folds without a hope of ever returning, or even leave them stacked in cryo capsules on a space hulk heading for the Rim until—one by one—their life support failed and they turned into dust. Ari van Blaiden might do any of those things, but once he'd agreed to take the settlers and find them a planet, it ceased to be Crowder's problem. Crowder tried to think of the thirty thousand settlers on the second ark as one unit, not as thirty thousand individuals.

He was going to be responsible for the deaths of the first arkload of settlers; he didn't want responsibility for the rest.

"What's your time scale on this?" Ari asked.

"They're already in transit, currently between gates. An unarmed ark, ripe for boarding. The crew know nothing."

Ari whistled. "You don't want much, do you?"

"You can do it." Crowder sounded confident.

"Maybe. But I want something else from you in return."

"What?"

"Cara Carlinni."

"I told you before . . ."

"I know what you told me, but I eliminated all the other possibilities. Believe me, I've been very thorough, and her workmate Jussaro was very helpful, eventually. She has to have left Mirrimar-14 with your man, Benjamin."

Crowder suddenly saw the opportunity smiling at him, one he would not have dared to contemplate before, but now his decision to gain Olyanda for the Trust had unfettered his conscience.

"We need to meet in person," Crowder said to the hologram. "Soon!"

"Crossways. Four days from now. Noon, local time, in the Koshee Corner House. Bring only one bodyguard and I'll do the same."

Crowder nodded agreement.

Chapter Eighteen

COLLUSION

CROWDER DECIDED THE FOUR-DAY WAIT had been worthwhile. He tried to keep the exultation out of his voice as he sat in a booth in the Corner House, one of the more upmarket establishments on Crossways. This meeting had gone much better than he had dared to hope. Ari van Blaiden had been totally courteous and even pleasant. His eagerness to skim tons of platinum ore from a prime site was probably his driving motive.

"We have a deal, then?" Crowder asked.

"I'll take the settlers off your hands, no questions asked, and skim my share of the platinum before the Trust moves in officially. It will take four or five months to get ore carriers into the vicinity. How does that work with your timing?"

Crowder tried to stop himself from smiling. "I can work around that. I have it on good authority that the FPA inspectorate will be paying a surprise visit in the colony's fifth month. We can't make a move until after that." An outright fabrication, but he wanted to make sure Ari didn't get there before his trap was ready to spring. "Don't jump the gun this time."

Ari swallowed the lie. The Five Power Alliance often checked on colonies, especially the ones that were politically sensitive.

"Agreed. Now, what about Cara Carlinni? What did you find out?" Ari leaned forward across the table.

"There is a discrepancy in the records. The woman we have listed as Benjamin's wife is a fraud. Your Carlinni, I guess. I can confirm she's on the Olyanda team as a comm operative."

"A Psi-1?"

"Yes." Crowder passed a dataslide across the table, and Ari docked the crystalline chip with his handpad and threw up a holographic display of port security footage.

Ari stared for a long time. "She's changed her hair, but that's her." It was as if the temperature in the room dropped by ten degrees.

The sudden change in van Blaiden's attitude left Crowder squirming. The feeling down the back of his neck made him want to find a nice solid wall to lean against even though it was exactly what he'd been hoping for.

"It's easier to settle a score on a planet with no peace-keeping force. I'll make sure she's waiting for you." He sowed the seed and hoped it would take root. He wanted Ari van Blaiden on Olyanda at just the right time.

"I wasn't intending to go myself. . . ."

Crowder had his wits under control again. "I thought I taught you better than that, Ari. The really important things can't be left to hirelings. That's why we're both here in person, now. After the FPA inspectorate leaves, I'll pull off the psi-tech team and leave Carlinni's cryo pod behind."

"I want Benjamin as well."

Crowder hesitated long enough to let Ari interpret it as reluctance. He sighed. "Very well. You can have both Carlinni and Benjamin. The settlers themselves won't be a problem; they're not armed. Any you leave behind will be dealt with later."

"How do you propose to do that?"

Crowder stared bleakly at him and then blinked. "That's for me and my conscience. I'll give your boys plenty of time to get in and out first. Perhaps they can see to the Cara business for you if you're not going."

"She has something I want. It's personal."

"Then I hear Olyanda is very pleasant in the autumn. I'll

let you know as soon as the FPA leaves. After that you've got a slim window of opportunity."

Ari van Blaiden grunted, but it was a low, animal sound, not at all designed to ease Crowder's nervousness. Crowder glanced around. He was pretty sure van Blaiden's minder, standing a little way off, was the ill-reputed Craike.

"Do we have a deal?" Crowder asked again.

"A deal." Ari nodded to Craike, who stood apart with Crowder's man, Danniri. Craike quietly settled the bill, ready for departure.

"Remember, it must be a discreet job," Crowder said. "You can scoop enough platinum to keep you in luxury for the rest of your life, but no one must ever discover where it came from."

"Understood. I'm glad you brought this to me, Crowder. I thought that our association had been irrevocably damaged after Hera-3."

"Hera-3 was a shambles. It nearly rebounded on all of us."

"Tell me, what upset you most, the fact that Craike went in too early or the fact that he didn't make a thorough job of it and eliminate all the witnesses?"

"He cost me a whole psi-tech team."

Crowder bit off the rest of his response. If Craike had followed the plan and waited until the psi-techs had lifted off, then Ben might have had suspicions, but he'd have had no firsthand evidence and no eyewitnesses. Crowder wouldn't have had to offer expensive pensions to buy off most of the survivors, and he wouldn't have to get rid of Ben and the remains of his team now. What a waste. Crowder bitterly regretted messing up Ben's life. The man had saved him; it was a foul way to repay a debt.

Ari waved dismissively. "If we'd waited, we might have missed the opportunity and some other outfit might have done just what I did."

"I know you, Ari. I know what drives you. You've done well for yourself in Alphacorp—at my suggestion, if you recall. It's worked out well for both of us, mostly."

Ari nodded. "I didn't give you enough credit for ambition, Crowder. I do hope our interests never clash."

Crowder looked into the younger man's eyes. Ari van

Blaiden was too hungry. It made him dangerous. He bluffed it out. "Think of me as a potential ally." How easy it was to lie once you'd started.

Crowder tried to suppress the thought that people would have to die in order for him to achieve his objective. In the grand scheme of things the Olyanda settlers and the psi-techs—even Ben—were just pawns. He had the moral high ground, doing what was necessary to promote the Trust's best interests, whereas Ari was working for himself, making the rules for his own dirty little games as he went along. Greed and corruption; it was everywhere.

If Crowder played this right, the van Blaiden problem would be solved soon, destabilizing Alphacorp while the Trust gained a fortune in platinum.

Checkmate.

✦ ✦ ✦

"You want me to schedule you into the survey runs, Boss? Are you crazy? You've got too much to do and, frankly, we don't need the help." Wenna looked up from her desk.

Ben ran his hand down the doorframe of the ops room in the LV.

"Don't try that, Wenna, I know what's got to be done and how many qualified people you have to do it. You'll be doubly up against it once Lorient's volunteers are installed. I'm not quite sure why he did that, but I'm sure somewhere in his brain it's connected to the platinum."

"I'm not sure he thought it through at all. Damn fool idea if you ask me, especially when in all other respects he seems to be trying to keep settlers and psi-techs apart."

Ben shrugged. "We can cope. I'll cover the areas of likely platinum deposits. If I take Cara with me, I can stay in contact wherever I am. You get the extra help, and I get to run off some energy. Besides, I'll go crazy if I sit behind a desk waiting for Lorient's next bright idea."

"And what about me? I need to run off some energy, too. This damned arm keeps me stuck behind a desk." She lifted her arm and then dropped it to her side again in an exaggerated shrug. "Do you know what my file says?" she continued. "Of course you do. It says 'Not recommended for active duty,' and that's a tough one to live with."

"I'm sorry, Wenna."

"Well, your duty here is as hampering to you as my arm is to me. The fact is you shouldn't be out in the field. You should stay here where it's nice and safe and hand out orders to the rest of us. As your second in command, it's my duty to remind you—"

"That the platinum must be covered up at all costs."

"Don't you think I know that? Hera-3—"

"I could have followed Crowder's orders and brought you all off Hera-3 safely."

"You didn't ask us to do anything that we wouldn't have volunteered for."

"Would you have volunteered to come back without an arm?"

"I came back. That's the important thing, and I have you to thank for that. What's done's done. We saved fifteen hundred people."

"It was a mess, Wenna, from first to last. The odds against us were stacked so high we couldn't see over them. *I* couldn't see over them."

"You and Ronan are a pair. He still won't look me in the eye because he thinks he let me down. You're still beating yourself up about all the deaths that you couldn't avoid. Survivor guilt, Ben. Get over it! You did the best you could with the knowledge you had, but you didn't know. You couldn't know . . ." She dropped her voice. "You couldn't know that our own people had sold us out. Even Crowder didn't suspect until afterward. Anyhow, the difference is we know about the platinum this time, and they don't."

She rubbed her shoulder as if just thinking about Hera-3 made her missing arm ache. "Was Crowder okay about the cover-up?"

"He wasn't happy, but he gave me his word. It goes no further."

"Then I'd ask what could possibly go wrong, but that would be tempting fate, wouldn't it?"

"Yes. There are too many things to go wrong. Our own

crew is the biggest danger. I trust the old team, but I don't know the new ones well enough."

"Agreed. The fewer people who are in on it, the better it will be."

"So schedule me in for regular survey work, and I'll cover the likely platinum areas. Cut down on the risk. I don't want to step on your toes, Wenna. You're still in charge of the section."

Wenna nodded. "What about Cara?"

"She'll fly with me."

"I meant are you going to tell her about the platinum?"

"No. She's not done mineral survey work before, so she probably won't spot it unless I'm stupid enough to draw attention to it."

"What happens if something goes wrong and the news of the platinum leaks out?"

"I asked Lorient to plan for that, but he won't, and I can make as many plans as I like, but as soon as I let anyone else in on them, I'm contributing to the possibility of needing to put them into action. If I had my own way, I'd sell the platinum to the outfit with the biggest guns and get the hell away to a new planet."

✦　✦　✦

Crowder didn't know Crossways well, but he asked around and paid well for reliable information. There were a lot of shady laboratories, but the biochemist with the best, or scariest, reputation was undoubtedly Janek. Knowing was one thing, getting to him was another matter altogether, although Crowder had one contact who might prove useful. Hammer worked in an altogether smaller and more discreet environment, manufacturing chemical mood solutions. Word had it that he was also one of Janek's agents.

Crowder took both Jusquin and Danniri. No sense in being incautious, especially on Crossways.

"Tell them we're closed for business, Tolly." The thin man in the stained lab coat didn't look up from his bench as the door opened.

"He tried to tell us that, but I think he's got a speech impediment," Crowder said pleasantly. "I think it might have something to do with losing his front teeth." He jerked his head over his shoulder to where Danniri had the unfortunate Tolly pinned against the wall, blood smeared over his jaw. "He's got a bit of an unpleasant way with him, your receptionist."

"That's what I pay him for." Hammer pulled his eyes away from the job in hand. "I expect he'll want double time for today." He glanced toward the outer office. "And his dental bills paid. I hope you gentlemen are calling in a commercial capacity and not about to start any rough stuff. If you're going to get boisterous, can you give me a minute to finish this first, please?"

"No rough stuff. We're here strictly on business."

Hammer grunted. It might have been relief or maybe satisfaction at his test results. He hit a button and the arcane glow from the apparatus subsided. "Are you buying or selling?"

Crowder crossed into the middle of the room and leaned casually against Hammer's bench. Jusquin stayed by the door to watch the corridor outside.

"Buying. I need something tailored for a certain situation. Something virulent but short-lived."

"I don't mess with that shit. Too dangerous." The chemist's voice hardened. "Go and see Janek if that's what you're after."

"That was entirely my intent, but I need an introduction. Professor Janek is not at home to casual callers," Crowder said.

"Neither was I."

"Your man, Tolly, is a pussycat compared to Janek's lab security." Crowder leaned forward. "I need to keep my liver in one piece to be able to use the virus after I've got it. The word on Janek is that he's as slippery as they come and likely to sell me talcum powder pills. Word on you is that you're straight if the price is right. I want you to act as an intermediary. Make sure I'm getting what I pay for."

Hammer grunted. "All right then, four thousand—in advance. That's just my fee for an introduction. What do you want?"

"A virus that has a one hundred percent kill rate, airborne, that will run through a whole planet in a matter of

months and then burn itself out so that the place is safe for
recolonization within, say, six months to a year. I need it
deployed in a grain shipment, which I will provide."

Hammer whistled. "You don't want much, do you?"

"I'm willing to pay for it."

"It won't come cheap, and it won't come fast."

"Do your best, Hammer."

Hammer snatched the proffered credit chip and nodded
sharply.

◆ ◆ ◆

Ben's first mapping run came soon enough. He'd be away
from the main compound for the whole day, so he needed a
strong Telepath with him. The electromagnetics on this
damn planet played havoc with regular comms. He never
really considered himself off duty. He searched for a reason
to ask Cara to join him and then got angry with himself.
Dammit, he shouldn't need a reason. She was an attractive
woman and he enjoyed her company. This stupid marriage
sham was getting in the way of a genuine relationship developing at its own pace.

He found her sitting at one of the plain, functional tables
in the canteen. As he slid into the seat opposite, Cara lifted
the lid from her tray and poked at the steaming contents of
the dish.

"I'm trying to decide what this is," she said. "It's got meat
in it, but I can't identify it." She took a forkful, put it into
her mouth, and curled her nose up.

"Well?" he asked.

"We didn't have alligator on the manifest, did we?"

He shook his head. "It's probably something local they're
trying out."

"Well, I wish they wouldn't, not without a warning."

"You could always go and complain."

"You're the boss. You go and complain."

"Are you kidding? I've declared the kitchen out of my
jurisdiction. Ada Levenson is more than a match for me.
Have you seen the way she wields a cleaver?"

"Coward."

"Absolutely." He laughed. "Actually, I think she likes me.

She keeps sending over hot meals if she notices I've missed dinner."

"That's even more scary. Euwww, just look at this." Cara poked at the contents of her tray again.

Ben felt like a gauche schoolboy about to ask a girl on a first date.

"I thought I'd go and take a look around. Wenna's short-handed in Mapping while she's having to devise a training program for Lorient's volunteers. Want to come with me?"

"Of course. Where you go, I go. I'm your comm Telepath."

"You have a choice."

She smiled. "Then I'd be delighted to accept your invitation."

He was surprised by the little tingle of pleasure he felt.

"Let's make an early start in the morning."

"I'll bring food. But it won't be this stuff." She poked at the unrecognizable meat again and pushed her tray away.

✦ ✦ ✦

Cara and Ben walked in companionable silence to the hangar and signed out a two-person flitter just before the sun was fully up. Cara flipped up the bubble top, stepped onto the swept-back wing, and climbed inside. Ben pulled the flexible harness across his shoulders, clicking it down firmly. It molded to his shape and locked.

"You or me?" Ben asked.

"Me, please. I need to log air time on these flitters."

She ran the checks and kicked in the antigravs to lift the flitter a meter off the ground. She taxied the elegant little machine out of the hangar and onto the landing pad. She cut the drive back to idle, while the antigravs' whine rose in pitch, then hit the alt control and felt the craft rise straight upward to a height of about twenty meters, plenty to give them a safe buffer.

"Ready?" she asked.

"Ready."

The main drive fired, taking over from the antigravs, and the craft shot forward and skyward. They circled, and Cara looked down on Landing, still no more than a work in progress, with half-dug foundations and trenches for pipework weaving between thin-skin warehouses for tools and raw materials just waiting for the settlers' resuscitation.

In the distance she could see Timbertown growing out from where the forest of broccoli trees met the river. Lorient had asked for some stone buildings, liking the site well enough for a permanent settlement.

Once they reached Ben's designated grid, she released the controls to him and sat back. Spending the morning as Ben's passenger in a Mapping flitter was much more relaxing than heaving crates out of a cargo shuttle. She hadn't had much experience with mapping teams, but Ben flew the kind of patterns she was expecting and ran routine surveys. They overflew a dense forest of trees that looked similar to Earth's giant redwoods.

"These don't look much like broccoli trees," Cara said.

"They're seeded," Ben confirmed. "Looks like bexan, to me. We had huge groves of them on Chenon."

When the original survey was done three hundred years ago, it was standard procedure that several pods of seeds were released into the atmosphere to see what might stick.

"Irresponsible husbandry." Cara scowled. "Lucky they haven't wiped out all of the native species."

"They're not native to Chenon, either, but I've always loved them. Not sure which planet they came from originally. Lunch." He changed the subject easily. "You brought it, so we might as well eat it. Shall we see the forest from ground level?"

He pointed to a suitable spot, and Cara skimmed the broad river, which poured out into a ribbon lake, and landed the flitter on its antigravs on a pebble beach.

"Wildlife?" Cara asked.

"Nothing bigger than a squirrel in the immediate vicinity." Ben checked the scanner.

As they floated in to shore, Cara saw that the trees were taller and greater in girth than even the biggest of the Californian redwoods were reputed to have been, but they were broad-leaf evergreens, closer in appearance to some of the Australian eucalypts than to Earth's northern hemisphere trees.

Oh, that's beautiful. She wasn't sure if she'd said that out loud, but she felt Ben agreeing silently.

The flitter grounded in a handspan of water on a firm sandbank and Ben lifted the bubble dome.

On the shore, the trees swelled above them like pillars in an ancient cathedral. Cara, unwilling to break the perfect silence, watched the play of sunlight through the broad, green leaves turn the surface of the water into a starry pool.

It's like one of those old English cathedrals. You know — all stately stone pillars and vaulted roofs. Even her thought was hushed.

"Make the most of it. We can spare an hour, but not much longer."

Cara dumped the cool carrier on the shingle shore and opened it up.

"You got chicken." Ben helped himself. "How did you manage that?"

"I asked the night staff, and said it was for you."

The chicken was good. Cara licked her fingers.

"Better than camp rations," Ben said.

"It certainly is."

Feeling better with chicken inside her, Cara sat back, leaning on her elbows, and breathed deeply.

"You know," Ben said, "there's been so much going on since we got here that I haven't had time to stop and smell the roses. This is great."

A small voice whispered in Cara's brain *it's only temporary.* If only she could break this neural block.

As if to echo her dark thoughts, a heavy cloud sailed in front of the sun and the light took on a strange greenish hue. A sudden chill gust, noticeably colder than the brisk spring air, slammed into them and was gone again. It almost took her breath away. Cara rocked forward and sprang to her feet. The trees blocked out a view of the sky, but over the lake the clouds gathered fast and the water looked like a darkening purple bruise.

Lightning cracked and the flash dappled the forest floor through the leaves. The air was still, but it was heavy with ozone and the promise of thunder.

"This storm is blowing in fast," Ben said. "Check with

base and find out what's happening." He ran toward the lake. "Let's get under cover. Go farther into the forest while I anchor the flitter."

Cara looked around, and the wind slammed into her, nearly lifting her off her feet before it died away again. She needed to find a safe place. The giants had probably withstood storms like this one for a few hundred years, but there was nothing to say that they wouldn't have branches torn off by the wind. The ones on the lake side were more vulnerable than the ones farther into the forest.

As if to remind her that even the giant bexans had a finite lifespan, she found a fallen tree, far enough away from the edge of the lake to act as a shelter. Beneath its trunk, down at the root end, there was a space just big enough to shelter them. She wriggled into it, twisting around so that she could see Ben while she contacted Wenna. The wind gusted again, and this time it didn't die back.

Ben reached the flitter, threw up the bubble hatch, and leaned over inside the cab. Then he stood up, clinging onto the grab-handle for stability, and locked the hatch down tight with his free hand. He let the wind blow him back up the beach, his body leaning back into it, fighting to stay upright.

"Move over." He threw himself down beside Cara and busied himself with his handpad, activating a sequence. Then he held his fist toward the shuttle. The bubble-top machine floated backward out into the lake, working on the remote. When it was far enough out, it sank until it was completely out of sight.

"There," he said. "That should keep it reasonably safe and make sure we get out of here afterward."

"If there is an afterward." Cara clapped her hands to her ears as a monumental roll of thunder boomed over them.

"What's happening in Landing?"

"Nothing. They've got no sign of a storm, but they're battening down the hatches and following this on long-range sensors. Some of our groups away from base are caught in it."

For fully ten minutes the world went mad. Even the giant trees couldn't stand against the wind and their trunks bent and swayed more than Cara would have thought possible.

There was no other choice but to keep down while the

storm raged around them. Cara and Ben huddled beneath the fallen tree, faces down in the earthy leaf compost that covered the forest floor. There was a movement in the dead tree roots and a small rodent-like creature made a run for their hiding place. Seemingly without fear, it skittered past their noses and down to the far end of the trunk, where the space beneath wasn't deep enough to accommodate a human.

I hope that nothing else calls this tree home. Cara aimed that thought tightly at Ben. "We don't need a leaper trying to share our space."

Their shelter shuddered as something, a branch from another tree perhaps, hit it. Cara flinched, and Ben put his arm across her back. She tucked her head into his shoulder, relieved she wasn't alone.

Then it was over.

The wind dropped as quickly as it had started, leaving the rain lingering for a few minutes before that, too, ceased and a mellow breeze raised the temperature back to normal.

They emerged from their hiding place, brushing dead leaves from their buddysuits. Ben called their flitter up, using the remote on his handpad. It rose out of the water, stately as a galleon, totally unharmed.

All teams, report. Cara connected Ben to the whole network of Telepaths. Messages flew at them faster than verbal ones possibly could. Thankfully, there were few casualties, though there was some damage to half-built houses in a settlement the residents had called Amory.

Cara felt Ben disengage from her mind. "We got away quite lightly," he said. "This time. But if one of these hits the settlers while they're out in the open, there will be some squealing. Hopefully, the worst of them will be over for this year before they travel. The meteorology team seems to think that this is the season."

✦ ✦ ✦

Are these people complete idiots? Ben fumed as he flew the four-man flitter to Amory township, one of the four most affected by the recent storm. Fliss Ruffalo, the psi-tech liaison at Amory, had called for help on behalf of the settlers. That was just peachy!

He really needed to be doing survey work, not babysitting settlers who couldn't look after their own supplies.

"This doesn't look good." Suzi Ruka sat in the seat beside him. Archie Tatum and Lewis Bronsen, a Finder, were in the back.

Set in a clearing just below a rocky gorge and on the edge of a broad forest of broccoli trees, the township of Amory was a mess. Houses had been smashed to matchwood, and the shallow creek that gushed out of the gorge had risen and swept away a wagonload of seed grain. On top of learning that Lorient's cooks had milled eight sacks of seed grain for flour, the loss prodded Ben into a grim mood.

The water still ran high between broken and muddied banks. Silt and deposited rocks half-covered what had been a road in the making. From the air, he saw tiny figures below picking through the rubble.

Ben landed the four-man flitter in a clearing below the town.

Suzi popped the door and stood on the sill, using the flitter as a vantage point. She narrowed her eyes and scanned the half-plowed ground. "Not good at all." She turned to the two young men occupying the backseats. "What do you think?"

Archie Tatum patted the bag of sensor bots in his lap. "I brought the boys to do structural assessments on the ruins, but even from here I can see what the report will say. It's all been blown to shit."

Bronsen ran a hand through his hair to smooth it. "Is that Fliss Ruffalo in a skirt?"

Ben looked more closely at the four settlers walking over the uneven ground to meet them and realized that the party consisted of three settlers and Fliss Ruffalo dressed in settler brown, not her usual buddysuit.

"Commander Benjamin." Fliss greeted them all as they climbed down from the flitter, but Ben noticed her eyes lingered on Bronsen a little longer than was necessary and Bronsen seemed almost shy. Ben got the impression he might have blushed, but on dark brown skin it didn't show. Fliss, however, a pale-skinned redhead with freckles, turned pink and Ben was pretty sure it was unconnected with the three settler men she was introducing.

"This is Wade Morgan, his brother Jonti, and their cousin Goff Parker. Goff is this region's blacksmith mentor and Wade and Jonti are carpenters, intending to set up a sawmill."

"Thank you for coming so quickly," Goff said as they took turns to shake hands. "We're grateful for your help."

Ben nodded. "Looks like you've taken a beating."

"It hit us at the wrong time."

"There's never a right time."

"I guess not. We'd got eleven timber frames up for houses, but not finished and—well, as you can see—they're finished now. With luck we'll be able to retrieve enough wood to make a very small garden shed. I guess we're starting over."

Archie Tatum gestured at the wreckage. "No casualties. You've got a storm cellar?"

"Caves. Back in the trees," Wade said. "We dropped everything and made a run for it. Fliss got all our animals in there, bless her. Otherwise we'd have nothing left."

"I didn't do it on my own," Fliss said.

"But we lost the seed grain." Jonti spread his hands wide. "Stupid of us to leave it exposed, but it all happened so fast. There must have been a natural dam burst farther up the valley. A wall of water hit the town like a hammer. We found an axle three klicks down the valley, but no sign of the grain. I guess the bags split."

"Well, look at it this way," Suzi said. "Some time in the autumn you'll find familiar looking wheat and barley growing wild downriver from here. It'll be time-consuming, but you can get out there and harvest the seed. Send your kids out to do it. Turn it into a game with a prize."

"Good idea, but in the meantime . . . We don't expect something for nothing . . ."

"There's a little spare seed grain for emergencies," Suzi said.

"Thank you," Jonti said. "We'll store it in the cave until we're ready for planting."

"Don't thank us," Ben said. "It's your grain."

They took a walk through what was left of the town. Fliss dropped back to walk with Ben while the Morgan brothers strode ahead with Suzi. Archie set his bots loose, checking over the ground, and Bronsen mounted the offered pony and rode down the valley with Goff in search of the remains of the lost wagon. Where resources were scarce, wheels and axles were more valuable than gold.

"They're good people," Fliss said. "I hate to see everything blown away like this. They don't ask for much, just get on with things as best they can."

"You've had no problems working with them?" Ben asked.

"None."

"Abandoned your buddysuit for a reason?"

"I lent it to Jonti's wife. She's been having a lot of back pain. It looks like chronic sciatica, nothing dangerous, but it's painful. The suit's been giving her analgesics until the district medic gets back from Royertown."

"Good move."

"She's very grateful. Said if she'd known, she'd have ordered a suit a long time ago. I didn't tell her how much they cost."

Ben laughed. "You like these people."

"I do. They're not what I expected."

Bronsen and Goff arrived back triumphantly with the lost axle and two wheels slung between their two ponies, arriving just in time for a hot meal of roast mutton, one of the casualties of the storm cooked long and slow over a communal open fire.

At least the timber came in useful for something, Ben thought.

The children got the choice bits, served up with a mash made of reconstituted paruna powder, which luckily had not been washed away with the seed grain.

Ben smiled to see the children so well looked after. Fliss was right. The more he saw of these people the more he liked them. They were the polar opposites of Lorient's hard-liners, yet they still lived within the Ecolibrian framework. These were the people who would make the settlement work. Not the administrators.

Chapter Nineteen

STORM

"SO THIS IS YOUR REAL CONSULTATION ROOM, Dr. Wolfe?" Cara found Ronan tucked away in what amounted to little more than a cupboard on the LV, close to the now redundant med bay.

"Cara." He looked up and smiled. "Just packing up the last of my stuff for my only-very-slightly-larger office in the new med-center. I thought that we'd go somewhere a bit more relaxing than a consulting room, though, if that's all right."

"Whatever." Cara was feeling nervous as it was, and to find out that they were going to have to make a journey before they could even start the monitoring session was just one more way of delaying the inevitable.

They walked across the compound in companionable silence, to a waiting flitter. Ronan took the helm confidently.

"Where are we going?" Cara asked.

"I told Ben I wanted to take you out of the camp. He suggested the lake you went to yesterday. Said you liked it."

"I hope there are no storms forecast."

"Not according to the long-range scanners. Trust me, I'm a doctor."

"I'd trust you more if you were a meteorologist." She grinned. "You'll like this place. It reminds me of being inside a cathedral, like the ones in Europe."

"I've never been to Earth," Ronan said.

"You're from Magna colony, right?"

"Yeah, a highly volcanic lump of rock in the Ortes System, which just happens to be well positioned to serve an eight-way jump gate hub. Specializes in shipbuilding. Freighters mostly. I hear Earth is beautiful."

"Parts of it are. The Saharan rain forest preserve is a man-made miracle, but some parts are still struggling. Australia's an overcrowded mess, the central cities still a dumping ground for all the displaced Chinese from the coastal regions. They've done some great preservation work on the historic European cities, though. I lived close to Old York for a time." With Ari, but she couldn't say that. "They've domed the medieval city to protect it. The Minster is magnificent. That's what this place reminds me of. If you close your eyes, you can feel it."

"Feel what?"

"Awe. Wonder. A sense of something immensely old and magnificent. It makes you want to whisper into the vastness of it to see if anything whispers back." She laughed. "Don't mind me. I get carried away. History from texts is dry and dusty, but it's never far from the surface if you open yourself up to it. Even here. Especially here."

They landed in the shallows of the lake.

She clicked back the harness and levered herself up out of the seat. "Oh, look. I didn't see those yesterday."

Down in the shallows, tiny silver-pink fishes, long and threadlike, darted from light to shade. Every so often they came up for air.

"Not fishes," Ronan said. "Amphibians, harmless according to Lee Gardham's wildlife reports."

"Pretty."

"Edible, too." He grinned and wrinkled his nose up. "But I wouldn't try them unless the alternative is starvation."

"Look there!" She turned to follow the blue-green flash of wings. Her excited words fell to the gentle earth, and silence flooded in to cover their tracks. "Humans are going to change this world, probably not for the better, but I'm glad I saw it like this."

They splashed to the lakeshore.

"Cara Benjamin, you're a romantic."

"Don't tell anyone, or it will blow my credibility."

Ronan laughed. "Welcome to my consulting room. Take a seat."

She chose to sit on the sand and Ronan sat facing her, his right leg touching hers. Body contact seemed to steady psi-techs.

"Nervous?" Ronan asked.

"Why? Can you feel me shaking?"

"No, it's just that I'd be scared if our roles were reversed." She nodded.

"Well, we'll just do some relaxation first, deep breathing. Clear out the jumble of today so we can start on yesterday ..."

His voice was low and gentle and not for the first time she wondered whether life would be very complicated indeed if he wasn't comfortably and certifiably gay.

Implants meshed and Ronan slipstreamed into her thoughts.

They went over what had happened since Cara arrived on Mirrimar-14, and Cara had no problems relating everything— even that first night with Ben. Ronan was easy to trust.

"What about before Mirrimar-14?"

Before Mirrimar-14.

She took it one step at a time.

Following rumors of psi-techs gone independent. A series of short hops on freighters and longer hops between worlds. Always dodging the authorities. Trying not to draw attention to herself while asking questions that no legitimate psi-tech would ask. Worrying as her available credits dwindled.

"Why?"

Escaped. She'd escaped from ...

She's in a holding cell. How long has she been there, doped up on Reisercaine and totally alone? Her bed is a hard board with no blanket or sheets and the lavatory is in full view of the observation hatch in the door. They've taken everything from her, even her buddysuit, so she's shivering in a thin shift, more like a hospital gown than prison garb. It's trilene, so she can't tear it; can't make a rope from it and hang herself—as if she would. They haven't even given her undergarments or shoes, and they feed her with finger foods; no cutlery.

She's had time to reflect on how she came to be here. That's what they want her to do; it's the first part of the softening-up process, before they begin Neural Readjustment.

She thinks about Ari. She's been thinking about him a lot lately.

Maybe it's her fault. She's made a big mistake, a bad choice. Two bad choices—though the second was the only one her conscience would let her make. Hooking up with Ari had been stupid, though it hadn't felt like that at the time. She'd driven a rocket sled through Alphacorp's first two unwritten rules. One: thou shalt not fuck thy boss. Two: thou shalt not fuck with thy boss' orders.

They've got her on a trumped-up mutiny charge after Felcon. She'd logged an official complaint, but Craike erased it. Now her protest is being treated as mutiny. It's grossly unfair. She's always done her best for Ari and for Alphacorp, and this is her reward.

Why are they going to all this trouble? It would be simpler to kill her. Plenty of ways to cover it up. Is it possible Ari has real feelings for her? Her face twists into a grimace. Strange way of showing it.

She hears the quiet shush of the airtight door mechanism along the corridor.

Footsteps and voices.

Ari. It's Ari.

Hope replaces everything else.

But then she recognizes the other voice. Donida McLellan. Psi-1 and then some. Sadist; bitch. She is to the psi-tech world what Ari's henchman, Craike, is to the physical one. There has to be something wrong with Ari to have two such perfect bastards doing his dirty work.

McLellan is speaking as they get near enough for Cara to make out the words. "Let me have another session with her, and I'll feel a lot happier about releasing her to you."

"Later." Ari's voice is, as always, warm and cultured with both an edge of friendliness and a tone of authority that makes it hard to go against him. "Have her brought up to my quarters. I think we can sort out this little aberration."

Little aberration. Does he think that her disobeying

Craike's orders to shoot down unarmed farmers is an aberration? She needs to tell her side of things. Now Ari's here, she'll get her chance . . .

"It's okay, take it easy."

She was on her hands and knees, retching into the sand.

Ronan knelt beside her and held her shoulders until she'd finished and her breathing had returned to normal.

She sat down again. "How'd I do, Doc? Did you pick up anything worth having?"

"Some, not a lot. Did you?"

"I . . . I know." She started to feel sick and dizzy again. She did know. Donida McLellan had said to Ari: *Let me have another session with her.* All that time in the holding cell had not been spent entirely on her own. What she remembered were false memories. All she needed to do was find the real ones.

"Next time," Ronan said. "Here, give me the start-card. I'll fly us home."

◆ ◆ ◆

Outside the LV, early the following morning, the whine of antigravs and the whirr of machinery, combined with distant thumps and bangs, announced that Serafin's builders were finally erecting an accommodation block. Cara tried to ignore it, but involuntarily winced when percussive bangs shook the ops room. Wenna looked up from her station and mouthed a cuss word.

"Anybody home?" Serafin West dusted off his hands on the seat of his buddysuit as he walked through the door. "You've got accommodation now."

"Does that mean I get a real bedroom?" Wenna asked.

"I've put you in the first broom cupboard on the left," Serafin said.

"Where have you put Ronan?" Wenna asked.

"Riser Five."

"Move him up. Put him in the room next to me. That boy's got to look me in the eye sometime."

"Wenna—" Ben started.

"What?"

Ben shrugged. "Nothing."

"You've got a damn good doctor half frozen because of something he thinks he's done wrong."

Ben nodded. "Go easy on him."

"I don't blame him for this, Ben." She gestured with the prosthetic arm and wiggled her fingers. "If I'd have been him, I'd have made the same decision. I was done for, but you were too stubborn to realize it. You could have gotten yourself killed trying to do what you did." She turned to Cara. "Thinks he has to save everyone."

Cara smiled. "I know. Sometimes it works out for the best."

"And one day it'll get him killed."

Cara felt a chill run down her spine. *Not on my account, I hope.*

"If you've finished talking about me as if I'm not here and not your boss . . ." Ben turned to Serafin. "You said something about having a room."

"Uh, yes." Serafin's attention had been taken by the exchange. "I've put you and Cara in the room at the far end. I've tried to give you a bit more space than usual. Tell me if it's a problem."

"I'm sure it will be fine," Ben said.

"And Wenna's right, by the way," Serafin said.

Ben looked up to the ceiling and gave an exaggerated long-suffering sigh. "Remind me again why I like working with you people?"

"Because we love you, really," Wenna said, and reached up to cup his cheek in her good hand.

Cara couldn't ever imagine anything like the relationship these people had in any Alphacorp team she'd ever worked with, but it felt good.

"Cara, here's your lock code." Serafin held out his hand and they fist-bumped to transfer the lock code to her handpad and then to Ben's. That's when the reality of the new room crept up and slapped her upside the head. Serafin had put them both in the same room. Of course he had. What else could he do without giving the game away?

✦ ✦ ✦

Would sharing a room with Cara—a private room—be a problem? Ben watched Cara head for the new riser to check it out. This was the disadvantage of keeping up the marriage sham. Well, he could cope if Cara could. It wasn't so much lack of privacy that was the problem. After all, they'd been sharing a dormitory with forty other people since they got here, but he found her presence in the cool of the night distracting. More than distracting if he was honest, but he'd promised her no strings and he was damn sure he wasn't going to crack.

He'd have liked to talk to Nan about it all, but the only way he could do that was through someone else's head, and if he did contact Nan, she was quickly going to figure that something was wrong. He felt guilty about not staying in touch, but it was better not to worry her.

When he took his pack into their new quarters, he found Cara sitting on the edge of one of the beds. She'd separated them and pushed them to opposite sides of the room, but she hadn't unpacked her kit.

"Ask Serafin to change the room for a single if you like. I'll bunk in with Gen," Cara offered.

"That'll look like my own wife can't stand my company."

When she looked at him sharply, he laughed at her. "A joke, okay?"

"I'm serious," she said. "You've got a heavy job. There'll be times when you need some breathing space."

"If I do, I'll kick you out. We can tell them it's a lovers' tiff."

"It's a long time since I've had one of those."

"A lover or a tiff?" He knew he shouldn't have said that as soon as the words were out.

"Both."

Ben caught Cara's sudden change of mood. Her former lovers were none of his business really, but dammit, sham or not, he felt unreasonably possessive, despite all logic telling him that even if she made a commitment to him—a big ask with everything that was going on with her right now—he could no more possess her than he could possess the air he breathed. *And yet she means as much to me as the air I breathe and the ground I walk on, even though I know*

*no more about her now than I did that first night on
Mirrimar-14.*

But he did know more. She was strong, resolute, kind,
compassionate, but she didn't put up with bullshit. She was
talented and beautiful, but she wasn't vain. She'd gone
through some kind of mental hell, but she was fighting back
and keeping her life together.

He shrugged and turned away, trying to remind himself
that she would have told him if she could.

Get a grip, Benjamin. Showing his feelings wouldn't help.
His noble intentions struggled against testosterone levels
that were off the scale. Maybe he could have damped down
his emotions better if they'd been separate, but the sham
marriage was a fragile link he didn't want to break.

"Unpack your gear. We'll probably be so busy we won't
coincide much." He dumped his bag on one bed, walked
out, and left her to it.

◆ ◆ ◆

"There's another blow coming." Cas Ritson broadcast a
warning. It caught Cara in the fresher. She dragged a robe
over her wet skin and padded out into the quarters she
shared with Ben. As usual, he wasn't there. She pulled her
buddysuit on, then ran down the corridor and across the
compound to the LV.

While her body was going through the motions of hurrying from A to B, her mind was already busy. The Telepaths
who were stationed at Landing immediately melded in gestalt. She locked in tight, and together they blasted out a
sharp warning to all the Telepaths with the survey teams,
wagon trains, and new settlements.

So far the settlers in the areas that seemed to be a target
for the sudden spring storms had established three new
communities, equipped with safe cellars. They'd had three
more violent storms, but none to equal the sudden squall
that Cara and Ben had experienced at Cathedral Lake. Unfortunately, the weather could change without much warning. This time four separate wagon trains were making their
way overland, exposed to the weather. Damn Lorient's do-

it-the-hard-way strategy. They could have ferried the settlers out in airbuses with no trouble at all.

Emergency! Storm alert! Cara relayed the information
to the Telepaths with the four endangered wagon trains.
*It's blowing in from the west. Seaboard Weather Station
gives no more than ten minutes warning. Secure your stock
and anchor anything you can tie down.*

Then the gestalt split to take on individual contact. Cara
kept a channel open for Ben, but also anchored herself to
Bick Rhinager, a Navigator scout traveling with a fifty-
vehicle wagon train across the southern plain.

Working on two levels took up all her concentration. She
stumbled her way to a chair in the ops room and flopped
down in it, vaguely aware of Wenna securing all the hatches
except the main entrance, waiting until the last possible moment before battening that down in case anyone was caught
out in the open and needed shelter. In the distance, the hangar doors rumbled to a close with the mechanics safely inside. They weren't in the main storm corridor, but they
would still experience a good buffeting from the strong
winds.

Hold the doors. She diverted attention from Rhinager
to the hangar door operator. *Ben's flying in; he's about two
minutes away.*

The doors rumbled open again, and she turned her attention back to the wagon train.

*We're totally in the open. I thought we were past the worst
of the spring storm season.* She felt Rhinager's fear pounding in her own chest. He was scared with good reason.
*We're unharnessing the animals and bringing them into a
circle.*

How many Dee'ells have you got?

*Five. They're already at work, trying to settle the beasts.
There's not even a hollow, so the wagons are all the protection we've got.*

"Have you got contact with Rhinager's train? Link me."
Ben came up beside her. Cara hadn't even heard his flitter
come in, but she was glad to see he was down safe. She
glanced up. Outside, she could see the tops of the broccoli

trees by the river beginning to sway with the first eddies of wind.

She opened up and brought Ben into the link with Rhinager.

Can you strip the polytarps from the wagons? Ben asked.

We're working on it.

Cara stayed with Rhinager as his transmission patterns became erratic and coherent thoughts turned to raw emotion. She pushed away as much of the secondhand fear as she could, but it was hard to remain separate.

She's huddled beneath a wagon, facedown on the moist earth, with her arms folded about her head. The wind is howling, snatching at her ears and blowing her hair flat against her head. She can hear the shouts and screams of terrified settlers all around her rising in symphony with the wind and knows that the worst is yet to come. Then there's darkness, turmoil, and terror. Her world turns upside down and the safe covering over her head disappears in an instant, whirling debris around her. Something strikes the side of her head, and she plummets into blackness.

When she came to, she found herself on the smooth floor. Ben was down there with her, holding her as though she was in danger of blowing away herself.

"The storm has eased." Ben loosened his grip. "Are you all right now?"

She nodded, not quite sure.

"Rhinager must have taken a blow that knocked him out. You went, too. Can you patch back to him? Is he still there?"

"I'll find out."

She shook the storm out of her mind and searched for Rhinager. She found him, fuzzy, but conscious.

Are you with me, Bick?

Yeah, but I've got a lump the size of a turkey egg on the side of my head. The wind just took the wagon. We got the canvas down, but it took it anyway. Shit. This place looks like a battle zone. Oh, hell ... There was a pause while Cara felt him staring round in disbelief. *We've got dead here for sure, and casualties, lots of 'em.*

Seaboard Weather Station has broadcast the all-clear, Cas cut in.

Rhinager, medical emergency teams are mobilizing now. What's your party's status? Ben asked through Cara's link. Cara sat back and let him take over.

A lot of casualties, human and animal. There's hardly a wagon left in one piece.

Cara opened up the link to give Ben access to anyone he needed.

Anna, how many emergency teams can you field? Ben asked.

Ten; medics and paramedics are at the transport pad now. Ronan's leading. I'm sending six nurses out, too.

I'm on it. Yan Gwenn cut in. *My pilots are warming up.*

How many more emergency teams required for the rest of you? Ben used Cara's link to broadcast to the whole colony.

Most of the wagon trains had been outside the storm path altogether and the settlements, including Landing and Broccoliburg, had fared reasonably well.

We've got one family trapped under rubble in Treagar Township. The message came in from one of the resident Telepaths.

"Serafin, can you handle that?" Ben looked across to the engineer, who nodded. "Take one of Anna's medics with you."

There was nothing else that the local medics couldn't deal with.

Given the advance warning, all the survey teams had been able to find shelter. Rhinager's party was, by far, the worst affected.

They divided the medical resources appropriately and launched four medevac flitters.

"Let's get on it." Ben sent out all the available crews, and Cara caught Serafin's order to get his Psi-Mechs airborne in case they were needed to shift debris.

"We'll need vets and Dee'ells, too," Ben said and Cara relayed that to Lee Gardham.

She ran across to the flitter bay three paces behind Ben

and slid into the backseat of a four-man machine. Ben hit the seat next to her and Gupta took the helm with Bronsen in the copilot's seat.

Three crews stay here on standby, Ben ordered. *The rest with us. Wenna, stay home and coordinate reports. Keep me up to speed with what's happening.*

You got it, Boss.

It took twenty-five minutes to reach the wagon train.

"Shit, look at that." Gupta voiced what they all felt at the sight of the devastation below.

The wind had scattered the wreckage of fifty wagons and three hundred lives all across the plain. Some survivors were obviously trying to help the injured, while others, dazed or hurt themselves, sat on the ground in small groups. A herd of horses and cattle milled and churned the ground.

The medevac flitters were not far behind, the drone of drives and the whine of antigravs filling the air.

Ronan and his team caught up with them on the edge of the debris field.

"Triage." Ben turned to Ronan. "Are you all right with this?"

Ronan nodded, his face a couple of shades paler than normal and his mouth drawn in a tight line.

"If you want backup . . ."

"I'll manage."

Cara wondered whether it was easier if you didn't know the people whose bodies were damaged, some beyond repair. Was it more impartial, impersonal? She suspected for an Empath like Ronan, it was always personal.

"Set up a triage point away from the wreckage." Ronan turned to Aster, his med-tech. "Usual drill."

"Can I help?" Cara knew the routine by heart. Locate and move the injured who can safely be moved, flag the ones who can't, and ask a medic to assess and stabilize. Deal with the ones who are savable; don't waste resources on the ones who aren't, until all the others have been attended to. She looked at the scene before her. There were going to be some lousy choices to be made.

"Ben needs you," Ronan said.

Cara turned to follow Ben across the wreckage field and

then turned back. "If it helps, Wenna said you made the right decision—last time."

"Thanks. It doesn't help. The right decisions are often the hardest ones to make."

She gave him a tight nod and turned away.

Chapter Twenty

TRIAGE

THE VETERINARY TEAM, LED BY LEE GARDham, was emerging from a flitter. The casualties, human and animal, would have the best treatment they could provide. Cara hoped it was good enough.

Rhinager limped toward her. He held a stark white pad to a wound on his forehead.

"I'm glad to see you're still on your feet," she said.

"There are plenty of poor bastards who aren't."

"Where's your captain?"

"I've not seen him. Injured, I think; maybe even dead. I don't know." He shrugged as if to say he couldn't do much about the fate of one man. "We could use some help with the beasts."

Cara flashed a message to one of the crews that hadn't been assigned yet and followed Rhinager to where animals were milling about, held in one area by five Dee'ells. They couldn't completely pacify such a large number of animal minds, but they could plant a boundary and keep the beasts that had not fled during the storm all together in one place.

Lee had recruited half a dozen able-bodied settlers to separate out the injured animals. She was already starting work and there was a sharp crack as another of the badly injured creatures was slaughtered. The stench of death was thick in the air.

Horses and ponies milled in a tight circle and set off the oxen. A Shire snorted and backed into a Cleveland Bay; the beast turned and snapped, causing a chain reaction. One of the Dee'ells turned to calm the ruckus and, using all her concentration, was slower on her feet than she should have been. A riding horse reared, staggered backward, and went down in a flurry of hooves, taking the young Dee'ell with it.

A scream knifed though Cara's brain, and pain seared her chest, spine, and legs. She staggered and reached out to block the signals. The pain abated, resonating as aftershocks. As the dust cleared, the horse rolled and lurched to its feet and skittered off into the herd again, leaving a still body on the ground. Cara ran, arriving by the stricken girl as the four remaining Dee'ells gathered to push the animals to safe ground.

Lewis Bronsen ran over from the opposite direction. "Fliss, are you all right? I felt . . . Oh . . ." He dropped to his knees beside the girl.

At first Cara thought the young woman was dead, but her eyelids flickered and she groaned faintly.

"It's all right," Cara said gently. "Fliss, is it?" She looked at Bronsen for confirmation of the name.

He nodded. "Fliss Ruffalo." He took the girl's hand.

"Lewis?"

"I'm here. Where does it hurt?"

"Nowhere."

That was a bad sign, Cara thought. One leg was twisted beneath her and her voice was weak, but the worst of it was the flashing red light on her suit cuff. Internal bleeding, probably crush injuries.

"The doc is on his way." Cara tried to sound reassuring. "We'll take you to Landing and patch you up."

"I don't think so. I can't feel anything below my neck, and I don't think I can move."

"Damn it to hell, I couldn't get here fast enough," Bronsen whispered.

"It's not your fault. No one can be everywhere at once."

"But it's Fliss . . ." he said.

Cara caught his emotion. "You two . . ."

"Lewis?" Fliss sounded panicky.

"Still here."

Ronan arrived with a paramedic and an antigrav gurney.

He checked the Dee'ell over and looked at Cara and Bronsen, shaking his head slightly.

Bronsen never moved from the girl's side, but tears streamed down his cheeks.

We need an emergency cryo unit over here. Ronan shot a message back to the medevac team.

We've already used the two we have. Cara caught the answer from one of the pilots. *There's another team on their way. ETA twenty minutes.*

From the look on Ronan's face it didn't look as though the Dee'ell had twenty minutes. "Listen, sweetheart, I've got a cryo unit coming. Just hold on. I'm going to give you the preliminary shots so you'll soon feel warm and sleepy. Don't worry."

"You're a bad liar, Doctor. I'm a Dee'ell, not a deadhead."

"It'll be touch and go, but if you're determined, you'll make it. I'm not going to move you until we can get you a cryo unit." He looked at Bronsen. "You're staying with her?"

Bronsen nodded.

Cara felt Ronan connect with Fliss and reinforce the feeling of optimism. His eyes glazed over. Cara realized what he was doing and linked with him as he lost himself in Fliss, trying to stabilize the internal bleeding.

That's better, Doctor. I like it much better when you're on my side.

She hadn't the strength to speak, but she could still use her telepathy.

Ronan. Enough, Cara said as she felt him begin to weaken. She tapped him firmly on the shoulder and said it again out loud. "You've done all you can."

With a judder Ronan came back into himself. "Thanks."

"You're welcome." It was too easy for a Healer to pour so much energy into a patient that he dangerously weakened himself.

Ronan administered two separate shots. "Go to sleep, now, Fliss." He waited until she was asleep. "Someone stay with her until it's over."

"I'll stay," Cara offered. She felt so helpless in the face of one more death. It was as if all the deaths were crystallized in this one.

"No, I will," Bronsen said. "I'm not leaving her."

Cara looked at Ronan, helpless. Bronsen was too emotionally invested to stay without support.

"I'll stay, too." A settler woman Cara hadn't even noticed spoke up from behind her. "Poor girl was trying to help us. It's the least I can do. You people are needed elsewhere. Go. Save lives. It's what you do." She sat cross-legged across from Bronsen. As Cara rose to leave, she tapped her on the leg and nodded toward Bronsen. "Husband?" she asked quietly.

"Might have been, eventually," Cara said.

Cara walked away with Ronan. "Isn't there any chance at all?"

Ronan shook his head. "If this was a one-off situation and if we had an available cryo unit right now, *and* if we could get her on the operating table with no further deterioration, she might live. We're not equipped to deal with massed casualties. If she goes to the top of the list, she'll take the place of others with more chance for complete recovery." He was silent for three strides. "Triage stinks, doesn't it?"

Cara nodded. "Did you get it right?"

"Yes," Ronan said.

"Sure?"

"Yes."

"Then will you please stop avoiding Wenna? She doesn't blame you for anything."

He took a deep breath and nodded.

"Good. Now, what can I do?"

"Help some of the walking wounded to the first aid area, then find yourself an emergency pack and start work; you can tie on a field dressing, can't you?"

Hours later Cara looked up from sealing a minor cut on the arm of an eight-year-old boy and saw that the work she could do was coming to an end.

"What do you say to the lady, Norrie?" the boy's mother prompted.

"Thank you."

"You're welcome, Norrie."

"We're all really grateful for your help, Miss," the woman said. "All your help. Might not have been much time to say so, but we are."

Cara nodded, almost too tired to smile. Numbly she went in search of Ben, who was talking to a hawk-faced middle-aged man. "Cara, this is Tellaman. He's the head of the new settlement and, now the wagon train captain is dead, he's in charge of the journey as well."

Cara looked at the settler for the first time. He held out his hand and she took it.

"Mrs. Benjamin, we have two children unaccounted for."

"We need a Finder," Ben said. "Where's Bronsen?"

Not a good idea. She flashed him a brief rundown of what had happened to Fliss and Bronsen's reaction.

"Sami Isaksten, then?" Ben asked.

Cara took a deep breath and let her mind range out to look for Sami. She was part of Gen's team, so that meant she'd drawn a trip to the coast for a few days. Somehow, having a direction to search in made it easier, and Sami popped into her head.

Sami, are you all right?

I'm with Liam. We took shelter in some caves while the storm was at its height. We're at Millertown. The people are all right, but the mill's a heap of kindling.

We need a Finder. Come as quickly as you can. We've got a couple of missing kids.

On my way.

Cara was with Ben and Tellaman when Lorient, Rena, and Jack Mario arrived in a medevac transport, returning from ferrying injured to Landing.

"Director Lorient," Tellaman shouted to gather those within earshot. "It's Director Lorient, Mrs. Lorient, and Mr. Mario." He started forward to greet the new arrivals.

"That's all we need," Ben said under his breath.

Lorient shook Tellaman by the hand and then hugged him like a father, even though Tellaman must have been a good decade older. Rena Lorient was quickly waylaid by a group of women and drawn into hearing their concerns.

"Commander Benjamin." Lorient acknowledged them with a nod. "Mrs. Benjamin. What a disaster." There was no bluster. Cara felt Ben's surprise.

"How many dead and injured?" Lorient asked.

"Two missing; seven dead including one psi-tech," Ben said. "Fourteen seriously injured, thirty-three needing further treatment or observation, and one hundred and thirty-five walking wounded out of a total of three hundred and four."

"What about livestock and equipment?" Jack Mario asked.

"The wind completely smashed more than half the wagons," Ben said, "and damaged most of the rest, though most of the chassis can be retimbered. Personal possessions and supplies are scattered from here to the northern ranges. Lee can tell you about the livestock better than I can."

Ben nodded to the tall, angular woman who had just joined them. She looked bone-weary, and her long straw-blonde hair was escaping from its ties.

"We're still counting. I've had to slaughter over forty head of cattle. I've got a bunch of settlers trying to butcher and preserve the meat before it spoils, but they could use some help. The sheep are all missing. I don't know if they panicked and ran or if the wind simply lifted them up and blew them away. I've got a flitter sweeping the area for signs now. The heavy horses mostly came though okay, but some animals have scattered and others were injured by flying debris or by each other in the panic."

"You said there were two people missing." Lorient turned to Ben.

"Little girls, sisters. Their father is on the critical list; he's already been shipped out for medical treatment. Their mother is still here, bruised but not badly injured. Sami Isaksten, our best Finder, is on her way here now."

"The mother, what's her name?"

"Ferina Roskayne, Director," Tellaman said.

"She must be distraught. I'll see her first and then, if you'll gather all the bereaved and walking wounded, I'll hold a meeting, see if I can give them something to steady them down. Jack . . ." He turned to his administrator. "Benjamin's emergency teams seem to be doing all the right things. I'll leave you to coordinate with them. I'll do what I'm best at."

As Victor Lorient strode purposefully toward the make-shift camp, Ben looked directly at Cara. She didn't need to be telepathic to know what he was thinking, but Lee Gardham came up to them, shaking her head, and voiced it.

The director never loses the ability to surprise me. The way he's been acting lately, I'd have thought he'd have blown a gasket over this, blamed us for not giving enough warning, and, yet, here he is, saying and doing exactly the right things.

I wish we could rely on it at other times, too, Ben said. *Still, let's be grateful for what we've got and start on the cleanup.* He switched to speech for Jack Mario's benefit. "Cara, when Sami arrives, you and I will take her up in a flitter and see what she can find. Get as many people as the cleanup team can spare. Follow the storm track on horse-back and check the immediate area thoroughly."

"Good luck," Jack said. "I wish I was coming with you. I feel so helpless."

"You'll be more use here, picking up the pieces," Ben said. "Rhinager will be your message service, either to us or to Landing. Just ask him if you need anything."

Jack nodded. "I'd like to bring in a settler team to help the families to pull all their stuff together."

"When we've picked up what pieces we can find, I think your settlers might appreciate a shuttle out of here to their destination. They've been through a lot and giving them a ride is the least we can do."

"Thanks. I'll talk to the director."

Sami arrived and turned all her talents toward finding the two little girls. They took a flitter up and ranged out wider and wider from the wagon train, making several overlapping passes, following Sami's directions. The farther away from the site they got, the more likely it was that finding either child alive would be a miracle.

"There." Sami was positive and Ben brought the flitter down to within a few meters of the ground. There was debris scattered across the grass. Sami nodded, and he eased the flitter down to one side of the spot.

Cara's heart was thumping. She knew that if Sami said they were here, then this is where they were, but part of her didn't want to find them. While they were lost, there was still the chance of a miracle.

"Here they are." Ben's voice cracked as he called them over.

Cara dropped to her knees in the debris beside two bodies. The three-year-old was battered and bloody, but the baby looked peacefully asleep, not a mark on her. Tears welled up and washed down Cara's face.

The body bags were way too big for the tiny bundles. They laid the little girls in the flitter and Cara contacted Bick.

We've found them, she said. *You'd better give Lorient the bad news; he'll probably be the best one to tell the girls' mother.*

I will.

There was a silent crowd gathered to meet the flitter when they arrived back at the wreck site. Disaster pulled a community closer together and there was no shortage of willing hands to take the bodies and do whatever was necessary.

"We're going to bury all the victims here." Jack Mario caught Ben and Cara by their flitter. "Director Lorient is going to conduct a service."

"That's kind of him."

"He wanted me to ask whether you wanted your young psi-tech buried here as well. She's as much a victim of the storm as any of the settlers. We'd be honored to have her resting with our dead."

"Thank you. That's a kind offer, but she has—had— friends who will want to give her a good send-off. We'll take her back to base."

When the last casualty had been flown out back to Landing, they lifted the body of Fliss Ruffalo onto an antigrav gurney and covered her over. The woman who'd sat with her in her dying moments led Bronsen by the hand and hugged him before she gently pushed him into the medevac shuttle.

"Thanks for staying with him," Cara said.

"It's not much, but it's the least I could do," the woman said. "Such a waste of a young life." She shook hands with Ben and Cara and every psi-tech within reach. "You all have our thanks for your help and our sorrow for your loss."

✦ ✦ ✦

As Cara's head hit the pillow back in her own bed at Landing, she realized that she'd gone nearly forty hours without sleep. She was beginning to shake internally, now that the adrenaline was wearing off.

Ben was still working, filing the reports of the search and logging the deaths of the settlers and Fliss Ruffalo.

Even tiredness could not keep away Cara's sick, empty feeling of loss. The death toll had risen to nineteen, including the two children. She hoped the girls' father would pull through. Anna said she thought he would.

Surprisingly, Lee had broken down when they'd arrived back at the wagon train with the two tiny bodies. She'd told Cara that she'd left her own daughter in cryo back on Earth in a Trust facility.

The thought of the little girl lying asleep, waiting for her mother, somehow disturbed Cara almost as much as the dead and maimed. The image of dead and sleeping children haunted her until she couldn't tell which was which. She was exhausted, but dreamless sleep wouldn't come.

"Lights."

The overheads came on at her command, and she threw back the covers, slipped her robe over her shoulders, and pushed her feet into light shoes. The pat-pat of her soft soles echoed down the dimly lit corridor. She passed Gen's room and Wenna's, both dark and quiet, but found that there was a light still on in the ready room.

"Cara, I was just making tea. Want some?" Ben looked up with a cup in his hands.

She nodded. "I couldn't sleep."

"It's been a hell of a day. Hell of a two days, actually."

"I keep thinking about those little girls."

"Don't."

"I know—there's nothing I can do now, and there's nothing I could have done then that would help." She ran her fingers through her hair. "How's Lewis Bronsen?"

"Ronan requisitioned a bottle of her best Scotch from Marta Mansoro's secret stash. She said he wasn't going to drink it without her, so the two of them have gone to get Bronsen roaring drunk. I thought about joining them myself, but I sent Wenna instead."

"Wenna and Ronan?"

"And a bottle of Scotch."

"Let's hope it works." She took the cup and sat in a chair with her knees up under her chin, sipping the hot brew.

They sat companionably, not talking until Cara had finished her drink. "I'm going back to bed." She nearly said, *Are you coming?* but thought he might misconstrue it as an invitation. "Good night."

◆ ◆ ◆

Lorient's volunteers had gone through the longest induction course Ben could possibly justify, but eventually they had to be incorporated into the survey teams. Wenna had drawn the short straw. He'd thought about giving them to Cara, but that seemed cruel—to the recruits. He figured Wenna would have more patience and that she'd draft in other tutors as she needed them. Maybe he'd suggest Cara teach them unarmed combat.

He tried not to smile as that thought crossed his mind. Instead, he drew his brows together and put on his stern face while he looked them over, standing or slouching together in the body of the LV. They were all men, of course. No surprises there, given that Lorient wasn't chancing any work liaisons leading to psi genes entering the settler gene pool.

He glanced at Wenna's tight lips. She knew why he'd agreed to Lorient's ridiculous suggestion, but she didn't like it.

Ben had misgivings, too, but he knew Lorient wanted his own men in the loop if news of the platinum broke. At least having novices klutzing around gave Wenna more than enough opportunities to lose the data they needed to lose. It was almost a win-win situation—almost. There was just that small problem that they were going to drive his teams mad, not to mention be a danger to themselves and others.

Back to the recruits. They looked like a mixed bag. He'd taken bets that half of them wouldn't stick it out, but that was okay. Natural selection was the first step in the weeding-out process. First of all he wanted to scare them. He'd already stated very firmly—on the record—that he took no responsibility for their safety. If any individual wasn't up to the job, he could put a whole team at risk.

He didn't try to be pleasant. He kept his face impassive and his tone even as he addressed the assembled settlers. "I should welcome you to survey work and thank you for volunteering, but I think you all know that having you here was not in our original plans. That doesn't mean we don't like you, or that we won't treat you well, but we have already had to interrupt scheduled work to train you and try to give you enough savvy so that you don't get yourselves—or anyone else—killed."

He looked at the recruits. Some took what he said with barely a flicker of irritation, a few looked positively offended, and a couple were downright angry. Watch the angry ones. The ones with a short fuse were bad news.

"You're going on active service now. Real survey work. I hope you can all take orders. I won't risk lives to pull one of you out of a self-created jam." He looked at the twenty-seven volunteers, an ill-assorted lot, all shapes, sizes, ages, and ethnic backgrounds. Half of them didn't look fit enough to take the kind of physical work that might be involved.

"Can any of you pilot a flitter?"

Only five sure hands went up and a couple wavered.

"Well, can you or can't you?" Ben asked one of the waverers.

"I took a few lessons."

The other waverer was a tall man, light-skinned with a shock of dark hair. "I had a license, but lost it again on a technicality. I can fly, though, if you aren't worried about Earth legalities."

"Did your technicality involve injuring anyone?"

"No." The man grinned. "The authorities didn't appreciate the way I used the vip lanes as a shortcut."

Ben nodded to Wenna.

"Name?" she asked the man.

"Max Constant."

Ben turned away while Wenna listed the other potential pilots and left her allocating volunteers to teams.

Jack Mario hovered in the doorway, and Ben went out to join him.

"Come to make sure we haven't eaten them yet, Jack?"

"I'm sorry. I didn't see this one coming or I might have talked the director out of it." Jack shrugged. "I feel responsible for their welfare. I'm sorry you got burdened."

"It's not your fault." Ben liked Jack. He reminded him of a more streamlined, younger version of Crowder, straightforward and practical. He was sensible enough to realize that without the psi-techs the colony would take decades to achieve what they could manage in a year.

Ben sighed. He turned his back to the room and dropped his voice so the recruits wouldn't be able to hear him. "Look, I know what I said, about sacrificing them if they got themselves into trouble, but you know that's not the case. My crews will do everything they can to keep your guys safe. How would it look if we lost them? You don't need to worry that we'll put them in danger, but I'm not going to tell them that. There are still no guarantees in this job."

"I believe you'll do your best."

"How's the director? We've not seen much of him lately."

Jack stared out of the window, avoiding eye contact. "I don't know, Ben. Truth?"

"Preferably."

Jack shrugged. "The director finds your presence here, that is the psi-tech presence here . . . intimidating, but he'd never admit it. He's even moved his own office to another building because I have Saedi Sugrue working with me. She's brilliant, by the way. You should promote her when you get home. Director Lorient's mind doesn't work on the same level as most of us. He's a very intelligent man, but he's truly phobic about anything psi, and he's gathered a small group of followers who feel the same."

"He has the backing of every one of your settlers. That makes him king," Ben said. "And I've noticed that, now that the settlers are in a strong majority, he's getting more of an emperor complex."

Jack turned back to face Ben and smiled. "You've spotted that, have you? It's hard not to be swayed by adoration. The people will do anything for him. That's why most of them are on Olyanda. He sold them a dream."

"Why are you here, Jack? You're not the type to buy dreams."

"I've known and admired Victor Lorient for most of my adult life. He gave me my first admin job when the big corporations managed to find good reasons for not employing an Ecolibrian, however well qualified. He's not always so . . ." Jack cleared his throat and changed his tack midsentence. "The director has a vision. It's a good vision, but he needs a good administrator to make it work."

"I'd be much happier if you were in charge and Lorient was confined to his pastoral duties. Where do you stand on the Ecolibrian thing? You're certainly not psi-phobic."

"No, I'm not. What about you? What do you think about us?"

"I want the colony to be everything you all want it to be. I just hope that the 'phobes can keep their feelings in check until we've finished what we were contracted to do."

"Me, too. I'll do everything I can to keep a lid on things."

They turned to watch the recruits taking their seats. Wenna would already have some idea of which ones she wanted to send back to prune the numbers down to the minimum number of fourteen that they'd agreed with Jack.

"This will be the first test—to see whether this lot can work with us," Ben said.

◆ ◆ ◆

There was a snatch in Cara's head; an outside interruption from the tech in charge of the flitter bay.

Cara, can you get Commander Benjamin over here, please. I don't know how to handle this. He just climbed in while I was working on the antigravs. He beamed a picture of Danny Lorient sitting in the pilot's seat of a four-man flitter with his finger hovering over the power control. *He says the commander gave him permission.*

Cara left her food untouched, glad for the excuse. "Sorry, folks—duty calls." She relayed the message to Ben across the room and saw him begin to move. They arrived at the door together and ran across to the flitter bay.

Danny had been a regular visitor to Landing, usually managing to tag along with Jack or sometimes get a lift on one of the groundcars with Saedi. His time in the hospital had given him an ease with psi-techs that the rest of his family didn't have. Or perhaps he was just less reserved, his condition giving him a natural innocence and an inbuilt confidence. Both Cara and Ben had taken to popping in to see him while he was recovering, and she suspected he'd made a wide circle of friends among the medical staff. As soon as he'd been allowed out, he'd headed for the landing pad. He liked to fly, and nothing his father could say would persuade him that the psi-techs were evil and that flitters would not be a part of their world in the future.

By the time they arrived in the flitter bay, Danny was firmly ensconced in the flitter. He had the antigravs on standby, but without the access codes, he wasn't going anywhere.

"Hello, Danny." Ben climbed up and sat beside him, smiling and casual.

"Hello, Commander Benjamin." Danny grinned broadly. "Can we fly now?"

"I don't think that would be the right thing to do without asking your parents first."

"I'm nineteen, now. I'm grown up."

"Sure you are, Danny, but your father is not just *your* father, he's in charge of the whole colony. We all need to ask his permission for lots of things."

"Even you?"

"Especially me."

"You're an abomination."

Cara felt her gut do a backflip. It was no wonder there was anti-psi-tech feeling if Victor tossed around words like *abomination* freely. What a bastard! She immediately stretched to catch Ben's reaction, but she felt his initial shock at the word well under control.

"Is that what your father says?" Ben's words were unruffled and gentle.

Danny nodded.

"Do you know what it means?"

Danny shook his head.

"It's not a good word, Danny. People who use it hate me because of the way I choose to be. I'm different from them. I'm a psi-tech. So are all the people here in Landing. We're all psi-techs, but that doesn't mean we're bad people. We're just different. The implants in our heads just help us to do our jobs better."

"I'm different, too. I'm a Downie. That's special."

"Everybody's special in their own way."

"That's good."

"I think so." Ben smiled.

"But my Mom and Dad don't like people to be different." Danny's face clouded.

"They like you." Ben tried to reassure him. "They like some kind of different, but not all kinds."

"I think they should like everybody."

"Sure you do. So do I."

"If my Mom and Dad say so, can we fly?"

"Of course. I'd like that."

Danny smiled and climbed out of the flitter. "Mrs. Benjamin, you're very pretty. Will you fly with us, too?"

"Sure, Danny." Cara found herself smiling back at Danny. He was a hard kid to resist. There wasn't a malevolent thought in his head. He opened his arms and hugged her, and Cara found herself hugging him back. It seemed so natural. Then he turned and trotted out of the flitter bay, heading back toward the groundcars to get a lift with the next one out. Cara watched him go.

Ben swung down too and joined her. "You've got an admirer."

"He's a sweetheart; not a bit like his father. You were really good with him," she said.

"I like him. He has the gift of happiness. And I think he has far more sense than most people give him credit for. He just doesn't always show it in the same way as everyone else."

Chapter Twenty-one

COUPLING

"I DON'T GET IT," GEN GLARED AT THE BOARD in Mapping. "Look at this frigging crew list. I lost Ro Napper, a perfectly good flitter pilot, got Casey Silk, who bailed after the first flight and went running back to Broccoliburg, and now I've got the mouthy one."

"Who?" Cara peered over her shoulder. "Oh, Max Constant. Tough luck. Though maybe it has something to do with you doing stall-turns out over the ocean with a rookie who's never been in a flitter before."

"You didn't tell Ben, did you?"

"I didn't need to. At least Constant isn't likely to barf all over the control console. Yan Gwenn was pretty chewed up over that and so was the cleanup crew, I guess. Silk wasn't too happy, either."

"How does Wenna expect us all to keep up the pace with brain-deaf settlers who are no more than ballast?"

"Wenna expects because Ben expects." Wenna's voice behind them snapped Gen to attention. "Got a problem with that?"

Cara tried not to snigger.

"I did ask all of you to treat the recruits gently." Wenna scowled. "You broke one on the first day."

"At least I didn't jettison him. I was seriously tempted. He was so slow I wanted to scream. He might have the rest of his life to spend on this planet, but I don't. I was in danger of falling behind because I was carrying a bloody tourist."

"Set the ground rules with Constant before you start," Wenna said. "I think he's got the potential to be useful, despite being a deadhead. He's quick on the uptake. I let Yan put him through his paces in a flitter. He's worth extra training." She picked up a sheaf of plasfilms and headed for the door. "You want to make section leader in a few more years. Deal with it."

"Do it tonight," Cara suggested after she'd gone. "If you have to chew Constant out, do it in private so he can start tomorrow's shift fresh."

"Ground rules, right." Gen sounded doubtful. "I guess that's what Ben would do."

◆ ◆ ◆

Max sat back in his chair in the corner of the dining hall and watched Gen Marling until she was out of sight. He'd made her mad, and he hadn't even worked his first shift with her yet. Even her hair bounced in sympathy with her mood. Women! He never had quite got the hang of understanding them. Psi-techs were even more complicated than the other kind.

But even when she was being authoritarian, Marling didn't throw her weight around without good reason. He didn't want to annoy her enough to be dumped from her team. Better do as she asked and shape up.

He hadn't expected to be working with psi-techs so closely, but he certainly wasn't going to turn down the opportunity to get out of the legions of field fodder. Maybe, after this, he could try and sneak into admin again. There were bound to be new opportunities if only he could stay around the central hub and not get shipped off to the back end of nowhere.

In the meantime, he'd landed on his feet. Survey work was more than interesting. He was getting a better introduction to his new planet than he would ever get from the ground, and his new boss was a definite bonus.

He mustn't think of Gen Marling as available even though she was one attractive woman. The rules were pretty firm, though they seemed pointless as far as the psi-tech women were concerned. He could understand that the gene pool for the new society shouldn't have any accidental bastards in it with psi-potential, but that should only restrict relationships between psi-tech men and settler women. One blanket rule shouldn't cover both sexes.

✦ ✦ ✦

After her shift, a fairly routine day of surveying and mapping the plains to the south with Ben and their new settler rookie, Mohan Razdan, Cara headed for the dining hall, collected her tray, and looked around for a place to sit. Ben was deep in conversation with Serafin. There was a spare place at their table, but sitting together in public put pressure on them to play Mr. and Mrs.

Wenna and Ronan together with Ronan's partner, Jon Moon, one of Wenna's cartographers, chatted animatedly at another table. Cara glanced around a little further. Gen was sitting by herself, so Cara headed over toward her table, not noticing that Max Constant was heading in the same direction until it was too late. He was on Gen's crew now, one of the few settlers who looked as though they were going to be useful. They reached Gen at the same time and Cara stepped back.

"There's room for two," Max said, and waited for Cara to sit down before setting his own tray on the table.

Gen looked at them both, and Cara sensed brief embarrassment.

Max looked up as if he wondered whether the two women were talking about him. Typical reaction of a deadhead in the company of psi-techs. Cara had given Max more credit. He didn't generally seem to be uncomfortable around them; in fact, she thought she'd heard someone say he'd worked with psi-techs back home. That was unusual for the narrow-minded settlers on this expedition.

Cara sat back and stared at Gen and Max. There was something very complicated going on here. Or perhaps it wasn't complicated at all, just very dangerous.

✦ ✦ ✦

Max had never felt more alive.

When he'd worked in accounting for Alphacorp, he'd got his kicks from sport, often a different one every year. Cave diving had been the most reckless. A successful cave dive was defined as one you came back from. He got wise to that after a couple of nasty experiences and decided the best cave dive was the one you didn't take. Hang gliding had been pretty cool, though, and he'd once—only once—done a base jump in a parasuit.

Exploring a virgin planet beat all of those. Doing it by the side of Gen Marling was icing on his cake.

He'd jumped at the chance of putting in extra hours with Yan Gwenn to upgrade his experience on ground-hugging domestic flitters to the more powerful workhorse models in use on Olyanda. Pity they weren't going to be left behind when the psi-tech teams finished their year. He'd relish being one of the few settlers qualified to fly. And surely that would get him out of doing carpentry for the rest of his life.

Today Gen had let him take the pilot's seat for the first time as they surveyed the coastal region. He flew the craft to a point above the high-water mark of a wide sweeping bay and let it settle into its antigravs. Then he cut the drive and sat back.

"No time to be self-satisfied, Mr. Constant. Get your brain into gear and let's get going." Gen was still on his case even though she knew she needn't be. He'd detected a softening in her attitude of late. The barbs still came, but there was no sting in them now that they'd developed a good working rhythm. Even so, she couldn't resist reminding him who was boss every now and then.

"Yes, sir, ma'am." Max saluted stiffly and grinned, turning the tables back on her. Before she could reprimand him, he was out of the flitter with the others and unpacking gear.

Liam Ryder, their exobiologist, a Dee'ell if Max understood that right, bent to examine the sand and to sample it for livestock. Gen and Sami Isaksten leaned in toward him and Max realized they were all communicating on a level that was totally beyond his reach. Not for the first time he felt a pang of regret that, as a teen, he'd been so convinced that Ecolibrianism was the answer to everything that he'd managed to avoid the routine psi-testing with the collusion of his (then) foster family.

Gen swept the coastline with a sounding device. "It's shallow enough for waders," she said. "But better turn up the heat on your buddysuits; the water is pretty cold."

"I'll work with Liam on that." Sami pulled the packs out of the flitter and tossed one to Liam with a grin. They waded about forty meters from shore to anchor the catch nets and were still only thigh-deep in water.

Max watched Gen watching the two of them working together. It was becoming very clear that, if Sami and Liam were not a couple already, then they soon would be.

"They make a good couple, don't they?" he said.

Gen jumped. "I didn't hear you coming up behind me."

"I thought you lot could sense us," Max said.

"Some can. I majored in telepathy and spatial awareness. I'm a Navigator, not an Empath."

"You seem sensitive enough to me." He ran his finger up the length of her spine and she shivered involuntarily. "See?"

She spun around to face him and took a step back, clenching her hands into fists. "Don't ever pull that kind of cheap stunt again, Constant. You know the regulations. Why do you keep coming on to me? What are you after?"

He stepped back and put both hands up in a gesture of surrender.

"Do I?" Hell, had it been that obvious? "I might just be teasing."

"I've given you the benefit of the doubt before, but this is once too often."

"Have you ever thought that I might just like you?"

"If you liked me, you'd leave me alone. What kind of a jerk are you? No fraternization between psi-tech and settler. None! If you haven't got that into your head by now, I'll lend you the rule book and you can do some homework."

He just stared at her, his defenses down. Her look began to twist his gut. "I've done my homework, but . . ." He shrugged. "I'm sorry. The homework files didn't tell me I'd meet anyone like you."

"Look, Max, I like you, all right? I didn't expect to, but I do. But it's not going anywhere. At the end of this year it will all be over. We'll be light-years apart."

"So? Is that any reason we shouldn't be . . . friends, now?" His gut was churning. "Look, I'll leave you alone if that's what you really want, but I think you feel it, too." He forced a bright smile. "We can keep it light and easy, Gen. You're not going to leave me pregnant when you go, are you?" He stuck out his belly and she half smiled. "There, now. That wasn't so bad, was it? We can just be friends if you like. No strings. No regrets. No sex. Well, I might let you change my mind about the sex if you twist my arm."

Who was he kidding? He lowered his voice to a whisper. "I'm going to miss you like hell whether I lose you now or lose you at the end of the year."

◆　◆　◆

Everything was going right for a change. Cara began to relax into the regular patterns of the job. Once the storm season ended, the settlement program ran like clockwork. Settlers were revived from cryo in batches, family groups of all ages between six and sixty were slathered in sunblock and given their wagons, horses, and whatever goods and animals they'd preordered and paid for. Then they set off across the plain— in large convoys—heading for their newly designated settlements all within a few days' travel of Timbertown and within reach of each other. The survey teams had identified a number of useful sites and Serafin's Psi-Mechs were busy linking them with a network of roads carved out of the ground by surfacing machines.

In large groups at Lorient's meetings the settlers might seem fanatical, but in small numbers and away from the heady emotions stirred up by rhetoric, they were reasonable, caring people with more interest in the practicalities of their new lives than with who was and who was not psi-tech.

Timbertown already boasted some permanent buildings, laid out by Serafin's crew with the settlers supplying labor and solid craftsmanship. Lorient's new hall—a central meeting place for the whole community—was half built, with engineers getting ready to lift the roof beams into place and Lorient's masons working on the detail. Once the masons and the psi-techs recognized each other's competence, they'd developed an easy working relationship. It would be a magnificent centerpiece for the new capital with a stone bell tower and a stained glass window featuring a dove of peace as its crowning glory.

The new communities were breaking and planting the ground, working toward self-sufficiency, and would soon be ready for the influx of thirty thousand settlers from the second ark ship. The settlers weren't lacking in farming expertise and Jack Mario had done a good job of making sure there were competent and confident agrarian leaders in each settlement with specialist craftsmen, blacksmiths, builders, carpenters, and potters as well as teachers, doctors, and midwives. They had the shared skills and enthusiasm to make the colony self-sufficient.

Everyone slowed down as the hot weather hit. A heat haze hugged the plain, though it was a little cooler by the sea and in the northern uplands. There were bouts of intense humidity, which made everyone uncomfortable and edgy, even the psi-techs in their buddysuits, though Cara could only imagine how uncomfortable the settlers were as they labored without the benefit of temperature regulators in their clothing or cool air in their living spaces. At least they knew it wouldn't last long. Olyanda, even here on its equator, would rarely top thirty degrees centigrade in midsummer. Every so often the clouds would clear, the humidity would fade, and for a few days the parched night air would crackle with all the glorious colors of the aurora.

Spring-planted crops now ripened in the fields, showing early promise of a good harvest. Fat cattle grazed in the pastures. Only the sheep were failing to adapt. Despite Lee Gardham's best efforts, they'd lost half of all the ewes that had been revived so far, and lambs from the in vitro tank stock weren't doing much better.

In the Mapping ops room Cara focused on the crew list and then read it again.

Damn. Gen and Max Constant had drawn another duty together, this time taking Lee Gardham with five shepherds and thirty sheep up into the mountains. Gen and Max; Max and Gen. Cara thought things had cooled between them, but was she imagining things? Lately they'd drawn more than their fair share of runs together, and it was beginning to look deliberate. They offered potential for a disaster waiting to happen, if it hadn't happened already. Dammit— they knew the rules, but Max had become a useful member of the team despite his irritating flippancy and lack of implant. There were times when she forgot he was a settler because he seemed so at home with the psi-techs.

At least they wouldn't be alone. The shepherds would be staying in the mountains, but Lee would be returning with Gen and Max.

Cara found Gen in the ops room and pulled her to one side. "You and Max."

"What about it?"

"That's what I was going to ask."

"It'll be okay. I can handle it." Gen pulled her arm from Cara's grasp.

"But . . ."

"I said I can handle it." Gen stomped off toward the flitter bays. Cara watched her go, surprised by her vehemence. Then her heart began to pound and she felt slightly sick with the weight of impending trouble.

It was already too late.

She hoped Gen *could* handle it. Cara considered getting Ben to step in, but dismissed the idea. He never interfered with any of Wenna's decisions, especially such an apparently routine one. Going to him with a simple request for a rota change would seem odd without an explanation, and Cara didn't want to get a black mark on Gen's record without absolute proof.

Cas Ritson stuck her head out of the office door. "Cara, can you tell Ben that Lorient has called a section heads' meeting this afternoon at the Central Hall in Timbertown. He asks if everyone can be there for the end of today's assembly."

"Any idea what it's about?"

"No. Maybe he wants to thank everyone for their hard work so far."

"Hmph. Is that likely?"

Cara paused, briefly, to relay the message. When she turned back to the notice board, Gen was already out of sight.

Damn, I hope she knows what she's doing.

♦ ♦ ♦

Cara pushed her way into the meeting hall, between settlers. Some said hello and nodded politely, others backed away once they realized what she was as if she had psi-tech cooties. Wenna, Ben, Serafin, and Suzi had arrived early. Cara tucked herself behind Ben into the only clear space in the room, returning his smile briefly. The pariah effect was a positive advantage in this heat.

Serafin compressed his lips together as if to keep from smiling. *I'm tempted to start a conga line through the crowd to see how many join in and how many run away. Who's with me? I bet we could clear the room in a minute and a half, tops.*

Ben's eyes crinkled in a half-smile.

Me. I'm in. Yan Gwenn made his way through the crowd to join them. Much as they had done for Cara, the settlers parted to let him through. He gave a shuffle in a one-two-three-step! A rhythm that no one outside their tight conversation would have recognized, but Suzi gave a soft snort and put her hand over her mouth to turn the noise into a cough.

Sorry. She took a deep breath and bumped a gentle fist into Yan's arm as he reached the group.

What did I miss? Marta asked as she slid into the lineup.

Tell you later, Cara said.

Anna? Ben asked.

On her way, Marta said. *She's been working with Saedi Sugrue to talk one of the settler paramedics through an appendix surgery in the Rollins Settlement. Routine stuff.*

I thought they had a qualified clinician at Rollins, Ben said.

They do. She's the one with appendicitis. Don't worry, the paramedic seems to be handling it just fine.

Victor Lorient stood on the platform with his back to a semicircle of chairs that usually held his immediate Council.

Today only Rena and Jack Mario were present. They sat, impassive, while Lorient delivered his set speech to encourage the last batch of settlers on their difficult journey. This lot were going the whole way by wagon, traveling north.

The psi-techs stood at the back of the room, biding their time, listening. Pep talks like this had been a regular occurrence as each group of settlers set off from Landing and passed through Timbertown to join the mass of colonists rippling outward from the center to make new lives for themselves.

Cara watched Lorient and examined the way he impressed himself on the crowd. Yes, he was fully in character as the charismatic orator.

The crowd yelled and stomped.

"We love you, Director," a woman shouted from the front row and the cry was met with a round of enthusiastic applause.

When he was dealing with the psi-techs, he was a different man. If only they could get through to him on some kind of human level. Pie in the sky. He didn't even think of them as human. His fear of psi-techs was so deeply ingrained that it would take more than their remaining time on this planet to make him see things differently.

Victor's voice was firm and strong. He was in full flow now.

"You will, no doubt, encounter many hardships along your way, but through it all you must hold firm to our ultimate goal, a free natural society without the abominations created by man. Go with good grace, brothers and sisters."

Hypocrite! His settlers are willing for us to give their tight-arsed society a kick-start. The man makes me sssick. Marta Mansoro's mental tone was so bitter she even managed to place a mental sibilance on the final ess.

Cara had heard Lorient's standard speech before, but the ripple of agreement that ran through the audience at the line about "abominations" always chilled her.

*I'm not saying it's right . . . * Anna Govan arrived and slipped in between Ben and Cara. *But you can see why he does it. These poor people are going into the unknown without the benefit of the industry and technology they've grown* up relying on. They've had to learn how to harness horses and milk cows by hand. They'll be breaking new ground with plowshares and spades, and when the supply of tools finally runs out, they'll have to make their own. They're going to be using manual skills our ancestors discarded centuries ago. If they cling to the security they're leaving behind, they'll crack at the first disaster. Better to remember technology as evil and deviant rather than life-giving and labor-saving.*

As long as he doesn't overdo it, Ben said. *There's still a lot of work to do, and until we leave, we need their cooperation, not their animosity.*

The settlers began to filter out, heading toward their wagons and their new lives. Lorient waited on the podium for the section heads to make their way to the front of the hall.

✦ ✦ ✦

I wonder why he called us in today? I have three harvest gangs working. Suzi Ruka was impatient. *I'd rather not spend time listening to this Eco-maniac.*

Victor Lorient waited until the last of the settlers had filed out and then addressed himself to the assembled section heads. "Come forward, please. I called you here today to discuss infringements of our charter." Victor delivered the words like stones dropping into a deep well.

Cara caught a sudden wave of emotion from him. High anticipation. Excitement. Self-righteousness. She tried to home in on it, but it dissipated, leaving barely an echo. Damn, if only Ronan were here. His Empathy was stronger than hers. She picked up a faint impression of numbers. Random numbers. Weird. She stood behind the others and concentrated on Lorient. He'd definitely changed from the man who'd emerged from cryo pale and shaking. She'd barely seen him for the last couple of months, but it seemed that as his empire had grown, his ego had expanded to go with it. All of a sudden he had no restraints. He was the highest law in the land, and his followers had given him executive authority. Where some men—Jack, for instance— would have treated that as a duty of care, it seemed that Lorient had treated it as a mandate to rule. What did he think he was creating here?

Watch out, she said to Ben.

He kept them standing at the foot of the podium, enjoying the superiority of height.

"One of our major concerns, when we contracted for the inclusion of your psi-tech support teams, was the interaction of your personnel and ours. Because of that, we laid down very clearly that there should be no social fraternization between psi-tech and settler. This rule has been broken."

Cara began to go cold. How could he know about Gen and Max? No. Keep calm. He couldn't know. This must be something altogether different. She kept her face straight and concentrated on breathing evenly. Lorient looked as though he was in a mood to show them that he didn't take this thing lightly.

"A mating. A copulation." He almost chewed the last word. "The woman in question, Mariel Fenec, is ours. She has been dealt with."

Cara was so relieved that Gen's dalliance hadn't been discovered that it took her brain a few seconds to catch up with Lorient's "dealt with." And then she began to get cold shivers.

Lorient continued. "The young man, Erich Coburg, falls within your jurisdiction and I would remind you that, to discourage this kind of behavior, he must be dealt with severely. Very severely." He paused for dramatic effect and then delivered his punchline using each word as a hammer blow. "I demand that you charge him with statutory rape and take the appropriate action."

Cara went cold all over. Coburg, one of Lee Gardham's junior exobiologists, was definitely in breach of contract, but that wasn't a criminal offense. Lorient was really going over the top.

"Wasn't the Fenec woman a willing partner?" Ben asked.

"Willing or not, intercourse was illegal." Lorient's eyebrows were drawn together across his forehead, his expression thunderous.

"The penalty for rape is too high a price to pay for a technical offense," Anna said. "I'm not prepared to carry out a chemical castration here on Olyanda, and neither will any of my staff."

"Director Lorient." Ben barely kept the anger out of his voice and Cara could sense his pent-up urge to act instead of debate. "We'll discipline Coburg appropriately, but it won't include anything permanent."

God, these people are primitive. Marta was not impressed. *What have they done to the woman? And what might they have done to Coburg if it was the other way round, one of our women and one of their men?*

Cut off his tackle with a rusty razor, I expect. Serafin's coarseness was probably a cover for his emotion. *Well, something like this had to come sooner or later, human nature being what it is.*

"Where's Coburg?" Ben asked.

Now that she knew to seek him out, Cara had forged a link to him already. She thought that he was nearby, but he was weak and confused, either drugged or injured. She hoped that, wherever he was, he was still in one piece and not suffering the fate that Serafin had suggested.

"We have him," Lorient said and nodded to two thuggish-looking men who'd been lounging near the door trying to look inconspicuous. "Tell them to bring Coburg in."

The emperor's palace guards, she said to Ben. *Already.*

The door opened and two more tall Ecolibrians supported a young man whose face, between the bruises, was deathly pale. They let him slump to the floor at the foot of the podium. Cara's stomach churned. What a bloody mess; no wonder she hadn't been able to get any sense out of him. She felt the reaction of mixed horror, sickness, and anger from all the psi-techs.

Anna stepped forward from behind the others. One of Lorient's heavies moved to grab her. Ben turned, but Marta was closer. She threw a punch straight from the shoulder with a gloved right. The heavy dropped like a stone. Marta shook her fingers. The glove probably saved her from breaking her hand.

Another heavy started to react, but Ben held up his hand and took his attention, shaking his head. "I wouldn't if I were you."

The man on the floor groaned, rolled to his knees, thought better of it, and then slumped again.

"Take your buddy to a first aider," Ben said to the second thug. "Man's got a glass jaw. He's in the wrong job."

Anna reached Coburg in four strides and dropped to her knees beside him. Cara saw the two heavies who'd brought him in begin to move forward. In the same instant she was aware of Ben gathering himself to intercept them. His emotions were on the surface, barely in check. It was a moment of infinite possibilities for further violence, but Lorient signaled his men to stand down and for someone to get the fallen thug out of the room.

Ben held himself steady, not making the first move.

Anna turned on Lorient sharply. "We should be looking at assault charges. You've half-killed him."

"He needs a prison cell." Lorient's face was stony, but, again, Cara sensed an unexpected flash of high emotion.

Ben stood protectively above Anna. "You had no right to do this."

Coburg's cuts and abrasions were recent enough to have opened up again, and there was blood on the floor.

"I've done what I saw fit, Benjamin. That's my job. Keeping your people under control is your job." His pointing finger took in Coburg and swung toward Marta. "If you don't do your job, I'll have to do it for you. You can have Coburg back. Make an example of him, or I will. Get him out of here before I change my mind."

"The charter is very clear about where your jurisdiction begins and ends." Ben's voice was hard.

"We're a long way from where that charter was written. There are a lot more of us than there are of you. Don't talk about legalities." Lorient dropped his voice to a low growl. "We'll be drawing up a new set of laws. New laws for a new world. My people are working on it now."

Behind Lorient on the platform, Cara saw Jack Mario lean forward as if to speak, but Rena put out her hand to restrain him. The heavies, Lorient's psi-tech-hating fundamentalists, no doubt, were a very solid presence. They wouldn't be much of a match for the psi-techs if it came to a skirmish, but this wasn't the time.

"Director Lorient," Ben said. "Have a care when drafting your new laws."

If he wantsss a war, he can have one. Marta Mansoro's telepathic voice hissed with anger. *He can fucking have one! We may only be three hundred strong, but he's never seen what we can really do. Just letting the engineersss loose would ssscare him ssshitlesss.*

Calm down, Ben said. *That's exactly what he's frightened of. We need to buy time. Get a medical transport and a security team here fast. Let's get Coburg to the med-center before Lorient changes his mind and we have a brawl on our hands.*

They're on their way, Cara chipped in.

I'll stay until they get here, Anna said. *And I'll make sure this bastard doesn't do any more damage.*

We'll all stay, Ben said.

Lorient came to the edge of the podium so that he towered over Ben. "I know you're all talking about me. Think-talking. Conspiring. Don't imagine that you can put one over on me, Benjamin. We have our own ways of doing things now."

He marched out, leaving his heavies not knowing whether to stay or follow. Rena rushed after Lorient, but Jack Mario was a little slower. He dismissed the heavies and looked across at the psi-techs. His eyes held an apology, but he said nothing.

Cara saw Ben incline his head very slightly to acknowledge Jack.

She wondered what the definition of certifiable insanity was. Though, if they put Lorient in a straitjacket, the fundies would start a war.

Chapter Twenty-two

RIOT

BACK IN MAPPING, WENNA MET THEM WITH A worried frown. "Sorry about Coburg, Boss. More trouble, I'm afraid. Cas has lost touch with Lee Gardham's party."

"When? Where?"

"Over the mountains. The last report she had was that they were on their way home, then nothing."

"Can you raise Gen?" Ben asked Cara.

She retreated into that peculiar stillness that Ben had come to recognize as a momentary absence from her own body as her mind ranged outward. After a few moments her eyes focused on his. She squeezed her lips together and shook her head.

His stomach churned. "Lee?"

She shook her head. "Lee's only a weak Psi-3, but I've never had any trouble contacting her before, whatever the distance. Now . . . it's as if she doesn't exist. Sorry."

"Dead?"

The thought filled Ben with dread. He'd lost too many on Hera-3. He'd promised himself no more.

"Or deeply unconscious."

He swallowed rising bile and took a deep breath. "Get

two Finders into the area. Divert Bronsen from the survey on Sector 41."

"I'll get Sami Isaksten airborne. I know she's on a rest day, but—"

He rubbed his forehead with his fingers. "Yes, Sami, she's damn good. Make sure they've both got full backup."

He desperately wanted to storm out and take a long walk to clear his head, but he didn't have that luxury. "Wenna, get four of your best survey crews flying a search grid. Send Ronan with a first-response team out in the medevac flitter. Have him establish a base near the search area. I have to deal with Coburg."

And just how was he going to deal with Erich Coburg? At best, the kid was an idiot; at worst, a starry-eyed romantic. Ack, that still made him an idiot.

✦ ✦ ✦

Leaving Cara to coordinate the search teams, Ben checked Coburg's records. He was a Psi-4 exozoologist with only a passive rating in telepathy. He was straight out of University with one six-month field placement on Toronto, the planet, not the city. He had good references and Lee Gardham had teamed him with a more experienced man and had been monitoring his progress. It was all down in his file. No cause for concern.

Ben walked over to the med-center, deep in thought.

"How's the patient?" He found Anna Govan in her office.

"Feeling very sorry for himself, but he'll live. He's got a broken nose and lost an eye. I can fit him with a temporary ocular implant, but not until the bruising has settled. The nose is going to take a couple of surgical sessions, too. Otherwise a couple of cracked ribs and the kind of bone damage to his right hand to show he landed a couple of good punches before they took him down."

"I'm going to get Gupta to assign someone round the clock to keep an eye on him. There's no sense taking chances."

"If you think it's necessary."

"I do. Is Coburg conscious? Can I see him?"

"He's had a mild sedative. Don't be surprised if he falls asleep on you. Room Eight. Don't be too hard on him. He knows he's messed up bigtime."

"Kid gloves, I promise."

If Ben had been going to tear him off a strip, he'd have changed his mind the instant he saw Coburg lying semi-reclined, the visible portion of his face pale between the bruising. His left eye was covered with a dressing and his right was barely visible behind the swelling.

Ben moved into his field of vision, and the young man tried to struggle into a sitting position.

"Sorry, son, I didn't mean to startle you. I guess I should have whistled first. How are you feeling?"

"Fine, sir."

"No, you're not. You feel like shit, but you're in good hands, and you will be fine, given time."

"Yes, sir." It came out slightly slurred.

"So I need your side of this story."

"Yes, sir. I'm sorry, sir. I let you down."

"You let yourself down."

"I didn't mean to, but . . . you know how it is, sir. You're from Chenon, too, aren't you?"

Ben nodded, realized Coburg couldn't see him and said, "I am."

"I grew up in Lomax County. My dad used to talk about you. Said if one farm kid could make it through psi-tech training, then so could another."

Lomax County was barely fifty klicks from the Benjamin farm. It wasn't an area teeming with sophisticated social circles. Ben remembered how naive he'd been when he'd hung up his mud boots and joined the Monitors.

"When I heard there was an opening on your team, I applied immediately."

"I'm flattered, Erich. Can I call you Erich?"

"My friends call me Ricky, sir."

The name grabbed Ben in the back of the throat. His nephew's name. A sudden memory of home washed over him. Paruna, tall as his shoulder, waving golden in the fields; the warm smell of cattle in the barn; the citrus tang of orange oil burning in the lamps in the atrium to keep the millen bugs away; Nan, his brother Rion and Rion's two boys, Kai and little Ricky . . . Ben's only family. He swallowed hard and dragged himself back to the antiseptic aura surrounding the sickbed.

"I'm flattered, Ricky, but you could have picked an easier job for your first assignment. You knew the rules when you signed on, so how come you broke them?"

"I didn't mean to. It just happened." He took a deep breath. "Mari's family had a Clydesdale mare, a gentle giant. They were intending to breed from her. There was an accident, the mare broke a leg. When a horse breaks a leg it's usually the end, but the family needed foals, even if the mare couldn't work, so they asked if we could do anything. We had the mare in a sling to keep her weight off the leg, and I went every day with a portable regeneration unit. Mari was always there, always so concerned, so determined not to lose the mare. I thought . . . we thought that we were winning, but a Clydesdale is a heavy beast to spend so much time in a belly sling. There was always a chance of complications." He shook his head and winced. "We lost the mare. Colic and a torsion. It was terrible. Mari was so upset. We were both upset. We'd invested too much time and emotional energy . . . It was only a hug . . . for comfort, but . . . it turned into more. And . . . things happened between us that shouldn't have. It was just one time, but . . . her brothers found us and . . . ."

"You know this will go on your record?"

"Yes, sir."

"When you're well again, you'll be confined to Landing. I'm sure Lee will agree that Calvin Tanaka can use you in the tank farm. No more contact with the settlers on any level. Understood?"

"Sir, yes, sir."

"You see even one settler coming and you turn and walk the other way."

"Walk the other way, sir. I understand."

He didn't tell the kid Lee was missing. One trauma at a time was enough.

✦ ✦ ✦

Cara spent the rest of the day at Ben's side, keeping him in touch with everything that happened as it happened. By the time Ronan had established a base camp, there wasn't time to do more than skim the edges of the mountains before they lost the light. Ben ordered the flitter crews to stand down, return to base, and be ready to search again at dawn.

"Plan on an early start. I want to be there by first light," he told Cara, sending her off early to get some rest.

"What about you? Don't you need sleep?"

Ben had fallen into the habit of staying up late so that Cara was asleep by the time he hit his bed.

"I'll be along soon."

Cara was so edgy that she was still dozing, half in and half out of sleep when Ben came into their room. He undressed in the dark silence and slipped into his bed without noticing that she was awake. She lay there tossing thoughts of Gen and Max backward and forward with the image of Coburg's broken face.

Eventually Cara felt herself in that half-life between waking and dreaming, and darkness closed in. She should be able to get back to reality, but somehow, she couldn't, and nightmares from the past played on her vulnerability.

Ari van Blaiden wavered in front of her eyes, then solidified. He stood over Ben's corpse. Then the picture shifted to Craike standing over a gutted riding beast on a mountainside on Felcon. Then it was Ari again, only this time Ari didn't back off as Craike had done. His arm swung upward and his hand was steady as he leveled a bolt gun at her. She knew with dull certainty that it would cut her in half from this distance, but Ben was dead and that was the only thing she could think about—Ari's finger tightening on the trigger. She couldn't move fast enough. There was nowhere to run.

Mr. van Blaiden wants to know that his secrets are safe . . .

"Oh, shit!" Cara sat up in bed and waited for her heart to stop pounding. Her hair was plastered to her head, and she was dripping with sweat from head to toe.

Bloody dreams. Bloody, bloody dreams! The long frustrating and worrying day had worn her out and brought her own fears tumbling back.

When this job was over, she'd be a sitting target. She

would arrive back on Chenon, in cryo, a pre-packed victim, unable to protect herself. And Ben would be just as vulnerable as she was. He was probably on the hit list, too; guilt by association. How convenient if neither of them woke up after the journey home. Ari could swing that. A bribe in the right place. A slight alteration in the dosage of the resuscitation drugs, and . . . end of problem. Even the transport home was vulnerable to attack.

She listened for Ben's breathing on the far side of the room and reached out with her mind. He was deeply asleep, exhausted. In all the time they'd been sharing quarters he'd never made a pass at her. If he did, would she turn him away? She couldn't deny a certain attraction, and—dammit—she felt guilty. If it wasn't for her, he'd have his choice of any of the single women on the psi-tech teams.

She felt guilty, too, for not telling Ben her suspicions about Gen and Max. This Coburg-Fenec thing had been magnified out of all proportion. If Gen and Max got caught doing the same, however, the shit would really hit the fan!

She forced herself to take a deep breath. All her unconnected fears crowded in on her. She should forget conjecture, concentrate on missing teammates, and not let the memories of Ari mess with her mind. Ronan said her memories were much closer to the surface now, but in some ways that made it harder.

Quietly she slipped out from under the quilt and pulled off her sweat-soaked sleepsuit. She hated wearing anything in bed, but sleeping naked was not an option, though she knew that Ben did. He was as unselfconscious about his body as she would normally be, but in this artificial situation that existed between them, she was discovering unexpected hang-ups.

Her bare feet made no sound on the cool floor, and the washroom door slid back with barely a whisper of noise. The shower's only sound was the spray of water on skin and walls. She let it wash away some of her fears as she massaged tense muscles with soapy gel. Old-fashioned showers might not be as efficient as fresher units, but she enjoyed them more.

She toweled her short-cropped hair dry and risked a couple of minutes under the blower, figuring that, if she hadn't woken Ben already, he would probably sleep through the soft hiss of warm air. Feeling much better, she padded back into the bedroom quietly, trying not to disturb him. She left the shower door open and the light on a timer to provide a soft glow for a few minutes.

She was still a little tense and she couldn't face climbing back in between the sweaty sheets, but she didn't want to start stripping them off right now. That really would wake Ben and he needed to be fresh for tomorrow. She pulled the covers back to air the bed and slowly and silently began to go through a relaxation routine, first with head and neck, circling round to find out where the knots were, then with back, shoulders and arms. Bending, stretching, tightening, relaxing.

There was no sound, but instinctively she knew that Ben was awake and watching. Aware of the fact that she was still naked, she reached for her sleepsuit.

"No. Don't do that."

She stopped in mid-movement.

"I was just enjoying the floor show. I'm not a monk, you know." There was a catch in his voice, but it could just have been the aftereffects of deep sleep.

A tremor of anticipation ran through her. What if she could forget Ari van Blaiden for one night? Her belly knotted with longing for Ben's arms around her, holding back the darkness.

"I know."

He propped himself up on one elbow and reached for the light, but only turned up the globe far enough to warm the room gently.

"Your skin looks like gold."

"I'm sorry. I didn't mean to wake you." She tried to ignore his eyes.

He sighed almost inaudibly. "It would have been a shame to sleep through that."

"I'm sorry."

"What for? Having a beautiful body?"

"For not sharing it."

He shrugged. "It wasn't part of the deal."

"Neither was keeping up this marriage sham for so long. You could find someone else if it wasn't for me."

"I don't want anyone else."

"You don't want me." She said it a little too quickly.

"I never said that."

"You need someone who can give you more than I can. Not just a body."

He was silent. He was a good man, a kind man, and he was her friend. When had that friendship become more? Had she even realized it before this moment?

"You've done so much for me, and I've given you nothing but problems." She moved over to his bedside and knelt down so that her face was just below the level of his, close enough to smell the warm, clean man-smell.

"Do you want me in your bed?" she asked.

He raised himself on one elbow, leaned over and put his arm round the back of her head, drawing her face to him. He kissed her lips very gently. "If I thought you wanted it, too, then my answer would be different. Go back to your own bed and let me get back to sleep before I change my mind."

She went.

✦ ✦ ✦

The alert came when Ben was deeply asleep; not quite dreaming, but holding to the memory of Cara, naked with dark shadows against her lamplit skin. It brought back memories of that night on Mirrimar-14.

Her voice shattered the image and rattled round his brain.

"Ben. There's a riot at the med-center. Settlers—looking for Coburg."

For an instant he didn't know where he was, but then his training took over. Adrenaline surged, and his mind cleared. He rolled upright and reached for his buddysuit just as Cara was reaching for hers. The other psi-techs were awake and staggering out of their quarters in varying stages of readiness. Cara kept a mental link open for Ben.

Emergency posts, he broadcast to all the psi-techs in Landing. *If rioting spreads, make sure that the base is secure. Fall back to the LV. Wenna, you know the drill.*

Backward, Boss. Don't worry.

Ben left Wenna to hold everything together in the LV. She wouldn't let him down.

Gupta, scramble. Teams one to five on the ground. The rest of you on aerial standby. Defense only. No aggression. Is that understood?

Gupta understood.

Everyone knew their places and moved quickly and efficiently.

Anna? Ben turned his attention to the med-center via Cara's connection.

As they tried to home in on Anna, they were hit by a wash of emotion.

Bastards. Anna's disjointed thoughts rang out. *Do something, for pity's sake. Oh! Bastards!*

Anna's thoughts cut off abruptly. Cara stumbled and Ben almost tripped over her. They looked at each other, each deeply aware that something was terribly wrong.

In the few minutes it took them to reach the med-center, it was all over. There were still people milling about, but the prime movers behind the riot had fled, leaving a trail of devastation and bodies.

Too many bodies.

Anna Govan lay where she had fallen in the entrance. Someone had tried to straighten her limbs. She looked surprised. There was a tiny entry wound in the center of her forehead, a jet pistol by the look of it, a clean shot. Someone knew how to handle the illegal weapon.

Ben shoved down the rising wave of anger.

The med-center doors had been smashed down. Another body was slumped close to Anna. Don Cooksey, one of Gupta's maintenance men. He looked like he'd been felled with a blow to the head, but not before he'd pumped anesthetic darts into four rioters. They'd probably wake up, but for now Ben didn't need to worry about them. There were a few psi-techs standing and sitting outside in a state of shock, as if they couldn't quite believe what had happened.

One of the med-techs was sobbing unashamedly while another tried to comfort him.

Gupta's men secured the building. The medics were already doing what they could to help the walking wounded.

Coburg was past all help, though. The young man's body, stripped and mutilated, dangled from a wire noose lashed to the arm of the stolen earth mover that they'd used to break down the door. A small fire burned below him, licking at his bare toes. He was past knowing.

Cara gave a small cry and closed off their mental connection. She turned away, and he could hear her retching.

Ben's guts were also trying to rise and choke him at the sight of Coburg's contorted face and bloody body, but he couldn't turn away. This was another death to carry.

Body count: three, he thought bleakly. I've killed three more. But it wasn't just bodies, it was individuals. He hadn't known Coburg well, but Cooksey had survived Hera-3. Not a close friend, but tied by a common experience. And Anna . . . He'd known Anna almost as long as he'd been in the service. For years she'd been talking about retiring to write up her research on mining diseases. Just one more mission, she'd told him. How many missions ago was that?

Serafin turned away from Coburg and shifted uneasily. "I wish I hadn't made that remark about cutting off his tackle with a rusty razor."

"I'll take him down," Gupta said.

"No!" Ben held out his hand. "Put a guard around him and bring Lorient here as quickly as possible. Make sure Jack Mario is with him and Mrs. Lorient."

"Mrs. Lorient?" Gupta was surprised. "This is hardly a sight for someone like her."

"That's precisely why I want her to see this," Ben said. "She can put pressure on Lorient more subtly and surely than we can."

"We've got some of the culprits." Gupta indicated the unconscious rioters. "None of them has any illegal weaponry, though. I'm going to enjoy talking to them when they come to."

"We need to know if Lorient was behind this," Ben said.

"I need proof. See if you can get me any firm evidence." He turned to the med-techs. "Who's senior here?"

"I am." Mel Hoffner looked up from where she'd been kneeling to check one of the unconscious rioters. "Until Ronan gets back anyway."

Oh, gods, he was going to have to tell Ronan that he'd got a promotion for the worst possible reason.

"Are you all right, Mel?"

"I'm not injured."

"That's not what I asked."

"I . . ." She looked toward Anna. "She stood between them and the rest of us, and they just shot her down."

"I know. I'm sorry to have to ask, but I need the ordnance from the murder weapon. You'll need to do a post mortem. On Don Cooksey, too, though cause of death looks pretty obvious."

She cleared her throat. "I'll see to it."

Cara came back to his side looking pale in the harsh floodlights.

"We won't forget this," Ben said. "But, right now, we have to contain this violence."

"And what if we can't contain it?" she asked softly.

"We can. We have to," Ben said. "There are three hundred lives at stake—two hundred and ninety seven, anyway. I'm not losing *this* team. If our situation here becomes totally untenable, we'll pull out after the second ark arrives with the rest of the settlers. We don't have the means to leave before then."

He didn't mention the Dixie Flyer. It was a last resort. But all of a sudden he was glad it was there, not for himself, but for the possibilities it offered.

✦ ✦ ✦

Cara wondered if it was Ben's Monitor training that enabled him to appear outwardly unflustered. She knew how angry he was, but he seemed to be able to push it aside and direct Gupta's men to secure the area and preserve evidence: images, measurements, DNA, prints, and witness statements.

Cara returned to her seat on the med-center steps and

stared at the ground until Ben halted by her feet and waited until she looked up.

"All right?" he asked.

"Better than he is." She kept her eyes averted from Coburg's gently swinging corpse. "Or Anna or—oh, I don't even know the name of Gupta's man. How terrible."

"Don Cooksey. He was one of my Hera-3 survivors."

Should she be surprised that Ben still felt proprietorial about that group of individuals, as if they were his continuing responsibility.

"A waste of a good life." Ben dropped down onto the step beside her. "Sorry to have to ask, but when the Lorients arrive, I want you to monitor their underlying feelings if you can."

"Am I looking for anything in particular?"

"A lack of surprise would be interesting."

"I'm on it." She straightened her shoulders.

"Thank you."

The sound of a groundcar announced the Lorients' arrival. About time. Ben stood up and heard Cara rise behind him.

"Ben ..."

He turned, glancing back over his shoulder.

"You won't do anything rash, will you?"

"Don't you trust me?"

"With my life, but . . ." She inclined her head toward Coburg then Anna and Cooksey. "They're yours and you always protect your own."

"I didn't do a very good job tonight."

"It's not your fault."

"I told myself that after Hera-3. It didn't help."

She reached out and rested her hand on his arm. He put his own hand on hers.

"Don't worry about me. I won't lose it." He took a deep breath. "You steady me. You know that, don't you?"

"I can hardly steady myself most of the time."

"You underestimate yourself."

❖ ❖ ❖

The groundcar drew to a halt, rocking gently on its antigravs before settling gently. Victor Lorient was first out of the front passenger seat. "What's all this about, Benjamin? Your man wouldn't say anything, only that it was important. An incident. Couldn't it wait until morning? I—"

"Good God in Heaven!" Jack Mario had held the ground-car door for Rena Lorient, but he stood frozen as Ben nodded to Gupta and two portable spotlights flashed on, illuminating Coburg.

Rena Lorient, emerging from the car, didn't quite scream, but her squeal of shock was audible across the compound. She reached out for her husband, but he was already striding toward the corpse and Jack caught her hand instead.

"What happened?" Jack sounded genuinely shaken.

"Justice by the looks of it." Lorient turned, and his eyes were bright.

Ben had never wanted to put his fist into someone's face as badly as he did at that moment. As if Cara knew, she moved up to stand right by his shoulder, her arm touching his. He let his anger sink back to a simmer.

"A riot. Your Ecolibrians." He waited for their reactions and glanced at Cara. "They went through Anna Govan and Don Cooksey to get to him. They killed the doctor that saved your son's life."

Jack and Rena knew nothing about it, Cara said. *I'm getting shock and horror from both of them. Jack's feelings are shot through with anger, Rena's with bewilderment.*

Good. As I'd hoped. What about Lorient?

Lorient had halted in front of Coburg's dangling corpse. He had his back to them, but that wouldn't hinder Cara's empathic abilities.

He felt Cara lean against him and he reached for her hand. She was trembling. *He's fucking excited. The bastard! Almost got a hard-on.*

He squeezed her hand. *Sorry. Can you stick with him? Did he plan this?*

I don't think so, but he's glad it happened. Stirred up resentment and hoped for a result would be my best guess. He's so focused on Coburg that he hasn't even taken in the two other deaths.

Thanks. I get the picture.

Hard to miss him. He's a high-reader. Emotions very near the surface. I've noticed it before, but never this clearly.

"What can we do to . . . help?" Jack had folded Rena back into the groundcar and walked over to Ben and Cara. "I'm so sorry. This is terrible. There must be something . . . Did Coburg have family? And, Doctor Govan . . . I'm deeply sorry. She was a good person. And the other man, Cooksey."

"Coburg has parents on Chenon. They'll have to be informed . . . probably not the detail. Anna Govan has an elderly sister still living, on Ferrina colony, I believe. Cooksey lost his wife a few years ago on Hera-3. He's been alone since then."

"Please express regrets of the colony administration. A few hotheads. We'll take steps to find out who."

Ben liked Jack Mario. He was the real brains behind the settlement plan. If only the politics of the situation would allow him to work with Jack and bypass Lorient altogether, but able as he was, Jack never seemed able to stand up to Lorient.

"We've got some of the culprits. Hopefully, when they wake, we'll discover the ringleaders."

Lorient turned, and Ben felt Cara flinch.

Go and wait in the med-center, he told her.

I'll stick it out.

He felt a rush of admiration for her. It wasn't easy for Empaths in a confrontation situation. He damped his own anger down even further so he didn't contribute to her problem.

"Director Lorient." Ben waited for Lorient to come to him. "Do you want to send someone to sit in when we interview the suspects?"

"Suspects?"

Ben explained about the anesthetized rioters.

"I want to see them."

"They're still out cold."

"I still want to see them."

Ben led him into the accident and emergency unit inside the med-center where four sleepers lay on gurneys.

"I don't know them," Lorient said, trying to hide the relief in his voice.

That's true, Cara said.

"You must have a fair idea who did this."

"No. No idea at all." He quickly turned away, avoiding eye contact.

"We do expect that you will deal with this, Director. Otherwise we will have to, and you don't want that."

"You have no legal jurisdiction here, Benjamin. None. It's our colony. You'll release those four to my associates."

"Erich Coburg was my responsibility, as were Anna Govan and Don Cooksey." Ben schooled his voice to a growl. "If I dragged the culprits back to Chenon in body pods, I would have interstellar law on my side. Don't think I won't do it if I have to."

"Of course we'll seek out the ringleaders." Jack Mario eased himself between the two men, ignoring, for once, Lorient's scowl.

"See that you do," Ben said.

As Lorient stepped inside the groundcar, Ben called Jack back. "What's the size of the problem, Jack? How many rabid fundamentalists does Lorient have? It seems to me that most of your settlers are reasonable people trying to get on with their own lives, but if this is what Lorient's fundies are capable of, we need to stop them now."

"Not as many as you might think, but they tend to be the ones who are hanging around Timbertown. They attend a lot more of the director's meetings and it reinforces a very negative message."

Ben stepped back for now. Maybe Jack just needed a small infusion of backbone and the will to stand up to Victor more firmly. This was a step in the right direction. He watched them climb back into the groundcar and give the driver the nod to leave.

"Do you think they will investigate?" Cara asked.

"I think Jack will try, but Lorient will protect his hardcore. I don't think there are many of them, but they stir up the easily led. I suspect the four that we've got are the led rather than the leaders."

"So what do we do? Are you going to release them to Lorient?"

"For now, but tag them with a subcutaneous tracking device so we can pick them up again when we need to. Gather evidence at the scene." He nodded to Gupta. "Take Mr. Coburg down now, please."

Gupta began to direct his team.

"Come on," Ben said, holding his hand out to Cara. "Let's go. We've got an early start in the morning. Gupta knows what he's doing."

He was quite surprised, but gratified, when she took it.

Chapter Twenty-three

SEARCH

BEN ROUSED BEFORE FIRST LIGHT, THOUGH he wasn't actually sure he'd had any significant amount of sleep. He had a jumbled memory of alternately staring at nothing, eyes wide open in the velvet-black darkness, or staring at the inside of his eyelids waiting for the blessed relief of sleep that never came. When he did doze, he saw Coburg's mutilated corpse or Anna's smiling face and heard her reassuring voice while staring in horror at the small round wound in the center of her forehead.

He was glad to dress and join the small flotilla heading for Ronan's base camp. Cara was already up and out of their room. He suspected she'd had a sleepless night as well. Ben piloted a two-man flitter with Cara at his side, holding open communications for the four flitters preparing to fly regular search patterns over rough terrain.

"How are you feeling this morning?" Ben asked.

She sighed. "Numb, but I won't let it interfere with the job."

He adjusted course and nodded. "I know we have a bit of a strange personal relationship, but I probably don't always remember to say that I'm very lucky to have you as a working partner, even if I don't always know what makes you tick."

"Should I take that as a compliment?"

"You should."

They were approaching the mountains when Cas patched through a call from Wenna. Cara held the link.

Ben. Wenna was agitated, her telepathic ability weakened by the distance. *Lorient's upset about Gupta asking questions. He says he expects you to be in his office by nightfall.*

Not possible. Tell him you're in charge, Ben said.

He's likely to try and call you. Be warned.

Thanks, Wenna. It's times like this when I'm grateful for this planet's EM interference. I really don't think I want to talk to him today.

Right on cue the radio link crackled.

Ben sighed. "At least it's only audio. I don't think I could stomach the sight of the self-righteous bastard turning purple at the other end of a video link." He made another minor course correction. "I've made every effort to placate Lorient up to now, but I'm running out of patience. There are three people who probably need medical attention, stuck halfway up a mountain. I'm not about to abandon this search in favor of going to a meeting with a megalomaniac."

Cara hit connect.

"Benjamin." The comm line crackled with ill-concealed malevolence. "Why didn't you tell me there was an emergency situation involving one of your psi-techs and one of my settlers? I have a right to know. Marling and Constant. Are the two of them alone together?"

"They were working together, that's all. We're taking a rescue team in now."

"But they are alone?"

There it was, the not-so-hidden subtext.

"You forced the volunteers on us, Director. Constant is actually one of the more useful ones. Don't be surprised when we give him a job to do." Ben's voice was still remarkably calm, given the way he felt. "Constant is with Gen and Lee Gardham. No need to worry."

"You can say that after Coburg?"

"Especially after Coburg. You're not trying to tell me that the Fenec girl was unwilling, are you?"

"Do you want to bring her before the council to find out?"   •

Didn't this man learn anything from last night? Cara flashed the comment across to Ben.

Apparently not.

Ben continued with Lorient's call. "Let it lie, now, Director. There's been enough unrest already."

"Don't try that one on me, Benjamin. Crowder told me I could trust you, but that's the problem, I don't trust any of you."

Cara saw Ben's knuckles whiten as he clenched them on the flitter controls. He took a deep breath. "Director Lorient. I think everyone needs to cool off. This mission will take as long as it takes. In the meantime, I'm going to pull my staff out of Timbertown, and I want you to take some time to calm your settlers down."

"Are you giving me orders, Benjamin?"

"I have the authority to take every one of my psi-techs off this planet if lives are in danger." Ben hoped that Lorient was getting this message loud and clear. "I'd say that last night was a pretty good indication that there is very little goodwill between your people and mine. Unless you want us to leave your settlers to sink or swim alone, I suggest you ease up."

"Is that a threat?"

"What do you think?"

Ben cut the comm-link and groaned. "What have I done?" He shook his head and rubbed his forehead with the fingertips of his left hand. "That was dumb. I should have sucked up to him again. That's what Crowder would have done."

"You don't know what Crowder would have done. He's not here and you are. I know how much you've bitten your tongue to keep Victor Lorient sweet. I don't think even Crowder would have had this much patience."

"Last night, when I saw Coburg hanging there, I wanted to smash my fist into Lorient's face. I still want to." Ben put both hands over his eyes. "I'm really not cut out to be a diplomat."

"But you didn't do it. You went for the best option."

Cara reached across and touched the back of his hand. He turned his hand over and grasped her fingers.

"Thanks. Moment of weakness over. We've got a job to do."

"Hey, if you need another moment of weakness anytime, I'm around."

He smiled at her. "I know. Thanks."

"It's not much, after all you've done for me."

"I'm not keeping a tally." He let go of her hand. "Someone's going to have to jolly Lorient along for a few days. Get hold of Saedi Sugrue. Tell her to find Jack Mario and have him contact me on a secure mechanical link. I might get some sense out of him."

Jack Mario came through within a few minutes.

"Jack. We've still got problems. You and I need to talk."

"You might be right." Jack sounded guarded, but there was something in his tone that gave a slight opening.

Ben took the opportunity that was offered. "Jack, I need to buy some time without your boss going off the deep end."

Jack made a noncommittal sound, but he certainly didn't spring to Lorient's defense. It must be bad if Jack was backing off.

"Have you got problems, too, Jack?"

"Look, is this conversation private? I mean like just me and you?" Jack asked.

"Cara's here. That's as good as private. She knows everything I know."

"I shouldn't be talking this way, Ben, but last night sickened me and it sickened quite a few others as well. We're not all fanatics, you know."

"I've told Lorient I can pull my people off planet. And I will, if I must."

"No!" Jack was obviously alarmed at the idea. "We need you here for the full term of your contract if we're going to have a chance of anything like a decent life in the first years of this settlement. You know that as well as I do. Even the director knows it. And the people—most of them—really appreciate the help you've given them."

"Lorient forgets very quickly when it suits him."

"He's confident that we'll succeed against any odds, but he's not always practical."

"He's starting to believe his own publicity. Jack. If the director isn't . . ." He paused, searching for the right word. "If he isn't *well*, perhaps he should stand down as leader, temporarily, of course."

"I hear what you're saying, but I couldn't force him to do that. He's up and down—erratic—but the man's a genius when he's working a crowd. Most of the settlers are here because they followed him back on Earth. They're looking to him as their head. What he says goes."

"Are you going to be able to calm the situation down a bit?"

"Mrs. Lorient and I are trying our best. She doesn't say much, but she's well aware of the problems. A lot of people go to her instead of to the director, especially the women. She has a natural bond with them. Not flashy like the director's but very real. She doesn't want to be disloyal, but last night's incident scared her."

"It didn't do much for me, either. Look, Jack, if you can do anything to keep the lid on this situation, I'd appreciate it."

"I don't know how long I can give you."

"Do your best. Wenna Phipps is the one to talk to while I'm not there, but if you need me, then contact me through Saedi Sugrue. You can trust her."

"Yes, I know. I'll do what I can," Jack said.

✦ ✦ ✦

The flitter droned onward through the morning. It had been a long night, and there was the prospect of an even longer day. Cara watched the rolling land below. It had ceased to look alien to her already. Even the broc trees looked normal.

And right now she wanted to see normal things.

She didn't want to think about last night, but Coburg's mutilated body seemed to be strung up just behind her eyelids and Anna's sightless eyes stared over her shoulder. She didn't need that right now; she needed to concentrate on Gen and Max.

She didn't let herself think about the possibility of finding a crash site and more corpses, especially if one of them was one of Lorient's settlers. As they flew steadily north, Cara continued to send out a steady stream of inquiry aimed at Gen, but couldn't raise her. They were in the shadow of the mountain range before there was a fluttering reply.

"Ben, I've got Gen! She's weak, but I've got her."

Cara brought Ben into the communication. "Can you get a fix?" he asked.

"I need a Finder." *Sami?*

Sami Isaksten was their best psi-tech Finder.

Here. She replied at once from one of the search-grid flitters.

I've got contact with Gen. Can you get a trace on her?

I'll try my best. Sami slipstreamed into Cara's link with Gen.

Okay, Gen, take it easy, Ben said through Cara. *Status report, please.*

Transport wrecked. Max . . . broken ribs I think. Bashed head, hurts, headache.

By the confusion, Cara took it that Gen was the one with the head injury.

Location? she asked.

North. Gen was positive on that one. She was, like Ben, a Navigator, not as talented in the "human compass" department as he was, but still sure of herself. *Northeast of where we left the shepherds. Ten klicks. Caves.*

Ben dismissed the rest of the search vehicles and alerted Ronan. Two rescue flitters and a medevac transport came together over the foothills and followed the course of a sharply defined valley into the mountains. Sami, tracking mentally, gave constant directions until they came to a spot surrounded by almost sheer rock walls. At the far side, a waterfall plunged down from the mountainside above.

They landed a safe distance away from the wreckage of the airbus. To one side was a sad, lonely shape laid out and wrapped in a survival blanket. Cara saw the body. Lee. Gen had not mentioned Lee. She'd been hoping against hope that it was because the gentle veterinarian was alive and well and not in any immediate danger, but Cara knew firsthand what concussion could do to a psi-tech's brain. It was possible Gen didn't even realize Lee was dead.

She heard Ben groan beside her. One more death for him to carry. He shouldn't, but she knew he would. She touched his hand and received a mute squeeze of the fingers in return.

A whistle from beyond the falls attracted their attention. Max stood by a cave mouth.

The flitters settled into their antigravs in neat formation close to the pool. Ronan emerged from the medevac vehicle. Leaving Sami with Lee, Ben and Cara followed Ronan to the cave. The young medic looked pale. Losing Anna was a hell of a way to get a promotion to chief medic. Cara could sense he'd bottled up his feelings, and she didn't intrude.

Max met them at the cave mouth.

"I'm sorry . . . about Lee. I couldn't do anything. I pulled Gen out."

Ben put his hand on Max's shoulder. "Let's see to the living first and then worry about the dead."

If you were going to get stranded anywhere, then finding a cave like this was pretty lucky. The floor was sandy and level and there was a smallish entrance leading to a large chamber. In the womb of the cave, Gen lay on a springy mattress made of vegetation stuffed into one of the emergency sleep-sacks. Max had rigged a light, using a power pack and parts cannibalized from the airbus, but even a soft glow seemed to hurt Gen's eyes, so it was positioned well away.

Ronan glanced at Max as he knelt to check Gen. "How are you?"

"I think I've cracked a couple of ribs. My chest hurts like hell, but if there was any lung damage, I'd probably know about it by now."

"You sure would. Here's a pain blocker. It'll make you more comfortable while you're waiting for me to finish with Gen."

He tossed a blast pack in Max's direction and turned his attention to Gen. "Cara, can you monitor me?" he asked.

Cara linked to him while he investigated Gen. He searched mentally for the injuries that were most in need of healing. Cara never lost her admiration for those who could direct their implant to tap into the electrical energy of someone's body and redirect the flow to enable the body to heal itself. It was easy for a Healer to lose himself in the job; to put too much energy into the task and drain himself.

Gen had a deep cut on her forehead, which was inflamed and puffy. Her right hand was severely bruised, probably with a couple of broken fingers. Max had strapped it up and now Ronan checked it, pronounced it satisfactory for the time being, and shaped a protective smart-case around it.

Throughout the examination Max stayed by Gen. She wouldn't let go of him with her good hand. Cara's guts began to churn. It had gone beyond a quick sexual fling. Gen couldn't hide her emotion while she was in this condition. It was coming off her in waves. As the shots began to take effect, Gen relaxed and let go, but Ben had noticed; Cara could read it in his face.

Ronan was deep in concentration now, not looking at Gen's external injuries, but using his psi-tech talents to explore for internal damage. Monitoring nerve and tissue, blood and bone, putting in a fix, where he could. Cara was following him, not really understanding Gen's internal workings but sensing Ronan's connection and the power flow. She crouched down by Ronan's shoulder in the cave, almost unaware of her own body until Ronan straightened up suddenly and, with a wrench, separated his mind from Cara's. She rocked back on her heels and landed on her backside.

"What's wrong?" She scrambled to her knees and shuffled forward, heart thumping.

"Nothing, sorry," Ronan said. Just a blip. "Going in again."

Cara linked and this time the exam concentrated on Gen's concussion.

Max was not familiar with this kind of treatment and he was agitated, giving away his feelings with every twitch, every look. It was just what she'd feared. They didn't need more complications after the Coburg-Fenec fiasco.

"Outside. Now!" Ben's temper had snapped. He grabbed hold of Max by the arm and almost shoved him out into the open air toward the waterfall where their voices would not be heard by the medic. Cara waited until Ronan had finished his examination, then followed. She had things of her own to say to Max Constant. Ben wasn't going to have all the pleasure of chewing him out. How could Gen have been so stupid after all the warnings? If this got out, neither Gen nor Max would be safe on Olyanda.

◆ ◆ ◆

Ben wasn't in a mood to take any bullshit. Lee's loss was still echoing in his brain—four people dead in two days—and now it seemed as though there was something going on here that was about to make life supremely difficult for everybody. "Okay, let's have the whole story." He felt like a parent whose son has just come home after an escapade. The first reaction was to yell at him for causing a fright, even when you knew you should be offering support.

"What?" Max tried hard, but it wouldn't work.

Ben wanted to punch him. "Don't play innocent with me, Constant. You and Gen."

"We're teammates."

Ben heard Cara come up behind them. He could tell she was angry—so angry he was surprised her footprints didn't sizzle. "I suspected you two, but I didn't think it had gone this far," she said.

"How far?" Ben asked Cara while never taking his eyes off Max.

"They're in love. Honest-to-goodness love." Cara nearly choked on the word.

"I do love her." Max said it in a defiant love-can-cure-everything type of voice.

Ben waved a hand to quiet him. "Before you start to yell that from the rooftops, let me tell you about Erich Coburg."

Throughout the story Max's face grew increasingly pale.

"Now do you see the problem?" Ben asked.

He swallowed hard. "It doesn't make any difference to me and her," Max said.

Before Ben could say anything else, Cara snapped. "That makes it better, does it? You're a selfish bastard." She was right in Constant's face, "You could have stopped this before it started. What happens to her after all this?"

He didn't reply.

"I'll tell you what happens. It's not enough that she loses you. She keeps thinking how unhappy you are, too. And not a thing in this universe can keep you together. Nothing. Then she loses her career. Then she falls apart, piece by piece." Cara was white-lipped and shaking with anger. Ben had never seen her like this.

"That's what happened to you, wasn't it?" Max said. Ben's attention swung from Max to Cara.

She turned, still angry. There were tears in her eyes. "No, that's not what happened to me. I didn't fall apart . . . I was ground into dust." She stormed off.

"That's what you get for messing with Ari van Blaiden," Max said, almost to himself.

"Ari van Blaiden?" Ben turned on Max, anger over Gen temporarily pushed aside.

"Cara's ex." He looked at Ben. "You didn't know?"

Things began to click into place. "Tell me."

"I worked for Alphacorp back on Earth. York office, accounts department. I processed her credit transfers and heard the gossip. You don't forget a face like Cara Carlinni's or a presence like van Blaiden's. I was surprised when van Blaiden ordered a stop on her wages.

"I didn't like to say anything when I recognized her here. I thought she might have been kicked out of Alphacorp, but I reckoned that was her own business."

A whole lot of questions dissolved into answers. Ari van Blaiden. She *was* in trouble. They were both in trouble.

✦ ✦ ✦

Cara sat on a rock and tossed pebbles into the turbulent pool at the base of the waterfall. With each disappearing pebble she cursed the power of love.

Ben came up beside her. She stared straight ahead and continued to toss pebbles, one by one.

He sat next to her and reached out one hand. She put a few pebbles into it from the small pile she'd collected, and he tossed one into the water.

"Is Max all right?" she asked.

"You were tougher on him than I was."

"Yes, sorry, it wasn't my place."

"That's okay, if you hadn't been so mad at him, I might have lost it altogether. That was a pretty good show you put on back there."

"It wasn't—a show, I mean."

"I've never seen you let go quite like that."

He threw another pebble.

"You should have told me about Gen and Max."

"It wasn't my place. I had no proof."

"You could have told me what you suspected."

"Go running to the boss? I made that mistake once before."

Her head began to feel muzzy. The warning signs that she was getting too close to betraying Ari and his business. Damn, She really wished she could get it out into the open. Ronan said she was ready, but she didn't feel ready.

"Do you want to tell me?" Ben's voice was gentle. She almost fell into it.

"You know I can't."

"Can't."

"That's right. Can't. Look, I don't like the thought that someone messed with my head, but it seems that they did."

"What can be put in there can be taken out again."

"Yeah. Right."

"When you get back . . ."

"If."

"When!"

"I'm going to collect my pay and hit the first ship for the Rim."

She tossed another pebble into the water. When she turned to look at him, he'd gone.

Everyone was busy with Lee's body and with Gen and Max. Cara wandered back into Gen's cave. They'd been lucky to find shelter, and Max wasn't bad for a rookie settler. He'd managed to rig up a small light using the emergency power pack in the airbus. Cara began to retrieve bits of scattered equipment, leaving the light until last. When she disconnected it, the cave was plunged into darkness. She reached for the cuff-light on her buddysuit. It stabbed into the blackness, illuminating a bright circle on the back wall of the cave. She stopped, frozen by the sight of the half-exposed nodes.

Her heart began to pound.

Platinum.

◆ ◆ ◆

Cara and Ben barely spoke to each other for the whole of the return journey. Ben had been in that cave. He was an experienced surveyor. He'd had every opportunity to discover the platinum, yet he hadn't said anything. What was he up to?

It was a tight-lipped little party that returned to Landing.

Tests confirmed Ronan's diagnosis of a serious concussion. Gen would make a complete recovery, but needed rest and quiet. Once that was established, Ronan didn't question Ben's request to move Gen back to her own room. Cas arranged for a Psi-3 or above to be on duty at all times to monitor her and, if necessary, to engage an isolation bubble that would prevent both intrusion from the outside and accidental spillage of Gen's thoughts while she was in her weakened state.

Gen couldn't concentrate properly or stand loud noises and she was tired all the time, but Ronan said that was normal. Emotional instability was also to be expected and, with the situation as it was at present, Ben tried to forestall problems by keeping her well away from outsiders.

Cara was the only person who could give Gen a shoulder to cry on. She wished this hadn't been forced on her, but once Ben had taken the decision to try and cover up the breach of discipline rather than punish it, Gen couldn't talk to anyone not already in on the secret. She had bouts of tearful depression. Even in her more sensible moments she was miserable. Cara had listened quietly at first, well aware of what a concussion felt like, but she was rapidly running out of patience. She wasn't the type of person to help anyone sort out their own feelings. Dammit! She couldn't even sort out her own most of the time.

"How's it going?" Cara let herself into Gen's room on the second day.

"Headache." Gen was sitting in the armchair with her knees drawn up under her chin—close enough for Cara to reach out and touch. Her skin held a grayish cast, and her black hair hung, limp and lifeless. She was allowed out of bed now as long as the room was kept dim and quiet.

"Have you taken . . ."

"Everything Ronan will give me. I keep trying to remember what happened. The crash, I mean, but I can't. I've got a few strange pictures in my head. Broken birds. Scaly imprints against the glass of the bubble. I hear Lee Gardham shout a warning in my head, and then . . . then nothing. I remember Max was there, though; whenever I woke up, he was there. He held my hand all the time and . . ." Tears began to roll down Gen's cheeks. She scrubbed them away with a fist. "I can't stand it anymore. I can't bear to think that I won't see Max again once he leaves for the coast. Ben's sending him to Seaward Base, you know. I'd give anything—anything—to get a return passage to Chenon for him. Would Ben . . ."

"It's too late to get a cryo unit for him."

"There will be spare . . . now . . . with Lee and Coburg . . ."

"Implant-wired. Suitable for psi-techs only."

"They could be reprogrammed."

"Risky without the right equipment. Do you want to get home and find a nine-month corpse where Max ought to be? Of course you don't." Lorient had insisted on no return routes for his settlers. He knew that some might want to jump ship, so he'd left no loopholes.

"There must be something."

"Maybe if Max was willing to put up with nine months of staring at the inside of a cabin with the ark crew."

"I'm sure he will."

"Better wait until Ben's in a better mood before you suggest it."

Cara shook her head, her own frustration rising. Gen was an intelligent woman. She'd had plenty of adult relationships. How come she'd thrown it all away for a smooth-faced settler with a sense of humor?

"You know, you're damn lucky Ben is covering this up for you." Cara perched on the end of the bed. "He's even giving you the opportunity to say good-bye to Max. It's more than I'd have done. I'd have had Constant out of here so fast he'd have beaten his own feet to Seaward Base."

"You don't know what it's like."

"No?" Cara tried to hide the rush of pain that she still felt when she thought of Ari. "Even if you're separated, you have the consolation of knowing that he loves you."

"That's supposed to be a consolation?"

"You'd prefer it if he didn't?"

Gen reached over and took her hand. "What is it? Ben?"

She shook her head. "You know what our situation is. Ben's never been anything but fair." Fair in their personal relationship anyway. She wasn't sure about the platinum thing. She'd given him a chance to mention it, but he hadn't. Was Ben as bad as Ari? Was Ari really all that bad?

"I thought you two were . . . you know. Ben's a good guy. I should know. Is there someone else?"

"Something like that."

"Someone you love?"

"No! I don't know . . . It was much more complicated than that. I can't help thinking that I might be drawn to him if I saw him again, even though I know it's the worst thing that could possibly happen. I don't know what love is anymore." The muzziness started to build up in Cara's head again. It's all right, she told herself. She was talking about feelings, not about Ari. Just feelings.

Chapter Twenty-four

DOUBTS

"GET ME THE GRAIN STOCK FIGURES." VICTOR Lorient pushed his chair back and rubbed his eyes. "Let's find out why no one has mentioned it." He turned and stared out of his office window into the busy street below. Timbertown was starting to feel like a real town. He wished the rest of this year was over and the psi-techs were well and truly gone from Olyanda. Then he sighed. He could wish all he damn-well liked; there was still over half their term to run. Benjamin had him backed up against a wall. Both Jack and Rena had persuaded him, individually— though he suspected them of collusion—to preach forgiveness and tolerance.

"Victor, dear, this is Jack's job. He's already checked the figures twice." Rena placed a bound ledger on the desk. "The stocks are all accounted for. There's less in store because two settlements needed resupplying after the storms."

"So Benjamin said, but why did he shuttle up to the ark ship to check a shortage. Did he go up there to alter the manifests?"

"It was months ago. You only have rumor to go on."

"And rumor of an extra grain shipment, which should have been here by now."

"Everyone has what they need."

"What about the psi-techs? The grasping bastards have hung onto all their grain. I think they're shorting us on live-stock, too."

"There's no reason they should."

"Them being them and us being us is reason enough. Get Jack in here and get rid of that spy in his office."

"There's no . . . Oh, you mean Saedi. She's only here as a comm-link. She's a very pleasant young woman. Very help-ful."

"Get rid of her."

✦   ✦   ✦

Cara woke and listened to the sounds of the room. Ben's breathing was deep and regular, a comfortable pattern. At least, it had been comfortable once, but now she found it irritating. No, irritating wasn't the word. She thought around the problem and had to admit to herself that she just wasn't comfortable with *Ben* anymore.

With all the important safety concerns for the whole mis-sion, Cara felt mean allowing something personal to eat at her, but in the three days since their return she'd watched Ben when she thought he wasn't aware of it. He hadn't logged the possibility of platinum at the mountain site. The recorder from the crashed airbus had mysteriously disap-peared, though she knew it was there when they first exam-ined the wreck. She'd seen it.

Was he trying to cover up the platinum? If so, why? Sometimes she told herself to trust her instincts. Ben was straight. Whatever he did, he had a good reason to do. At other times she recalled that she had thought the same about Ari van Blaiden. She didn't want to fall into the Ari trap again, get involved, and then regret it.

Ben rolled over in his bed. She needed to get up and out of their room now, before he awoke. Very quietly she pulled back the covers, grabbed her clothes, and headed for the shower. Five minutes later she was fully dressed and ready to leave.

"Cara."

Ben's voice froze her hand halfway to the door.

She heard him sit up, but didn't look round.

"We need to talk."

"No."

"Cara?" He said it softly, but it was still a command.

She turned around.

"What's the matter with you? You've hardly said a word to me since we found Gen. Have I done something to upset you?"

"You've been busy. A lot on your mind with Gen and Max and the Coburg thing and people wanting to pull out early and . . ." She realized she wasn't being very coherent and ground to a halt.

"Not too busy to talk to you. In fact, I've missed talking to you. Gen and Max—well—we'll sort it out somehow. I feel sorry for both of them, but for now I have to keep them apart. It's for their own good."

Did it mean more to him because he and Gen had been lovers once?

She shrugged. "You're under a lot of pressure. I told you when we first started to share that there would be times when you'd need your own space. It's not fair to you, having to share with me. You've got a tough time of it. Decisions to make."

"You being here doesn't affect that."

"Gen needs someone to look after her for a while. Someone to shield her at night when her dreams spill over. I thought I'd volunteer. I can move my stuff into her room."

There was a long silence. She didn't look Ben in the eyes, then Ben said, "Of course." His voice was strangely neutral. She might have asked if she could borrow a pen.

She turned to go.

"Cara . . ."

"Yes?"

There was another long pause.

"Nothing. I'll see you later."

❖ ❖ ❖

Ben spent the next few days trapped behind his desk, hamstrung by administration, not daring to go too far afield in case the situation with Lorient boiled up. He worried that Cara and Ronan might have noticed the platinum in the cave, but Ronan had been concentrating on Gen, and Cara had been too emotional about the whole situation. It had been a lucky escape.

He'd been dubious about Lorient's decision to hide the platinum, but it seemed to be working. He was beginning to think they might even get away with it.

He wondered how much of Lorient's current empire building was linked to his knowledge of the platinum. Maybe he needed to have a long talk with Lorient, but just at the moment that probably wasn't such a good idea.

There was a new problem, another minor irritant. Saedi had returned from Timbertown and reported that Lorient thought the settlers were being shorted on grain. There was a shortage, but Saedi believed that was because some of Lorient's camp cooks had milled some of the seed grain for flour, one of the dangers of not having proper control of the stores once supplies had been moved to Timbertown. Lorient had then checked the early logs for manifests and had got hold of the story that Ben had cooked up about the grain shortage on the ark—nothing more than an excuse to shuttle up there and get a very private message to Crowder—had added two and two and made six. It was a good job Crowder had promised an extra grain shipment. Saedi had ventured an opinion that nothing less would appease Lorient.

Ben needed to talk to Crowder direct. He'd spoken to his Telepath, Ishmael, several times, via Cara or Cas, but, despite requests, Crowder had avoided speaking to him personally. Ben was uneasy. He'd have bet his life on Crowder. Damn it, he was betting his life on Crowder. His and every other psi-tech on the planet, and probably the settlers' lives, too. He wanted to know that there was a transport on standby. He damn well wasn't going to lose another psi-tech team. They were relying on him to get them home safely.

They trusted him.

Which was more than Cara did.

He didn't know what to make of Cara lately. Their good working rapport had slipped away for no reason that he could figure out. He was surprised just how much knowing the identity of Cara's former lover disturbed him. Out on the Rim, Ari van Blaiden's reputation, if you knew who to ask, was for ruthlessness. Now he added up Cara's veiled references and wasn't far off an answer that made sense.

He wanted to say all this to Cara now, but she seemed to be slipping further away from any intimacy, physical or emotional. Perhaps she just needed more time, but dammit, hadn't he given her enough? Maybe things would never work out between them. Maybe that had never been on Cara's agenda the way it had been on his. Maybe he should have said something sooner instead of being so bloody understanding.

He sighed and got up. No use chasing himself in circles. Better get on with something solid. He needed to check on the vet team in general and Calvin Tanaka in particular. Ronan might be a natural replacement for Anna, but stepping into Lee Gardham's shoes was not going to be easy for Tanaka, who was good at his job, but lacked the people skills to be a good leader.

He found Wenna in the ops room.

"I'll be across the river if anyone needs me."

"All right, Boss," Wenna said.

Ben decided to walk. The weather was warm and dry after a three-day bout of strong summer rainfall. He nodded to the pair of security guards on duty by the bridge and crossed over to the animal rearing station that they tried to refer to as the nursery instead of the tank farm, in case their words were overheard by settlers.

Calvin Tanaka, veterinary scientist and specialist in artificial womb technology, met him at the entrance. The facility took natural livestock embryos, cryogenically stored, and reared them to maturity in tanks. It was the only way they could supply the settlers with enough domestic livestock for their gene pool.

"Calvin, how's it going?"

"Good. It's going real good." Calvin was a lively young man, more optimistic and less cautious than his predecessor. He led Ben into the long, low riser where animal embryos at various stages of development grew in their artificial wombs, cushioned by amniotic fluid.

"We broke our own record with this last batch of sows and I'm sure we can do even better next time." Calvin was like a proud father. "I've increased their intake of—"

"Good. Well done. No problem with the settlers?"

"I've been dealing with Elder Lenten. They come over every week and take the newborns for intensive rearing. I was a bit worried about the fourteen-klick journey to Timbertown, so I keep them here for an extra week now, but the settlers are managing well. They're very good with livestock."

"And how about the rest of your team? The administrative work? Not too much of a strain?"

"I'm getting used to it. I hadn't expected a field promotion . . . I miss Lee."

"So do we all."

✦ ✦ ✦

In the shadow of the deserted half-built lighthouse on the rocky headland above Seaward Base, Max Constant waited impatiently for the love of his life. He jiggled from one foot to the other, paced the length of the wall and back again, and then leaned against the block-work with a sigh.

Serafin's builders had raised the external skin to a height of seven meters. The tower section was already growing out of the west wall and there were plans for a lookout station on top with a lamp-room to guide the fishing fleets at night using good old-fashioned candlepower like the very first lighthouses had done.

From here, Max had a magnificent moonlit view over two wide curving bays to the north and south. Seaward Base, spread along the southern bay below, was little more than a collection of prefabricated buildings and a row of boat sheds alongside the foundations for permanent homes. Those who had an eye to the weather were making sure that their sheds were secure even before their homes were finished. You can sleep in a boat, but you can't catch fish in a house.

A shadow detached itself from the larger darkness of a pile of building materials. "Don't you know how to stand still?" Gen asked.

"How long have you been there?"

"Long enough to know you'd be useless in a situation where stealth was required."

"I can be stealthy. I'm here every night being stealthy. Six days, Gen. Six whole days. I've missed you so much."

She chuckled and pulled him into her arms. "I only got the all clear for active duty yesterday. This is the first chance I've had to get away without anyone noticing. I'm supposed to be in the foothills doing a timber survey, but I've taken a slight detour."

"More than slight. Will they notice?"

"I'll fly through the night to make up time, and I can fix the flight recorder. They might notice I'm asleep on my feet, but that's all."

"I was beginning to think I'd never see you again." Max buried his face in Gen's collar and breathed in her scent.

"I told you we'd find a way," Gen said.

"You did."

"Are they treating you well?" she asked.

"I'm mostly working with Jon Moon."

"Ronan's partner."

"Yeah, I think the good doctor has asked him to keep an eye on me. Anyhow, we're charting the coastline most days. He's good to work with: fair, even-tempered. I'm actually learning a lot. If you were here with me, it would be perfect."

"You and me and baby makes three."

"What?"

"I'm pregnant."

"What?" The cogs of his brain whirred without connecting to anything.

"Pregnant. I'm keeping it. Do you mind?"

Did he? A flash of how family life with Gen might be lit up his imagination and then all the reasons why that could never happen crowded in and snuffed it out.

"Mind?"

She pulled away from him. "I shouldn't have told you. It doesn't change anything, does it?"

"Yes. Yes it does." He pulled her back into his arms. "Do I mind that you're carrying my child? Of course I don't mind. It's . . . wonderful, amazing. Do I mind that we might never be able to bring our child up together? Yes, I mind that. I want us to be together forever, but I don't know how I can make that happen."

"I do, or at least I think I do. We have to get Ben on our side. When the second ark comes—"

Hope stirred? "I can go home with you?"

"Not in cryo. The pods we have are calibrated for psi-techs. Lorient didn't want an easy way off planet for anyone. This was designed as a one-way trip, but the ark crew doesn't travel in cryo. It would be a boring journey. Nine months staring at the inside of a tiny cabin. With me. And Baby."

"I don't care how boring it is. What's nine months compared to a lifetime?"

"I'll talk to Ben when the time is right. In the meantime, keep a low profile."

"I'll not put a foot wrong. Promise. The psi-techs will find me all cooperation from now on."

"You'll have to settle for visits when I can. I'll try and do it with permission next time."

"Soon?"

"I hope so."

"I do love you."

"I know."

❖ ❖ ❖

Even though she'd moved out of their shared quarters, Cara was still working with Ben. It had been ten days now and she'd observed a definite pattern. She'd started to keep a log of what was missing from the reports, and it was obvious, even to her, that Ben was leaving out a proportion of heavy metals, anything that might lead a geologist to suspect platinum. It was a good cover-up. She couldn't expect confirmation of that from the rest of the team. Youen Biggs was so wrapped up in his search for native wildlife that he might as well have had his head up his backside and Mohan Razdan, their token settler, was a nice guy, but a real rookie. Cara privately thought that's why Ben kept him on their team in particular.

Ben probably thought he was safe. She'd never told him about Felcon. He didn't know she'd had experience—a bad experience—on a platinum planet. He probably figured she wouldn't be able to recognize platinum.

Wrong, Commander Benjamin.

She was watching him. Waiting for him to make a mistake.

Something, maybe loyalty or maybe fear of finding out what she didn't want to know, prevented her from discussing it with anyone else, and fear of finding out that she was right stopped her from confronting Ben. Instead she watched, helpless, as he faithfully mapped the sparse iron and tin deposits and charted areas which would yield fossil fuels, but ignored the greatest find of all.

She knew that the settlers probably wouldn't want to make use of it now, but there would come a time, a thousand years hence, perhaps, when the planet would be open again. The Trust, or its descendant companies, would make contact and look for trade agreements and profits. Then the platinum could give the native Olyandans a very nice starting point for their interplanetary financial security. But only if they knew it was there. Only if it *was* there! Was Ben planning to sell the information to some mining corp with a rip-it-out mentality?

This was just the sort of situation Ari would have taken advantage of. Natural resources to be plundered—and no one would notice for at least a thousand years. It was obscene. It was immoral. Was Ben planning a similar scheme? Wait until the last minute, then rip out the platinum and—good-bye Olyanda?

Cara had trusted Ben with her life. She owed him more than the nagging suspicion that seeped like a fog through the dark alleys of her mind. Why couldn't she trust him? That question died half-formed. She had trusted once; bitten the fruit already and found half a worm.

After two long days charting the estuary, Cara lay in her little bed, wanting desperately to be able to close her eyes and let sleep take her somewhere safe. Ben's early morning starts were beginning to tell on her. They'd be up at first light, working from dawn until dusk and spending the evening hours logging their worksheets before falling into bed, exhausted.

She found sharing a room with Gen irksome. To be fair, Gen was away from base more than she was here now that Ronan had given her the all clear to return to duties. She'd transferred to contact work and was monitoring the wagon trains heading down toward the southern marshes. She carried overnight gear and often stayed away for several days at a time. However, when she was home, she was a noisy roommate. Cara had learned to sleep through her nighttime ramblings and sleep-talk, and tactfully kept quiet each time she got out of her bunk for a pee, but this time something was really amiss.

By the sounds coming out of the washroom Gen was not well. Cara kept quiet, knowing that the last thing *she* wanted when *she* was throwing up was someone inquiring solicitously if she was all right. However, a crash and a thump brought Cara reluctantly out of her covers. Gen was in a heap, naked on the floor in a sorry state, kneeling over the pan. Cara put her hands on the girl's shoulders, more as a gesture of support than anything else and, when she had finished throwing up, brought her a clean moist towel and a cup of water.

Gen was a mess. Her face was gray and drawn, its usual golden undertones sunk into sallowness, and her eyes were pink-rimmed. Cara helped her up. Gen's hands went to cover her naked breasts. It wasn't a gesture of modesty; her nipples were dark, standing out against her light brown skin. Cara and Gen had shared a room for long enough for Cara to recognize the changes in Gen's body, the heaviness in her breasts, the slight thickening of her waist. She put her hand out to Gen's belly.

"When's it due?"

Gen's eyes filled with tears. "I'm not sure."

"How? Aren't you clipped?"

Gen shook her head. "I was in a relationship once . . . and I had it reversed, you know, because . . . and then it didn't work out. I've been taking shots ever since." She took a deep breath and squared her shoulders. "And I decided to stop because . . . well haven't you ever felt . . . you know . . . ?"

Cara handed Gen a wrap, feeling more like her mother than someone her own age. "I've never found anyone I wanted to have children with." The thought of Ari as a father made Cara shudder.

"One day you might. I did. I never thought it would be a

deadhead, but so help me, I love Max and I want his baby even if I can't have him."

"You'll have to tell Ben."

"What? No! I can't. Not yet."

"You'll have to."

"No! Please, Cara. Don't tell him. Please. Promise."

"You won't be able to hide it."

"I'll tell him when the time is right. Promise."

"When?"

"When I'm ready. When I can."

"Make it sooner, not later."

◆ ◆ ◆

"You wanted to see me, Director?" Jack Mario hovered in the doorway. "I've just spent a very frustrating half-hour trying to make the radio work. I don't suppose you'd change your mind about Saedi Sugrue?"

Victor stared at him until Jack looked away. Was Jack getting too fond of the woman? Psi-techs were dangerous, even to someone as stalwart as the redoubtable Jack. But he had more to worry about right now. "Have you seen the grain figures?"

"Yes, of course, They're all in order."

"Have all the sacks weighed. They may be underweight."

"I'm sure they're not."

"I saw Benjamin's face when I reminded him that there were thousands of us and only three hundred of them. He didn't like it."

"Confrontational politics are not the way forward, Director. Please don't push the psi-techs."

If the bastards pushed him, he'd damn well push them back.

"Not scared of them, are you? There's no need to be. I've got my followers. Remember who's boss here, Jack. The people have put me in charge, and they'll keep me here."

"Is that what it's about, power?"

"Personal power? No. Far from it. It's about responsibility. If I thought I could trust anyone else to keep the psi-techs in their place, I'd resign tomorrow. I'd move Danny and Rena to a settlement by the ocean and take up fishing."

He shook his head. "You're all too soft. You see them as human."

"Did you call me, Dad?" Danny pushed the outer office door open.

"No, son, I didn't." Victor's voice softened. "But now that you're here, you could go down to the kitchens and get us a cup of coffee."

"I haven't got time, Dad. I'm going up in a flitter with Mrs. Benjamin."

Danny turned and vanished out of the room.

"Danny!" Lorient was at the door in seconds, his heart thumping. "Danny! Come here. Where did you say you were going?"

"For a flitter ride with Mrs. Benjamin."

"I told you to stay away from Landing."

"Mom said it would be all right."

"Your mother?" Rena had surprised him lately, making decisions he would never have expected. She'd given him a hard time over . . . certain things that had happened. He wanted to overrule her, but he found himself worrying about the gap that had opened up between them.

"I wanted to go and visit the Seaward Settlement," Danny continued. "Mrs. Benjamin is going there. It will take me seven days if I go by wagon. You said I should make my own mind up about things, now I'm grown."

Jack said softly, "You can't argue with that. And she's a good pilot, he'll be perfectly safe."

"Thanks, Dad." Danny took Lorient's silence as permission and skipped off down the corridor.

"They have their uses, our psi-tech friends." Jack watched until Danny was out of sight.

"They might be useful, but they are not friends."

◆ ◆ ◆

She hadn't quite promised, but Cara felt she should give Gen the opportunity to tell Ben the news herself. For the next five days, running survey missions, working with Ben every day, Cara worried that Gen's secret was about to burst out of her mouth. She felt as though she had it written across her forehead and was only surprised that Ben didn't sense what was going on inside her head. Not telling him was just one more brick in the wall between them.

Then Ben announced that they'd take a few days to catch up with admin. Wenna had been bugging him because she wanted to get airborne again and there were also things that needed his attention on the ground. Cara was grateful for the break, but Gen's occasional presence in the ops room as she logged in and out on her own survey trips added even more pressure. They exchanged conspiratorial glances and Cara covered up for Gen's tendency to make late starts because she was spending a lot of time in the bathroom in the mornings, but despite all her exhortations, Gen still shook her head when Cara asked if she was going to tell Ben today.

On the sixth day Ben stalked through the ops room with a face like thunder, looking neither to right nor left, but as he passed Cara, sitting at a workstation, he paused, said, "Get Gen in here, now," and strode into his office.

He knows. Cara's stomach lurched.

✦ ✦ ✦

"Miss Marling, sit down, please. Do you have something to tell me?"

Ben kept his voice low and even. This was a conversation he didn't want to have. He felt sick inside. *Out with it, Gen, don't make me drag a confession out of you. Not you of all people.* All of a sudden his office felt half the size and short on oxygen.

Gen didn't sit and Ben saw by the set of her jaw that she wasn't going to make this easy. Fine. If she wasn't, then he wasn't. He tapped the datacrystal on his desk.

"I can read a buddysuit upload and I know what elevated hCG levels mean. How long did you think you could keep your pregnancy secret? Were you going to wait until it was obvious?"

Gen glared at the datacrystal. "How many times do you check through all the suit readouts? Someone told you."

"So you told other people before you told me."

"Not exactly."

"Who knows?"

Gen shrugged.

"Who knows?"

"Max."

"You've seen him since he went to Seaward Base." He didn't make that sound like a question.

She hesitated.

"You have!"

"I love him."

Ben closed his eyes and concentrated on breathing slowly, in and out. In and out. "What do you see in him? He's nothing but a chancer."

"He's not. He's funny, kind, sweet, passiona— Are you jealous?"

"Don't be ridiculous."

"We used to—"

"A long time ago. We were good together once, Gen. It's over."

"It wasn't over until you brought Cara to Chenon."

"Now who's jealous?"

"I am so not jealous of that relationship. You're both heading for a fall. Why do you think she's bunking in with me?"

"Let's keep to the point. You're pregnant. Who else knows about it?"

"Cara guessed. Ronan probably knows. He scanned me. He must have. . . . ." She touched the fading bruise on her temple. "It's not Cara's fault. I made her promise not to tell. She didn't, did she?"

"Cara did not tell me." *And that's another obstacle between us. Oh, fuck, what a mess.* "You know what happened to Coburg. Three lives lost, and the Fenec girl wasn't even pregnant. What do you think will happen if Lorient finds out?"

"Does he have to find out?"

"Not if you don't have the baby."

"Are you suggesting a termination?"

"I can't force you. This isn't the Militaire."

In the Militaire, such matters were routine on long away missions where pregnancy could endanger the soldier and her unit. Things were generally more flexible in the colony service.

Generally.

But he had a duty of care.

Generally, in the colony service, your colonists weren't trying to find excuses to kill you.

"I can count as well as anyone, Gen. Your baby's due about the time we're scheduled to leave Olyanda. You can't safely undergo cryo while pregnant. If you have the baby here, it can't do cryo for the return trip. No infants under six; the mortality rate is too great."

"There's another option." Gen looked at him under lowered eyelids. "I have the baby before we leave and Max and I, and the baby, go home the long way, awake on the ark ship."

"An ark ship only has two pilots awake on rotation. It isn't equipped for families. Babies are fragile; emergencies happen: colic, fevers, any number of small ailments that an adult would fight off but a baby would need urgent medical attention for. You'd need a medical team. It's hardly practical."

"So you are suggesting a termination."

"I'm asking you to consider your options. If you've done this just to ensure Max gets a ride back to civilization . . ."

"You think that?"

"I don't know what to think. You were heading for a promotion, Gen. It seemed to be what you wanted. Now what do you want?"

"I want Max, and I want this child. I've never felt like this before."

"Think about it sensibly. You don't want Max to end up like Coburg, do you?"

"I can't think about it sensibly. I just keep thinking that I might have to leave Max behind. I've really fucked up, haven't I?" She gave a rueful shake of her head. "In more ways than one."

"Yes, I'm afraid you have. Don't make a decision now. Go away and think about it. We'll talk again in a few days."

The best solution for Gen would be for Ben to give her the Dixie to get her and Max off planet and away from danger, but the Dixie was Ben's back door, his only escape plan if he needed to get Cara out of danger. He wasn't ready to relinquish that unless it was the last option. Gen obviously wasn't even aware of the little flyer's presence. He pressed his lips together in a hard line. No, he wasn't going to give her that get out, at least, not yet.

◆ ◆ ◆

The barrier between Cara and Ben grew more obvious each day. Judging by their wary watchfulness even Youen Biggs and Mohan Razdan had noticed. The easy banter of the early days had dried up. They flew a shift, manned the surveyors, took soil and bio samples with the efficiency of robots and with about as much humor. The nearest they got to smiling was at Youen's delight in finding another creature to add to his list of discoveries.

Coming to the hangar early one morning, Cara spotted Ben in a dim corner, talking to Yan Gwenn. She was about to join them when she realized what they were examining. The bulk of a machine, half as big again as a four-seat flitter, stood draped in polytarp. The corner of the covering was open and exposing the drive casing, instantly recognizable as the space-scarred Dixie Flyer. What the hell was that doing here? Was Ben thinking of leaving?

Everything clicked into place. How much platinum could you get in a Dixie? She blinked away tears and retreated until she was out of sight.

How much?

Enough.

Chapter Twenty-five

CONFESSION

EATEN BY SUSPICION, CARA DECIDED TO ASK for reassignment. Then she changed her mind on the grounds that she should stay close and find out exactly what Ben was up to. They were charting the eastern highlands, which were old in geological terms. Wind and weather had shaped the landscape, and where the high land met the low there were vast tracts of dust desert. Ben put the flitter down and cut the drive. When the dust settled, they all climbed out into the dry heat of late afternoon. Clouds of fine black powder puffed around their feet with each step.

They had to be doubly careful to watch out for a number of stinging insects, irritating but not deadly, though one liked the taste of human blood and could cause nasty allergic reactions in some people. The settlers had taken to calling them skeeters, even though they bore no real relationship to their Earth counterparts. Youen was one of the unfortunate ones who came up in angry welts with just one nip; when he sensed one in the air, he generally climbed into the flitter until the danger was over. Despite lathering himself with repellent cream or wearing a protective net, he was still a magnet for them, as though he wore a flashing illuminated sign on his head that said, *Fresh blood here.*

Where dust gave way to rocks, heat reflected from the smooth table surface scoured clean by the arid wind.

Mohan tested a boulder prior to sitting down. "Yeowch! You could fry an egg on that. I think I'll stand."

Youen emerged from the flitter and scanned the area for any flicker of alien life, then began to delve in rocky cracks and turn over stones to see what lurked beneath.

"Ready?" Cara prepared to monitor Youen. He had a tendency to fall over his own feet while his mind was pre-occupied elsewhere.

Ben shouldered a pack of geo-sensors and walked past her, heading north to check the substrata for anything un-usual. He'd made it a rule that no one went off alone, but he didn't offer to take Mohan.

Cara broke off from monitoring Youen before he'd really got started. "Going alone?" she asked.

He stopped and turned. "And if I am?"

One rule for you and another for the rest of us, is it? She switched to a tight telepathic band.

I'm not taking Mohan because he's not got enough savvy for this kind of job, and you're too busy.

You didn't even ask.

Would it have made any difference if I had?

Cara was, for once, totally at a loss for words.

Ben turned, walked back, and threw the geo-sensors into the flitter. "Take a break," he told Mohan and Youen. "I need to talk to you," he said softly to Cara, but the softness in his voice was offset by the steel in his fingers as he took her arm, almost dragging her along with him as he strode across the rock and down onto the soft surface, stirring up dust with every step.

"Something you can't say in front of them?" she asked as they got out of earshot.

"It's something I can't say in front of anyone else." His face was as stony as the desert. "I need to know what's wrong."

"Wrong with what?"

"Don't play that game! Wrong with you. Wrong with me. We used to be friends and now you cut me out. Why?"

"I don't cut you out. Nothing's changed." She wouldn't meet his eyes.

"Everything's changed. Even Youen and Mohan keep their heads down in case they get them bitten off."

She didn't answer.

"Come on. What is it . . . Is it Ari van Blaiden?"

"What?" Her head snapped up. The dizziness threatened to overwhelm her, but she pushed it away. *It's too late. He knows. And I didn't tell him.*

Mr. van Blaiden wants to know that his secrets are safe.

"What about . . . ?" She couldn't even bring herself to spit out Ari's name.

"He was your lover."

"How . . ."

"Max let it slip. He used to work for Alphacorp accounting. He assumed that I knew, since I am your husband."

"In name only."

"We can remedy that." His hand clamped tight on her arm, and he stood still and yanked her up close.

The fire in his eyes was pain, not lust.

"You wouldn't . . ."

He breathed out sharply, let her arm drop, and stepped back a pace. "Dammit, Cara, don't you know me well enough by now? Don't you trust me?"

"I thought I did."

"And now you don't?"

"I want to . . ." She looked at him. Tears of emotion and frustration were about to let her down and come spilling out. She took a deep breath.

Now or never. If she didn't tackle him about it right this minute, she'd always wonder. "Tell me about the platinum. Tell me why you're not logging it. Tell me why you've got the Dixie Flyer hidden in the hangar. Tell me there's no conspiracy, that you're not on the take. Look me straight in the eye and tell me."

"What?"

She had all her psi-tech talents stretched toward him. He could lie, but he couldn't fool her. She would know.

"Platinum?" He looked bemused. All she was getting from him was puzzlement, genuine surprise.

"You're not going to tell me there isn't any." She almost spat it out.

He closed his eyes for a moment and then half nodded and looked at her. "There's platinum. I didn't think you'd done enough survey work to . . . Well, never mind. Why do you think I saddled us with a single-minded dreamer and a green settler?"

"Then why aren't you logging it?"

"Hera-3."

"What about Hera-3?"

"It was overrun by pirates, just like the official records say, but using weaponry that could only have come from one of the big corporations."

"Alphacorp." Cara suddenly went cold all over. Did it have Ari's stamp all over it?

"Or even the Trust," Ben said. "What chance do you think this colony would have if the Trust or Alphacorp or any of the megacorps knew the extent of the platinum deposits? The more people who know about it, the more likelihood of careless talk after the mission ends. By the time Wenna analyzed the data and spotted the platinum . . ."

"Wenna's in on this?"

"She found it. Came to me with it, scared as a rabbit. Wenna and I have done all the surveys of the platinum areas personally. That's why I was so keen to get out from behind a desk and into the field."

"And the Dixie Flyer?"

"It's there because of you."

"Me?" She stared blankly at him.

"I thought if you were really in trouble, you might need a way out."

It was the truth. She could sense it. But still something didn't quite fit. "Why didn't you tell me that was what you were up to?"

Now it was his turn to look uncomfortable. "When I brought you here, I didn't know about the Neural Readjustment or the Ari van Blaiden connection."

"Would it have made a difference?"

"You were his lover. Might still be. Cara, how do I know you're not working for van Blaiden?"

"Ari's spy? How can you think that? You got me off Mirrimar-14. He was trying to have me killed."

"It could have been a very good cover story. Even you might not be aware. Maybe you'll wake up one morning and something inside your head will have triggered and you won't be you anymore."

They were nose to nose, surrounded by nothing but desert and their own team in the far distance. His words landed like a solid blow. Maybe she would. Her legs felt as though they couldn't take her weight and the skin on her face felt icy despite the heat. She tried to swallow the lump in her throat.

"I know," she said. Her voice felt tiny out here in the desert. "But . . ." She cleared her throat. "I won't let it. There's too much of me in here." She put her hand to her head. "Don't think I haven't had doubts, because I have, but that's why I believe that whatever they did to me wasn't finished. Ronan . . . Couldn't he tell?"

"He doesn't know you like I do." Ben stepped forward and put his hands on the sides of her head, then bent his own down until his forehead touched hers. "Open to me. All the way."

She jerked her head back. "It's a two-way thing; do you trust me enough for that?"

"Just do it."

She did as he asked and their foreheads connected. She felt his skin hot and dry against hers. After the first inkling that Ben was reading her emotions, she got nothing but a warm glow. This man loved her steadily, truly, and deeply. When he released her, she stared at him as if seeing him for the first time. She'd known his feelings all along, if only she'd let herself believe them, but suddenly she did believe, and it pulled the rug out from under her feet, made her feel weak at the knees, slightly breathless. She fought the realization away so she wouldn't have to deal with it right now, hoping she'd not transmitted it before their two-way contact faded, but afraid that she had.

"I've had all the pieces of this puzzle in front of me since the day we found Gen and Max," Ben said softly. "I kept taking them apart and not liking the look of them. I was hoping—I don't know what I was hoping. Whichever way I put the pieces together, I didn't like the result. Cara, I need to know. I need to know everything and I need to know now. Can you tell me? I'll help you deal with the block if I can."

Should she? Could she? If she did, she couldn't make matters worse.

She took a deep breath.

A wave of nausea hit her—*Ronan says I'm ready to tell*—but she fought it off. *It's too late, he knows.*

Mr. van Blaiden wants to know that his secrets are safe.

The nausea got worse, and her head started to spin until she felt as though she was going to pass out. She must have stumbled forward because the next thing she knew she was in Ben's arms. She leaned her face against the tough hide of his buddysuit, feeling the heat on her cheek.

"I can't," she whispered. The sickness retreated, but she knew it was just waiting for her to try again.

"Ronan says you're ready."

"He told you that?"

"He said I'd have to be patient, and I've tried, but I can't just sit around waiting any longer. I need to know I can trust you." He pushed her away to stand on her own feet, turned, and started to walk toward a rocky outcrop. "There's shade over here."

She followed.

"Here, these rocks will keep the worst of the sun off."

They also cut them off from the flitter where Youen and Mohan were waiting.

"Sit."

She sat in the shade and Ben flopped down next to her. Above them, the clear deep blue sky began to waver and the aurora crackled into life, cascades of lace rippling as if disturbed by celestial winds.

"Talk."

"About?"

"Anything. Stuff that's not blocked. Start with your childhood if you like—he's hardly blocked that."

"My parents split up when I was—oh, let's see—seven, I think. Mom's a marine biologist with a receiving implant and Dad was a hydro engineer, a Psi-Mech. I spent some time with him and some with her, racking up cryo because it was the cheap way to travel. Then Mom got another new boyfriend that she was pretty serious about, but we didn't get on, so I was shipped off to the Erin colony where Dad was on the engineering team for a new dam project. I was supposed to stay with him permanently."

It hurt to think about it, even now. "I was so self-absorbed that I completely failed to pick up his spiraling depression until his line manager flagged it up. He was advised to check into a rehab program if he wanted to retain any chance of keeping his Psi-4 status. He seemed better after that, but I think he was mostly putting on an act for my sake. He died in an accident, if it was an accident. The report was inconclusive because of previously assessed suicidal tendencies. Besides, there wasn't much left of him after he fell from the dam wall into a swarm of digger bots."

Her voice cracked. "I couldn't go back to Mom, so I spent almost a year with Grandpa Carlinni on Earth—in Cornwall. He was old. I guess we'd all spent so much time in cryo that the years had slipped past for him. He was clever, though. He'd been a professor at Oxford University. He got me a scholarship to Aurax, the Alphacorp boarding school for psi-gifted kids in the Saharan city of New Tamanrasset. I got my implant at the age of fifteen and graduated to Academy One on the outskirts of Paris three years later.

"I left the Academy as a Psi-1 with enough points on my degree to walk into any job I wanted, so I opted for extra training and then Special Ops. By the time I was twenty-four, biologically that is, I'd worked my way up to Number Three. I went to Earth to take the next set of exams, and that's when I got headhunted by the Spearhead Teams. They were offering instant promotion and almost twice the pay with a fast track up the ladder for Psi-1s. I did a couple of years with them as a Number Two, and then . . ."

She swallowed, clenched her teeth, and bit down hard to keep the nausea at bay. *Ronan says I'm ready.*

"And then I got assigned to Alphacorp's Special Ops headquarters in York. That's when I got mixed up with Ari. When Ari and I first got together, he was sweet. I know that doesn't seem possible, but he was. Sweet and funny and . . . passionate. He had this saying, you know, about how his operatives shouldn't ever expect drums and trumpets and that a job well done was its own reward."

"Crowder used to say the same thing," Ben said. "I used to tell him he was bullshitting us, but he was right. Psi-techs will never get a parade. We do what we do, but it's always best not to draw attention to our differences. Deadheads will never truly figure us out and mostly they prefer not to."

She closed her eyes and leaned her head against the rock . . .

❖ ❖ ❖

She's in Ari's garden house on the edge of the city. York is beautiful in the spring. The window is open, and she can smell the night-scented stocks outside. She's never lived in a house with a garden. Ari must be loaded.

She sighs and then shields her thoughts from him, even though she knows he's not psi-tech. Loaded in more ways than one. She rolls over on the bed. The silk sheet moves with her. She stretches and smiles. Ari rests his elbow lightly on her belly and traces delicate patterns on her breast with his fingertip.

They're in that limbo place between lovemaking and the real world.

He nuzzles her forehead and leans right over her, propped up on one elbow. Now he tastes the small faint scar on her shoulder and licks salt from her skin, his tongue traveling across the swell of her breast.

After a lifetime she remembers to breathe.

❖ ❖ ❖

Her body reacted to the memories of sex with Ari, and she yanked her mind to the present.

"He . . ." She cleared her throat. "He asked me—no—he *told* me I was going to be his lover and then he persuaded me to work for him."

"You already worked for him."

"A job within a job. He said he needed to know how things worked at the kind of level he couldn't get from read-

ing official reports. It didn't seem so bad; not like telling
tales—I mean—he was in charge of the whole thing. I
agreed and . . ."

"To being his lover or to working for him."

"Both. He's just not the kind of man you turn down.
He's—well—forceful, I suppose. I don't mean he coerces
people, it's just that he's got the kind of personality that's
hard to resist. What Ari wants, Ari gets."

"And what did you want?"

"Then? Ari. No doubt about that."

"And you continued going on away missions?"

"Yes. I wanted my career, too. We both decided that was
the best thing, at least for the time being. I knew there'd be
some problems. There was the aging differential for a start,
with me doing missions with cryo travel, but Ari didn't like
to be tied down and I knew he took other lovers while I was
away and . . ."

"And did you?"

"I could have, I suppose, but I didn't. With cryo, my sub-
jective time away was shorter than his. Besides, do you really need to know that?"

"Just curious. Go on. You were going to tell me about
being Ari's spy."

"That makes me sound like I was selling him secrets. He
was entitled to know, you know."

"Would he have been entitled to know about the platinum if you'd been assigned to a mission like this one?"

"Did you tell Crowder?" She saw his face and knew that
he had. "Anyway, that's not a fair question to ask. The circumstances here aren't the same. This isn't Alphacorp. I'm
not the same. If that's all you're bothered about, then this
conversation ends here." She made as if to get up, and he
reached out for her arm.

"I'm sorry. Go on. Yes, I told Crowder. The raw platinum
data had already gone in the weekly packet before we spotted it. I needed someone to put a stop on it at the other end.
Tell me about Ari."

She bit her lip. Nausea settled in the pit of her stomach,
but she forced herself to ignore it. There were things about

Ari she could tell. It wasn't all classified information. Ari; it was a big subject. Where to start . . .

"I loved him. It was as simple as that. We were marvelous together and I hated being away from him, but gradually . . . gradually I came to appreciate that our relationship was stronger for being episodic. The time away made the time we had together more intense. I can't quite pin down the first signs of change. I didn't want to think about it at first. He did age more than me, of course, but it wasn't just that. He developed a cruel streak. Maybe he had it all along and just kept it well hidden at first. Sometimes it seemed to be nearer the surface and . . . oh, small things. Intimate things. Let's just say he changed, and I didn't like it, but by the time I knew I wanted out, I was stuck with it."

❖ ❖ ❖

She's trying to tell Ari that she wants to quit, but he won't listen.

"I don't accept resignations from my special people," he says, and the tone of his voice is final.

"Ari, you don't understand. I'm not cut out for spying, and I don't like deceiving people."

"You're excellent at it, I don't want to lose you."

"You won't lose me. I'll still be with Alphacorp."

"Ah, no, that's not possible. Do you know what happened to the last person who tried to resign from my team?"

"No."

"No one else does, either, though I think Mr. Craike might have some idea. I left the severance up to him."

He emphasizes the word "severance."

There's a long silence.

❖ ❖ ❖

"Ari's not the kind of man you just up and leave. Anyway, I was still in love with him, addicted to him, I suppose. Does that make sense, or am I rambling?"

"I get the picture."

"It all came to a head when I was posted on a trouble-shooting mission to Felcon."

Another wave of nausea hit her.

"You've lost all your color. Here."

He handed her a pouch of cool water from the pocket of his suit. "Is it the block?"

She sipped and nodded.

He held out his hand and she took it, feeling Ben's strength and energy flowing in her direction.

"Fight it. You'll never have a better opportunity. You're halfway there already."

She swallowed hard. He was right—*Ronan says I'm ready*—but it felt like she had an egg stuck in her throat. *It's my free choice.* A headache sat just behind her eyes and she tried to will it away. *I will not be ruled.*

Mr. van Blaiden wants to know that his secrets are safe.

I will not be ruled!

"I was leading a section and Robert Craike was in charge of the mission."

"Craike!"

"You know him?"

"By reputation. Go on."

"The platinum extraction company—a subsidiary of Alphacorp, but I didn't know that at the time—and the local farmers were head-to-head over a land dispute. The miners were stripping minerals out of land that wasn't theirs, and the farmers were justifiably outraged. Alphacorp promised that ore would be shipped off planet for processing, but then they began laying foundations for a hyper-processing plant, and you know what that does to land."

Ben nodded.

"There wasn't enough farmland on Felcon to share it with platinum mining and processing. Very much like Olyanda, the habitable regions were too small, the surface deposits just right for strip-mining. Anyhow, before we arrived, there had been a couple of inept sabotage attempts on mining operations and the situation was ready to erupt. Our brief was to find a peaceful solution, but they sent us equipped with heavy weapons and live ammo. I should have realized then, but . . ."

She stopped talking to breathe deeply, aware that she was gripping Ben's hand hard.

"Craike's no peacemaker."

"He didn't even try. He deliberately provoked trouble. He backed the farmers into a corner. They retaliated. It was a bloodbath.

"I took a stand against Craike and gave my team the option. Four bailed—too afraid of Craike, and I don't blame them—but the rest stuck with me. We confronted him outright . . . did it by the book, Alphacorp regulation 1041: procedure for censuring a superior officer on active duty. I didn't expect him to concede gracefully, but I didn't expect a stand-up battle, either.

"He killed Arak, my Number Two, just blasted him without warning, and shot the knees out from under Nathan and Lori Goss. Then he ordered the rest of us locked up pending trial for mutiny. Up until then it had been a legitimate protest, but one of our jailers told me Craike had reported Arak, Nat, and Lori as killed in action and had erased my official complaint. That's when we knew we were in deep shit. He could just dispose of us, and none of us trusted him not to do it. The three of us managed to escape: me, Torrence, and Brina, who'd had some personal trouble with Craike earlier. We headed across the Araspika Desert on crestedinas to where we knew the farmers had an enclave that hadn't been touched by mining, but we never got that far.

"Torrence was injured in the escape. We didn't realize how badly because his buddysuit looked after him, but when we stopped, I saw the burns."

✦ ✦ ✦

She's holding Torrence in her arms in the glaring white noon. Felcon is a pig of a planet. Here, on the edge of the Araspika Desert, the heat is formidable. Each breath tastes like an oven.

She tries to shelter his face from the sun with her body, but it's a futile gesture. An energy blast from Craike's bolt gun has cooked a thick line across his chest. He's done well to get this far. Maybe she should have kept going and let him die on the move, but she wants to believe he still has a chance.

Common sense tells her to leave, but she can't, even though she has nothing to offer but companionship in Torrence's last, lonely minutes. His buddysuit has administered painkillers, though its damaged circuits are failing now, and he is, as far as she can tell, free from pain and trapped in a narco-haze.

She considers surrender—get him into a cryo capsule and home to a proper medical facility—but it's already too late. Craike won't show any mercy.

Torrence's breath rattles in his throat, and then he doesn't breathe in again. There's nothing more she can do. Leaving his body on the hillside she takes off across the desert, riding a crestedina.

She's exposed against the baked earth with nowhere to hide. She can't outrun the flitter, but the thought of that bastard, Craike, makes her try. She touches her heels to the crestie's flanks. It grunts and stretches out into a lope. Keep it up. Each bound takes her closer to safety. She clings to the balance strap, pulling herself tightly into the saddle; one slip on this uneven terrain and she's done for.

The flitter sounds seem to be directly behind her now.

She daren't look round, but she can imagine the forward mounted lasers aiming at her. She feels as though she has a target painted between her shoulder blades. There's an empty ache where she expects the blast to hit.

It doesn't.

The machine roars low overhead, barely missing her. The crestie, oblivious to all but its rider, runs on. The machine circles and comes at her again.

She's lost. There's no need to run the crestedina into the ground. The realization bumps in her belly and, despite the heat, a cold sweat beads her skin.

She eases up and the beast slows and stops, its coffin-shaped head down and its breath coming in snorts through the soft flaps of its nose. Torrence's riderless mount is way behind, but it keeps running until it catches up.

She slides from the saddle with her knees trembling, though whether it's fear or exhaustion she can't say. Quickly she strips both saddles and bridles and smacks the crestedinas on the rump to set them off down the hill. They shamble away, but then lose momentum, stop and begin to whiffle for sand-spiders between the skeletal remains of the sparse spring grasses.

The flitter glides in, drops its speed, and settles into its antigravs, landing lightly. The bubble top swings open. Three buddysuited figures spring out like mobile jack-in-a-boxes, with weapons primed. She leaves her sidearm in its holster; she doesn't want to kill teammates, and she can't kill Craike without going through them. Craike emerges at a more leisurely pace. He knows he's won.

"Five down, one to go," he says, raising his energy-bolt gun. "Funny, I thought you'd be the most difficult to catch."

Cara looks past the muzzle, stares him straight in the eyes, and says nothing.

She grapples with the adrenaline clutch in her belly and pushes the all-too-real fear out of the way before it chokes her. Craike's finger begins to close on the trigger. He swings his arm sideways in an arc and the blast of energy from the bolt gun cuts the legs out from under her crestedina. It goes down with a single bellow. He continues firing and the blast sears through its belly. Blood and intestines splatter over the dried-up ground. The stomach-turning stench of gore and baked shit rises in the heat. Torrence's crestedina begins to bray very loudly, continuing until Craike blasts half its head away.

He levels the gun at her. His smile is carved into his cheeks, but it doesn't reach his eyes.

"Don't think Ari van Blaiden can protect you now," he says.

"You're talking instead of shooting, Craike. Maybe you don't want to upset Ari after all."

Craike nods to one of the men. "Put her under," he says.

The man slaps a blast pack to the side of her neck. She feels something cold and sharp. Her knees give way. Then nothing.

✦ ✦ ✦

Cara looked up at Ben, but his questions had stopped.

"This next bit is going to be difficult, I think."

"Here." He opened his legs and pulled her to sit between

them so she was leaning with her back against him. Then he gripped her with his thighs, wrapped his arms around her, and leaned his forehead against the back of her skull. She felt cocooned and safe.

"Open."

She let him into her head and brought all the memories she needed to the front and shared them. They attacked the block together . . .

❖ ❖ ❖

She's in a holding cell, cold and scared.

Scene shift. Donida McLellan is smiling at her, and the smile is anything but pleasant.

Scene shift. Ari is standing turned away, fixing a drink. The carpet is warm beneath her bare feet. She feels a rush of lo . . . don't go there!

Shift. Ari's doubled up on the floor, crouched over his groin.

Shift. She's grabbing him from behind, reaching for his throat. Squeezing, pinching.

Shift. He's out cold, and she's staggering under a wave of sickness, but reaching for his buddysuit and then seeing his handpad.

Shift. She's downloading information.

Shift. She's fighting to control her breathing, walking down the corridor trying to look as though she has every right to be there . . .

Shift. She's out into the light.

Shift. She's on her knees heaving up bile.

❖ ❖ ❖

"Enough," Ben said.

She turned and looked at him over her shoulder. His skin had taken on a gray sheen. He'd shared the nausea and the blackness. Halved the effect, helped her to bring memories from behind the block.

"The handpad. You've got information that could wipe him out."

She nodded.

"He knows about it?"

She nodded again.

"And you think he was close to catching up with you on Mirrimar-14?"

"Craike was on the station."

"It wasn't Craike who caught up with you in the cargo tunnels?"

"No, that was one of Ari's agents who tried to muscle in on Craike's territory. Maybe he thought he'd get a promotion."

"You think Craike killed him?"

"Probably. His throat was cut. It's Craike's style. He likes blood." She started to shake.

"It's all right now. You've gone as far as you need to. I understand. Everything."

"Ari . . ."

"I understand about Ari, too."

"Ben, it's not that I don't feel for you. If we'd met before . . ."

"We didn't meet before, and there are no what ifs. We're in the here and now, and Ari's history."

"If only . . ."

"If you want it to be you and me, it can be."

She leaned into him and relaxed. Maybe it could. "I'll work on it."

Chapter Twenty-six

ESCALATION

CARA FELT A NEW OPTIMISM AS THEY FLEW back to Landing, but she knew immediately, when they landed, that something was wrong. As they docked in the flitter bay, Wenna came to greet them personally.

"Sorry, Boss. You're not going to like this. Just got the message on mechanicals, from Lorient himself, that you're wanted in Timbertown for a section head meeting."

"What's it about this time?"

"Officially or unofficially?"

"Either. Both."

"Officially I don't know. Unofficially I'd say it's a lot to do with the fact that Gen Marling has pretty well told everybody that she's pregnant."

Cara felt her heart thumping. How could Gen be so stupid?

Ben cursed under his breath. "Has she named the father?"

"No, and she says she's not going to. But there are a lot of people making intelligent guesses."

Cara caught Ben's look, and they bolted for Ben's office where there was privacy. His emotions were near the surface and she could read him quite clearly. He was angry, but he was also genuinely amazed. "Why? Why tell everyone now? Why couldn't she just keep it quiet for a bit longer." He looked at Cara.

"Fear, I think."

"Fear?"

"She didn't want to lose the baby. She was frightened you'd press her to have a termination."

"What does she think I am? It's her body. Why am I surrounded by people who don't trust me?"

Cara put both hands up, palms outward. "Don't count me. I'm totally trusting. Now, at least."

"I don't know how we're going to make the best of this situation. Who can we trust in the Seaward Base team?"

"Ronan's partner, Jon Moon."

"Good. Use Ronan and Jon to get a message through to Constant. Tell him to take a break and go on a long camping trip. I won't have a repeat of the Coburg affair. There are times when I think Max Constant doesn't deserve to keep his balls, but I'm damned if Lorient's going to pull a stunt like that again!"

The communication only took seconds. "Done."

"Dammit. Where's Gen?"

"I'll see if I can find her." Gen wasn't difficult to find, but she was barely coherent. Cara pulled out of the conversation as soon as she'd gleaned the basics. "She's in Timbertown. Lorient's got her, but she's not been harmed. She's freaked out in case Lorient goes after Max. Do you want me to patch you through to her?"

"Just tell her we're on our way and not to give away any information at all. Nothing. Just wait until we get there."

✦ ✦ ✦

By the time they reached the hall in Timbertown the other section heads were gathering. Cara pushed her way in with them.

Victor Lorient looked like a man under considerable stress; gaunt face, deep-set eyes, prominent nose, and his skin had lost its bloom. Behind him, Rena Lorient sat stiffly in her upright chair. She'd developed frown lines and her hair had faded to the color of old ice in just a few months.

She'd soon look like Lorient's mother instead of his wife. Jack Mario, sitting next to Rena, shuffled uncomfortably and looked anywhere except at the eyes of the assembled psi-techs.

Lorient glowered at them. "I am aware that you all try to get away with telling me as little as possible about your activities."

"You have our daily reportsss, Director Lorient." Marta rose to the bait.

"Red herrings, Miss Mansoro. Red herrings! So many reports that if I were to spend my time checking them I'd only be halfway through before you were all off planet."

It's taken him quite a while to work that one out. Marta had not found her task here easy. She fought a constant battle to balance demand for resources against supply and had to cope with the added burden that Lorient called her in regularly to complain that essential stores were being diverted from settler to psi-tech. She couldn't disguise her scaly skin, but she always wore her buddysuit closed all the way up her neck to cover her gills when visiting Broccoliburg.

Lorient continued, "Another flagrant breach of the charter has come to my attention."

"Victor! We don't know that for sure." Rena Lorient's voice was quite sharp.

"Then why won't she say who the father is? We all know she was marooned for several days with the settler member of her crew."

"I'm sure that I have no need to tell you that we're talking about your Miss Marling. Perhaps we could ask her to join us now."

Gen was ushered in. She was tight-lipped and had a *what-have-I-done-now?* kind of expression. She saw Cara, and her mouth twitched in a failed attempt at a smile. Cara nodded back, not daring to take her attention from the link she was holding open.

"Miss Marling. I would remind you that as an employee of the Trust you signed an agreement not to breed while on active service and also for this mission you signed a contract expressly forbidding sexual relationships between settler and technical crew."

"That's correct." Her voice was strong enough to carry to the assembled section heads and the hangers-on from the administrative staff.

"Then can I ask, just to clarify matters, you understand, whether you are, indeed, pregnant?"

"That's none of your business."

He scowled. "Not unless your baby is fathered by a settler. If you won't divulge the father's identity, you must be trying to protect him."

"It's a breach of her employment contract," Ben said. "A matter entirely for the Trust to deal with. There's no law that says any woman has to reveal the father of her baby."

"There can be by tomorrow." Lorient tried to stare Ben down. "This is a special case. Trust Law is hardly applicable here. It's Olyanda law that counts." He turned to Gen. "When you crashed your airbus some time ago, you were left alone with Max Constant, the settler assigned to your crew, yes?"

"That doesn't make Max the father of my baby."

"Then who is?"

Shall I offer to do a DNA test? Ronan asked.

Not a good plan unless you're willing to fake the result, Cara replied.

Any bright ideas? Serafin asked.

Not unless you can come up with a psi-tech father before Lorient hauls Constant's ass here. Ben's answer was blunt. *How about you, Serafin, do you fancy fatherhood?*

Let's be realistic, who would go for a shriveled old prune-face like me, 'cept, perhaps, Suzi? How about Calvin?

My wife would kill me. Calvin Tanaka was married to one of the tech team's vets.

Dammit. I don't need this. Cara caught a private thought before Ben's broadcast one, *Cara, play this for all its worth now, and we'll straighten it all up later.*

"Well, Miss Marling. We're all waiting." Lorient loomed over Gen, but she held out against his bluster.

Ben cleared his throat, "No need to get heavy, Director. Gen is protecting someone, but it isn't Max Constant, it's me." The announcement fell like an unexpected summer storm. There was a surprised hush, and then everyone seemed to be talking at once. "Thanks, Gen. It was a nice try." Ben walked up and put one arm protectively around her shoulder. "Sorry, Cara. I wish you hadn't found out like this." He looked across to Cara, who stood somewhat stunned. She hadn't quite got his drift, but now she understood. It could be worth two lives. Play it for all it's worth. Right.

"You bastard, Benjamin!" Cara spat out the words. "And as for you . . . I thought you were my friend." Gen reeled back and began to protest her innocence, but Cara saw Ben's arm tighten round her shoulders.

"Is this true? Can you prove it?" Lorient almost growled.

"I don't have a certificate if that's what you mean," Ben snapped, "But if you must know, Miss Marling has a rather fetching little mole on her left breast,"

"And—er—Ben's got a small scar near his groin." Gen took her cue.

"You brazen bitch!" Cara squared up to them. "And as for you, Ben Benjamin, a scar a little further over might have done more good!" *Duck.* She swung her arm and let fly with a resounding backhand, but instead of avoiding it, he took it on the jaw.

She didn't wait to see what happened next. Holding her jarred knuckles with her left hand, she marched, stiff-backed, out of the room and down a corridor and only stopped when she was well out of earshot. Her breath was coming in sobbing gulps and she was so well into the part of the wronged wife that she found she felt slightly hysterical and had tears trickling down her face. She leaned against the wall. It was cold and hard and she smacked her head into it. She hadn't expected to feel like this. She knew it was only a sham, but then so was their marriage. She felt as though she had lost something precious which she'd only just begun to find. Rubbing her eyes clear, she slipped quietly out of the door and into the bustle of the city still raw with building scars.

◆ ◆ ◆

Max would have liked Seaward Base if only Gen had been by his side.

He pulled mapping duties with Jon Moon, and when he proved not altogether incompetent for a deadhead, Jon started to schedule him in with some of the other psi-techs. The settlers steered clear of him, unsure of his loyalties, but that was fine. He didn't much like hanging around with settlers, not since he heard about the poor bastard they'd butchered. Yeah, okay, maybe they weren't all bad, but he couldn't trust any of them. If they found out about him and Gen, he'd be toast.

He concentrated on keeping a low profile, doing his job to the best of his ability and not pissing off any of the psi-techs. It seemed to be working. He had an easy relationship with Jon, and Rufus Greenstreet had actually asked for Max to be assigned to his mapping run.

Gen wasn't likely to appear again any time soon, but Max made a habit of walking up to the lighthouse every evening, watching it grow, block by block.

The roof trusses were in place now, thanks to a building gang newly arrived from Landing. Gen had sent him an honest-to-goodness letter in the courier pouch and he'd read it so often that he thought the ink might fade.

I'm going to ask Ben about the return trip soon. Right now it's not a good time, but I want you to know how much I love you. I'll try and get a flight to Seaward soon. Please be patient. You're always in my thoughts.

He could feel the letter, warm in his shirt pocket, as they returned to Seaward. Rufus let him land the flitter in the shallows of the bay. He'd never done a water landing before, but Rufe talked him through it and he dropped the two-man machine right on target to settle into the bobbing waves, floats deployed.

The sight of Jon Moon running across the beach toward them, his face deadly serious, cut short Rufe's congratulations. They popped the bubble top, and both men jumped down and splashed the few strides to shore.

"What's up?" Rufe called out when Jon got into range.

"Message for Max."

Max's first thought was that something had happened to Gen. His pulse began to pound.

"Is . . ." He almost asked if Gen was all right, but the reason for his transfer was still a secret, or he thought it was. You could never tell with psi-techs. Benjamin had told him not to sound off about it, and no one had mentioned anything.

"Is everything all right at Landing?" he managed to say.

"As far as I know, but there's a message to tell you to take yourself off for a camping trip for a few days and don't make contact with any settler groups. Have you been up to something you shouldn't have?"

"Me?" Max did his best to shrug, but his shoulders had knotted.

"Take an emergency pack out of the flitter and here, some supplies. Rendezvous at Hewart Point seven days from now. If it's not me or Rufe in a two-man flitter with more supplies or a recall, take off and don't look back. You're on your own."

Max didn't ask any questions. Guessing that it was something to do with Gen wasn't the biggest leap of logic he'd ever made.

He could feel her letter in his shirt pocket right now, so even though he couldn't read it, he was comforted by the words.

Rufe shoved a pack into Max's arms and Max shouldered it, knowing it contained an all-weather sleep-sack, single shelter, and a compact kit that contained everything from fishing hooks and a knife to water purification granules and a basic med kit.

A sudden memory of the crash, dragging Gen out of the wreckage, finding Lee dead, hurling up his last meal, retrieving the kits, starting to think about what to do next, and common sense kicking in. Shelter, first aid, water, food. . . . Survive until someone found them.

Now he'd better hope that he could survive without someone finding him.

"Thanks, Jon. Rufe. See you in seven days."

He headed up the path toward the lighthouse. The sun had just fallen into the sea and painted the cloud-fingered sky salmon. He had an hour, maybe an hour and a half, before it was too dark to see where he was putting his feet. How far could he get?

The construction gang had packed it in for the night. Max skirted a stack of timbers cut for purlins. Above his head the roof trusses soared against the afterglow like dinosaur ribs.

A shadow moved. Max's heart skipped a beat. "Gen?"

"Max Constant?" The voice was male and low.

"Who wants to know?"

"Get him, boys."

Three figures came out of the darkness. Max was buffeted to one side, then the other and something flung over his head. His hands were yanked behind him, and he hit the ground with lung-emptying force.

He started to yell, but the head covering was pulled roughly back and a rag stuffed into his mouth. He hardly had time to see the face of the man leaning over him, but in the moonlight all he knew for sure was that he had light-colored hair. Then the bag was shoved back over his head, and he was yanked to his feet. The rattle of a bridle and the stomp of a hoof told him that his assailants had come on horseback. Some of Lorient's fundies?

With a sick lurch of his stomach he remembered Gen's letter in his shirt pocket. It was as good as a death warrant.

❖ ❖ ❖

Sometimes Ben just didn't get Cara. She'd played it well in front of Lorient and his cronies, but now she was acting cool and distant in private as well as in public. It was probably easier to keep up the pretense all the time. You never knew when someone was watching.

Besides, he had enough to think about.

The order for Max's arrest hadn't been rescinded despite Ben's confession.

The tension between settler and psi-tech heated up with the weather. Ben set Gen the task of keeping a running file on all incidents, partly to keep her mind off Max twenty-six hours a day, and partly because he didn't want her too far away from where he could keep an eye on her. He wanted to see if he could pin the anti-psi-tech activity down to one small group or trace it directly to Lorient. He had plenty of suspicions, but no proof.

Within the space of three days a psi-tech man, one of Serafin's mechanics, was beaten nearly senseless for picking up a settler child who'd fallen over and skinned his knees on the street in Timbertown. In Landing, there was a brawl when a group of settlers arrived with a wagon insisting on grain they believed was being kept from them. Several other small incidents stopped short of an all-out fight. Marta had a close call when she was hassled by a gang of young thugs. She only escaped them by taking to the river and staying underwater until help arrived, saved by her gills.

Lorient had a list of psi-tech misdemeanors for Ben to deal with—all trivial, most imagined, but it was indicative of the settlers' mood.

Ben gave the whole psi-tech team a strong lecture about not being pushed into using their talents against the settlers, no matter what the provocation.

Lorient, eloquent and convincing, took to holding meetings daily and he wasn't preaching reconciliation anymore. Settlers traveled klicks on foot or horseback to hear him. The fanatics began to wear Ecolibrian symbols depicted in a variety of ingenious ways, embroidered onto clothes, painted onto skin, or as homemade jewelry. Within a few days, those not wearing symbols were being picked on by those who were. The pressure was on to conform.

Lorient wanted the psi-techs gone, and for their part the psi-techs would have been happy to finish the essential jobs and leave as soon as the settlers from the second ark, due soon, had been revived, but Ben still hadn't had any direct contact with Crowder.

Seven days after Max left Seaward Base, he failed to turn up at the rendezvous point.

◆ ◆ ◆

Victor Lorient locked his office behind him and strode up the hill to his house. It was quite small for his status, but he liked to appear modest.

Outside the house was a stable. Though groundcars were available for the first year if he needed them, the settlers' official policy was not to use equipment that would not be staying on Olyanda after the tech teams left. Victor wasn't much for horseback riding, but he could manage. Rena said she preferred the little square cart pulled by a pony, and he was pleased to see that she was learning how to harness and groom the animal herself even though Danny was always willing to do it for her.

Where was Danny today? The boy was often out and about somewhere, since he'd taken to hitching lifts on flitters. Victor didn't like that idea, but the flitters would be gone at the end of the year and, overall, he was pleased that Danny was adapting well to the new environment. He was much better off in a world where the pace of life was slower.

A figure moved in the shadow of the stable. Thinking it was Danny, Victor paused and turned. The figure had ash-blond hair that was almost white. Taris, not Danny. He ambled over unhurriedly, hoping that Rena hadn't noticed.

"I told you not to come here."

"Sorry, Director. I missed you at your office and I wanted you to know that I found something."

"This way." Victor led Taris behind the stable to an embryonic vegetable patch that Danny had begun to dig. Broccoli trees on the north side offered shade from the sun and shelter from the watchful.

"Well?"

"Director, you're not going to like this."

"Just tell me, Taris, I'll make up my own mind."

"I went snooping around Landing. In the animal barns across the river, they're supposed to be breeding critters, but they've got a shed full of tanks. There's a lab and all sorts of machinery. The critters in the tanks were just half grown—not even big enough to be born . . ." He pulled a face. "I swear, Director, it looked like cloning to me. I couldn't keep my dinner down."

Victor had been pressured into allowing the tanking station. The psi-techs promised that they'd only rear natural embryos, but if Taris was right and they were cloning, what monstrosities might they be rearing?

"You've done well, Taris."

"Thank you, Director. What are we going to do about it?"

Victor was torn between the desire to rip out the abomination and the knowledge that his name was on the agreement. He'd not agreed to cloning, however.

"Only . . ." Taris' voice was wheedling. "I've got some friends who feel just as strongly as I do about this and they say it shouldn't be allowed."

"You've told others?"

"Only a few. I felt so bad when I got home that . . ."

"I see." Victor took a deep breath. The decision was made for him. If anyone knew that he was allowing this to happen, he'd be less than a leader in their eyes. Taris had taken the decision away from him.

Victor took a deep breath. "You're sure you have friends you can trust?"

Taris looked up at Victor's face, and there was the light of zeal in his eyes. "I do." He turned away with new purpose.

✦ ✦ ✦

Cara's unease grew. Whenever she passed through Landing or Timbertown, she felt as though everyone was watching her, saying, "There goes Ben Benjamin's wife; he's thrown her out for another woman, you know." In Landing she kept getting messages of sympathy or strange looks from those who wondered what was wrong with her to drive Ben into Gen Marling's bed.

This was the woman who had decked the head of the psitechs in front of a hall full of onlookers. This was the woman whose best friend had taken her husband. This was the woman whose husband thought so little of her that he hadn't even bothered with the courtesy of a separation before bedding one of his staff.

Cara had moved out of Gen's room and into a single one that was hardly bigger than a closet. She took to spending her spare hours there and suddenly felt able to do what she hadn't felt able to do since escaping from Ari: she opened up what she'd stolen from his handpad and started to go through it systematically. Some of it made sense and some of it didn't, but a pattern began to emerge, and Felcon was barely the tip of the iceberg. It was obvious that, as well as the information from his own insiders in Alphacorp, he was receiving information from someone in the Trust, and there was some kind of special force—illegal, she presumed—set up to do some very dirty work, indeed. She wanted to share what she'd found with Ben, but she still wasn't officially speaking to him except when necessary for work.

She'd taken just about as much as she could. When she went for her regular checkup, she'd had to sit the stress test twice for Ronan to correlate results. Ronan had rested his hand on Cara's shoulder and said, "Get it out into the open."

"It's Ben."

"Of course it is."

"I know this thing with Gen is only a sham, but I thought we were over the worst and now we're apart again."

"Talk to him."

"I'm not sure I can. Oh, I can do the everyday stuff, but the personal stuff is much more difficult."

"You can't resolve anything until you talk. It's time."

Ronan's words stayed with her as she got back to her little room and stripped off the light coverall she wore beneath her buddysuit. She stepped into the shower and set the jets to maximum. It was all Ben's fault. He should have found someone else to play the part of Gen's lover. Why did it have to be him? Was there something between them? There certainly had been.

She knew that was ridiculous, but she worked up a temper as she worked up a lather. In the end she couldn't stand it any longer. She pulled on the first clothing that came to hand, soft pants and a stretchy top, took a deep breath, and marched purposefully to Ben's room. She passed Gen in the corridor.

"You look as though you mean business," Gen said.

"I need to talk to Ben."

"Reconciliation time, huh?"

Reconciliation? She didn't think so. She didn't really know why she needed to see him or what she hoped to achieve, she just did. Maybe it was make or break time.

Gen fended off a pair of nosy onlookers in the corridor who'd seen the look in Cara's eyes. "Give them some space." Cara heard her say, "There's not much privacy here at the best of times. I'll personally kill anyone who disturbs them tonight." Then the door closed.

Ben came out of the shower with a towel round his waist, just finishing the tight braid in the back of his wet hair. There was a bruise on his cheekbone from where she'd hit him.

"Hello, Cara. I thought I heard the door."

"Hello, Cara? Is that all you can say? Come on, you can do better than that. How about, 'How are you?'"

"Well—how are you?"

"Do you really want to know?" She was beginning to feel out of control and she fed the feeling; let it go; ran with it.

"What's all this about?"

"I've been collecting words of sympathy. Have you any idea what people are saying out there?"

"Words." He shrugged, a what-can-I-do-about-it kind of shrug.

"Words that I've had enough of. I feel like a prize idiot!"

"Ah, now we're getting down to it. Your feelings are hurt."

"And shouldn't they be? I am the wronged wife, after all."

"Are you?" He finished plaiting the braid, turned, and poured himself a cup of tea from the hotpot in the corner.

"What?"

"You're certainly not wronged, and you've never been a wife." He put his cup down untouched. "When we first came here, I thought . . . I hoped that there might be a chance to turn our relationship . . . into something more solid, but I guess the whole van Blaiden thing screwed that. Maybe that's over, maybe it isn't—I guess time will tell. In the meantime, this situation is just another sham. Don't get upset. At least it's doing somebody some good."

Suddenly she glimpsed something fragile which had eluded her for longer than it should have. Damn. Ronan was right. But Ben was being as annoying as hell, and he wouldn't be having that kind of impact on her unless she really cared—cared more than she'd let herself admit. Well, she wasn't going to make a turnaround now and fold like a wimp. How could she retrieve a relationship she'd never had in the first place? She'd promised to work on it, but was there anything there to work on?

"It's not doing me any good at all." She hid her confusion in petulance.

"Don't you think I've had my fair share of flack? And Gen, too? The adulterous husband and the deceitful friend. At least you're the innocent party."

"Yes, well, I want out."

"Out?"

"Let's make our divorce public." She sounded bitter, even to herself.

"If you want to, but we both knew what we were getting into."

"Did we? I wonder. I thought we had a friendship." She blinked away tears. After their heart-to-heart in the desert she'd thought all their personal problems would resolve.

"We did, but we could have had more."

"More what? More sex?"

"You've got to have some sex in the first place to have more sex. And I don't count the night we met."

"You've waited all this time to throw that in my face. What's the matter, didn't you enjoy it?"

"Very much. But you didn't." He dropped his voice. "I'm not talking about sex, I'm talking about love."

He came up close, and she could smell the soap on his damp skin.

"What moves you, Cara?" he asked. "What touches you? I'm damn sure it's not me." There was an echo of *I wish it was*.

It wrenched at her. Why couldn't things be simple between them?

"What makes you tick, woman? Ari van Blaiden? What did he do to make you love him so much and yet be so afraid to love again? Was he so good in bed?"

She shuddered, remembering Ari in bed: powerful, athletic, greedy, ruthless, excessive. Sex with Ari was sometimes painful, often exhilarating, always draining. She'd been riding an emotional high, and the fall had been long and hard. How could she love again when love was so damaging?

"It is possible." Ben's voice was gentle again.

"What?"

"To love again."

Had she been broadcasting? How could he have read her thoughts so well? Maybe he didn't need to be empathic to know what she felt.

"Is it?"

"Yes. If you want it badly enough."

Did she? She replayed the past. Ari. Ben. Ari. Ben.

*Mr. van Blaiden wants to know . . . *

Bugger Mr. van Blaiden.

Ben was warm and real, whatever he said, she knew he loved her and—go on, admit it—she loved him, too. The Ari in her mind was her own version of Ari van Blaiden. She'd clung to the image of the past for too long. It would destroy her if she didn't break free from it. Did she want to be free to love again?

"I think I do."

"Not good enough." He turned away from her, and she saw a tear of water from his wet braid run down the muscles of his back.

He was being hard on purpose. She supposed she deserved it. She'd trampled all over his feelings since that night on Mirrimar-14. If she was entirely honest with herself, she'd known right from the beginning that she'd touched him. She'd used him without giving anything back. Now was the time for giving. Giving and taking. Because she wanted to and not because she felt obliged.

She touched the rivulet, cutting it with her finger, felt the tension in his skin, in his whole body.

He turned.

She looked up at him. "I know I do."

"And you've got to trust me." He took her hand, curled it into a fist, and brushed his lips across her knuckles.

She nodded, not trusting her voice.

He bent his head forward and kissed her. It was gentle, warm and inquiring. His face was still damp from the shower. She pressed forward into him and returned the kiss, feeling a surge of excitement in her belly. A feeling that she'd almost forgotten. She let herself go.

Her arms wrapped around his neck involuntarily. He slipped the hem of her top up over her head and bared her upper body. Then, while she struggled to pull off the offending garment to free her arms, he ran his hands up from waist to underarm and then slid them round to the swell of her breasts.

She gasped involuntarily and pulled away. Was this just her hormones kicking in?

No, it wasn't. This was real. How could she have been so stupid for so long? Ben had been here, waiting for her to make her mind up, and she'd almost missed the moment.

It's never too late. He was in her head, but she didn't question it. Instead, she opened up her fears and her longings to him, implants meshing, and slipped a tight cocoon around their emotions to keep the rest of the world out.

A confusion of senses followed—physical, sensual, emotional—until they lay on the bed, exhausted, in a tumble of covers and clothes.

Perhaps she slept. She was floating in that halfway stage between reality and dreaming. She knew Ben now. There were no secrets between them. She knew the beautiful but brittle first Mrs. Benjamin and what it was like to make love to Gen Marling. She knew about Ben's worries that Crowder was playing politics with the whole Olyanda colony. What had she given Ben in return?

Poor Ben. He knew now what it was like to be screwed by Ari van Blaiden, in both senses of the word, and . . . She sat bolt upright as she remembered something and said, "I'm sorry."

"Sorry for what?" He was warm and sleepy.

"Sorry if I thought of Ari while . . ." She blushed.

"It won't happen again."

"What if . . ."

"I tell you it won't. Do I have to prove it?"

He reached up for her and they fell back among the covers.

Chapter Twenty-seven

CONSEQUENCES

BEN WHISTLED QUIETLY UNDER HIS BREATH as he logged in his ident to use the two-man flitter in the end transport bay. It had been two days since Cara had given herself permission to be whole again. Two wonderful days and even better nights that put him in a good mood even Lorient couldn't dispel. There was a low-key conspiracy among his team to keep the situation under wraps.

"Ben," Suzi called to him down the length of the hanger. "Cas said you were going out. I wanted to ask you something. Did you know Calvin suspected someone had been snooping at the tank farm?"

"Snooping?"

"He found a door forced this morning. Gupta is checking it out."

"Keep me informed. To the uneducated eye there's not much difference between tanking and cloning."

She nodded and went in search of the young vet.

Ben turned back to the flitter.

"Hello, Mr. Benjamin."

Ben recognized the voice behind him immediately. "Hello, Danny."

"Are you flying again?"

"I'm going to Timbertown to see your father."

"Can I come? I got a lift here in a groundcar. I need to go home now."

"I can take you."

Danny scuttled round to the other side of the flitter and jumped into the passenger seat.

Ben climbed into the pilot's seat. Under minimum power, he rolled the little machine out of the bay and set it up on its antigravs.

Danny was grinning again. "I like flying," he said. "I'll miss you when the psi-techs go home."

If you do, you'll be the only one. Ben's thought went unsaid.

✦ ✦ ✦

Cara felt as though she had just shed one outgrown skin and her new one was pulsing with life. She had given up all idea of following convention and was on duty with Gen, overflying some of the smaller watercourses between Timbertown and the next largest settlement. They'd decided to brazen it out together.

Gen was coping with the pregnancy much better now that she was able to admit it. Ronan had given her something for the sickness and confirmed that everything was progressing normally. She should have been full of optimism, but she was still fretting over Max's disappearance.

"He's keeping his head down, probably camping out somewhere quiet," Cara told her, but Gen wouldn't be convinced.

"He'd get a message to me somehow," she said.

"How? Be realistic." But privately Cara thought that she might be right. Jon Moon and Rufe Greenstreet hadn't found any sign of him. It was time to get a Finder out to look for Max.

They completed their sector and set a course for home. Cara had the controls. She flew in along the valley, over new settlements upriver from Timbertown. Trees had been felled and timber stacked for natural drying on the edge of the lumber camps. One or two structures in the settlements were at the foundation stage and several more had been marked out on the new town plan. Until homes were completed, the settlers would live in their wagons and in tents.

Timbertown, its street plan now well-defined, the meeting hall complete and several wooden houses already occupied, looked as busy as an ant colony from this height. Below them, the road to Landing was full of traffic. Another flitter registered on her screen some distance away. Cara knew instinctively it was Ben. Her mind reached out for his, and she was rewarded with a warm feeling of love. He was heading toward Timbertown with Danny Lorient in the passenger seat.

"Look." Gen pointed. Far ahead along the road there was a slim plume of smoke rising across the river from Landing.

Cara's belly knotted. *Ben. Smoke.* She gave him the coordinates and he swept round.

I see it. Fuck! It's the tank farm. Gestalt.

Cara handed the controls over to Gen and forgot about the immediate operation of the little craft. She opened her mind on a broad channel. Cas, safe in the ops room at Mapping, and Saedi, returned from Timbertown, joined her mentally to hold the combined minds of every psi-tech in the immediate area.

Emergency procedure. Ben gave the instruction through the gestalt, but individually, everyone was already following the carefully worked out routines.

On our way. Yan ordered the emergency vehicles airborne.

A blast of pure panic from psi-techs in the tank farm cut through, threatening to drown all other communication. It held many voices, but barely anything was coherent or recognizable.

There was pain, panic, and fear—each emotion powerful enough to overwhelm the unwary.

I'm on it, Cas said and split off from the whole.

Cara felt a wave of relief. Cas would monitor the disaster area to act as a lifeline for those inside it. Freed of that responsibility, Cara slammed down a shield between the gestalt and the psi-tech distress from the burning area. The thin plume of smoke was now a sticky black column billowing upward. Flames licked through the sections of roof that had already melted and dropped. Emergency vehicles doused the area with fire depressant from the air and water from the ground. Cara could see a corral of med vehicles surrounding an instant riser that inflated and formed an on-site emergency room. Ronan's people would already be in action beneath its cover. Damn, but they'd be missing Anna.

Gen circled the site above the level of the airborne fire-fighters, and Cara looked down. A bioplas structure should be resistant to flame. It didn't burn like that without help.

✦ ✦ ✦

Ben let his flitter's height bleed away, circling a short way above Gen and Cara. Beside him, Danny bounced up and down in his seat harness.

"It's not fair, Commander Ben. Not fair. People get hurt. Nasty, dangerous fire. Not fair."

Ben shut Danny out of his consciousness, keeping track of the situation through the gestalt. Gupta's men already had the flames under control, but estimated casualties were high. There had been at least twenty psi-techs on site, though not all in the main building. Ronan had only accounted for thirteen of them so far, and one of those was already dead.

"It was naughty. Very naughty. They shouldn't play with fire, should they?" Danny was still babbling, getting incoherent and tearful.

"Steady on, Danny. We can't help anyone like this." Ben took a few seconds to calm him down.

"It was bad. Mr. Colchek is a retard." Danny picked the worst insult he had in his vocabulary.

"Who?" Ben was suddenly interested.

"Mr. Colchek and Taris. I saw them down there on the road." Danny pointed to the Timbertown road. "They're both bad men. I don't like them. My Dad likes them, but I don't."

"What have they done, Danny?"

Danny shook his head and put his face in his hands melodramatically. "Oh, Commander Ben, don't get mad with me. They're the ones who get rid of the horrible things."

"Horrible things?"

"You know, clones and 'bominations."

Ben did know.

"Where did you see them?"

"Down there as we came to see the fire." Danny pointed again to the Timbertown Road.

"You're sure?"

"They were on horses. Taris has very white hair. That's why I noticed."

Ben circled the flitter and aimed it toward where Danny pointed.

Cara, did you catch all that?

Yes. I'm with you.

Gupta, who can you spare? Ben asked.

Three groundcars are on their way, Green Four, Five, and Six.

Thanks.

Cara opened up a link between Ben and each of the three groundcar drivers and their crews.

What are we looking for? Green Four asked.

Two men, heading toward Timbertown on horseback. One is white-blond. Ben looked into the distance. *They can't have gone far, but let's be sure. Groundcars make all possible speed to Timbertown. If you don't spot them, set up a roadblock and check everyone passing through. We'll fly the road. Cara, with me. See if we can catch them in a pincer.*

It was hard to spot two riders in the steady traffic that rolled between Timbertown and Landing each day, but Ben flew low to one side of the road, and hovered on the anti-gravs while they checked every face. Danny pressed his nose against the plasglass and kept up a running commentary. Gen and Cara went out on the left wing to make sure no one broke away.

"There." Danny saw the two horsemen and started to get excited.

They were on the road, trying to hide themselves between two grain wagons. Ben came in low behind them. Cara to the front. The two riders broke away from their fellow travelers and pushed their mounts forward into a gallop across the grassy plain, but Green Five and Six roared past them and circled back. Caught, they pulled up while Green Four closed the circle. The two flitters came in close, whining on their antigravs. The horses danced nervously.

Tranqs. Ben checked the tranq gun carried on every flitter for unexpected encounters with any of the native nasties. He calibrated the dosage for a human. Danny bobbed and swayed against his safety harness in a state of high excitement. "Danny, sit still and don't move, do you hear me?"

"Sit still." Danny nodded, scrunching down into his seat. "Don't move."

With the tranq gun in the holder and both hands on the controls, Ben dropped the flitter to the ground and abruptly cut the antigravs.

"Stay where you are, Danny." He hit his own harness release, threw up the bubble canopy and jumped up on his seat with the tranq gun in hand. Both riders broke for different gaps at the same time. The white-haired one, Taris, aimed for the other side of Cara and Gen's flitter and the dark one, Colchek, aimed between Ben and Green Four's groundcar.

Ben recalibrated for a horse and fired. His air-dart smacked into the rump of Colchek's mount; the animal ran on a few paces before it stumbled and fell. Behind him, he felt Cara's mind-link close down and he glanced back to check on her. The second horse was down as well, and he had a brief image of Cara launching herself over the wing of the flitter with Gen standing in the copilot's seat, a tranq gun firmly held in a two-handed grip.

The second crewman from Green Four jumped out of his groundcar and onto the downed rider. He yelled and rolled back. Ben saw blood spurting from a knife wound high on his inner arm.

Leaving Danny still strapped into his seat, Ben launched himself at Colchek, who was stumbling to his feet by the prone body of his horse, knife still in his grasp. Ben didn't stop. He went for the knife hand before the man could get a proper grip or stance. He twisted it viciously and heard the satisfying crack of bone. The man screamed.

"Keep still, you bastard, or you won't live to answer for what you've done."

The crew of Green Six was there within seconds. Ben looked up. Where was Cara?

◆ ◆ ◆

Everything happened in slowmo. Cara was aware of Ben going for the other fugitive, but she focused on her own quarry.

The white-haired man, Taris, hit the ground running as Gen's tranq dart stopped his horse in mid-stride. He ran like a whippet, but Cara leaped over the flitter's wing, dropped to the ground, and pounded after him, in front of the Greens by twenty paces. She got close enough and sprang to bring Taris down with a classic tackle. There was a brief moment when she knew she'd mistimed it, then she was too busy trying to deal with the consequences. She went down heavily with her chest on the back of Taris' booted feet. The air whooshed out of her lungs and she gasped, trying to ignore the pain in her breast. She crouched to bring her own feet under her trying to get a balance.

Taris recovered before she did. He was good. Good enough to have been combat trained—unusual for a settler. They were both still on the floor when he rolled round and shoved a weapon up to her head.

"That's far enough." Taris grasped her shoulder tightly with his free hand. "Get up quietly. Don't make any sudden moves."

She locked away panic and did as she was told. He rose with her and then shifted the gun's position and buried the muzzle in the side of her neck. It wasn't a tranq gun, in fact, it felt heavy enough to be a bolt gun. Briefly, she wondered how he'd obtained one of those. They were illegal on most civilized worlds, and doubly so on Olyanda where the biggest weapons the settlers had were crossbows and a variety of hunting blades. Even the psi-techs were strictly limited to tranquilizing smart-darts.

Taris transferred his grip to Cara's left arm and shoved her in front of him as the Greens approached with Ben close behind them.

The moment was frozen. Cara opened up to the psi-techs.

She felt Ben's surge of fear for her before he subdued it. In any critical situation fear could be useful, but it was too damaging if you let it get the upper hand.

"Get back," Taris yelled and he pushed Cara forward within a few meters of her flitter, always keeping her between himself and the approaching Greens. Gen was still standing on the seat, tranq gun in hand.

"Drop that," he said. "Set the drive on standby and climb down."

Take your time, Gen. Ben edged forward slowly.

"Climb down, unless you want to come along instead."

Slowly Gen climbed onto the wing-step, taking her time, exaggerating her movements.

Good girl, Cara thought. Anything was worth a try if it distracted him for even a second.

Cara fought for breath, dizzy with pain, but she didn't think she'd broken anything. She felt the way Taris had his weight distributed; she leaned slightly, testing for weakness; looking for some way she could overbalance him without his finger jerking automatically on the trigger.

"Mister Taris, that's bad." Danny Lorient released his harness and bobbed up in the passenger seat of Ben's flitter like a target at a fairground shooting gallery. Cara felt shock run through Taris' body. Maybe he thought Danny's pointing arm held a gun—whatever his reasoning, he swung around in alarm, aimed, and fired. Cara had no inkling of his intentions. She felt him move and a crack jarred her eardrum. She saw Danny fly back and fall slack in his seat while at the same time Ben yelled, *Down!*

She flung herself away as hard as she could, twisting to one side. The Greens, between Ben and Cara, dropped without question as Ben hurled something, then launched himself forward to follow it up. A knife flashed through the air above Cara's head and buried itself up to the hilt in Taris' shoulder. The gun fell from useless fingers. Cara rolled away and came to her feet as the Greens closed in.

Ben lunged forward. She flung her arms around him, partly because she needed to and partly because she saw the look in his eyes.

Let the Greens see to him, she said. *Danny . . . *

Danny's body lay crumpled and broken in the passenger seat, a black-and-bloody burn rupturing the upper half of his chest, his head thrown back and his breath coming in ragged gasps.

✦ ✦ ✦

Cara's arms and the Greens' efficiency came between Ben and murder. Or would it have been justice? Ben's head swam with the horror of it. He thought that seeing red was just a figure of speech, but his vision darkened and red blood pulsed in his vision.

The choking smell of burned flesh would stay with Ben forever. Bile rose in his throat, and he swallowed convulsively. He felt Cara shaking against him. Neither of them moved for what seemed like an age until Cara eased herself free of his protective arm. The paramedics had arrived quickly and were doing their best, but emergency cryo wasn't an option for Danny.

"Get a message to the Lorients." Ben said.

"There's no psi-tech in Timbertown. Lorient sent Saedi back, remember?"

"They should be with their son." He pinched the bridge of his nose and screwed up his eyes against tears that were close to the surface.

Cara tried the mechanical comm in her flitter, but the static washed out the signal.

"Get a message to Jack," Cara said. "Let him tell them."

"No. I feel useless here. Let's go. By the time the paramedics get Danny to the med-center, we can have the Lorients in Landing."

Cara grabbed his hands and dragged him a few paces away from the medics. "It's not your fault!" Her voice was full of anger. "Did you pull the trigger?"

"I put him in harm's way."

Cara pushed him, hard. "You can't see the future. Taris shouldn't have had access to that kind of weapon. If he did, it was because someone allowed it to be brought here against colony regulations."

"If I hadn't given the kid a lift . . ."

"He might have wandered over to the tank farm and been caught in the fire. He might have fallen from a horse and broken his neck."

"And he might have walked home safely. And lived to a ripe old age."

"He might. Would that have been your fault, too? He's not dead yet. Ben, you can't take on the guilt for this. If you carry the souls of everyone you've ever lost on your shoulders, you'll end up collapsing under the burden. You're still dragging the weight of all your dead crew from Hera-3—and Anna, Cooksey, and Coburg, no doubt. And likely Lee Gardham as well. You can't save everybody, no matter how hard you try. We're in a dangerous business. People get hurt out here in the vast deeps where there's precious little law and no backup. And, as commander, you're the one who has to bury them." She scrubbed tears away with the heel of her hand. "But then you need to let them go. Let them sleep easy in your memory. You're not to blame for Danny. You couldn't have known about the bolt gun; couldn't have known about Taris. Cut yourself some slack."

He shook his head. He couldn't afford to cut himself any slack. There were too many people depending on him.

❖ ❖ ❖

The rest of the afternoon passed in a blur of hurry-up-and-wait.

The Loriets allowed themselves to be shuttled to the med-center and such was their distress at Danny's condition that contrary to Cara's expectations there was not a single word of recrimination. It would come later, no doubt, but for now all their concern was for Danny.

Ben and Cara sat in the med-center lobby while Danny was in surgery. When he was transferred to a high-dependency room, the Loriets were admitted and Ben and Cara dismissed by Ronan.

"Go and get some rest, both of you," he said. "We're at full capacity here with the casualties from the fire. Get out from under my feet."

Saedi transferred back to Timbertown at Jack Mario's request. Jack took up the reins from Victor seamlessly.

A day passed.

Ronan had said if Danny could get through the first day he stood some kind of a fighting chance. Rena and Victor never left his bedside, though he wasn't conscious.

Cara began to hope that Ronan was a miracle worker. He spent some of his off-duty time at the boy's bedside, putting in a fix, as far as he could. The bolt gun had damaged Danny's heart, and there was no alternative but to replace it with an artificial one, a short-term solution which would not be sustainable once the psi-techs left the planet. But it was not only Danny's heart; his lungs were compromised, too.

Partway through the second day, Lorient asked to see Ben.

"Shall I come?" Cara asked, half hoping Ben would say no. She wasn't sure she could face the overwhelming emotion that Lorient would be likely to be transmitting.

In answer, Ben kissed her on the forehead and left alone, returning barely half an hour later looking strained.

"Bad?" she asked.

"Bad enough. He's in shock, barely knows which way is up."

"He knows about Taris and Colchek?"

Ben nodded, "But I don't think Rena's aware. If she finds out . . ."

◆ ◆ ◆

After three days, Victor began to hope that Danny would pull through. He didn't remember a time when he'd not been sitting by the boy's bedside, watching the machines like a hawk in case there was some kind of change.

Rena sat on the opposite side of the bed, her hand on Danny's, though the boy wasn't aware.

Dr. Wolfe had said this was a medically induced coma, for Danny's own well-being. It kept him pain-free and gave him the best chance of recovery. Their other alternative would be to put him into cryo and ship him back to Earth. However, given his previous reaction to cryo, that would likely kill him anyway.

Victor had brought one of their own medics in for a second opinion and had been told in no uncertain terms that the psi-techs had the best chance of getting Danny through this and to agree to whatever they offered in terms of tech if he wanted his son to live.

"We've done everything we can," Dr. Wolfe had told him. "It's up to Danny now."

Victor had been so distraught he'd even forgotten to keep the numbers running in his head.

Dr. Wolfe had called regularly, not getting too close, but sitting quietly in the room, his eyes closed. What was all that about? He'd asked the nurse and had been told that Dr. Wolfe was a psi-tech Healer. Victor's first reaction had been to tell him to get out, but seeing Rena's face as she held Danny's hand, he thought that any chance was better than none.

Rena hardly spoke. Did she suspect?

Victor felt a sick dread rise to choke him. Taris and Colchek. How could it all have gone so badly wrong? He'd never intended . . .

But he'd never curbed them, either.

On the fourth day, Dr. Wolfe asked if he could speak to them both together.

"Will he live?" Rena had asked, her eyes hollow and dark with lack of sleep and pain.

"There's been no improvement. It's time to bring him around and see what happens. It could go either way."

Rena looked at Victor.

He couldn't read her expression. Did she blame him?

"He could die," Rena said.

Dr. Wolfe nodded. "He could live."

"Will he be in pain?"

He shook his head. "No, though there may be some discomfort. That's no bad thing. He needs to fight. Sometimes a patient's conscious will to live makes all the difference. We think it's the best chance Danny has."

"Will he know us?" Victor felt as though his own heart was trying to rise in his throat and choke him.

"He should."

Rena nodded. "Then let's do it."

Victor found himself nodding.

Dr. Wolfe made some adjustments to the drips that fed into Danny's cannula. "You should be the first people he sees when he wakes. Tell him—"

"We know what to tell him," Rena said.

Dr. Wolfe nodded and stepped back.

Victor lost track of time, but when Rena sat up straight and squeezed Danny's hand, he knew that the boy was awake.

"Mom . . . Dad." Danny's voice was weak, but he managed a smile.

"How do you feel, son?" Victor asked.

"Funny."

"Funny ha-ha or funny peculiar?" Rena dropped back to a question from Danny's childhood.

"Funny pec-u . . ." Danny couldn't quite manage the word but his eyes said he understood the joke.

"We love you, Danny," Victor said.

"'Course you do, Dad."

Rena choked back a sob.

Danny squeezed her hand. "I love you, too. Can I go flying again, soon?"

"As soon as you get better. You can go flying as many times as you like," Victor said. "I'll come with you."

"Me, too," Rena said.

"Commander Benjamin will have to get a bigger flitter." Danny smiled, but the expression froze on his face. The monitor flashed red, and Dr. Wolfe stepped forward to check it.

"Is he . . . ?" Rena asked.

"He's sleeping again," Dr. Wolfe said.

Twenty-six hours later, a day of Victor staring at Danny's pale face willing him to live, Dr. Wolfe admitted that he was not going to wake up.

Victor sat and watched the machine recording the beat from his son's artificial heart, but it wasn't life. Rena still held onto Danny's hand, but there was no longer any hope.

When Dr. Wolfe finally suggested switching off the machines, Rena broke down and howled over Danny's still body. Victor tried to comfort her, but she shook him off and gave him a look of pure hatred.

She knows, he thought.

And he didn't know what scared him most, losing Danny or losing Rena.

❖ ❖ ❖

"Are you all right—really all right?" Ben asked when they were safe in their room, a lifetime later.

"I'd really begun to hope Danny would . . ."

"I know. Me, too."

They'd spent the last few days between the clearing-up operation at the tank farm, the med-center and the riser where the two arsonists were behind a solid wall of Gupta's guards. There was no way they were going to give those two over to the Ecolibrians without some assurances.

Jack Mario was desperately trying to keep a lid on the settler situation, but rumors already blamed the psi-techs for Danny Lorient's injuries despite all Jack's information to the contrary. Jack had eventually been forced to call a public meeting to calm down the crowds and, in Timbertown at least, had firmly reminded them that Danny had been shot by one of their own using an illegal weapon.

The death toll at the tanking station reached six, including both Calvin Tanaka and his wife. Two more were still on the critical list and there was one other with injuries that would keep her hospitalized for a long time.

"If you really want to know, I'm not all right at all," Cara answered Ben's question. "How about you?"

"I've been better."

He held out his arms and she folded herself into them, their buddysuits rubbing together like thick hide.

"Here, let's get out of these." Ben unfastened Cara's and helped her to peel it off and she did the same for him. Then they stripped off the lightweight undersuits and dropped them in the laundry. They shared the shower, soaping and massaging each other's aches away. Cara's left breast still showed a yellowing bruise where she'd landed on Taris' boots.

"You should go to Ronan with that." Ben ran his hand across the blotchy skin.

She shook her head. "I've got some arnica gel. It's old-fashioned, but it works."

"Here, then. Let me."

They climbed into bed together and he smoothed the gel onto her skin, then held her very gently until they fell asleep.

Chapter Twenty-eight

ABANDONED

★*THE ARK'S GONE.*★ CAS RITSON CUT INTO Cara's first caff of the morning. She crossed to the bed and prodded Ben awake, linking him through to Cas before the importance of the words sank in.

Gone?

She felt Ben make the transition from sleep to full consciousness in a moment.

I just tried to uplift today's colony log to their matrix as usual and they're not there.

Perhaps their system's down, Ben tried to rationalize.

I tried everything before I called you. There's no matrix, no mechanical comm-link, and no one within parsecs with an implant. In short—there's no ark.

Ben sat up and swung both legs out of bed.

"If Cas says they've gone, they've gone," she said. "They could already be in the Folds if she can't raise Molloy. I'd say that was a good definition of *gone*." Cara let the link drop. "They weren't supposed to leave before the second ark got here. Does this mean we're stranded?"

Ben's mouth compressed into a grim line. "Looks like it. Damn." He reached for his buddysuit.

"You said Crowder was sitting on the platinum information," Cara said.

"Let's not jump to conclusions. It might be nothing to do with—."

"He's stranded us because he's going to send in raiders." Cara felt the color drain from her face.

"Not Crowder." Ben pulled on his trousers and shrugged into his top.

"You sure you trust him?"

"I know Crowder. He's devious, but he's a friend. He's not above being manipulative to get what he wants, but what he wants is always what he considers to be the right thing. He's not out for personal profit. He's a Trust man, through and through. Everything he does is to advance the Trust, and his only personal ambition is to sit on the Board. He says he'll be chairman one day, and I believe him."

Cara crushed her caff cup and threw it into the recycler. "What better way to get a seat on the Board than to deliver a whole planet-load of platinum?"

"No, you're wrong. Dead wrong."

"I've been searching Ari's files. I'm beginning to understand devious. He talks to someone in the Trust, but he uses a code word." She dragged on an undershirt and then hopped about pulling on the lightweight leggings she wore beneath her buddysuit. "I hope I'm wrong, but Crowder's the one not answering messages. He's the one not sending the transport ship to take us home. If it's not Crowder, then who is it?"

"There's always the chance that one of ours has put two and two together."

Cara dragged on her buddysuit in two halves and locked them together. "Only a Psi-1 or a strong gestalt of class twos could send a message off planet and I doubt either Saedi or Cas could do it without me feeling their power usage, and certainly I'd feel the pull of a gestalt, so besides me, you, and Wenna . . . there's only Crowder." She fastened the shoulder clasps and stood up.

He looked at her steadily. "And I've got to believe it wasn't you, if I want to stay sane."

"It wasn't me."

"Maybe he's let the information slip, or someone's stolen it. Maybe the ark . . ."

"Crowder," Cara said firmly. It was the only conclusion that fit. He was too good at what he did to let that kind of information slip.

Cara tasted Ben's bitterness. It was an echo of how she'd felt when she'd discovered Ari's duplicity. He shook his head.

"That's what I thought about Ari, but I was wrong."

"I need to talk to Crowder, direct. Not through Ishmael. Can you do it?"

She nodded, sending her thoughts snaking out into the blackness of space through the Folds, homing in on Chenon, searching for just one among thousands. She knew Crowder, knew his voice, his face. She'd been in his mind. She should be able to find him, no problem. Distance was only a barrier if she let herself believe it was. She searched and searched again. Nothing. At last there was a little flicker of surprise and then it was as if a gate slammed down.

"He's shielding. His damper's up to maximum."

"Do whatever you have to do to crack through."

"I might need a gestalt. I'm a Psi-1, not a miracle worker."

"I don't want to panic anyone else, yet. Maybe I can get reassurance from Crowder. Will you try alone first?"

"Okay."

She sat on the floor and crossed her legs, finding a good mental balance, clearing all the rubbish and settling herself into a deep meditative state. Could she manage a triad with an uncooperative third at this kind of distance? There was no real reason why not. The only limitations were those she set herself. *Believe it.*

She drew her energy into the calm space she'd created in her center, pushed away thoughts of the enormous distance and instead she fixed on Chenon and then on Crowder himself, seeking outward, imagining herself like a missile locked onto its target.

She fired.

But the target wasn't there. Instead of Crowder, Cara's thought impacted on a queasy amorphous blob. It was him, but it wasn't, and she certainly couldn't communicate with it. If she'd been standing, she would have fallen. As it was, she rocked backward until Ben caught her and held her steady.

"What do you need?"

She blinked and looked through him. Her focus had fractured completely, her temples beginning to throb.

He bent her arm and checked the vital signs on her cuff. She didn't need the buddysuit readout to tell her that her adrenaline levels were at maximum and her heart rate was up and off the scale.

"Cara."

"I'm all right." She stumbled over the words. "But . . . but I couldn't get through. He's deactivated his implant. He definitely doesn't want to talk to us."

Ben bent her forward and shoved her head down between her knees, then he knelt behind her and rubbed her back and shoulders gently until she sighed and sat up.

"I'm sorry." She put both hands over her eyes and tried to breathe away the disorientation.

"What happened?" he asked.

"It was like running through syrup." She rubbed her eyes. "I couldn't fasten on anything. It was definitely him, but not him. There was something blocking his implant—deliberately. Either his damper's got a modification I've not come across before, or he's on a suppressant drug—Reisercaine, perhaps. Someone with a basic receiving implant could survive on that for long periods if he really doesn't want to talk to us."

Ben swore. "He'd have to be desperate to do that."

She nodded. "I think . . ." She waved at her handpad. "There might be answers here. Ari's files."

"See what you can find." Ben squeezed her shoulder.

✦ ✦ ✦

Cara settled herself at the table in their room and began systematically checking Ari's files. If the answer was in there, she'd find it. She hoped for Ben's sake that she was wrong about Crowder, but that brief noncontact had been enough to convince her that whatever was wrong involved their boss on some level. Why shield like that otherwise?

She was grateful that Ben left her to it. He brought her fruit tea midmorning, put it by her elbow, and left without saying a word. At noon he placed a bowl of chowder on the table, then dropped a kiss onto the top of her head. "Any luck?"

She didn't raise her eyes from the holographic display. "Possibly. Ari definitely has an informer in the Trust, but I don't know who, and he's hired in mercenaries more than once. There's a lot of routine stuff to filter out, but I'm looking for anything relevant to platinum or piracy or . . ." Her skin went clammy as her eyes spotted a name. "Oh . . ."

"Just 'oh'?" Ben asked.

"When was Hera-3?"

"Hera-3? You've found something?"

"I think so. It says H-3 and it's late '94." She turned her wrist and let Ben see the display.

He flicked to the next screen and the next and the next, then he bumped fists with Cara and copied files to his own handpad. "Got the bastards at last."

The catch in his voice betrayed his emotions. She grabbed him and held him tight. "That's good, isn't it?"

He pulled back and sighed. "Yes. It's good, but . . ."

"So Hera-3 was Alphacorp?"

"Alphacorp and the Trust. Combined. I knew that someone had to have sold us out, I just . . . I didn't suspect . . . a combined job. That makes it a lot more complicated."

"Why would you? I didn't suspect Ari for the longest time. Even when I began to think something might be going on, I tried to find excuses for him. For a while I tried to convince myself it was Craike working alone."

"We have to bring everyone together: section heads plus Lorient and Jack Mario. I'm not sure how I'm going to . . ." He let his hands fall limply to his knees. "Give me another half hour with those files and then I'll bring what I've got to the LV."

◆ ◆ ◆

Cara stood outside the LV and watched the skies above Landing. What was she expecting? They'd known this would be a tricky assignment. The settler situation was critical enough; they didn't need to be screwed by their own side, too. The warm summer wind ruffled her hair. The intense heat and humidity had already gone out of the season. Autumn wasn't far away. For a change, Olyanda wasn't trying to fry them or blow them away. It was hard to think that invaders from offworld might be on their way to rip minerals out of the planet.

Jack Mario walked across from stores. He'd dropped everything and hitched a ride on one of the regular supply cars. Cara led him into the meeting where Ben waited.

"Lorient?" Cara asked.

"He says whatever it is I can handle it. It's only been three days since the funeral."

"I understand, but this is big. He should be in on it."

"We're all here now," said Marta Mansoro, sliding in through the door. "What's it all about, Boss?"

"You're here because I trust you," Ben said. "That's trust with a small t. Right now Trust with a capital T is a dirty word."

Cara counted bodies. Fourteen with herself and Ben. Wenna, Gen, Cas, Suzi, Serafin, Ronan, Gupta, Marta, Yan, Archie, Saedi, and Jack.

Jack looked uncomfortable, especially when Ben asked him if he'd told anyone about this meeting. "If you're planning anything against Director Lorient, I should warn you that my loyalties have to lie firmly with the settlers."

"We wouldn't put you in that kind of position," Ben said. "It's much more serious than that and it directly concerns the long-term welfare of the whole colony. The director already knows about it."

"So what gives, Boss?" Suzi spoke aloud out of respect for their silent guest.

"How much of a surprise would it be to any of you to know that this planet is rich—and I mean rich—in platinum?"

"Platinum? Wow." Yan Gwenn whistled.

Cara watched all the faces. Wenna knew already, but by the look on her face, Gen had worked it out, too.

"What are the implications?" Ronan asked.

"Doesn't that depend on who knows about it?" Suzi glanced at him sideways.

"Precisely," Ben said. "I would have sworn that no one off this planet knew, except for . . ." He hesitated. "Crowder."

"Crowder's all right," Wenna said. "He's straight."

"I agree. If we can't trust Crowder, who can we trust?" Cas said.

Cara shuddered. She had her own views on that.

Ben continued, "I'm just telling you all the facts." He took a deep breath. "We discovered the platinum early. Wenna spotted it in the logs from Gen's flyer on the day of the first storm. At Lorient's insistence we kept it quiet, but there are huge deposits on this continent. Who knows what else there is hidden under the polar icecaps and the glacial plain."

"Boss, how big is huge?" Suzi asked.

"Difficult to estimate without a more detailed survey, but it's probably got the potential to be bigger than Suran Sixteen."

"Shit! That's the sort of thing any of us might risk a lifetime's reputation on," Yan said.

"We might, but we won't," Cas said. "It's only money."

"And it's power for the corporations, and that's what it's all about." Cara leaned forward. "They'll do whatever they have to do to maintain power for themselves, especially if they can block a rival in the same move."

"Look, what does this all mean?" Jack asked. "You say the director knows about it?"

"He does. I wanted him to sell the mineral rights and buy a new planet right at the beginning, but he wouldn't. Platinum is good news and bad news. Yes, it's worth a fortune, but everyone with a bigger stick than you is trying to take your lottery ticket before you can cash it in.

"Lorient decided to bury the information about the platinum, but that was dependent on Crowder cooperating. We thought—I thought—that Crowder was totally trustworthy, but now there are things happening that I don't like," Ben said. "I think there's a major player looking to score, or even two major players." He leaned forward. "Unless we tell the FPA about the platinum, which means we get legal pirates instead of illegal ones, we might as well be dead for all we can do from here." Ben's fist clenched.

"So what's happened to bring all this to a head now?" Ronan asked.

"The ark's gone and I've just been given answers to questions I've been asking for a long time."

"The ark?" Jack half stood and then dropped back to his chair. "But that's impossible. It hasn't finished unloading our supplies."

"I wish it was, Jack. We're on our own."

"The second ark?"

"If it arrives."

"Crowder promised to send transport. What about the arrangements for us to go home?" Suzi Ruka said.

"I just get a load of waffle from Ishmael. I've had no response from Crowder at all. Cara's tried to contact him, and he's shielded." Ben let that information sink in.

Cara had never seen so many stunned faces. Desolate would be a better word.

"The bastards don't intend to let us leave, do they?" Serafin asked. "Not if we know about the platinum."

"Cara has a few more pieces of the puzzle," Ben said. "There's a connection you're not going to like."

"I should tell you about Ari van Blaiden," she said.

Mr. van Blaiden wants to know ...

Get out of my head!

The nausea hardly bothered her at all now.

She talked without interruption until the whole story had been delivered from beginning to end, though she caught Jack's eye as she glossed over the sham marriage. It didn't seem to matter now.

"You're saying this Ari van Blaiden person is some kind of pirate? If they come in here to rip the platinum out, what happens to the colony?" Jack asked.

There was a loud silence around the room. They all looked at Ben.

"I'll tell him," Wenna said. "On Hera-3 they wiped out a whole colony. We figured the big money was behind it, either Alphacorp or the Trust. Now it looks like it was both, but we had no proof until now."

"How could they . . ." Jack began.

"Because space is big and even a whole planet is a very

insignificant part of it." Ben took a deep breath. "Cara had the answers all along, but she couldn't access them until she beat the neural block. We've been through Ari van Blaiden's files, and his mole in the Trust might be Crowder."

The room broke out into a babble of incredulity. Everyone had trusted Crowder. He was their boss, their lifeline. He'd saved their individual and collective butts times without number.

Cara felt as though she was the only one who'd never trusted him, never felt he was on her side.

Ben held his hands up for silence. "I'm sorry. I know how you feel. I don't want to believe it either."

"Boss, how could it be Crowder? You saved his sorry ass on Londrissi," Cas said. "We're small-fry in any power games, but how could he do it to you? Hera-3 nearly damn well killed us all, you included."

Marta turned to Ben. "That's why you wanted the Dixie Flyer," she said. "Have you got a psi rating in clairvoyance that you're not telling us about?"

"The Dixie was for Cara's benefit."

Cara would have protested her part in it, but Cas didn't give her time.

"You've got a flyer here?" she asked.

Ben nodded. "I was hoping I wouldn't need it."

"Then we've got options," Serafin said.

"I want to try and contact someone I think may be able to help, before we try anything else."

"Crowder?" Cas asked.

Ben shook his head. "Mother Ramona on Crossways. Even her spies have spies. You wouldn't believe how many top-ranking officials she's fixed things for. After that, possibly, someone has to go back home, to Chenon, and do some digging. We have to know for sure who's behind this."

"That's you, isn't it?" Cara asked. She didn't want to see him leave, but she knew he was the only one who could effectively access the system.

"No one else would find the answers. It's a two-man flyer." Ben looked around at the group. "Unless anyone has any serious objections, I'm going to take Cara. Not just because I love her . . ." Cara heard his words with a shiver of pleasure. "But because a Psi-1 on comms will be useful, and because if Ari van Blaiden is involved, she's a sitting target here—even more than the rest of you."

There were no objections.

"I just used up a whole lot of energy trying to contact Crowder," Cara said. "A gestalt would make life easier for the Crossways contact."

Cas and Saedi both linked implants with her. She took the focus and put Ben right up front. She gathered all the implants in one by one and molded them together. It was a bit like making a snowball, and when the ball was tight and firm and perfectly round, she hurled it.

✦ ✦ ✦

Mother Ramona.

*Gods, it's the middle of the night. Benjamin? It is you? Still alive? I was so sorry to hear . . . *

Ben felt Cara's mind retreat, leaving him to talk to Mother Ramona. When he'd finished, she let the link drop and everyone looked at him. The weight of their expectations settled on his shoulders.

"According to all the official records, this colony is in the grip of a plague—a local virus no one can find a cure for. It's deadly, and we've been quarantined."

"Well, can't we just tell them that there's no virus?" Archie said. "We've got three Psi-1s here—is there anyone we can't reach?"

"There's a quarantine notice out on this planet," Ben said. "No one will break that, no matter what we say and who we say it to. If we were really infected, we'd say anything to get help . . . or at least that's the way logic goes." He felt a headache building up behind his eyes.

"What about the second ark?" Jack asked.

"It's supposed to be here any time now—if it's coming."

"What does that mean?" Jack asked.

"I wish I knew."

"Thirty thousand souls. What have they done?"

"Possibly nothing, but if we make a big fuss and set people off asking questions and searching, the easiest way to dispose of them is to push their ark into the Folds and not bring it out the other side. Realistically, there's not much we can do from here, not yet. I've asked Mother Ramona to see if she can trace the vessel. Something that big has to have been logged through gates, and there's a limit as to which gates it can use. She'll find it."

Jack's face was a mask of surprise, shock, and shattered dreams. Eventually he took a deep breath. "So do we think van Blaiden's on his way, or is it Crowder?" He rubbed his forehead with the back of his hand. "And does it matter which one of them is screwing us?"

Everyone went quiet until Cas voiced the big concern. "If we're under quarantine, then there's no rescue. If they think there's a rampant virus loose on the planet, they won't send anyone. Ever. Again."

"We're on our own," Suzi Ruka said.

Ben was aware that Cara had said very little yet. He desperately wanted to talk all this through with her, see if she had an angle on it that he hadn't seen. "Not quite, Suzie," he said. "We're on our own with a planet full of platinum, ten thousand settlers, and some contacts who aren't ruled by either the Trust or Alphacorp." He turned to Jack. "We'll have to mine some of the stuff now. Enough to fund some kind of resistance or at least secure a loan on good faith to buy what we need to set this thing straight."

"I wouldn't blame you if you all just bought your own way out of here and took enough platinum with you to retire to somewhere safe," Jack said.

Wenna rubbed her prosthetic arm. "That's not our way."

Jack shrugged. "Why can't we just offer to sell them the platinum? Hell, we can give it to them if it keeps the colony safe."

Cara shook her head. "How much do you know about platinum mining and refining for use in the jump gates, Jack?"

"Nothing . . . well, next to nothing anyway."

"On this scale it's destructive. There are several igneous reefs with high concentrations of ore, but much of the platinum is spread thinly over a wide area of alluvial deposits. The easiest way to access it is to strip-mine, spoiling vast tracts of land. It takes over three metric tons of ore to pro-

duce a gram of platinum, and getting that ore is wasteful.
Then there's the refining. There's pollution from cyanide,
heavy metals, and acid mine drainage. Exposure to platinum salts has adverse health risks, and that's before they
start processing it for the jump gate rods. Believe me, you
don't want that on Olyanda."

"Besides . . ." Ben took over. "If Olyanda was auctioned
off on the open market, the price would be higher than either the Trust or Alphacorp wanted to pay. Neither of them
wants to get into a bidding war."

"And we couldn't do an inside deal?" Jack's voice
sounded close to panic.

"Not legally."

"Do we care about legal?"

"Not entirely, but the megacorps want to retain the appearance of legality."

"So we're fucked."

"Not if we can help it," Ben said. "We've got enough platinum to buy help, the biggest problem is whether we can do
it before the raiders arrive."

"Are we going to fight for the planet?" Jack asked.

"No, we're going to fight to leave it," Ben said. "Try and
take your settlers somewhere safe. Find them a nice
platinum-free planet. I only said it couldn't be sold legally.
If whoever we sell it to has the firepower to hold it, they get
to keep it."

He looked around at the sea of faces, but really only
wanted reaction from one.

Why did I ever doubt you? she asked on a tight band
that was meant for him alone. *Even Jack's fallen naturally
into letting you make plans.*

But have I made the right plans?

*In a lose-lose situation, coming up with any kind of plan
is difficult enough, but protecting the people is paramount—
and that's what you're doing.*

He felt a warm glow. He didn't need her approval, but he
was glad to have it.

"Cara and I will take ore samples and surveys to Crossways. I've got a contact there, so we'll do a deal and hire a
transport fleet to come and get everyone."

"Ten thousand of us," Jack said. "In cryo? That took months."

"We don't have months," Cas said. "And we don't have the cryo units."

"It will take four superliners," Ben said. "Or a fleet of smaller transports . . . Let me see what Mother Ramona can come up with."

"What about the towns? The farms? The animals?" Jack asked.

"Abandon them. Turn the livestock loose, leave the towns and farmsteads as decoys."

"It's all a bit . . . radical, isn't it?" Jack looked dazed. "What if you're wrong? What if they don't come?"

"They will," Cara said.

"Hope for the best, but plan for the worst." Ben said. "By the time this plan is underway, we should have confirmation one way or the other. If we're wrong, all you'll have to do is round up your animals again and bring the settlers home."

Cara leaned forward and put a hand on Jack's arm. "If we're right—and you do nothing—your settlers will be sitting targets when bombs fall on your towns. Which would you rather do? Act and look foolish, or don't act and die?"

"I'll ask the director."

"No, Jack," Ben said. "Time's past for asking. And with all respect, the director isn't in the best frame of mind right now. I'm telling you, and then you tell him. This is how it's going to be. We'll send psi-techs to every settlement, and I'd like a settler representative, one who's got the gift of the gab, to travel with each of them to make sure your settlers understand this is for real and that cooperation is required."

"Tell them about the platinum?"

"No, that'll just complicate matters. Tell them we've landed in the middle of a territorial war we knew nothing about. Tell them it's aliens."

"Aliens!"

"Joke. Tell them anything they'll believe."

"They might believe in aliens."

"As if."

"Right. Territorial war it is."

"That's almost true. This is the territory. Good man . . . and, Jack?"

"Yes?"

"How are the Lorients?"

"Really?"

"Yes, really."

"I've never seen them like this. After the initial shock Rena's holding up better than Victor, but she's barely talking to him."

"Does she know Lorient sent Colchek and Taris?"

Jack shuddered. "She might have suspicions, but 'sent' may be too strong a word . . . 'inspired' is closer, I think."

"Are you sure about that? Lorient thought the tank farm was the equivalent of cloning, and Danny was pretty sure they were Lorient's men."

"Well, sadly, we shall never know."

"Surely you'll put them on trial?"

"There will be a hearing. The result is a foregone conclusion. Colchek and Taris will get what's coming to them."

"I'd like to testify."

"I'll pass that on, but you understand that we have to minimize the grief, and . . . we want our director back."

"Oh, I get it," Cara said. "There won't be any connection found between Lorient and the arsonists, will there?"

"Under other circumstances I'd push them on that, but right now there are too many other people to worry about."

As the meeting broke up, Gen grabbed both Cara and Ben by the arm and pulled them aside. "You've got to do something about Max," she said. "He's in trouble. Otherwise, he'd have turned up somewhere or contacted us somehow. And if he is out there somewhere, laying low, he won't know any of this is happening—he'll be left behind. I know you don't like him, Ben, but, please, let me send a team of Finders out looking for him."

"I have no feelings for him one way or the other," Ben said. "Although he's caused his fair share of trouble. Yes, start Sami Isaksten searching. See if you can locate him and bring him in."

Chapter Twenty-nine

CLASH

*B*EN! CARA!* GEN'S TELEPATHIC SHOUT, CLOSE
to panic, cut across Cara's breakfast in the dining hall.
Emergency.

Gen. Steady. Cara reeled under the onslaught and
shoved her plate away. Ben was over by the counter collecting his own tray, but he was already in on the conversation.
He could hardly avoid it; Gen was frantic. Cara's brain felt
like it had been hit by an electric shock. A rainbow of colors
danced behind her eyelids. She gritted her teeth. *Slow
down, Gen, what's the matter?*

*They put Max on trial this morning in Timbertown.
Found a letter I . . . Got some liar to say they'd seen us together. He's scheduled for execution with Colchek and Taris.
Victor's just announced it. They all cheered. Cheered! Do
something. They're going to burn them.*

It was the mental equivalent of a sob. *Burn them!*

Cara felt something nasty crawling between her shoulder
blades. Ben had made a crack about burning Max at the
stake—how ironic. So much for justice.

Gen. Ben butted in. *When and where?*

*Tomorrow at sunrise. They've got them all locked up in
the undercroft at Central Hall right now.*

Where are you?

Still in Timbertown.

Come home, Gen. We'll figure something out, Ben said.

Gen wanted to stay close to Max; Cara could feel it without words.

Ben's right. Come home, Cara said. She closed down the communication and hurried straight to the Mapping office.

By the time she arrived, Ben had told Wenna what was happening.

"Uh-huh, Boss, I can see what's coming. Let someone else break Max out."

"Who?" Ben asked.

"Gupta, maybe. He can look after himself."

"No, I can't ask anyone else to do it. This isn't official business."

"Ask for volunteers."

"I wouldn't put anyone else in that position."

"Dammit. Ben, you can't do it on your own," Wenna said.

"He won't be on his own," Cara said. "I'm going, too." She saw the look on Ben's face.

"Don't argue, Ben, she's right," Wenna said. "And you'd better let a few others in on the deal. You'll need backup. I'd volunteer myself, but I couldn't trust this arm one hundred percent. I'll work control for you from here, though."

Ben nodded to Wenna. "We'll do it tonight. Can we get Serafin's schematics for the building?" He turned back to Cara. "We'll need a team that's good in a tight corner. Ask Ronan if he's willing to join us and . . . Archie Tatum with a score of sapper bots." He grinned, but the smile didn't quite reach his eyes. "That should give us an edge."

❖ ❖ ❖

In the entrance to a half-finished building, right across from the Central Hall in the center of Timbertown, four shadows blended into the darkness.

Cara tugged up the collar of her work-worn settler coverall. She pulled a cap down over her hair, rubbed at the smudged dirt on her cheeks, and breathed deeply, fighting down the butterflies that danced in the pit of her belly.

She looked across at Ben, another shadow inside their quiet cocoon. He seemed calm on the surface, but she could feel that he was ready for action, functioning on several levels. He had the plan uppermost in his mind with an awareness of their group actions and each individual's own part. Timing was critical.

The hall lights shone through the high windows across the street as settlers attended a silent midnight meditation before the executions. Just around the corner, nestled in the shade of an alleyway, Gen sat in a standard four-man groundcar with the cargo space stripped and padded to take two more passengers. It had been there since before dark. A few minutes ago, Gen had casually walked from their shelter and slipped into the driver's seat.

Lorient's disciples had already started to build a fire pit in the market square. Cara could see the glow from here.

Barbaric, Ronan said on a narrow band that went no farther than the four of them. *This is all about revenge for Danny's death, and it's a huge warning to anyone else who steps out of line.*

Ready? Ben looked to Archie.

Archie licked his lips and nodded.

Gestalt.

On Ben's signal, Cara linked them together. What one knew, all knew. Cara, Ben, Gen, Ronan, and Archie became one being with five separate mobile units, each capable of individual thought yet working as a team in a way which a deadhead could never understand.

Archie slipped away quietly, and Cara was aware of him approaching the base of the bell tower with a posse of tiny spider-legged engineering bots, known as sappers. He sent them on their way up the walls, controlling each one with precise ease as they drilled and lasered, tunneled and levered.

The midnight bell began to chime. Nine—ten—eleven— and CRACK! The splitting of timber released such tensions that it sounded like a projectile weapon. The two main beams supporting the bell shifted, and there was an almighty clang as several tons of bronze alloy dropped to lodge crosswise in the tower against a beam which was not designed to take its weight.

Instant panic gripped the crowd. Archie relayed the scene

as he quietly slipped away. No one individual could be heard above the clamor. Those inside were jostling each other in the doorways to get out.

Several people came running from the market square and were trying to get in to see what was happening. Cara, Ben, and Ronan ran with the rest. A small side door swung open, unlatched by a bot, and they slipped into the shadows to find Archie waiting.

Hold on—I have to put the lights out.

Archie ran back to where he had a view of the body of the hall. Cara could feel him retrieving the tiny sapper bots one by one and sending them to each light source. The candle flames flickered and died, and there were yells and bumps. No doubt someone would find an oil lamp and re-light it, but until then, the confusion provided a good cover. When he came back, the four of them ran down the steps that led to the undercroft, their soft-tread boot soles making little noise on the stone floor.

There was no light at all, but they were all wearing infra-red beamers and night-lenses so with Serafin's schematic in their implants and the Ben-talent for direction pushed to the fore there was no error. They arrived at a strong internal door.

Barely pausing, the part of them that was Archie silently sent a bot to flip a few levers inside the mechanical lock. They waited to see if anyone in the room had noticed. The Cara-Ronan part sensed six deadheads in the room. Max and five guards? Unlikely. Probably Max, Colchek, and Taris with three guards.

The prisoners must be shackled; otherwise there would be more than three guards. It was Ben's thought, but they all understood it simultaneously.

The guards were well-insulated from the noise of the evacuation upstairs. Cara shut herself off from the fear that was bouncing around in the undercroft from the condemned men, and tried to concentrate on the guards. They had a kind of swagger-feel about them that said they were armed.

Maybe less sharp than unarmed men might be, she said.

Ready? On my mark. Go! Ben kicked them into action.

As they burst through the door, Cara dropped to the right and Ben to the left, drawing eyes away from Archie and Ronan. Ben carried a fist-sized stone in one hand that he'd picked up outside. He lobbed it at the groin of the first figure and the man folded in two. Cara took the second one, rolling in under his aim as he brought his weapon into play. She pushed him backward and went for his arm, slamming his elbow hard into the stone wall. While his gun fell from numb fingers, she put him out with a single anesthetic dart from her smart-dart gun.

She looked round. Ben was just straightening up from the third man. It had only taken seconds so far.

Ronan ran straight to Max. He'd been roughed up, so he didn't look pretty, but he was still on his feet.

Colchek and Taris were backed against a wall, shackled as Max was, with no regard for the cast on Colchek's arm.

Here, Archie. Ronan signaled him over, and Archie crouched over Max's wrists and ankles. The tiny sapper bot disappeared inside the lock mechanism and the shackles fell away.

Out now, Ben said and motioned toward the door.

"What about us?" Colchek called out.

"What about you?" Ben's voice was hard.

"They're going to burn us."

"Yes."

"Take us with you."

"Take us, or we'll tell them it was you took the freak-lover," Taris said.

"Take you so you can burn some more of us?" Cara pulled off her hat, and they recognized her immediately. Their faces sagged.

"But you're right. We can't leave you to burn," Ben said. He pulled a tranq gun from the back of his belt and leveled it at them. "One shot will put you to sleep for hours. You'll just wake up in time for the bonfire party. Two shots are enough to drop a bull, so you could die, depending on your constitution. Three will kill you for sure."

Cara saw Ben's face was pale and strained. She couldn't imagine that he'd just pull the trigger, but letting them burn alive was also unthinkable, no matter what they'd done. She realized she was holding her breath, not knowing what he'd do; not knowing what she herself would do if she held the gun.

"You've got a choice," Ben said. "You can tell me who set up the burning at the tank farm, or you can die right here and now."

"Go to hell," Taris spat at him.

Ben pulled the trigger.

The tranquilizer dart hit Taris in the thigh. He stared at it, wide-eyed.

"Five seconds. Make your mind up," Ben said to him.

"Fuck you." The anesthetic reached his brain and Taris slumped back against the wall, falling awkwardly against his shackles.

"What about you?" Ben asked Colchek.

"Please . . ."

"You have the same choice that he had," Ben said. "Don't make such a stupid one. You've got a slightly better chance of not ending up as barbecue if you agree to go public with your story."

"I . . ."

"In another three minutes this building will be dropping around your ears. Who told you to burn the tanks?"

"Kill him and let's go," Tatum said.

"Tell him, Colchek," Cara said.

"The director. May we be forgiven. The director told Taris that fire cleanses—but I didn't mean for Danny to get hurt, honest."

"You just won a temporary reprieve," Ben said. "Unshackle him, Archie."

Archie sent the little bot to flip the mechanism in Colchek's shackles.

"What about him?" Archie nodded at Taris. "You can't leave him. If he doesn't die when I drop this building, he'll finger us and they'll burn the poor sod alive in any case."

"We can't take him, either. One extra body will tax the groundcar space as it is. We can't take two." Ben took a deep breath, and his mouth clamped into a tight line. Quickly, he pumped two more darts into Taris' prone body. A cold shock ran through Cara, and, in part, some of it was Ben's own reaction that she was feeling. He hadn't taken any pleasure in the act.

"Max, can you walk?" Ben asked.

"Yes, I think so."

"Good. I'll feel much safer with Colchek out cold, but we can't carry two of you." Ben leveled the tranq gun at Colchek and shot one dart into his thigh.

"You promised . . ." Colchek's hands flew to the dart as if he could pluck it out.

"It's only one dart. You're not dead yet," Ben said.

As Colchek's knees buckled, Ronan and Cara caught him between them.

"Let's get out." Ben went to Taris' body and pulled the three darts out of it. The pinpricks wouldn't show by the time they'd finished.

"Drag them into the hallway." Archie indicated the guards. "That part won't fall."

He and Ben grabbed the three unconscious men and pulled them, one at a time, to safety.

Ben straightened up. "Time for Archie's wrath-of-God stuff," he said.

There were more sounds of chaos from upstairs. By now, most of the crowd was safely outside the building. Archie slipped away again, heading back to his bots in the body of the hall. The voices of the crowd turned to shouts and screams as loose masonry began to fall inside the bell tower. The bell crashed to the ground, but no one was injured. Then, slowly, the fabric of the building began to crumble, starting with the bell tower. The final few, still in the building, stampeded for the doors. Some people elbowed each other out of the way; others helped those less able. A small group of people carrying an unconscious man went unnoticed. Miraculously, or so it seemed, the building held together long enough for everyone to get out, then, stone by pseudo-gothic stone, the tower twisted and fell, taking out the end wall which in turn brought down a major part of the roof and the upper galleries.

The morning would find a dangerous shell with nothing

left whole except part of the undercroft and the south wall with its huge stained glass window depicting the dove of peace. If the psi-techs left the settlers to clear most of the site by hand, it might be several weeks before the last bit of rubble was sifted and it was known for certain that Max and Colchek were missing.

Quickly. Gen had the groundcar ready. She swung the door open and flung herself out of the driver's seat to sit in the back with Max. The vehicle wobbled on its antigravs as they bundled the unconscious Colchek into the storage space and Ronan climbed in with him. Ben took over the controls with Cara by his side.

Make room. Archie reached the groundcar last and pushed himself into a space not meant for passengers.

Within minutes psi-tech emergency squads from Landing responded to frantic pleas from the settlers. They landed their flitters in the street. Teams of paramedics and rescue workers poured out of flitters and onto the pads. As the first pilot lifted off again to make room for more incoming craft, Ben coaxed their seriously laden craft out of the alley and joined the traffic.

"What are we going to do with Colchek?" Cara asked. She deliberately didn't mention Taris.

"Seriously embarrass if not ruin Lorient if he tries to stir up any more trouble."

"Where are we going to keep him in the short term?"

"Cryo. We'll keep him in a med freezer."

"And what about Max?" She nodded toward the back where Gen was in Max's arms. "Wherever he goes, sooner or later someone will recognize him. Are you going to freeze him, too?"

Ben looked uncomfortable. Cara suddenly realized why.

"You're going to have to take him off planet instead of me. There's no choice, is there?"

"Not much. Dammit!"

"It won't be for long." Cara tried to keep her tone light, but tears of disappointment were choking her.

"I hope it won't be for long." He reached out and took her hand in the semidarkness. "I'll come back and get you."

"Maybe Crowder doesn't intend to abandon us. He might still send a personnel carrier for us all. I might be in cryo, so just stick to your specialty."

"What's that?"

"Being there when I wake up."

"You can count on that."

She didn't mention the possibility of not waking up.

✦ ✦ ✦

Lorient is telling everyone that the psi-techs want to destroy the colony. That message came from Saedi Sugrue in Timbertown. Cara was in the Mapping office, feeling like a spare part as Ben prepared to leave. *He's just announced that he'll take a meeting. I think you should come.*

Cara cut Ben straight into her communication.

We're on our way. Ben stood up and his chair clattered over behind him. "I think we've pussyfooted around for long enough. Let's go in force. This could get nasty."

Gupta. Ben used Cara's link. *We'll need twenty of your best men, all armed with smart-darts. Bring sound grenades in case we need to do crowd control.* He took a deep breath, gathering his thoughts. *Ronan, have a medical team standing by, too, and, Wenna—*

"Here, Boss." Wenna was right next to him and spoke aloud.

"Make sure this place is well protected. It could be a diversion to draw us away to leave Landing open, especially if they've got snoopers out looking for Max and Colchek."

"Will do."

"Yan." The pilot was standing by the door. "Get my Dixie ready to go, and put Max in there with a pilot—Gen, you can do that job—if there's any sign that the settlers are going to tear Landing apart, get airborne, and we'll arrange a rendezvous point."

Cara saw Max open his mouth.

"Don't argue, Max," Ben said, "It's as much to keep the Dixie in one piece as to save your neck."

Ben and Cara ran for the hangar. Gupta's security team, twenty men armed with smart-darts and sound grenades, piled into flitters alongside them. Cara linked everyone in gestalt. In only minutes they all set down in tight formation on the perimeter of an angry crowd.

◆ ◆ ◆

Ben leaped down from the flitter, Cara close behind him. Gupta's men fanned out, ready.

An impenetrable crowd of people had gathered outside the ruined hall where the Dove of Peace window stood like a monument above the ruins, cracked but not shattered. A wooden platform had been hastily rigged where the debris had been cleared.

Up on the platform, Lorient was just stepping forward, his hair whipping around his face in the back-blast from the antigravs. Even at this distance he looked haggard. Behind him, Jack stood alone. No Rena. Was that significant?

"My friends, we have all been betrayed." Lorient's voice rang out. "And, look, our betrayers are here." He pointed at Ben and Cara and swung his arm to encompass the twenty men in black buddysuits with smart-darts held ready.

He had the complete attention of the crowd. "Shall we suffer freaks and abominations to live among us?"

There was a roar of "No" from several hundred throats.

"That's more than enough," Ben said to Cara. "It's time to get some attention ourselves." He linked into the gestalt. *Set your sound baffles.*

He clicked his cuff control pad and set his, feeling the background noise retreat to barely a murmur.

Cara nodded. *All set.*

Gupta confirmed. *Team all set.*

Ben took a small sphere from his belt pack and rolled it into the middle of the crowd. It began to shriek with ear-splitting volume.

His suit shifted the phase on the sound waves to cancel the noise out in the immediate vicinity of his ears, but Lorient's congregation scrambled to get out of its way, falling over themselves and trampling each other in the rush. The screamer cut a swathe through the crowd.

Come on. Ben signaled, and moved forward.

Cara, Gupta, and fourteen of Gupta's armed men slipstreamed after him before the Ecolibrians recovered from the noise and closed in behind them. The rest of Gupta's crew stayed to guard the rear.

Ben jumped onto the platform, Cara close behind. The security men took up their position at the base, with their smart-darts armed and another screamer primed.

Lorient rushed forward through the noise, but Jack leaped, his face a mask of pain, and grabbed Lorient's arm. As Lorient shook him off, Cara got close enough to make contact. She seized Lorient by the hand and put a twist on his wrist that immobilized him before Ben could give in to his anger.

Any excuse would do. Ben really wanted to smash his fist into Lorient's face.

Not here, Cara warned. *Not with all his followers watching. You'll be playing into his hands.*

Don't you trust me? he shot back at her.

With my life, but maybe not with his right now.

Dammit, she was right.

Relax. Point taken.

The screamer stopped.

"Jack . . . Jack!" It took two tries for Ben to get through to Jack. He was shaking his head and rubbing his ears with both hands. "Jack, as soon as this lot start to get over the screamer, they're going to be fighting mad. Say something, anything, to quiet them down and give us some time with Lorient. Don't worry, I'll not hurt him, tempted as I am."

Cara let go, and Ben pushed Lorient toward the back of the platform. "This way, Director. We need to talk."

Lorient turned and pulled back his arm as if he was going to take a swing at whichever one of them he could reach first.

"That would be a big mistake," Ben said. "Listen, before you do or say anything else, because you and I hold your colonists' future in our hands. I want them to survive. What do you want?"

"I want you freaks away from here, back to where you came from."

"Before or after we try and find out who's trying to screw us all?"

Lorient paused for breath long enough to enable Ben to launch into what he had to say.

"Here are the facts. One. The psi-tech force here is on your side. We think someone is going to make a bid for the platinum, and we're the only thing that's standing between you and them. Two. The rest of your colonists in your second ark are missing. Three. If you want to save your people, you are going to have to work with us. The sooner we arrive at an understanding, the better for us all because, believe me, there may be more of you than there are of us, but if you back us into a corner, we can fight dirtier and harder than you ever dreamed possible."

"Are you threatening us?"

"Haven't you listened to anything Ben said?" Cara interrupted. "We're trying to help you, but you're too damn blind to see."

"There's one more thing," Ben said. "Your thug, Colchek, didn't escape. We have him and he's prepared to sing his heart out about you. What will your followers think then? What will your wife think?"

Cara saw Lorient's face crease with pain.

"Now, do you want to talk?" Ben asked.

✦ ✦ ✦

Cara stood back in amazement and listened, not to Ben, though she heard everything he said, but to the emotions coming from Victor Lorient. The answer to their problems hit her like a shower of bright sparks and she quickly joined with Ben to pass on everything she suspected.

Ben heard her thoughts and his eyes widened.

"He what?"

Lorient's mouth closed.

"Hold still, Director." Cara reached up and brushed Lorient's hair from his forehead. Along a shallow wrinkle line, almost invisible unless you were looking for it was a fine surgical scar. "There's no scar when an implant goes in because it's seeded on the tip of the finest hollow needle, but to deal with it once it's started to grow through the cortex needs a surgeon of consummate skill. He's had an implant deactivated and partially removed." She turned to Lorient. "Director, you used to be one of us."

"It can't be done," Ben said. "It would kill him, or drive him insane, and I don't just mean paranoid, I mean a blob of gibbering jelly."

"They don't remove it—it spreads too far too fast—but they can disengage the functions if surgery's done quickly enough after the first phase of implantation. A girl in my unit at the academy had a psychotic reaction to the implant and opted for deactivation. It's risky, though, a last option. What would drive a man to apply for an implant, take the time and effort to pass the exams, the psych, and the physical, and then want out almost immediately?"

She spoke directly to Lorient, all her senses open to his every feeling.

His eyes darted from her to Ben and back again. Lorient's face went from beet red to ghostly pale.

"I . . . Call it rebellious youth. I wanted to show my father he was wrong. It split the family in two. And he wasn't wrong. When the damn thing was installed, I found . . . I could control people."

"You were a broadcasting Empath?" Cara breathed.

"More than that. I didn't just make suggestions or transmit my feelings. I said do something, and they did it. Have you any idea just how that makes a man feel . . . the power . . . ?" He shook his head. "I was terrified. Terrified and exhilarated and joyous, but . . . no one should have that kind of power."

Cara could think of many who would leap at the opportunity. All credit to the man that he hadn't.

"What did you do?" Ben asked quietly.

"They tried to persuade me I was special, that they'd look after me, but, you know the kind of looking after they had in mind. Keep me in a facility until there was a need for my talents, then bring me out, turn me loose to persuade someone to their way of thinking, and then stuff me back in my box." His mouth set in a stubborn line. "I had them deactivate the thing and take out what they could. I knew the risks, but I'd rather die than have that kind of power over people. I didn't die. After rehab, I went back to my family and begged their forgiveness. That's how I know the depth of evil embedded within each implant. Only a sinner can know the true depth of sin. I threw myself into serving the Ecolibrian movement. Tried to tell myself I could be normal again. I guess I was looking for redemption."

"But it's still there, isn't it? Most people just call it charisma."

"It's not the same. Not as strong. I can ignore it, mostly. I don't connect with it. I'd never use it for personal gain."

"No one is suggesting that you do," Ben said.

"Danny inherited it, didn't he? Natural psi? I infected him." Victor Lorient put both hands to his face. "May I be forgiven."

"Danny was a wonder," Cara said. "There wasn't anyone on this planet—psi-tech or settler alike—who didn't feel better after meeting Danny. He radiated goodwill to everyone, because that's what was in his heart, but your actions didn't infect him with psi ability. That's not the way it works. Believe me. If Danny had any innate talent, it was genetics alone and nothing to do with your implant."

There was a long silence.

"Director Lorient . . ." Ben stepped forward.

"Get away from me!"

Cara caught Ben's look of helplessness. *Let me try. You're too much of a threat.* She used a very tight thought that bypassed Lorient.

"Director Lorient." Her light touch on his forearm snapped him ramrod-straight and he stared at her, wide eyed. "Honestly, you didn't infect Danny."

He just shook his head, and Cara didn't know whether she could overturn the beliefs of more than half a lifetime.

"What now?" Lorient said. "Discredit me in front of all of them?"

The crowd was louder than before.

"What good would that do?" Ben stepped forward. "Listen. Your people are getting angry. They want you." He paused. "Calm them down. Prepare them for what's to come. Your secret's safe with us."

"Please, Director Lorient, otherwise people are going to get hurt," Cara said.

"Blackmail." Lorient's face was an emotionless mask. He knew he'd lost this battle, but he was covering it up well.

"Negotiation," Ben said.

"Director, Commander Benjamin. Please come, now!" Jack called to them.

Lorient stepped forward and Ben followed him.

"Psi-tech-bas-tards. Psi-tech-bas-tards." The crowd had started to chant.

Gupta's security guards stood shoulder to shoulder, facing down the crowd.

"Please." Victor Lorient stepped forward. "Please, calm down and listen very carefully."

Cara felt all his powerful charm come on line. Implant or charisma, it made no difference. The crowd would do whatever he said. They had a breathing space. She hoped it was long enough to let Ben get the information they needed from Crowder.

✦ ✦ ✦

Standing in the hangar with Ben as Max said his good-byes to Gen and stowed his small bag on board the Dixie, Cara wanted to scream: *Don't leave me*, but instead she just hugged Ben briefly.

"I'll call you twice a day, on schedule."

There's a storm coming in. Eastern Seaboard Station gives about eight minutes' clearance. Cas Ritson's message cut across their good-bye.

"Ah, that's it. Summer's over. Olyanda's trying to kill us again. You'd better get off before you lose your window."

"Storm . . ."

"We'll manage. Can the autumn be any worse than the spring?"

"I . . ."

"Go."

"Love you."

"I know."

She reached up and their lips connected one last time.

Then he was out of her arms and into the Dixie, closing the hatch with a soft, reassuring click.

She stood in the shelter of the hangar doors as the little machine lifted on antigravs and rolled out onto the pad. It soared upward and dwindled to a bright star in the daylight sky. Moments later the first icy blast of an autumn storm sent her reeling into the doorframe as dark green-gray clouds roiled in. This one was going to be a doozy.

Chapter Thirty

JOURNEY

BEN'S CONNECTION TO CARA STRETCHED tight, then tighter still like a piece of elastic under too much strain. He wanted to let go and twang back to Olyanda to be with her again, but duty and grim determination drove him on.

Two days to the Invidii Gate and nothing to do but chew over the situation. Crowder, van Blaiden, platinum. Max was no help—he was mooning over Gen when he wasn't throwing up in quarter-G.

Cara's first call was brief. The storm was still raging overhead, pinning everyone down in bunkers, caves, and storm cellars. By their second contact it had abated and flared up again.

I should have stayed.

Good job you didn't stay.

They both spoke together, then laughed.

We're managing, Ben. No one was caught in the open. You just do what you set out to do.

A day later the storm on Olyanda had blown itself out completely, and life was returning to normal. He mentally kissed Cara good-bye as he prepared for the jump into fold-space. By the time he emerged at the other end, the distance would be enough to limit them to brief, essential communications.

"Can I do anything?" Max asked.

"You ever flown a Dixie before?"

Max shook his head. "I feel like a spare part."

Ben refrained from saying that he was.

"I want to help. You left Cara behind in order to get me off Olyanda safely."

"It seemed to make sense at the time."

"Thank you. I'm not sure, if our situations had been reversed, that I'd have abandoned Gen to save you. I miss her so much already. You . . . you can talk to Cara?"

"She can talk to me. I'm not much of a Telepath."

"What's it like, having someone in your head?"

"Depends who it is, but . . . well, there are protocols for that sort of thing. You learn them early and you learn them fast, but most of us already knew we had some kind of latent talent before we got tested."

"I was never tested."

"Never? How did you manage that?"

"A series of foster homes, all Ecolibrian. I moved around a lot. I wasn't always the easiest kid. I guess I fell through the cracks, and, of course, none of my various foster parents hurried to volunteer me."

"Did you want to avoid testing?"

"I wanted to avoid any kind of authority when I was twelve, didn't you?"

"I probably had it easier than you." Ben recalled his teenage years. "My gran brought me and my brother up, and she was a psi-tech herself, a diplomat for the Five Power Alliance before our parents died, so testing was just something you did. My brother tested positive but refused an implant. He stayed on the farm, which was all he ever wanted. I won a place at the academy on Chenon and later spent a couple of years training on Earth after signing up with the Monitors."

"If I wanted to have a receiving implant, could I get one at my age, or do you have to be fitted with them when you're young? I'd like to be able to have Gen talk to me."

"It's never too late, but they're expensive, and you'd have to learn how to use it. The older you are, the more difficult it is to adjust, but if you're determined . . ."

Max nodded. "I am."

"Then talk to Mother Ramona when we get to Crossways. In the meantime, we'll reach the Invidii Gate in three hours. Better get some sleep beforehand because you sure as hell won't get any in the Folds."

"What about you? Don't you need sleep?"

"I'm okay. I'm used to this. I catnap when I can."

"You mean I'm flying with a pilot who sleeps on the job?"

"Not in foldspace—as for the rest of it, relax. There's an onboard computer."

"Machines."

"Don't trust 'em?"

"I don't know what to trust, and that's a fact!"

Ben could empathize with that.

Max let his head roll back, and for a while Ben thought he was sleeping, but at length he opened his eyes again. "Ben?"

"Yes?" Ben looked up from his screen.

"The Folds."

"Yes?"

"I've heard that they can do strange things to your mind. Is that a psi-tech thing or . . ."

"Or will it affect you, too; is that what you mean?"

"I guess."

"It affects everybody—or at least it's affected everybody I've ever flown with, psi-tech or de . . ."

"Deadhead. It's okay; you can say it. I've heard it often enough before."

"Sorry."

"But the Folds . . ."

"I don't know what's out there. It's never the same twice. Everyone sees something different, and you have to keep on telling yourself it's not real, except sometimes it is, and that's when you're in deep shit."

"But the gates are safe, right?"

"Mostly, the bigger gates are, but they take longer and we haven't got that luxury. We're going through the Invidii Gate because it's smaller, faster, and less well monitored. It's normally only used for unmanned freightpods. You can't send the big passenger ships or cargo hulks through. They pull too much mass and . . ."

"And they're too valuable." Max felt a cold weight settle in his stomach.

"Right."

"But you've done this before, haven't you?"

"Yes, or gates like this. Never this particular one."

"Oh, great!"

"Don't worry. It's a gamble, but the odds are good."

Max unclipped his harness and sat upright. "How many ships disappear?"

"You don't want to know. Even one ship that doesn't make it is one too many."

"Do you believe in anything? I mean, a god or anything like that?"

"God? No. And I thought Ecolibrians didn't believe in a supreme being either, just the oneness of nature; what they used to call the Gaia Theory before the Ecos made a quasi-religion out of it."

"We believe that when you die, your atoms are reabsorbed into nature to start at the bottom of the food chain again only, well, in space that wouldn't happen, would it?"

"Maybe. Eventually. We're all made of star stuff. Look, theology isn't my strong point, Max. I guess I'm pretty simple in the philosophy department. You do the best you can with what you've got and try to go through life in such a way that you leave people better off than they would have been if you hadn't been there. Sometimes you can do that in big ways, sometimes in small ones."

"And if that puts you in the firing line?"

"You have to decide whether something's worth fighting for, or even whether it's your fight."

"And is Olyanda your fight?"

"I guess. I'd rather it wasn't, but there's no one else. That makes it mine."

"You could have walked away—or flown away—and taken Cara with you."

Ben made a course correction and didn't reply for nearly a minute. Then, at length, he said, "Don't think I didn't consider that."

"You're a hero, Benjamin. I guess I'm not."

Crowder had sometimes accused him of being a white knight, but no one had ever accused him of being a hero. He'd always associated heroism with a particular brand of gung-ho stupidity. All he was doing was what his conscience wouldn't let him leave undone.

"Hardly." He shrugged. "We'll be entering the Folds in ten minutes. If this is your first time, you should make use of the head before we get there. Don't say I didn't warn you."

Max eased himself out of the couch and to the cubbyhole that passed for sanitary facilities on the flyer. They'd not wasted much space on it, but it was effective. He peed, hearing the recycler kick in.

He strapped in to his couch again. "Is it really that bad?"

"Buckle up tight." Ben leaned over and locked Max's harness.

"Why'd you do that?"

"Because I don't want you getting up and throwing yourself around the cabin trying to fight off some hobgoblin from your nightmares. Just keep telling yourself they're not real."

"And if they are?"

"Tell yourself they're not."

Max took a deep breath. "If you're trying to scare me, you're succeeding."

"Good. Just remember, if any of those hobgoblins turn out to be Gen-shaped, they're definitely not real."

Max nodded.

"Right. One minute." Ben's hand moved over the control panel, and the shield opened to reveal myriad stars beyond the thick, radiation-proof plasglas.

"Oh, gods, it's . . ." Max stared.

Of course, his first time in space, conscious anyway.

"Beautiful," Ben said. "Terrifying."

"Both."

"That bright star isn't a star at all. It's the Invidii Gate beacon."

As they neared, the brightness resolved itself into two silver disks, hanging in space. Between them, a deep black void waited.

"Here we go." Ben cut power to the computer and took over the helm.

"I thought you said you used the computer?"

"Not in the Folds—it can get as confused as a human."

"And you?"

"I'm a Navigator. This is what I do, find my way through uncharted territories. Don't worry, I'll not be catnapping."

The black void grew and grew until it filled the viewport.

"It's not so ba . . ." Max's voice cut off abruptly into an incoherent gurgle.

"Niagara Falls in a barrel," Ben said through gritted teeth.

◆　◆　◆

Shapes and faces swim in the blackness outside the Dixie and inside, too, though here the blackness is less tangible, more like it's in Ben's head. People he's known, distorted out of all proportion like some bizarre surrealist painting. They loom and fade, loom and fade. His grandmother, ex-wife, brother, school bully, Lorient, Crowder, faces of comrades lost on Hera-3.

Strange wyrm-like shapes swirl through the little craft, entering through the skin of the Dixie, taking a good look around and exiting the same way, as if nothing is solid. None of them is as big as the void dragon he saw last time, though they could be its baby cousins. If the fold-creatures were from his imagination, he had a really good imagination, inventing detail down to their yellow, reptilian eyes and the prehensile claws on the fronds attached to their lower lips like deadly beards.

He adjusts the Dixie's course, feeling as though there's nothing between him and the vast deep. His fingers connect with something cold and slimy. He turns and sees Max, or his remains, half decayed, lolling in his harness. He jumps, but his own harness holds him strapped firmly to the couch. Then the corpse grows flesh, sits up, and pukes.

It's not real. It's not real. Please let that not be real.

But Cara is real. She's outside in the void of space, naked and smiling. No, that definitely isn't real. Not outside the flyer. Then she's inside, still naked, but this time not smiling.

Her face is suffused with pure lust and she's all over Ben, no longer a corpse, but alive and . . .

Max yells out. Ben wonders whether he's seen the same images, but it's no matter.

It's not real. It's not real.

Then, with a whoosh and a pop, it's over.

✦ ✦ ✦

He shook Max's arm. "It's over. Wake up."

"What? I . . . Get off her . . ." Max's eyes were slightly unfocused. He took a swing at Ben, but Ben dodged easily.

"Is this real?" Max asked, intelligence returning.

"If I said it was, would you believe me?"

"I don't know."

"Well it is, and you only threw up once. Well done."

"I threw up? Sorry." He looked around but could find no evidence.

Ben laughed. "Only once. Or maybe you didn't. That's good going. Here, drink this."

"Coffee?"

"Sorry, water."

Max took it. "So what kind of demons did you meet in the Folds?"

"You don't want to know."

The jump through the Invidii Gate landed them one day away from Crossways. Ben tried to prepare Max.

"Crossways is a dangerous place," he said. "Watch your back and watch mine, too."

"I've heard of it, but I'd always thought it was a myth."

"Well, it isn't, and whatever you heard is probably true."

"Not your first trip, then?"

"No."

"Maybe you're not such a clean-living, straight-up white knight after all. Crossways doesn't sound like the sort of place heroes hang out."

"Shut up, Max."

Once through the low atmosphere docking bays, Ben hailed an auto-cab, and the little tub-shaped vehicle bounced them halfway round the circumference of the station.

"Who is this Mother Ramona?" Max asked. "What does she deal in?"

"She doesn't deal in narcotics, and she doesn't deal in death. That's good enough for me. Just be polite, speak when you're spoken to, and if she offers to make love to you on the couch, don't refuse."

"But . . ."

"Don't refuse. She considers that very impolite."

◆ ◆ ◆

"Ben Benjamin." Mother Ramona held out her hand, and he took it. "I've secured you both passage on a freighter heading for Chenon." She looked at Max.

"Who's your shy friend?"

Ben didn't have to be empathic to know how uncomfortable Max was in Mother Ramona's lair. He was trying hard not to stare at her, but his eyes kept resting on the marbled skin displayed to excellent advantage by her low-cut dress. Maybe the Ecolibrian in him was having a hard time with the fact that she was an exotic, but the man in him was definitely drawn by the cleavage.

"Max Constant, one of my new business partners."

"Finished with the Trust?"

"I think it's finished with me."

Max shuffled his feet. Ben hoped he'd not act like an ass.

"So, you said you had something to trade. What are you selling?" Mother Ramona pushed the clutter to one side and perched on the edge of her workbench. Her skirt fell open to reveal her elegant pale legs. Ben tried not to smile. He knew she was doing it for Max's benefit.

"Platinum. A lot of platinum. Or rather—potential platinum."

"Ah." She nodded.

"Can you broker a transaction? For a percentage, of course."

"Of course."

"And I'll need a short-term loan against it."

She raised an eyebrow.

"Let me show you the planetary survey."

A few minutes later Mother Ramona looked up from the reader and nodded. "You've got your loan, Benjamin."

"Good. Do we need to go through channels? Is Chaliss still running Crossways?"

"Chaliss was a thoroughly unscrupulous man. He met with . . . an unfortunate accident. My dear friend Norton Garrick seems to have stepped into his golden slippers. Garrick and I go . . . way back." She patted the couch absentmindedly and smiled. "I'll make arrangements in return for the appropriate commission."

Mother Ramona looked straight past Ben at Max, who shuffled again. "What else do you want?" She turned to Ben.

"You're sure you can trust Garrick?"

"He's a businessman."

"Can we buy his loyalty?"

"Platinum buys you a whole lot of that, especially from me."

"I know. That's why we're here. Will it buy Garrick? Is his word good?"

"I can vouch for him."

"You're that close?"

She smiled.

"Can you set up a meeting with him? I have something to attend to first on Chenon and then I need to talk to Garrick. There's big profit in this for everyone."

"Oh, Commander Benjamin, I love it when you talk dirty."

Briefly he told her everything he knew about the situation, including Cara's relationship with Ari van Blaiden. When Mother Ramona agreed to a deal, she stuck to it. Buying loyalty from a stranger seemed to be a lot more secure than trusting a friend.

"You know what I think?" Mother Ramona leaned forward. "Since the Trust has already said you're all as good as dead, they're playing for keeps."

"The colony is in the way, and so are the psi-techs. I guess one big calamity now stops people asking questions later," Ben said. "Who worries about the dead? They'll hold a memorial service and move on. It'll blaze in the headlines and on the space-log for a while, then everyone will forget."

"According to my contact on Earth, the Trust's Board got the same story that was released to the public. The settlers have been wiped out by a virus. They've promised a thorough investigation, but naturally they're cautious because of possible infection."

"That must have caused a huge stink on Earth," Max said.

Mother Ramona's blue hair fell across one eye as she nodded. "But the news broke after the second ark ship left, so the top Ecolibrian heavyweights were all out of the way. The FPA is smoothing it over with the other fundy factions with a sweetener from the Trust."

"Any news of the second ark?" Max asked. "There are thirty thousand settlers still out there somewhere."

"Nothing yet. I've got spies out. We traced it through three gates and then lost it—in the records anyway—at the Dromgoole Hub. I've got people checking their databanks and jump logs. We'll find them if there's anything to find."

"Since there isn't a plague, do you think we can presume that whatever is happening on Olyanda isn't happening with the knowledge of the Board?" Ben asked.

"That would be my educated guess."

"Is that good or bad?" Max asked.

"We'll never find out sitting here," Ben said.

Mother Ramona stood up. "I'll make a call about the platinum. Then I'd like to get to know your new associate."

Max watched her leave the room and breathed out. "What does she mean by get to know?"

"I warned you about the couch."

"Yes, but she's . . ."

"What? Older than you? A criminal? An exotic?"

"She's not Gen."

"This is for Gen, and for Cara, and the Ecolibrians. Don't let me down."

"Uh—I won't, but bits of me might."

Mother Ramona came back to the doorway.

"I've found a lab that can test your samples right away and certify them. My driver will take you."

Ben nodded.

"Take two of my enforcers," she said. "The lab's straight, as far as straight goes on Crossways, but don't take stupid risks." Mother Ramona handed Ben a credit chip and waved him to the door. Then she turned to Max.

"And now, Max Constant, tell me all about yourself. Is this your first visit to Crossways?" She stepped forward, smiling.

❖ ❖ ❖

Cara settled down to contact Ben at the appointed time.

Hello, love.

Hello, yourself.

Where are you?

Mother Ramona's den. Where are you?

Our bed.

Ah.

She caught the echo of thoughts that made her heat up in all kinds of unexpected places. She giggled.

What's new? she asked.

This afternoon I deposited more credits in the bank than I ever thought to see in my lifetime. I've got a clean account, DNA matched and totally legitimate. Crossways has an excellent banking system. How about you? You sound tired.

We've been cleaning up after the storm. The settlers have been uncommonly cooperative, but Lorient has been giving us grief over the arrival of the wheat shipment.

It arrived? Crowder can't send a transport home, but he can send an extra shipment to back up a false story. What's going on?

It's a drone pod. Probably been on its way for some time. It landed on the floodplain by the estuary off course by almost a hundred klicks, thanks to the storm. I tried to tell Lorient that we've more to worry about than using resources to retrieve something we probably won't need, but he's taken prairie wagons to get the seed. Damn stupidity. It'll take him

days to get there, even presuming there are no more storms.
She paused, conscious of the fact that Ben didn't need bothering with her troubles. *The upside is that it keeps him out of our hair for a while.*

Have you got a psi-tech with him in case of emergency?

No. He won't have any of ours anywhere near him. He's taken a mechanical comm unit, much good may it do him on this bloody planet.

You can't help someone who won't be helped. You take care of yourself, you hear? Get back in touch tomorrow. We're leaving here tonight for Chenon.

Stay safe.

Always.

She tried not to make a disparaging remark. He was good at taking care of others. Himself? Not so much.

✦ ✦ ✦

Max ran his hand across what was left of his hair, now cropped to stubble. He studied his reflection in the mirror in Mother Ramona's den. He hardly recognized himself in the practical flight suit.

Ben's long hair lay in strands on the floor. Ben caught his eye and shrugged as he fastened his own buddysuit neck. "It'll grow back. Got your ID straight?"

Max nodded. "Ric Dubeau. How do I address you if I'm supposed to be your assistant? Are you Fredo or Mr. Damiani?"

"I'm a freelance systems engineer. That probably doesn't rate formal address on Guaylar. Call me Fredo."

They left the Dixie in dock on Crossways. Ben paid a hefty bribe to make sure she stayed untouched, and they caught a freighter to Nevitz Station. From there they hopped a regular shuttle to Chenon. In less than twenty-six hours they were docking at the spaceport with forged papers and altered ident chips. Max's heart hammered so hard that he felt sure the immigration officer would hear it and pull him up, but the false ident was obviously good enough.

Max envied Ben, who seemed to breeze through the whole procedure as if he hadn't a care. Once through security, out of the terminal, and into Arkhad City, however, Ben exhaled sharply, and it was only then that Max realized he'd probably been equally nervous.

"Do you know where we're going?" Max asked.

"Somewhere I've never been before. Somewhere well away from my apartment."

"You have an apartment here?"

"I did, presuming my grandmother hasn't disposed of it already. Did Mother Ramona say how long ago they pronounced us dead?"

"If she did, I didn't register it. Sorry."

"No worries. I don't intend to try and contact Nan. I don't want any attention drawn to her or Rion and the family. My apartment's on the south side. We'll try the east of the city."

Max was grateful that Ben knew his way around. They checked into an unremarkable three-room business suite in a mid-range hotel, the kind of accommodation a reasonably affluent freelancer might afford between jobs. It had the advantage of being hooked up to every communications net on the planet.

"I need sleep," Max moaned as he dropped his bag on the common room floor. "My body clock is completely scrambled."

While Max tested the bed, looked in closets, and examined the plumbing, Ben ordered tea and sat straight down in front of the comm console and computer matrix.

"I'm going to try and get past the office security systems at Crowder's HQ," Ben said. "I need to access the main database."

"Can they trace you back to here?"

"Maybe—if they're looking, but not if I'm careful. Look, Max. You don't have to get involved. You've got a life of your own to sort out. I brought you back because you'd be dead meat on Olyanda, but you can please yourself, now."

"I told Gen that we'd find a way for us to stay together," Max said.

"Nearly getting yourself toasted by Lorient's heavies is a hell of a way to do that!"

"Yeah, I thought I made a very thorough job of it."

"What will you do now?"

Max had intended to cut and run, and find a bolt-hole big enough for himself and Gen and Firstborn, but when it came to the crunch, it didn't feel right. "If it's all the same to you, I'll come along for the ride, at least until it gets rough. I'm not saying I'll be any good at the rough stuff. I'm a natural-born accountant, but I don't like the idea of thirty thousand settlers still frozen on a transport somewhere. It scares the hell out of me that these kiddies might just leave them floating—or worse. It could have been me on there."

Ben nodded. "Fair enough. I'll not deny it'll be useful to have backup."

"Even from me? I thought you thought I was a pain in the butt."

Ben shrugged slightly. "Gen's a friend. I trust her judgment."

"Thanks. I'll not let you down. I've got a vested interest in what happens on Olyanda. I want Gen away from Olyanda, safe, with me. After this is all over, I'll probably get a job with some private firm, cooking their books. Legally, of course. I've worked for Alphacorp, so I've got all the right qualifications. It's boring." He shrugged, "But, hey, I'm good at figures, and it's steady. With a family to support I'll need the credits. I'm kinda looking forward to being a family man. I might even apply to work for the Trust. I reckon they owe me."

"Would you get in?"

"I'll keep the Ric Dubeau identity. I've got a few strings I can pull in the records department. Someone I knew from Earth who transferred here to Chenon, in fact. I'll probably be able to get a posting on one of the better colony worlds and take Gen with me. Olyanda's given me the taste for colony life."

"You have a contact in the records department?"

"Yes."

"A good contact?"

He shrugged. "I've not seen her for a while, but good enough. An old girlfriend."

"Then we might be able to take a shortcut through Crowder's systems. Can you get in touch with her?"

"I think so."

"Do it."

Max tapped Ben's handpad showing local time. It was the middle of the long night.

"Oh, okay. Let's catnap now, and then we'll be fit for action when everyone wakes up."

Chapter Thirty-one

CONFRONTATION

BEN AND MAX SHOULDERED PAST WORKDAY pedestrians along brightly lit traffic canyons gouged between slab-sided buildings, open to the black night sky far above. Ornamental gates gave way to a sudden oasis of calm. Max had made the call first thing in the morning and arranged a meeting here in a public park near the records building at morning break. Morning was relative on Chenon, but false daytime was almost convincing. The park was a showpiece of botanical engineering with multihued flora from a dozen worlds competing to catch the eye. It was too manicured after Olyanda.

They strolled to the appointed spot, third bench from the rotunda, beneath the spreading branches of a chestnut tree, a magnificent Earth specimen, and waited in silence.

"Max?" The woman who approached them was small and dark, not pretty, but lively. "Max? What have you done to yourself?"

Max's bruises were fading now, but they still showed yellow around his eyes.

"Not self-inflicted, I can assure you. Lorin, this is a good friend of mine." No names, no rank. "We need a favor and it's a big one."

"Am I going to regret this?"

"I hope not," Ben chipped in quietly. "But there are lives at stake. Maybe lots of lives. We need information."

She looked to Max, her eyes wide.

"It's important, Lorin."

"What have you gotten yourself into, Max? You can't just expect me to break the law without knowing what it's all about. You and I go back a long way, but . . ."

"Just talk to . . . to Fredo, and make up your own mind. Please. It's important."

Ben took Lorin's arm and with a sideways glance at Max led her over the dusky pink of the garden's well-manicured lawns. When they were out of earshot, Max saw them turn to each other and begin to talk, heads close. At one point Lorin started to walk away from him, and Ben called her back, still talking intently. Then, after about five minutes, he stopped and backed off, hands spread apart as though he'd said all he could say and was waiting for an answer. When he didn't get one, he started to turn away, yet even from this distance Max could see Lorin mouth the word: wait.

When they walked back, Max could see the tightness on Lorin's face.

Ben raised one eyebrow slightly. "I had to tell her . . . about the . . . deal."

"Ah, yes, the deal," Max said.

"I agreed a hundred thou."

"Fair enough."

"In a coded account." Lorin looked somewhere over Max's left shoulder and then down at her feet.

Max nodded.

She half smiled, a facial movement that didn't reach her eyes. "I should have asked for twice that, shouldn't I?"

"Lorin . . ." Max said.

"Oh, don't worry, lover. I said a hundred thou and I meant it. What do you need?"

"A copy of planetary contract EXC116/Sec18," Ben said. "And I need to know whether planetary survey EXC116/RB809 has been filed and if so under what classification." He didn't need a copy of the file; it was the data from Gen's first survey. "Is that too much to ask?"

"That doesn't seem so top secret."

"It's not top secret. Probably not even classified . . . but make sure you don't leave a trace. I don't want anyone to know the information's been accessed."

"No problem."

"Here's where to send it." Ben held out his handpad and Lorin met him knuckles to knuckles.

"All right. Be waiting. Two hours." She left quickly without looking back.

"Well, I didn't expect that!" Max said as they watched her retreating figure. "I thought we might talk her into it for the sake of being on the side of the white hats, but . . ."

"Never underestimate the power of wealth."

"Yeah . . . I guess."

✦　✦　✦

Two hours later Ben accessed the Trust's computer system from a public terminal in the transit lounge at the port, found the documents he needed already sitting in the anonymous mailbox he'd set up via Mother Ramona before leaving Crossways. He forwarded them to Mother Ramona and downloaded a copy into his handpad, confirmed the credit transfer, then got out fast in case anyone had traced Lorin's snooping.

Back in his hotel room, he sat at the reader and stared intently at the screen. What it revealed pulled Ben up short even though he had been half expecting something like it.

"Come on, what gives?" Max hovered impatiently.

The more he read, the less Ben liked. "It's not good news. The planetary contract . . . Aww, shit." He read the next bit and realized what they were up against. "The jargon is legalistic, but basically there's a penalty clause. Olyanda is owned by Remagen, a subsidiary of the Trust. It's been leased in perpetuity, rather than sold. Here, look. It's leased to the Ecolibrians via the FPA for the express purposes of colonization. In the event of the planet being left to lie unused, or it ceases to be used for anything other than its primary purpose, i.e., domestic and agricultural, the lease reverts to Remagen, i.e., back to the Trust. In the event of the settlers wanting to relinquish the planet for any reason, the lease has to be offered by them on the open market."

"Well, they're already too late to do anything about that," Max said. "The colony's already established."

"Read it again." Ben had worked out the implications. "If the colony fails, the planet belongs to the Trust again. And that includes the right to mine platinum. If the colony is abandoned or if it dies—that is, if all the settlers die— the Trust takes the whole lot back legally. But if the settlers sell the lease to the planet it has to go on the open market, so the Trust enters a bidding war with Alphacorp, the FPA, and anyone else who can scrape up billions of credits."

They were already preparing to do it. The settlers and the psi-techs were already reported as dead or dying. Now someone would have to make sure that came true one way or another. The story of the virus would scare off the independent observers until the area was declared clear. Very neat. That would even give whoever it was time to wipe out the unprotected settlers, cream off a portion of platinum and cover their tracks before handing over the planet to the Trust.

Ben smashed his fist on the table and sat back, eyes closed. Deep breathing until he trusted his voice not to crack. "If Crowder's behind this," he said very quietly, "I'll kill him myself." What was platinum worth? Was it worth all those lives? To some, no price was too high to pay, especially if they weren't paying it.

◆ ◆ ◆

"I've got to see Crowder." Ben paced up and down their shared hotel sitting room until Max got dizzy watching him.

"You must be mad." Max sat up on the couch and switched off the holovid, which he'd been trying to concentrate on and failing.

"Probably, but he's the key to all this. He knows what I need to know and the only way I'm going to find out is by confronting him. I'll beat it out of him if I have to. I wish Cara was here. At least she'd know if he was lying. I don't trust myself. I'm too close to him."

Max felt hollow in the pit of his stomach, not for the first time. All his life it had seemed that whatever he did wasn't important, but now things that he'd done had really hurt people. He'd fucked up, bigtime. "I'm sorry."

"What for?"

"If it hadn't been for me, you'd have had Cara here." Max bit his lip. "Look I don't know how to say this. I'm not very good at apologizing, but I've been pretty selfish up to now. I didn't think about Gen's feelings when I started coming on to her. It was just a bit of a laugh—a pretty girl and all the more tantalizing because it was forbidden, but somewhere along the way I got bitten. I really do care about her, and I've discovered that I really do care about the colony, too. So whatever I can do, count me in. I'm with you all the way."

Ben nodded. "You're all right, you know, once you drop the window dressing." He checked the time on his handpad.

Max felt as though he'd just been handed the biggest compliment he'd ever received.

Ben didn't seem to realize he'd said anything special. He continued, "Crowder usually works later than anyone else. Use your Ric Dubeau identity and call him at exactly 32.10 this evening, audio only. Say you're an old friend of mine from the Monitors. That should give him some explaining to do and ensure he's still in the office after the shift has gone. I hope you're a good actor. I shall expect you to be so grief-stricken that he takes plenty of time to tell you what a wonderful person I was."

✦ ✦ ✦

Cara was late getting in touch, but Ben couldn't wait. It was well past dusk as he negotiated the HQ perimeter—not daring to risk the main gates. His buddysuit gave him a certain anonymity, and he had a generic entry code rather than his personal pass, which would surely have been wiped out of the matrix by now. He'd certainly lost his Level One clearance.

He strolled through the parking lot as if he owned it, punched in the door code for the goods entrance, and pushed off into the antigrav shaft, facing away from the camera plates and staying close to the safety ladder in case someone spotted him on one of the vid-circuits. The building was never totally empty, even at night, so one more uniform, more or less, wouldn't cause any excitement unless his face was obvious.

Up on the first floor all the lights were on standby, except for Crowder's office. As he made his way silently along the corridor, Cara's personality flickered into his head. He felt a shiver of warmth.

Hello, love, having a busy day? he said.

*You wouldn't believe what these damned settlers . . . *

I'm three paces away from Crowder's office.

Mind if I listen in?

Be my guest.

Ben stepped silently through the door. Crowder was hunched over the com trying to sound sincere. "He was my most trusted team leader, Mr. Dubeau." The bastard even managed to sound emotional. "And he was a good friend. I'll miss him."

"Now if only you'd told me that when I was alive, I'd have asked for a pay raise." Ben enjoyed the look on Crowder's face. "Take it steady or you'll have a heart attack."

"How did you get here?"

"Not important. Do you want to ask me why I got here?" Ben paused, though no answer was forthcoming. "But then, you know why, don't you? I want to know what you've got planned for Olyanda. I know half of it already. Now you can tell me the other half. Let's start with why you didn't trash the platinum data."

"I did."

"Come on. How long have we known each other?"

"Too long for this sort of suspicion," Crowder said.

"Then give me proof, or give me a reason."

"Ben, dear boy, do you think I would abandon you? I've got a shuttle coming to pick up all my psi-techs. Of course, you'll all have to disappear, officially, but there'll be a credit bonus that will keep everyone quiet, even you."

"I won't say I can't be bought, Crowder. Everyone's got a price, but mine isn't money. Tell me about the platinum."

"Okay, okay. The platinum . . . it's too important. Ben, the Trust is my life. I've given everything to it. My youth, my wife, everything."

"That was your choice."

"And I made it willingly. The Trust . . . Believe me, Ben, I'll be chairman of the Board one day. Maybe even one day soon. I'll make it to the top, and I'll take you with me. But we'll not get there by ignoring a platinum planet. Olyanda will give us an edge over every other trading company in the whole of the known universe. We'll stomp Alphacorp into the mud."

"You can't take me with you to the top. I'm dead, remember?" Ben saw Crowder's body twitch twice as if he'd tapped his foot.

"Dead, yes. I am so sorry. I owe you my life . . ." Crowder sat back in his chair, his eyes clouded.

A flicker on Crowder's face gave away another presence in the room. Ben spun to the left. There was a sizzle in the air, and the bolt beam scorched a channel in the wall. He jumped back out of the line of fire with a curse.

Danniri and Jusquin, Crowder's bodyguards, came at Ben from opposite sides. Instead of going for either, he ducked low and emerged between them, making their hand weapons useless without the danger of hitting each other. They suffered a fatal moment of indecision.

Ben's hand flickered to the dark buckle on his belt. With one twist the cross-shaped centerpiece snapped off as it was designed to do, revealing four chisel edges as sharp as razors. Ben skimmed it sideways toward the right-hand man. It buried itself in his throat, severing artery and windpipe. Blood began to spurt high from the wound, spraying the wall and floor.

Even as Ben made his move, Jusquin's booted foot connected with his ribs. He rolled with it and twisted, almost landing on Danniri's bloody corpse, slipping in the pooling blood. The lifeless fingers still held the bolt gun. Ben grabbed it, twisted again, and fired. Jusquin fell and lay still.

"That's enough."

Ben stared straight into the muzzle of Crowder's jet pistol.

"Two down, one to go. Would it be me next, Ben?"

"Not until I'd wrung every bit of information out of you that I could."

Crowder leveled the gun. It was lightweight, but it would still make a mess of him at this range. Ben didn't have a chance against it. He got to his feet slowly.

"Go on, then. You said you owe me your life. Is this how you repay your debts?" He didn't take his eyes off Crowder as he straightened up. "From this range you shouldn't have any problems, though the blood might stain your shirt. What's one more life on top of all the rest?"

Crowder's hand never wavered. His eyes remained steady, but he didn't fire.

"It's not quite the same as killing people on another world, is it? Give an order. Make a payment. That's easy, but this . . . this is messy." He flicked an eye to the bodies on the floor. "It's messy and very personal. Is it worth it?"

Crowder didn't even blink.

"If it's your scheme, it will be well planned. Who are you sending in? Does the Trust have its own black-ops fleet? Or have you done another deal with Ari van Blaiden? Tell me, Crowder . . . all the time you were standing by my side at the Hera-3 hearing, were you laughing out of your arse?"

Crowder shrugged, but his hand never wavered. Ben kept on, hoping to get him talking. If he'd had the guts to pull the trigger, he'd have done it by now, but one wrong word could push him right over the edge. He kept his voice low, tried to give Crowder the impression it wasn't too late to offer him a deal.

"Cutting communications was a good idea. We thought you were on Reisercaine, but . . ." Ben nodded to the small pins in Crowder's lapel. "Neat trick, a double-damper. Leave us stranded, without resources, then divert the second ark. It was very clever. I would have thought, though, that you'd have sent a transport to lift us all off Olyanda, get us out of the way. You didn't need to lose your psi-tech team if you'd been prepared to wait until the end of the year. Haven't you lost enough psi-tech teams?"

An irrational laugh bubbled up through Ben's subconscious. "You never intended for us to survive, did you? With or without platinum, we were going to be lost in the Folds on the way home. You put the Hera-3 survivors together to get rid of the last witnesses, and you were willing to lose the rest of the team to get rid of us. The platinum was a complication you didn't expect, but you were willing to make use of it."

"Not lost." Crowder's voice cracked. "Just mislaid in cryo. A hundred years would have done the trick. Believe me, Ben, I never intended any harm to you or your team, either on Hera-3 or Olyanda, but . . ."

"But platinum trumps all other considerations." Ben exhaled sharply and shook his head. "I trusted you, Crowder. I trusted you with my life . . . and theirs. What next? Airborne attack? Neural blast bombs to turn us all to zombies, then send in a mop-up division?"

Crowder didn't blink. "Better make a deal for yourself, Ben. You're too late already. Probably . . . let's see, seventeen days Earth-time by the Exan Gate . . . about four days too late."

"We came by the Invidii Gate."

Crowder turned pale. "When did you leave? Had the grain shipment arrived?"

Ben's scalp began to crawl. "What does it matter?"

"Had it?" Crowder almost screamed. His gun wavered just a fraction.

Ben didn't miss the opportunity. He flung himself sideways and slammed against Crowder's desk, knocking the furniture into his legs. Crowder staggered and sent his float chair crashing into the wall. Ben vaulted over the desktop, grabbed the gun, and dropped with one knee on Crowder's chest, pinning him to the floor.

He replayed everything Crowder had said in his mind, then married it up with the official reports. Plague. Shit.

"Biological strike, Crowder. That's why you want to know, isn't it? Did I leave before or after some deadly bug was released? In which case, am I infectious now?"

Ben put his face close to Crowder's and breathed out.

"What might I be infecting you with? Something neat like an altered flu bug or an anthrax-based killer, or something truly messy, like Ebola. Here you are. A present from Olyanda."

"No! You don't know . . ."

"Don't know what? How bad the plague is? Tell me, then.

What have you released—bacteria, a virus, neurotoxins?"
Ben put the jet pistol against Crowder's neck.

"Pull the trigger. If you left after the grain arrived, you'll
be doing us both a favor. Use it on yourself next."

"What have you done? What is it?"

"Endaemia. In biological terms, a chimera, a superbug. A
weapon from more than one viral source. Now, for God's
sake, tell me when you left and how long you've been here."

Ben pulled Crowder up from the floor, then shoved him
down hard on the float chair which wobbled dangerously
until he jammed it against the wall. "Tell me more."

Crowder pinched his lips together and shook his head.
Ben grabbed Crowder's ear and twisted hard, immobilizing
him with the pain, then he shoved the muzzle of the gun
into Crowder's crotch until the man winced. He released
the pressure on Crowder's ear without letting go completely. The trouble with getting information with pain was
that the information was likely to be what you wanted to
hear, not necessarily the truth, but Ben had known Crowder
a long time.

"There's nothing you can do." Crowder choked back a
sound that was halfway between a giggle and a sob.

Ben pushed the gun harder into Crowder's soft flesh and
was rewarded with a gasp that could have been either pain
or fear. Whichever it was, Ben had Crowder's full attention.

"I haven't got much time, Crowder. If I pull the trigger, it
almost certainly won't kill you, but you'll wish it had."

"All right. All right. But it won't do you any good. It's already too late."

"Tell me!"

"A killer. Human-specific in this form. Airborne. Virulent
as all hell." He started to move his fingers in a universal
cutthroat gesture, but more pressure from the gun stopped
him. "It's fierce, but it's fragile. Lifespan of six months, but
that's enough to do its job. Within a year the planet will be
safe again."

"But if I'm already infected, then it's too late. Is that it?
Is there nothing that can stop it?"

"Not before it's swept through the rest of the populated
galaxy."

Ben shoved his rising panic to one side. She was still there in his head, sitting quietly, not interfering. *Did you get that, Cara?*

All of it.

And the grain shipment?

There's a chance the settlers may not have reached it yet. If they haven't, I'm going to kiss Victor Lorient for doing it the hard way.

Get on it.

Already moving. Her mental contact snapped off, leaving a sweet ache where she'd been.

Ben dragged Crowder to his feet. "You'll never get away with this. It's too big."

"You're wrong. It's precisely because it is so big that no one will question it. Never underestimate greed. Even if I reveal the whole thing to the Board, all they'll do is sniff at my methods and then take every advantage of circumstances."

Ben jammed the gun against Crowder's neck again. "What about the second ark? What have you done with it."

"It's safe. Safe. I'm not a monster."

"You could have fooled me! Safe where?"

"The Arcturus System. A fresh planet. Safe. Tell me. You're not infectious, are you? You'd have blown my balls off by now if you were." Crowder turned on his negotiating voice. "You're not stupid, Ben. Forget all this. It's already too late to do anything for the poor sods on Olyanda, but there's still time to save yourself. I'm sorry it worked out like this. You're my best man, you know. Your only flaw is your integrity. You're too honest. Too honorable to finish me off now, even though I know you want to. My flyer's in the port. Take it and get out. You'll fare well enough on your own. I've always had you pegged for resourceful."

Ben tightened his grip on the gun. His palms were beginning to sweat slightly, and his ears felt as though they were being bombarded by white noise. This wasn't real. He would have trusted Crowder with his life. He wanted to pull the trigger. No one else would ever be able to square it up for the settlers and the psi-techs.

"You're wrong, Crowder. I'm not honorable enough."

He weighed up the choices. Kill Crowder now. Satisfying, but what if the thirty thousand were not safe on Arcturus? Take Crowder prisoner? The possibilities of being able to get him out of the building and off planet without a firefight or a miracle were remote.

"An honorable man would kill you right now. I'm leaning toward expediency."

He'd have to leave him here. Crowder wasn't going anywhere, though next time security would be much tougher to crack. And there would be a next time. Once the thirty thousand were safe, Crowder was a dead man and honor would be satisfied.

"You're not going to hurt me." Crowder's voice slipped past negotiation and into manipulation mode. "We go back too far. Get out while you can, Benjamin."

"There was a time when I would have died for you, Crowder, but not anymore. You might still be useful, so . . ." Ben put the gun close to the side of Crowder's head and pulled the trigger.

The gas propellant exploded. The bullet took half of Crowder's ear with it and buried itself in the wall where its explosive charge gouged a ragged crater in the medonite. Crowder's shriek was lost in the fierce crack from the weapon, and he fell to the floor clutching his ear. Blood poured through his fingers as he whimpered with pain.

"Consider it a kindness, Crowder." Ben's voice was low and barbed. "With only one eardrum you're less likely to hear the ghost of a colony, screaming in the night."

❖ ❖ ❖

Late night on Chenon was dusk for Cara. She leaped to her feet by the riverbank where she'd come to chat to Ben in private. *Listen up, everyone. This is an emergency. I need the exact coordinates for the wheat delivery pod right now.* Cara flashed a broadcast. She quickly explained what she'd gleaned from Ben's confrontation with Crowder. *If that pod's open, we're all dead.*

What one knew all knew, and though there were one or two psi-techs on the verge of panic, the practicalities of the situation quickly asserted themselves, swayed by the consensus. The last thing they could afford was to run around in circles.

Gen was on duty in Mapping; within a minute she'd come back with the coordinates.

I'm on my way. Wenna's thoughts were thick with sleep. She'd worked the night shift and was catching up with her rest. Cara could feel her scrambling for clothes and trying to manipulate her arm into some sort of working condition.

No one knew how close the settlers were to the wheat pod's drop zone. The best they could do was to get there before them if that was still possible.

I'm closest. Sami Isaksten broadcast from the Seaboard Station. *I can get there in about six or seven hours.*

How many people can you muster? Cara asked.

Only three of us. There's me, Jon Moon, and Rufus Greenstreet.

Get in the air as fast as you can! We're on our way.

Cara felt Cas take over her open comm-link to coordinate the action. Gupta's security team was the first airborne, with Wenna riding up front, followed closely by Archie Tatum and another Psi-Mech, who launched in their bot-carrier. The rest of the psi-techs raced for every available flitter.

Saedi Sugrue grabbed the last two-man flitter and headed in the opposite direction to everyone else, toward the half-built city. *I'm not sure it can do any good, but it won't do any harm. I'm going to get Jack Mario.*

Cara.

Ronan?

I have the medevac flitter on the landing pad.

On my way. The medevac flitter was the fastest emergency vehicle they had. Cara sprinted for the hospital, taking the stairs to the roof two at a time and almost falling into the passenger seat clutching the stitch in her side.

Hold on. Ronan slammed the safety catches closed and hurled the sleek vehicle skyward with cursory pre-flight checks.

Cara's heart thumped in her chest.

"Do we have a plan?" Ronan asked.

"Yeah—improvise." Cara shrugged. "I don't know. I suppose just telling them the truth and having them believe us would be too easy."

As they overtook Gupta's flitter, he waved at them. *Hey, Doc, if they've opened this thing, will it do us any good to fry them all where they stand?*

Cara went cold all over. She looked at Ronan and he shrugged. "If the bug's airborne? It depends on what's gone into making the little critter. I hope I don't have to take a guess." *I don't know, Gupta, and that's the honest truth.*

I brought engineering explosives—flashburners. Gupta's thought trailed off in a wobble as if he could barely bring himself to voice the idea. *I'm just saying, that's all. What? I don't like it, either. Okay, I'm sorry I mentioned it.*

But the thought hung in the air. Cara tried to ignore it but wondered whether she could be responsible for burning anyone she suspected of being infected. She stared at the blackness beneath their wings, hardly seeing it for the horrors behind her own eyelids. If the cargo pod had been opened, everyone was dead anyway. Why not attempt to save some by sacrificing others? She blinked twice and pushed away thoughts of what might never happen, knowing that it could be their last desperate act if all else failed.

Chapter Thirty-two

RACE

BEN HEARD A NOISE. THE DISTURBANCE HAD alerted security. He pocketed the gun, retrieved his bloody buckle, and slipped through the door that Crowder's heavies had come in by. This area was off limits to most of the staff. Crowder had his own way of getting in and out of the building when he needed privacy.

Ben dropped the lock behind him and ran, soft-footed, down the corridor, not trusting to the antigrav shaft, but taking the emergency stairs. On the ground floor, he doubled back into the security room. One man was in there, flicking rapidly through the recordings.

"Looking for a picture of me?" Ben leveled the gun.

The guard stiffened but didn't turn round.

"I've got no quarrel with you, Scully, so just pass me the slide from that machine."

"Commander Benjamin? I'd know that voice anywhere. But they said you were . . ."

"Dead? They exaggerated. That's it. Don't turn around, just pass the slide backward." Ben got close enough, grabbed the slide, and then stepped back out of reach.

"Scully, I've got a problem. Have you ever known me to lie?"

"No, Commander." Scully's voice wavered.

"Then I'm not going to start now. For your own sake, you never saw me tonight. The recorder wasn't rolling. There's no record of what happened in Crowder's office. Do you understand?"

"Yes."

"I mean, do you really understand? Because if you get this wrong, you're dead. Crowder won't want any witnesses. The life of one security guard won't outweigh that one single, simple fact. If you say you saw me, you're a dead man, and it won't be me pulling the trigger. Now do you understand?"

"Yes, Commander Benjamin. I do. I really do."

"Good man. And you might think about getting a transfer to somewhere far away—soon—and take your family with you."

Ben slipped quietly out of the door.

✦ ✦ ✦

"Get your stuff. We're leaving now." Ben slammed into Max's hotel room with his bag already in his hand.

"I'm coming." Max knew when not to argue.

In less than five minutes they were on their way to the port, and Ben had explained everything.

"But how can he do that? Mass murder . . . I mean *mass* murder. I'd never thought about that before. At what point does murder become mass murder? Two, twenty, two hundred . . . two thousand? How can one human being do that to . . ." He subsided into silence.

"Have you heard back from Cara yet?" Max asked for the fifth time since they hit the fast lane for the port.

"You'll know as soon as I do." That wasn't strictly true, of course, but Ben couldn't see the value in turning over the what-ifs one more time.

"Have you got ice in your veins?"

Ben took a deep breath. "If I give in to what's inside me right now, I won't be any use to anyone. Get a grip."

"Hey, I'm not trained for this. You were a Monitor."

"Nothing trains you for losing the ones you love. I've done it once. I'm not about to do it again if I can help it. You can either help me, or you can set up house on Crossways and keep Mother Ramona company."

Max took a deep breath. "Her couch is a bit too soft. I'm with you."

"Okay, then. Keep it together, or keep out of my way." Ben glanced across and caught Max's anxious look. "Before I went to see Crowder, I set the recording system to survey his office. The whole lot, Crowder's plan. Everything— including me killing the heavies—will be right there on the recording. There are three copies." He handed one to Max. "I dropped the third off at my apartment. My family will find it if they look hard enough."

He should have contacted Nan any number of times since this thing blew up. Dammit, he could even have called the farm on a public link while they were on Chenon, but the more they knew, the greater the danger. He didn't want his family involved.

He swallowed hard. "Whatever happens, Crowder's not going to get away with this."

The words *whatever happens* chased themselves around his brain. Ben slammed his fist into the side of the control panel. The pain in his knuckles helped to counteract the ache in his soul.

✦ ✦ ✦

Please let them have bogged down to the axles in estuary mud or been headed in the wrong direction. Cara scanned all sides with an infrared scanner for Lorient's wagons while Ronan kept them flying low and fast.

"How long?" Cara asked.

"About six hours. Get some sleep."

"No, you might miss them in the dark. Two pairs of eyes are better than one." She tried the radio comm again, but got only static. "Damn this planet. Damn the damn settlers. Why the hell couldn't they take a Telepath?"

A cool gray dawn crept slowly over the horizon and painted the sky a dirty off-white.

Finally there was a blip on the scanner.

"There!" Cara pointed. "I can see the hoop of a wagon."

Ronan adjusted their course and Cara tried the radio again, only to get a burst of the usual static.

"Still no radio contact?" Ronan asked. "Even when we're within visual range?"

"Uh-huh." She shook her head. "And I don't think we're in visual range. That's only a single wagon down there."

It was, indeed, a single wagon. They circled it, but the picture told its own story. A dead horse lay close by. There were no other heat sources, no other signs of life.

"They can't have left long ago," Ronan said. "That means we have a chance."

"Yeah, but how close are we to the site?"

"Close." His mouth was set in a grim line.

We're here—landing now. Sami Isaksten reported.

What can you see? Cara responded.

Wagons. Oh, fuck! By the way they're drawn up—tents pitched, horses hobbled, fires burning low—I guess they've been there a while. I can see the pod, it's half-buried, but there's no one around it. I can't tell whether the hatch has already been popped. Looks like they arrived late yesterday and have been camped for the night. I can see a few people stirring. No one looks sick.

Whatever you do, whatever it costs, if that hatch is closed, don't let them open it.

Sami, Jon Moon, and Rufus Greenstreet against a mob. Cara glanced sideways at Ronan and swallowed hard. Jon Moon was his lover.

We're going down, Sami said.

Cara tried the radio again, but it yielded nothing. "I bet the bastards don't even have it switched on!"

They've seen us, Sami said. *They're coming out of their tents.*

"How long?" Cara asked Ronan.

"Eighteen minutes."

Eighteen minutes, Sami. Stall them. If they haven't opened it, tell them the truth. Tell them it's a virus. Only, for goodness sake, tell them to wait eighteen minutes.

No one talked about what would happen if they had opened it, but Cara was aware of a tight conversation between Ronan and Jon. She didn't pry.

She kept a light contact while Sami landed her flitter just

off to one side of the pod and came face-to-face with a delegation of suspicious settlers. What could three of them do?

"Can this thing go any faster?" she asked Ronan.

"You think I'm not gunning it to the max?"

She shook her head. Sami Isaksten, Jon Moon, and Rufus Greenstreet were hardly their most authoritative figures. Lorient probably wouldn't even recognize their faces.

"Don't blow it, Sami," she breathed.

Ronan put out a reassuring hand. "She's level-headed. She'll manage. Jon's great backup, he . . ." His voice cracked.

Now it was Cara's turn. She clutched Ronan's hand, hoping to be of some comfort but finding nothing to say. Finally, as they came within sight of the pod and Ronan needed both hands for a landing, Sami's jubilant cry hit them all like a ray of sunshine.

It's still sealed. Thank the gods your ancestors worshipped and all their little angels. The pod's still sealed . . . but Lorient's not buying the plague line. It's the truth, for goodness' sake!

Stall him. We're here.

Below them, the estuary was at least three klicks wide with soft brown mud stretching out on either side. Where mud turned to coarse grass, Cara could see a circle of hooped wagons and a metal pod, about the size and shape of an airbus fuselage, scored and scarred by its journey through space.

A crowd had gathered.

Cara didn't know whether she'd have any more success than Sami, but she had to try. Maybe she could get through to Lorient. Before Ronan had powered down, she was scrambling out of the hatch, ducking under the swept-back wing, and running toward the crowd gathering at the pod. She could see Sami, Jon, and Rufus standing defensively between the settlers and the hatch.

A settler she didn't recognize tried to tackle her, but he wasn't combat trained and his balance was completely off. She sidestepped him, sent him crashing to the soft ground, and raced for the pod. Lorient turned to face her and motioned to his settlers to stand aside. Dragging in a steadying breath, she walked through the men—always the testosterone mob—and placed herself between Sami and Lorient, nodding at the psi-techs. Sami gave her a grateful look, and all of them gave her a telepathic greeting. She saw Jon Moon look anxiously to Ronan, who was pushing through the settlers.

I told him it was a plague, but he didn't buy it. He thinks we want the wheat for ourselves, Sami said. *I thought he knew about the platinum. Isn't he expecting dirty tricks?*

I don't think he knows what to expect. I don't think he knows which way is up. I think Danny's death has unbalanced him completely.

Cara quickly took stock of the situation. The pod had sunk up to its middle in the soft floodplain, and the main cargo hatch was half-buried and would have to be dug out by hand before it could be opened. There were seven wagons drawn up in a circle and about twenty men—no, make that twenty-four men; she'd just spotted more coming out of the far wagon. Oh, fuck, they had smart-dart rifles, probably loaded with enough anesthetic to drop a bull; not fatal, at least not singly, but a shot from one of those things would put anyone out for long enough for them to open the pod.

"Mrs. Benjamin, I might have known . . ." Lorient eyed her warily.

"Director Lorient. We have to talk."

"There's been enough talk already," one of the younger men called out.

"Enough, Ed," Lorient said, but the man stepped forward threateningly and Lorient had to put out his hand to reinforce his order. "We said we'd take care of the wheat. It's ours. How can it be contaminated when it's been packed in a sterile environment?"

She took a deep breath. "Deliberately."

His face showed a range of emotions, but shock was quickly replaced by rage. "How dare . . . Are they trying to starve us to death?"

"Starve, no. Director, can we talk privately?" If she could just get him alone, she could pour the information directly into his mind and he would know with absolute certainly that she was telling him the truth. And she was prepared to tell him the truth—all of it. But he just stood rigid. He wasn't going to let her have her own way, and she could hardly let anyone guess that she could get inside Lorient's head, least of all his own people. She tried another tack.

"We're all in this together. Someone wants this colony to fail, and they're not bothered if the psi-techs get buried with it. This pod is carrying a bioengineered plague, courtesy of the Trust."

As twenty-four voices supplied a soundtrack of surprise, anger, and disbelief, Ronan reached them and stood between Cara and Jon Moon, touching Jon's hand in acknowledgment and receiving in return a tight little smile and a mouthed: missed you.

Now they were five. Odds of five to one—easy!

"Suppose we believe you." Lorient quieted his men. "And I'm not saying we do."

"That wheat's ours!" The young man called Ed shouted out.

"You're welcome to it." Rufus Greenstreet, about the same age as Ed, bounced up and down on the balls of his feet, his pale face offset by florid pink circles on each cheekbone. He was close to losing it. How many weather techs ever had to face a mob?

"Settle down, Rufe. You're not helping," Cara said as Ed moved forward with intent.

"Ed!" Lorient snapped out a command, and the young man stopped in mid-stride.

"If we wanted your wheat . . ." Cara raised her voice. "We could have beaten you to it and had it removed from the pod and shipped out on an airbus while you were still dragging your wagons over the floodplain."

"Maybe you did. Maybe you don't want us to open up the pod and find it empty." One of the older men that Cara didn't know by name stepped up on the other side of Ed.

"Where's the logic in that? No, don't tell me," she said as he drew breath. She mustn't get sidetracked. Victor Lorient was the one she needed to convince. "Director, please."

Should she try mind to mind or would that freak him out completely? In the distance she could hear the sound of flitters, the rescue squad.

"There's more of the bastards," Ed shouted. "Quick, let's get the wheat before their reinforcements arrive."

The crowd surged forward past Lorient as the five of them stood their ground, meeting the first wave of settlers head on.

Victor, listen to me. If you let them open the pod, we're all dead.

Cara just had time to fire a message at Lorient and hope that there was enough residual implant to enable him to receive it before Ed came charging in and she twisted aside from his vicious tackle and dropped him with clubbed fists to the throat, not elegant, but effective. After that, it was a melee of ducking, punching, kicking, and generally trying to stay in the game without letting them pin her down, hoping the others were doing as well . . . or better. She took a ringing slap to the side of the head, saw lights crackle across her vision, and blinked hard to clear it.

"Steady." Ronan hauled her upright when she didn't even realize she'd gone down. How long could they keep this bunch occupied? How long before someone slipped behind them? All around her were jostling bodies and the sounds of fists on flesh and scuffling feet mixed with curses and exclamations.

Ronan's steadying hand vanished. She ducked a wild punch and slammed her elbow into her closest attacker's gut, hearing a satisfying grunt of pain, but someone grabbed her from behind, and in stepping into him she tripped on someone already down and staggered. A second pair of hands grabbed her by the waist, and the man behind her got an arm around her throat and yanked her even further off balance. Totally lost, she closed her eyes and let herself go completely limp, hoping to fool them into thinking she was unconscious and letting her drop out of their hands. Not a move to try when someone was trying to kill you, but these guys weren't trained killers.

Never underestimate an angry, frightened man. As she flopped onto the ground, someone's boot toe connected with her ribs once, twice. Pain shot through her side. She felt a rib crack and the knowledge was almost as damaging as the pain because now she knew it wasn't going to stop and that one more wrong move could puncture a lung. She waited for the third kick, but it never came. The scuffle moved past her.

Groaning, she rolled over and came to her knees, muttering obscenities with what breath she had left and wondering whether she had any fight left in her.

"Mrs. Benjamin." A solid hand slid under her arm and hauled her up to her knees. Pain shot through her chest, and she almost retched. "Did you mean it?" Lorient stared down into her face. He looked like a man waking from a bad dream. "Is it true?"

Swallowing hard, she put the memory of Ben's confrontation with Crowder to the front of her mind and opened her thoughts to Lorient. *I can't lie to you. Not like this.*

"Enough! Stop!" He was on his knees in front of her, his arm not so steady anymore. "You're hurt. I'm . . . I'm sorry. What a damn mess!"

"Ribs." She found that drawing breath to speak hurt like hell. "No matter. Stop them opening the pod."

She felt blackness closing in on her, and she must have passed out for just a couple of seconds because the next thing she knew was that Lorient had gone and she was still on her knees. Cursing like a trooper at each jolt, she staggered to her feet as the ground shook.

A roar went up and the fighting petered out with cries of alarm replacing shouts of anger. The pod shook and rolled and began to sink further into the soft ground until the hatch was completely obscured.

Sorry we're late for the party. How's that? Archie Tatum sounded self-satisfied.

Gives us some thinking time and some talking time. Thanks, Archie.

Archie's bots had undermined the pod and sunk it firmly into the ground so that the settlers would need shovels to dig their way to the hatch. Thinking time, indeed. In the meantime, Cara could see that Lorient had pushed his way to the front of the crowd and Gupta's security team had efficiently secured the area. The fighting petered out as quickly as it had begun, but there were casualties on both sides. She could see Ronan still on his feet. Definitely handy in a scrap, that doctor. Jon Moon was with him, though clutching a bloody nose. She couldn't see Sami or Rufus.

Everybody all right? she asked.

I think I'm going to be sick, Rufus replied.

Sami? But there was a gaping hole where Sami had been.

She's over there. Ronan started toward a figure on the ground.

Cara took painfully slow, short steps to where Ronan and Jon bent over Sami. At first Cara thought she was unconscious, but Ronan put his hand on her face and closed her eyes. "Neck snapped," he said. "She's gone."

"Gone? Oh." Cara felt her knees buckle and she sank to the ground besides the lifeless psi-tech, clutching her side, but hardly noticing the pain anymore. She didn't move when Ronan sat down beside her and put his hand on her ribs, though she was vaguely aware that the pain subsided.

"I sent her, Ronan. It's my fault," she whispered.

"She held them off for long enough for us to get here. Together, we held them off long enough for them to get here." He indicated the security team. Cara could see Gupta and Lorient talking intently, but no one was making any move toward the pod. "If you hadn't sent her, the pod might have been open by the time we got here. She saved the day. Saved the settlement. You made the right decision."

But all Cara could think about was that she'd gotten one of Ben's team killed.

Chapter Thirty-three

DEAL

BEN AND MAX MADE IT BACK TO CROSSWAYS in record time with only two shuttle transfers, and within an hour of docking were settled into Mother Ramona's den, sitting on her couch in the station's early morning, each clasping a hot drink. Ben sipped his without really tasting it.

Mother Ramona pushed some books aside and sat on the desk opposite them both. "I did some digging. You were right about the plague originating on Crossways. Where else, really? The cargo pod was routed by a man called Hammer through Janek—he runs one of the shadier laboratories here, and we've got some shady ones, believe me. Apparently there was a delay, which Janek didn't communicate to your Mr. Crowder. Something to do with a dockside sweetener for handling biohazard cargo."

"There's a chance, then, but why haven't we heard? They should have found it by now. Can you lend me a tame Psi-1 to send a message to Cara?" He scrubbed his eyes with the heels of both hands. "That plague was meant to take us all out, psi-techs and settlers alike. Crowder shafted us all."

"Bloody, filthy plague." Max's drink slopped over his hands and he hurled the cup away, splashing its contents across the floor. "I'm sorry . . . I didn't mean to . . ."

"No matter. It's only a rug."

"It's the waiting . . ." Max said.

Mother Ramona handed him a cloth and then left them alone to wait.

And wait.

Finally Cas Ritson came through. Her touch was more abrasive than Cara's, and Ben could sense she was backed up by Saedi Sugrue adding extra power.

It's all right.

Relief washed over Ben, and he grabbed Max by the shoulder and nodded to him, turning his back as the man dissolved into tears.

Where's Cara?

Infirmary. She's got a busted rib. There was a dustup, but they held the settlers off long enough for Gupta's team to secure the pod.

How bad?

Ronan's doing intensive therapy. She'll be fine by the time you get home.

Ask her to contact me as soon as she can.

Ben . . . Sami didn't make it.

*Sami . . . *

There were five of them between the pod and the settlers, and things turned ugly. They held off twenty-five of Lorient's boys until we arrived. Saved our butts for sure.

Sweet little Sami. Twenty-eight years old and as good a Finder as you could want. She had family on . . . Ben thought back . . . one of the colony outposts in the Kindred System. Parents and a brother if he remembered rightly. They'd probably have already been informed that Sami had perished in the plague. Should he contact them and let them know how she'd really died? Maybe not. Not yet anyway. If there was the opportunity later, he would. He owed it to her.

But Sami had succeeded. Cara had succeeded. The pod had not been opened. Crowder had lost. Ben realized his own cheeks were wet, too, and he wiped them with the heel of his hand.

"We should celebrate." Max looked up. "I want to get roaring, stinking drunk."

"Celebrate later. We've won the first round. We still have a planet lousy with platinum and a colony of obstinate blockheads to deal with."

Max looked at him. "It's not over?"

"What do you think?" He turned to Mother Ramona. "Did you fix up an appointment with your friend Norton Garrick?"

"With my fiancée, Norton Garrick." She grinned. "I did."

"A shrewd alliance." Ben inclined his head in a semi-salute. "I'd like you to come with me. I have a proposal for you both—one I think you'll find . . . challenging."

"I like a challenge."

"I know." He grinned.

✦　✦　✦

The following morning Ben found Mother Ramona in her den, curled up on her couch with a book. He suspected she lived in there, even though the rest of the house was cool and spacious.

He waited until she looked up. "Hey there, business partner."

"Hey, Ben."

"Sorry to disturb you, but I want to add something to our shopping list."

"Something impossible, no doubt."

"A jumpship."

She dropped the slim book on the couch, and its screen went dead. "Now, you're in the realms of fantasy. There's nothing available on Crossways, either to hire or buy, equipped with its own jump drive."

"I just have a feeling that I need to win all the time I can get. What about the ones that aren't available?"

She thought and then began to laugh.

"Are you fussy who we steal it from?"

He shook his head. "I can't afford to ask questions."

"If we can get the ship I'm thinking of, you might appreciate the irony. It belongs to a mutual friend."

"Crowder?"

"Ari van Blaiden. He's been known to use Crossways as a port of convenience. He uses a false ID, of course, but that doesn't fool me."

"He's not here now?"

She shook her head. "But his ship is."

"Where's Max?"

"In the garden, mooning over his woman. She must be quite something."

"Gen? Yes, she is."

"I thought so. When a man's invited to seal a bargain on your couch and doesn't shut up, for one minute, about the woman at home, it's a sure sign of an incurable romantic."

"He did that? I'm sorry. It wasn't very polite."

"No, don't worry. In its own way, it was charming, and in his own way, so was he. I'll enjoy working with him, but don't worry, I'll give him a break from the couch." She laughed, deep and throaty. "Besides, he'll be busy."

"I hope I . . ."

"You were, as ever, a perfect gentleman. Cara is a lucky woman. I'm glad it worked out for you."

"Let's hope we get a happy ever after."

"I'd wish you luck, but you make your own luck, Benjamin."

"How can I fail with you and Garrick on my side?"

"Let's not count the ways."

◆ ◆ ◆

Ben didn't ask how Mother Ramona arranged for a team of crack thieves and obtained the docking codes for Ari van Blaiden's ship. All they needed to do was to get past the security guards. A small task if you said it quickly enough.

The *Raider* was a state-of-the-art jumpship with its Alphacorp registration insignia filed off and renamed the *Solar Wind*. Ben had a satisfying feeling that his gain was Ari van Blaiden's loss. Luckily, its owner was off-station.

No doubt his platinum had paid for both the ship and Mother Ramona's loyalty, but he'd started to think of her as a friend, though he couldn't tell at what point their relationship had crossed that invisible line. Maybe it was on her couch, but there was more to it than that. If she trusted Garrick, then he'd trust her judgment.

Max looked over his shoulder as he studied the ship's specs. "Nice piece of kit. I always wanted my own spaceship, and I guess this is about as close as I'll ever get. You sure I can't come with you?"

"You can be more use here, and you'd be a liability on Olyanda. Lorient's moods are up and down like . . ."

"Mother Ramona's skirts?"

Ben grinned. "Hush, she'll hear."

"You do know how to fly this thing, don't you, because there's an awful lot depending on . . . ?"

Ben looked at him and raised one eyebrow. "Relax, Max. I'll bring Gen back."

Max cleared his throat. "Good luck, then. I'd say keep in touch, but . . ." He touched his temple. "Maybe I'll have a receiving implant fitted while you're away. It's not like I can't afford it now."

"Swallowing your Ecolibrian principles already?"

"Oh, you know, other people have principles, I have . . . ideas."

"Well, don't get big ideas while I'm gone. Look after our finances and stay out of trouble."

"I'm good at that. Finances, I mean." He nodded, half held out his hand to shake, then changed his mind and left quickly, passing Mother Ramona in the doorway.

Ben watched him leave. He wasn't bad at trouble, either.

"Will you please stop him from getting himself killed on Crossways without me?" he asked.

Mother Ramona laughed. "He'll be all right. I'll give him a bodyguard."

"I think he'd be better off with a nursemaid."

"I'll give him Derry, then. He's been round the block a few times. Knows how to keep a low profile."

"Thanks."

"Are you sure you've got everything, Benjamin?" Mother Ramona's eyes were all concern.

He nodded. "You know what to do?"

"I do."

"You've got all the dirt on Crowder and all the Hera-3 evidence as well?"

"Safe."

"Good. If anything happens, feel free to use it to your own advantage. Break him, and split the Trust and Alphacorp wide open. Don't give them the opportunity to shaft anyone else."

"Trust me."

"You're a strange woman, Ramona, but, actually, I do."

"Mother Ramona, to you."

"I always wondered why *Mother Ramona.*"

"What else would you call a woman of the cloth?"

"You?"

"I took holy orders on Eldibane when I was eighteen—you know what that means on a pleasure planet. I arrived on Crossways when I was twenty-five. There are more places to serve my god than in a nunnery, you know."

Ben laughed. "And how many people do you tell that to when you're cementing your deals on the couch?"

"You're not the first, but you're the only one I haven't killed—so far." She grinned. "Believe that if you want to."

"I think I will; it makes me more comfortable."

"You take care."

"I'm not planning to die out there."

"Good. I always thought that life had some higher purpose in mind for you."

"Now you're getting philosophical."

She laughed. "Just saying."

"I guess this is good-bye, then," Ben said. "For now."

"For now."

She gave him a brisk, brief hug and turned to leave.

❖ ❖ ❖

Bravery came in many forms. It was easy in the midst of action when adrenaline was running high, but in cold blood it took more determination. Ben wasn't a thief, but a man could change if he needed to, and Ari van Blaiden could afford the loss. It was time to make a move.

Ben sat in an auto-cab with three men, dressed, like him, in buddysuits and identified only by their code names of Bravo, Echo, and Papa. They waited on the transit line just outside the residents' moorings. Delta, Oscar, and Sierra were in the car behind them. Through the thick plasglass wall Ben could see that the private dock was as different from the cargo port as you could get. Wide open spaces and normal atmosphere. The ships all gleamed in the gentle lighting.

"Nearly time to go," Echo said.

Ben wondered whether Echo might be a woman.

You all right?

Ben nodded and pulled on his own face mask and infrared lenses.

"Time. Go!"

Bravo pushed the door open, and the lights in the transit tube winked out. They jumped out of the vehicle and hit the ground running. The door clicked shut behind, and the little tub zoomed off.

Bravo led the way through doors, normally heavily alarmed and guarded, but now open and quiet. They crossed the wide walkway crouching low and strung out so as not to make an easy target.

"Hold." A challenge came from somewhere to their right, and Papa dropped to one knee and fired a smart-dart at a figure moving in the darkness. There was the sound of a body hitting the floor.

Anesthetic. Ben might have become a thief, but he wasn't a killer—at least not without good reason. But if anyone fired at them, the ammunition would be live. They were lucky; they crossed halfway to the Vantix dock before someone caught on. There was no preliminary warning call, just a steady stream of fire, slightly high and wide, thrown off by the tracer scrambler the team of professional thieves carried as part of their equipment.

There was the *pfft* of another smart-dart being released and a yell as someone in the Vantix compound fell.

A second volley of firing found its range. The ground at Ben's feet erupted into splinters as a blast of energy hit it. He leaped sideways and kept running. There was no cover to be had. He hoped the power backup had been as well-sabotaged as the lighting circuits. The Vantix guards had night-sight goggles, but the darkness still gave them some advantage.

The firing stopped.

"Now." Ben sprinted for the ship they'd targeted. The three other code-named thieves from the Alphabet Gang had taken out the rest of the guards.

"Quick." It sounded like Papa's voice.

The ramp was already down.

Ben ran up it and, in the low-level lighting of the flight deck, found the pilot's chair and eased into it. Behind him, he heard a scuffle and a muttered oath.

"Shit." Papa's voice came out of the darkness.

"Leave him." That was Echo.

"Is he hurt?" Ben asked.

"It's all part of the job." Bravo said, and the ramp swung up as the door swung down. "There's an exit point nearby; he'll make it."

"I suggest we go now," Echo said to Ben. "Speed would be good."

Ben set the power levels at maximum and released the docking clamps.

"Papa?" he asked.

"Clear of your thrusters. Bravo, Delta, Oscar, and Sierra are all on board," Echo said. "Just get us out of here."

"I hope your man in control has done his job."

Ben lifted the *Raider* on its antigravs and slotted it into the access tube with barely a meter to spare from fin to wall. As the shield doors closed behind them, the outer doors opened up in front. He felt the mass of the craft, slower off the mark than the Dixie would have been, and compensated.

Without warning, the outer doors began to close.

"Strap down," Ben yelled.

He kicked in the aft thrusters and the *Raider* sprang for the door, screamed sideways onto its wingtip and through with barely a whisker to spare.

"Shit!" This from Sierra, but the rest of the company were professionally cool.

"Rendezvous in nine minutes," Echo said.

Ben put some space between him and Crossways before someone filled it with pulse-cannon bolts.

The Dixie hung in space at the appointed place. A second transport hovered nearby. Ben maneuvered so that the Dixie was beneath the *Raider* and then sent out the grapple and brought it safely into the hold. When the air had cycled, the door opened and a sixth anonymous thief appeared, dressed in a plain, black buddysuit like the others. He tossed his cargo of evac suits onto the deck, one each and a spare since Papa hadn't made it.

The five thieves didn't remove their masks. Ben could pass them on any street, any time, and never recognize them.

"My thanks," Ben said. "Your transport awaits. I suggest you make a move. I don't want a send-off party from Crossways catching up with us."

"Air lock ready to cycle," Oscar called across.

Oscar put on his helmet, the last of the thieves to finish suiting up. He clicked the seal closed.

Ben watched the six of them transit to the waiting transport.

As they safely slid inside the transport, he checked out the ship. This was no runabout; it was a fleet cruiser big enough to store the Dixie in the hold, but it could still be flown by a single pilot plumbed into its nav and tech systems.

He felt the hum as he connected to the ship, and one by one the ship's systems opened up to him. "Oh," he said out loud as he found the weapons modifications, and then again, "Oh, yes." He grinned to himself. "Thank you, Ari van Blaiden."

He'd asked for a ship with a jump drive, but he'd got much more. This baby had weapons systems, a stealth-net and crew quarters for thirty. She'd certainly been a black-ops ship and he wondered whether she'd been one of the ships that had attacked Hera-3. All the better if she had; she could make amends now. He let his mind wander deeper into the ship's systems. *Oh, sweet.*

He tried not to think of her as stolen goods. A little worm in his brain said: *Maybe you're doing the galaxy a favor if she's a black-ops ship.* This ship was a perfect toy. He briefly entertained fantasies of rescuing Cara and roaming round the galaxy in the *Solar Wind*, free of the Trust, taking jobs for the good guys only. Ack! Crowder had been right; he did have White Knight Syndrome.

He felt his way deep into the ship's system, set a course, fired up the jump drive, and watched for the telltale no-star blackness sitting like an octopus with tendrils of *nothing* misting out from its rim. At times like this he envied those with a belief in the afterlife. Jumping without the gate beacons needed a certain kind of madness or desperation. Some adrenaline junkies did it for fun. He shuddered.

The Folds beckoned, loomed. Then with a rush that took his breath away the *Raider* was inside the nothing, a place that didn't exist. In the deepest Folds of space the fabric of space-time was stretched very thin and compressed like pleated paper. At that point, even the finest of on-board AIs became erratic. What demons might he find this time?

In the intense blackness, amorphous gossamers of color and light swirled briefly and vanished again. The Folds were unfathomable. It was as if they carried the whole history of the universe plaited into a single strand. Sometimes it was random; sometimes he saw, quite clearly, the double helix of human DNA. One infinitely small part of the strand was Ben's own.

There were other strands, too. His parents, shriveled to dust, floated across his vision. His Nan, two brown boys in her embrace. A group of men, lost in a swamp, and a stringy boy leading them to safety. The dawning realization that they didn't feel the certain pull of home like he did. The letter granting him a place in the Academy. His first active command in the Monitors during the Garnier insurrection, bending orders so he could save civilians. The smuggler vessel apprehended on the Rim with eighteen hysterical Burnish refugees in its hold, destined for the illegal exotic trade. The fight with Columbar to keep mercenaries out of the mine dispute. The confrontation over bribes with Sergei, his boss. The hollow realization that his file was marked E for "expendable." The surge of anger as Sergei came at him with a tangler; the satisfying crack as he broke both Sergei's arms. Crowder's job offer. *I need a man with brains who knows which way is up.*

Cara. In a shimmering dress so fine it left nothing, and at the same time everything, to the imagination. Cara. Strung out and helpless. Cara. Unbearably angry, her fist swinging toward him. Cara.

The ship burst out into realspace and the visions faded, leaving an ache of emptiness.

Chapter Thirty-four

PREPARATION

WENNA'S NEWS THAT BEN WAS APPROACH-ing Olyanda brought Cara to her feet in the middle of the dining hall.

Rain poured down, but she rushed out into the compound with no thought for getting wet. For once, she wasn't wearing her buddysuit and within minutes her uniform was drenched. She grabbed a groundcar from outside the LV, shaking rain droplets out of her eyes, and headed for the ship. While she drove, she took a deep breath and reached out with her mind.

Ben!

Cara!

The emotion nearly overwhelmed her. She echoed it back to him, leaving him chuckling.

Our personal life will have to wait. She caught the mental equivalent of a sigh. *We need to talk to the settlers.*

She heard the *Raider* before she saw it emerge from a cloud bank and land on the edge of the plain. Ben had barely reached the bottom of the ramp before Cara ran into his arms. They stood there together in the rain.

"Oh, I've missed you," she said.

He didn't reply, but he held her so tight she thought he was never going to let her go.

"You're wet," he said at length.

"It's raining."

"So it is." He grinned and kissed her again.

It was easy to get lost in the sensation, but when Cara came up for air, she sighed and stepped back, looking closely at the *Raider* for the first time. *Solar Wind*. Her knees turned to jelly and her head began to buzz.

"Where did you say you got the ship?"

"I didn't. Mother Ramona . . . sourced it for me."

"On Crossways?"

He nodded.

"Ben, that's Ari van Blaiden's ship."

He grinned. "Payback."

"What was it doing at Crossways?" Cara's heart was fluttering like a butterfly's wing. *Mr. van Blaiden wants to know . . . Breathe.* "Ben, is Ari on his way here?"

"How could he be? With Crowder's plague let loose, this planet shouldn't be open for business for at least six months."

"I just have a very bad feeling. If Ari has access to Crowder's files, he'll know about me and about the platinum. If he doesn't know about the virus, what's to keep him away? He's coming."

"Get in the car." Ben propelled her into the front passenger seat and slid behind the control panel. They rose on antigravs over the uneven ground. Cara stared at the inside of the front screen without really seeing it, trying to reach some connection that was lying just behind her eyelids. Ari van Blaiden was coming.

Whichever way she looked at it, she arrived at the same answer. "Follow my logic, Ben: Crowder and Ari have been working together, but it's a devil's bargain. They hate each other."

Ben looked at her sideways.

"Isn't it obvious? Am I adding two and two and making six? Look, who's Crowder's biggest rival in Alphacorp? If Crowder could somehow entice Ari van Blaiden to Olyanda, the plague rids him not only of the colony and the Hera-3 witnesses, but of one more big problem—Ari himself. It's very sweet. Crowder gets two birds with one rock. Profit and revenge combined."

Ben shook his head. "That theory only works if you presume Crowder has made the connection between you and Ari and can use you as bait."

She nodded. "Worrying, isn't it?"

"We need to talk to Mother Ramona." Ben's face was drawn and a muscle danced along the side of his jaw, betraying his tension.

"You're thinking you should have killed Crowder." Cara put one hand on Ben's arm. "It's one thing to take someone out in the heat of the moment when they're coming at you armed to the teeth, but you're not a cold-blooded killer, Ben, and I wouldn't want you to be. Besides, Crowder might have a part to play yet."

✦ ✦ ✦

Victor Lorient eyed the groundcar with suspicion and then looked to its driver. Saedi Sugrue. He'd always been suspicious of the woman, but she'd never been anything but unfailingly polite despite his rudeness. What was she made of?

"Director Lorient. I've come to take you to the meeting as arranged," Sugrue said.

"Aren't you going to get in, Victor?" Rena stepped round him and climbed into the backseat. "Good morning, Miss Sugrue, very kind of you to come and collect us."

"Morning, Mrs. Lorient. Is Jack—Mr. Mario—coming?"

"I'm here, Saedi."

Jack came huffing up the hill dragging his coat on over one shoulder. He didn't wait for Victor but climbed into the front seat next to the psi-tech. Victor had little choice but to step into the backseat next to his wife. She shuffled over. It might have been to make room, but Victor was pretty sure it was to keep herself separate from him as she had since Danny's funeral.

"Saedi, I heard about Sami Isaksten," Jack said. "I wanted to tell you how very sorry I was."

"Thanks, Jack."

"Yes, Miss Sugrue, my condolences also," Rena said. "She did us a great service."

Was it Victor's imagination that she gave him a look out of the corner of her eye?

"We saw a large craft coming in, yesterday," Victor said. "One we didn't recognize."

"Commander Benjamin."

"So what's this meeting about?"

"I really couldn't say."

Couldn't or wouldn't, it was all the same. The psi-tech set the car on its antigravs and Victor hurriedly strapped in.

The ops room was full, but luckily there was a corner they could squeeze into when Sugrue dropped them at the door. Jack shook a few hands as they entered, and Rena greeted Benjamin cordially. Cara Benjamin pointed to a chair where Victor could sit without being too close to any of the psi-techs.

He looked around. All of the section heads were there. The only one he didn't recognize was a young woman wearing an insignia of the vet team. Of course, both Tanaka and his wife had died in the fire at the tank farm. Most regrettable. He swallowed hard. It really was most regrettable. How could he have let Taris and Colchek get so out of hand? He was glad, so glad, that Taris was dead and he hoped he might never have to deal with Colchek again. No one, not even Jack, knew that Benjamin's lot had snatched him. They all assumed he'd been crushed out of recognition in the meeting hall collapse.

Benjamin called the meeting to order. "Back to plan A," he said. "We need to evacuate. Quickly."

"I thought we had six months before the Trust made its move," Victor said.

"So did we," Benjamin said. "But Cara's sure, and I agree with her logic, that Ari van Blaiden will arrive first. There's a significant movement of unmarked ships through the Crossways home space. Mother Ramona was unable to get their identities, and that in itself is worrying because all the regular mercs and criminal gangs are known on Crossways. Half of them are based there."

"And you think it's Alphacorp?" Jack asked.

"Not Alphacorp, Ari van Blaiden. We think he's working for himself," Benjamin said.

"And has he . . . Do you think he . . . ?" Victor couldn't

find the words. "The second ark ship. Did you find out what happened to it?"

Ben shook his head. "I'm afraid not. Crowder said Arcturus, but Mother Ramona hasn't been able to confirm that. I swear, Director, I will make it my priority once the Olyanda situation is sorted out. In the meantime I've got people out looking. Good people."

"It's all . . . too much." Victor put both hands up to his face.

The room was too small, too stuffy, too . . .

He needed to breathe.

All along he'd treated the psi-techs as enemies while the real enemies were the organizations that were supposed to bring order to the galaxy.

"Are you all right, Director?" Cara Benjamin asked. He looked up, barely seeing her through unfocused eyes. "Director?"

"Someone get the director a drink of water." He wasn't even sure who said that, but moments later Jack was pushing a cup into his hands.

"I'm all right." He took a sip. "All right. Go on." He circled his right hand. "Please."

"The good news is that they can't ignore the laws of physics," Benjamin said. "Ore carriers and mining barges are too big to route via the faster gates. Since I've stolen van Blaiden's jumpship, hopefully his only jumpship, he's going to be arriving by one of the regular jump gate routes and that will slow him down. It's my bet he won't arrive without backup, so the Invidii Gate is out because it can only take small ships. Even so, we've probably only got days, or a few weeks, at most. Mother Ramona is arranging transport to Crossways for all of us, but she's hampered by the laws of physics as well. The bigger the ship, the longer it will take. She's sourced two cruise liners, big ones, and a few smaller transports."

"What about the *Solar Wind*?" Cara Benjamin asked.

Victor struggled to catch up. "That must be the ship that landed yesterday. Did Benjamin say he'd stolen it?"

"If we cram people into every available space," Benjamin

said, "she can maybe take sixty at a time, ninety if they take turns to breathe in and out. Gen, do you feel up to doing shuttle runs?"

"You're giving me your new toy to play with? Sure thing, Boss." Marling was the pregnant one.

"Pick your own copilots. If van Blaiden shows up, get back to Crossways and sit out the fight. She's armed, so get a couple of Gupta's maintenance men to work tactical. If you get into a situation, however, I'd prefer that you turn tail and run like hell."

"Understood. Is it okay if I take Jon Moon? He's a Psi-3 Navigator. Cara, how about you?"

She shook her head. "I'm staying here with Ben. When he leaves, I leave."

Ben continued, "If and when van Blaiden arrives, the psi-techs and any settlers still not evacuated will disperse to the forests in small groups, guerrilla style, and be ready for anything."

This was all going too fast for Victor. "Are you sure all this is necessary?" He spread both hands. "Can't we just tell them we give up? Tell them we're leaving?"

"We know enough to be able to identify them. They won't want witnesses. The object of the exercise is to survive until the new owners get here."

"New owners?"

"Evacuation is a damage limitation exercise at best," Ben said. "But I think I've found a permanent solution."

"You have?" Victor heard his own voice come out like a squeak.

Ben grinned. "I've sold your planet."

He struggled to sound authoritative. "You've done a deal with the Trust?"

"Uh-uh." Benjamin shook his head. "I've sold to the biggest criminal consortium in the sector."

"You what?" More than one person said that simultaneously and all heads turned to Ben. Victor wasn't the only one to look shocked.

"Olyanda is about to become a subsidiary of Crossways," Benjamin said. "Norton Garrick and Mother Ramona are on their way here with a fleet of pirates. Only, in this case, the pirates are the good guys. They get the mining rights for as long as they can hold onto them which, with their fire-power, should be a very long time. They've had practice."

Victor's brain started to catch up with the conversation. "And we get our lives, is that it?" he asked. Had the psi-techs made a grab for the platinum after all?

"Plus you get five percent of the profits," Benjamin said. "Which, believe me, will make the new Ecolibrian colony—wherever it ends up—very, very rich."

He'd never wanted to be rich, just safe and free to live the way he believed all men should live. Still—rich—he supposed that was infinitely better than dead. "And can we trust these . . . criminals?" he asked.

"Actually, we can. They have nothing but their reputation and their wits to survive on, and so both are impeccable . . . within their given dispositions."

"And what do you get out of it?" Had the psi-techs taken the biggest share for themselves?

Benjamin just grinned. "I cut the psi-techs in for one per-cent. And before you say anything about profit motives, my crew has lost everything, too. They can never go back to what they had. Some of them have families they may never see again. They deserve a stake for their future and they're going to get it."

"That's very fair, Director," Jack rumbled quietly at his side. "Very fair, indeed."

"All right," Lorient said. "You're not going to get any ar-gument from me this time. Just get my people out of here safely." He glanced sideways at Rena. "I want my wife on the first ship out of here."

"Victor, no," Rena began to protest.

"Yes. Someone has to look after the evacuees. Jack can supervise gathering everyone together. I won't leave until the last person is safe. That's my job."

"With Mrs. Lorient's permission, the first flight leaves just as soon as ninety people are on board," Benjamin said. "First thing in the morning. Hand baggage only. Lives are more important than possessions."

✦ ✦ ✦

After everyone had departed, Ben slumped in a chair in ops.

"Well done," Cara said.

He looked up at her. "Lorient didn't make the obvious snap judgment? After all that's happened, I wouldn't have blamed him in the slightest if he'd accused us of trying to get rid of the settlers so we could keep the platinum for ourselves."

She shook her head. "He looked like an old man. For the first time ever I think I felt sorry for him. You think he's learning at last?"

"I hope so." Ben shrugged. "Nothing I can do about it anyway."

"So quit trying, at least for tonight. You look dead beat," she said.

"I probably am if I stop to think about it. That's how I've survived so far—by not stopping to think."

"Do we have a chance?" Cara perched on the edge of a desk.

"We stand a chance of getting a few thousand settlers off planet or hidden before things get nasty." He shrugged. "After that, we'll see."

"You need some sleep. Go to bed." Cara took his hand and held it to her cheek.

"Only if you come with me."

Cara ignored the half-smile on Wenna's face as they headed for the door. In their room, she turned up the opacity of the window to maximum and shut out the gray daylight. Ben sat on the edge of the bed, not moving. She undressed him like a child and rolled him into bed, then quickly stripped off her own clothes and slid under the covers. They held each other tight until Ben drifted off into a deep sleep.

Cara lay still and listened to his even breathing, making sure he wouldn't wake, and then let herself think about Ari and what the consequences might be of seeing him again. Was anything else hidden inside this head of hers waiting to trip her up?

❖ ❖ ❖

The following morning Gen, Jon Moon, and their hastily assembled crew took the first bunch of settlers off-world.

Rena Lorient led them on board, calming them all with kind words of reassurance and barely looking back at her husband. Cara wondered whether she was pleased to get away from him and whether he was secretly relieved to be free from her disapproval. There seemed to be a chasm between them since Danny's death.

Settlers and psi-techs worked together. Why did it take the threat of imminent death to suddenly make people realize that their similarities were more important than their differences? Even Lorient was working with them, if not exactly relaxed, at least resigned. Cara wasn't sure how much of it was an act and how much was genuine. How long would it last before his personality flipped again?

Yan Gwenn's airbus crews collected settlers from the outlying farmsteads first. Two of Mother Ramona's smaller carriers arrived on schedule and took six hundred passengers safely away to Crossways. The first cruise liners arrived three days later and though they took a further six days to load, they carried away almost four thousand to safety.

The autumnal weather was on their side so far with no more fierce storms and only a minimum amount of rain. Despite Lorient's best efforts, however, the settlers were angry and upset at having to leave their new farms behind, farms that had already taken their blood, sweat, and tears and—in some cases—the lives of their loved ones. Three villages refused point-blank to leave their homes until Lorient himself commandeered a two-man flitter and a pilot and went ahead of the evac teams to warn the settlers and explain as best he could. Chastened by the director's admonishment, they cooperated, but unwillingly. After that Lorient undertook a whistle-stop tour of all the settlements, sympathizing, explaining, cajoling, wheedling, and only when all else failed finally ordering them to toe the line or be left behind.

"I never thought I'd actually warm to the man," Cara said, watching Lorient climb down from his flitter in Landing at the end of a very long day. "But he came through."

"Yes, he has." Ben put his arm round her shoulders and gave her a brief hug. "I hope we come through for him. At this rate it's going too slowly. We need a Dunkirk."

"What's a Dunkirk?"

"Something that happened way back on Earth in the mid-twentieth century during a civil war. British troops and their allies were trapped on the beaches of Northern France about to be captured or wiped out by an encircling enemy army. They were saved by a fleet of little ships: fishing boats, pleasure steamers, ferries, and anything that could float. That's what we need now. Can you connect me with Mother Ramona?"

◆ ◆ ◆

The little ships began to arrive in the evening on the third day. Some could only take four passengers, but others could take twenty or even thirty at a pinch. Every one of them was welcome and every one of them would be paid well for their services when the platinum started to pay off. In the meantime they took promissory notes from Norton Garrick.

Altogether, they evacuated almost four thousand settlers in four hundred and thirty-two vessels. A hospital ship took the patients from the med-center, including the cryo unit that held Colchek. Cara hoped Max and Mother Ramona had adequate accommodation organized at the other end, but Crossways was the least of their worries.

The influx of little ships all ground to a halt with a storm warning.

They'd evacuated approximately nine thousand settlers, leaving around seven or eight hundred and some lonely graves. Cara had helped to bring in the settlers from outlying settlements, but once the storm kicked in, she was pinned down in Landing with everyone else.

"Tired?" Ben steered her toward their room.

"Yes, but . . ."

"No buts. Sleep now. Work tomorrow."

The storm raged outside. Temporarily safe in Ben's arms, Cara tried to sleep, but couldn't. Thoughts of plague, Ari, and platinum chased themselves around in her head. Eventually, she must have dozed off because she dreamed.

She's surrounded by dark, as thick as velvet. She can feel it running through her fingers. Ari's voice comes from somewhere beyond it. "It's not over until I say so."

Then a different voice, a woman's voice, drums though her brain. "Mr. van Blaiden wants to know that his secrets are safe."

She woke, cold with fear. She could feel Ben awake, too. His arms were still around her.

"You cried out," he said. "Nightmare?"

"My imagination's working overtime. I dreamed that Ari was already here on Olyanda. It was so real." A little thrill of anticipation, tinged with dread ran, unacknowledged, through her body.

"You're so sure it will be Ari in person?"

"Oh, yes."

"You're not on your own this time."

"He'll come because of me. This is my fight, Ben."

"That makes it mine, too."

He leaned up on one elbow and kissed her. She put her arms up around his neck and pulled him closer. Ben was warm and solid. She needed him tonight more than ever to help drive the ghosts away.

Long after Ben had drifted back into sleep, Cara lay awake. The echoes of their lovemaking still tingled through her body. Ben and Ari; Ari and Ben. A direct comparison was impossible. They were so very different. She loved Ben. Of course she did. The feeling had grown without her even being able to detect when like and respect turned to love. But did that mean she had stopped loving Ari van Blaiden? Could she be in love with two men at the same time? Reluctantly, she had to admit that just because she loved Ben, it didn't prevent that clutch in her guts when she thought about Ari. Fear, loathing, and love. She couldn't separate any one from the others.

✦ ✦ ✦

Incoming. Wenna's warning came as the storm died away in the deep blue just before dawn.

Sure? Ben asked. It wasn't the first blip they'd spotted; the magnetic storms played havoc with their instrumentation.

Mother Ramona's spotter saw a fleet of at least nine ships emerge from the gate, but they're not from Crossways.

Ben sent a message via Cara to every psi-tech. *They're here. You know what to do. Good luck.*

In the half-light they scattered, moving deep into the woods, taking the remaining settlers with them.

Cara contacted Gen and Jon Moon on the *Solar Wind* just as they were about to enter foldspace for the return journey. *Go back to Crossways. You can't do any more here. The few settlers who are left will have to scatter with the psi-techs.*

"Let's get out," Ben said. "Everyone clear on what happens next?"

They were.

Cara ran for the horse barn to meet up with Ronan, Gupta, Archie Tatum, and Yan Gwenn. She took the reins of a bay mare, patted her on the neck, checked the girth, and mounted quickly. Ben swung into the saddle of an iron gray. One by one, the rest of the team hoisted themselves aboard their mounts, some more easily than others, though all psi-techs were supposed to be trained to operate all forms of transport, including animate ones.

Cara's mare caught the excitement of the moment. She tossed her head and danced on the spot. Cara took a moment to settle her down. Then they all clattered over the pontoon bridge, past the shell of the tank farm, and across the plain toward the nearest finger of woodland, a ten-klick ride accomplished without incident. Once there, they retrieved the first stash of food and equipment. Sharing the load between them, they moved deeper into the forest toward the base set up for emergencies. The going got much easier once they were under the heavy canopy of the broccoli trees, thankfully just as dense now as in the height of summer.

They heard four craft, heavy freighters by the sound of it, roar overhead and farther away there were sounds of lighter craft and the unmistakable sound of a series of explosions coming from the direction of Timbertown. A quick check with Wenna reassured Cara that everyone was clear and that she and Lorient were safely hidden with a mixed party of psi-techs and settlers, including Jack Mario and Saedi Sugrue, well away from the town.

"Glad we didn't have to say I told you so to the survivors." Cara glanced across at Ben.

He nodded. "I didn't necessarily want to be proved right. I'm surprised they haven't hit the LV yet."

"I think Ari wants me in one piece." She shuddered.

"Well, he's not having you. All we have to do is stay out of trouble for another few days," Ben said. "Mother Ramona should be here soon with a fleet."

All during the first day they kept on the move, traveling steadily. They could hear light craft flying search patterns, but none came close enough to spot them with heat scanners.

That night they slept under bivouac shelters, quickly erected between trees with polytarps, their buddysuits providing insulation from the cold, hard ground, though Cara found snuggling up to Ben an enormous comfort.

"It'll be all right," he whispered.

"You don't know that."

He didn't answer.

◆ ◆ ◆

On the second day they heard a flitter overhead. It was not one of their own as Yan Gwenn had taken care to immobilize them before they left by removing the drive couples. As the flitter came closer, they pulled up their horses and dismounted, crouching underneath their mounts so that the heat signatures would look like nothing more than a herd of wild creatures.

"Whoa, good girl, steady," Cara told her surprised mare, thankful she'd never shown any inclination to cow-kick. She crouched there while the flitter circled, but then it moved on, and she breathed a sigh of relief.

"Did that work?" Cara asked.

"Let's hope so," Ben said. "If not, I guess they'll be back."

Their woodland base was well camouflaged, just a few rustic timbers hastily felled with flash-cutters and roofed with polytarp and fronds of a fern-like native plant. The horses were safe enough, corralled together close by, and they had a stash of ration bars. They slept together, always with at least two people on watch turn and turn about.

When it was Cara's turn to go on watch, she took a rat-bar, a small smart-dart pistol, and stationed herself to the north of the camp.

One minute she was walking the perimeter, alert for anything untoward and the next she was running soft-footed toward her destination, with a vague memory of having immobilized Yan Gwenn with a single dart, leaving him unconscious on the leafy floor. Her feet kept moving while her mind said stop. Feet won. She reached down for her pistol and found the holster empty. She tried to access her implant to contact Ben, but found a wall between herself and the technology she had relied on all her adult life. She opened her mouth to shout, but no sound came out.

Heart pounding like a kettledrum, she put all her effort into controlling her feet and managed to slow them down to a steady jog. She reached for a tree, smacked her hand into it painfully, but didn't manage to get a firm grip.

Try to turn . . . turn . . . turn. . . .

But her feet knew where she was going even if she didn't. She knew who would be waiting for her when she got there, however. Fear washed over her in waves. In the back of her mind she recognized the voice that had plagued her intermittently since Sentier-4. *Mr. van Blaiden wants to know his secrets are safe.*

So much for breaking the Neural Reconditioning. She never knew this part of it was here, waiting to be activated. Damn Ari van Blaiden to hell and back. Her mind failed her, but even as she whirled into blackness, she realized her feet were still moving.

When she came to her senses, she was standing in a clearing. Her feet had stopped, her hands were shackled behind her back, and standing barely a meter in front of her, leering—there was no other word for it—was Robert Craike. Behind him, an anticipatory grin on her face, Donida McLellan.

Oh, fuck!

◆ ◆ ◆

Ben quartered the ground again, wishing that Sami Isaksten was still with them. She'd have been able to find Cara instantly, or at least pinpoint a direction. It was barely three hours since Ronan had been alerted by Yan Gwenn's return to consciousness that something was wrong. Morning light filtered through the canopy and although they'd found Cara's trail, it had dead-ended in a clearing.

"They must have had antigrav sleds," Gupta said. "There's a horizontal abrasion on this tree trunk at about the right height, but no vehicle tracks or hoofprints or footprints leading away from here. They could be anywhere by now."

Cara said van Blaiden wanted her, but how had they'd taken her with such surgical precision unless she'd knocked out Yan herself and deliberately gone out to meet them? He wouldn't let himself think that she'd done that on purpose.

"There's another rationale," Ronan had said when Ben had finally voiced his fears. "We thought she'd broken the conditioning, but sometimes these things run deeper than anyone realizes. There could have been a sleeper element built in, just waiting to be activated."

Ben couldn't reach Cara's mind, but he knew his own telepathy was weak. When Ronan couldn't reach her either, he began to really worry. Could she be dead already? He thought he might know if she was, but that could just be a lover's conceit. He stretched his awareness out as far as he could but only sensed a steady nothing.

Cas' settler group was the closest, and they had Bronsen with them. Gupta took Cara's mare and rode off to meet him in the forest and bring him to join the search party.

Cas formed a link from where she was; through it, Ben contacted all the parties to check on their status. Everyone else was safe and accounted for, but Lorient's party was in chaos and Wenna was spitting feathers.

He's gone to freaking Landing. Thinks he can negotiate with the invaders. She was just setting off after him. *Don't worry, Boss, I'll catch up with him.*

Chapter Thirty-five

TURNING

CARA'S HEAD SWAM. WHERE WAS SHE? HER cheek pressed against floor grating and her arms, half-numb, were fastened behind her back. The amount of feeling left in them was pure pain. She took a deep breath and ran her tongue round her mouth. Ugh, she'd been drooling. How long had she been unconscious, and what had they given her?

Ben? She reached out through her implant, and the world shifted. There was nothing there except a sickly emptiness. Reisercaine. She recognized the psi-suppressant from her time on Sentier-4. Being on her own was the loneliest, most frightening feeling she'd ever experienced. At least during her time on the run she'd deliberately isolated herself from her implant. She'd been in control and all the time was buoyed up by the knowledge that she could switch it on again anytime. Now she was at the mercy of someone else. She tried to recall what it had been like before taking the test and coming up psi, before the academy, but she couldn't recreate what it felt like not to be connected.

This place looked awfully familiar. She was in the body of the LV. From this angle she could see into the compound that had been her home for months, though now there were sleek personnel carriers there as well as combat skiffs about the size of flitters, but faster and armed.

She heard a voice and her world shifted. Ari! After so long.

"Well, Miss Carlinni. Awake, I see." She recognized this other voice as well, female and mean.

"Ari. Where is he? I want to see him."

"Good." Donida McLellan's face came into her field of view, canted over at an angle "He wants to see you, too, but first we need another little talk." The face vanished.

"Bring her."

Cara heard the command and then yelped as someone gripped her arms and hauled her upright, propelling her toward the door of the little cubbyhole that used to be Ronan's office. Ronan. The image of the young medic conjured the memory of the stone lodged between her fingers. Remember.

Remember Ari.

She loved him.

Which one—Ari or Ben?

Was there a difference?

"In here." McLellan's voice came from somewhere out of Cara's line of sight. "Sit her in that chair. Strap her in. Now, leave us. Carlinni, this is going to hurt you a lot more than it's going to hurt me."

A mind bored into her own.

Cara's world went black.

✦ ✦ ✦

There wasn't much Ben's group could do except move on from their last position and wait for Bronsen to catch up to them. Ben prowled the perimeter of their new camp until Archie growled at him to get some rest. When he did finally fall into a light and troubled sleep, it was interrupted in the early hours of the morning by powerful thoughts from Saedi Sugrue.

Wenna went after Lorient, and now I can't contact her.

"Ronan! Wake up. Listen in to this." Ben tossed the first thing that came to hand, a rat-bar, in Ronan's direction. It struck the medic somewhere in the middle of his sleeping bag, and Ronan came awake with a muffled curse.

You think they've been taken by van Blaiden, Saedi?

I just got one brief burst from Wenna. Something about a scary woman.

"The scary woman's got to be Donida McLellan," Ronan said.

"McLellan?"

"Who else could kick-start Cara's conditioning?"

"Oh, shit! We've got to find her. And Lorient. If he's gone to try and cut a deal with van Blaiden, he'll be presented with a contract for the sale of one planet. If Lorient signs it, he's dead meat, and so is the colony."

◆ ◆ ◆

"Cara? Cara, are you all right?"

"Ari?"

"Oh, thank the gods." Ari's handsome face, fuzzy as if through water, began to clarify. "I thought we'd lost you. Here, sit up."

A strong arm lifted her up, plumped up pillows behind her back, and eased her gently back onto them, then rearranged the covers. She was in a bed, an air-mattress bed that was big enough for two. The room looked vaguely familiar, but right now all that mattered was Ari, his blue eyes twinkling and his blond hair falling casually over his forehead.

"Ari." She pulled him to her and they held each other for what seemed like an eternity, but she never wanted to let go. She breathed him in.

"I thought we'd lost you, girl." Ari pushed the hair out of her eyes. "This has been the toughest assignment yet, but you did it. You were so deep under cover I thought we'd never get you out again. They almost broke you."

"I left Alphacorp. Ran away. You're not my boss, now."

"No. False memories. A cover. Deep cover." He kissed her forehead. "Don't worry; it'll take a while to get your bearings. You've had a rough time, but you delivered the goods. We've got the platinum for Alphacorp. It all went just like we planned . . . well, except for you having to sleep with Benjamin. I'm sorry about that. Was it bad?"

Benjamin. A memory came into her mind.

She's lying in a bed in a room in the visitor center on Mirrimar-14 with a naked man next to her. There's warmth radiating from him, but they're not quite touching. She feels chilled even with the tingle of sex still reverberating in her belly. She's only slept with him to get passage off-station. Benjamin has been considerate, kind even, but he's not Ari. She closes her eyes tight to lock in the tears and takes slow, even breaths.

She's thinking of Ari, and she mustn't or she won't be convincing.

Benjamin reaches across to pull the sheet up around her shoulders, his hand brushing against her breast in the shroud-darkness of the room. She flinches before she can stop herself. Damn, she shouldn't have done that.

"Did I hurt you?" He raises himself on one elbow, his voice full of concern.

"No. You were wonderful."

She tries to make him feel good, but she's not sure he's buying it. It's a good job she's had the full conditioning, or she probably wouldn't be able to fool him, but she more than half believes the story about Ari herself, so she's pretty sure she can carry it off. Mrs. McLellan is a genius.

"The memories will fade, sweetheart. I promise."

"I . . . slept with Benjamin, Ari."

"Don't worry about it."

"How long was I away?"

"Over two years, nine months of it in cryo, so it's not been as long for you. For me, it's been an eternity."

He leaned over and nuzzled her ear. She yanked her head back.

"Ari, I'm sorry. Give me time. It all feels so strange."

"Of course. What am I thinking! I'm just so pleased to have you back." He laughed. "Hell, woman, I've missed you. Get some rest. There's a guard on your door. It's for your own protection, you understand; the crew here are all new, except for Craike and Mrs. McLellan. I wouldn't want one of them to get trigger happy at the sight of a stranger."

"I am tired."

"Sleep, then."

She slept, comforted by the knowledge that Ben and Wenna, Gen and Max, Jack Mario and Victor Lorient were now safely in her past and she was back where she belonged.

✦ ✦ ✦

Ben pulled his horse up on the edge of the forest. In the fading light the LV and buildings at Landing, ten klicks distant, were barely shapes. To one side, on the landing pad, was a single sleek cruiser plus the more unfamiliar shapes of bulbous ore carriers and a flotilla of smaller skiffs, armed, no doubt. Ben had seen skiffs like those before—on Hera-3.

"We walk from here." He dismounted and unsaddled the gray, then gently pulled the bridle forward and let the bit drop out of the animal's mouth. "Go on, get lost. Enjoy the rest of your life." He slapped the horse on the rump and watched as it trotted off.

Ronan nodded and followed suit.

"My arse was sore anyway," Gupta said.

"I dunno. The horse was a welcome relief after being on foot," Bronsen said. "I was just getting used to the idea." He was still riding Cara's bay mare. "Ah, well, back to wearing out my shoes." He dismounted.

"Think yourself lucky it was horses," Gupta said. "I once had to ride a camel. Evil-tempered beasts, and they spit."

"Will someone help with these?" Archie Tatum had a case of mini-bots retrieved from his saddlebags. "I've got one case in my backpack already."

"Aren't there bots stored at Landing, Arch?" Bronsen asked as he took the box.

"I hope so, but we might need help to get at them. These little babies are all-purpose workers: drill, cut, laser, clamp. Too useful to leave behind. Serafin divided them out between us."

Ronan nodded toward the landing pad. "Van Blaiden's come in force."

"Yeah." Ben fastened the collar of his buddysuit. "He came expecting to be able to scoop platinum ore and leave, and maybe pick up Cara on the way, with or without her consent. Now he finds the whole scenario has changed. Instead of as much time as he needs, he's got a few days at most before a fleet bigger and nastier than his is breathing down his neck."

"You reckon Cara will have told him everything?"

"We can't presume she hasn't."

"So why isn't he scooping and running?" Bronsen asked.

"He hasn't got time," Archie said. "Best drill bots in the world won't quarter-fill one of those ore carriers in a couple of days."

"He's making it up as he goes along now." Ben scowled. "If they've got Lorient—and we have to assume they do—it opens up new possibilities for them. If I were van Blaiden, I'd get Lorient to sign the planet over to Alphacorp, claim a finder's fee, and leave a muddy legal battleground. Mother Ramona and Garrick might find themselves facing the wrong end of a task force from Alphacorp, the Trust, and the FPA combined." He groaned. "I might have started a war!"

"So we get Lorient out before he signs anything, plus Wenna and Cara," Ronan said. "I'm not leaving Wenna behind again."

Ben tried not to add: if Cara wants to come, but he thought it.

"Okay, a ten-klick hike, gentlemen. Let's go."

✦ ✦ ✦

Cara turned over in bed, opened her eyes, and blinked. The room was dim with early morning light filtering in from the high window. It looked familiar for a moment, but then she blinked again and it seemed like a hundred other rooms in a hundred other risers—plain, impersonal, functional. She felt relaxed and rested, at peace with the world. Shower first and then . . . find something to eat. She padded barefoot to the washroom; no surprises there, just the facilities and a generic wash kit and towel laid out for her use.

Gratefully, she pulled a little sonic from the pocket in the wash kit and popped it into her mouth, counting to thirty before she spat it out and rinsed. That felt better. She set the shower to lemon and bergamot and stood under the pounding water spray. So much nicer than a sonic fresher unit.

As she emerged from the washroom, wrapped in the towel and still a little damp, the outer door shushed open and Ari entered. Over his shoulder she could see a guard—for her benefit, of course—and an anonymous corridor. Briefly she wondered why the guard wasn't wearing standard Alphacorp grays, but then her attention was taken by Ari waving a jug and two glasses.

"It was the best I could do," he said, pouring amber liquid into the glasses and handing one to her.

She sipped it. "Apple juice?"

"I told you it was the best I could do. Powdered apple juice at that. Some bastard stole my spaceship with the good stuff on board. I wonder who that might have been."

"Not my fault. I told you where to find it."

"Yeah, Crossways. It'll have been melted down for scrap by the time I get there."

"You want me to go get it?"

He laughed. "No. I've got better plans for you."

He reached across and pulled one corner of the towel. It fell away and she leaned into his hands. Instead of the expected gentleness, his fingers were demanding against her flesh, gripping, squeezing. He found her nipple and pinched. She gasped and arched against him, warmth flooding through her.

He pulled her to the bed, cursing when in his haste he almost missed his footing and sent the lightweight frame skating up against the wall.

"Ari . . ."

He smothered her neck with kisses, dipping his head to her breasts, nipping at her skin. Dizzy, delirious, she gasped and pulled away.

"Ari, don't . . ."

But it was too late. As her shoulders hit the bed, he was on top of her, his hands recalling passions, demanding responses. There was a brief respite while he ripped off his clothes and then he was on her again, knee jammed hard between hers and hand reaching down between them, playing her like a musical instrument.

And she sang for him.

Oh, she remembered now, remembered all too well, remembered pulling him into her and wrapping her legs tight round his back and urging him on with a twist of her hips and whispered words so that it would be over sooner.

This wasn't how it should be between two people.

He finished and rolled off her, reaching for his trousers and huffing with satisfaction. "I missed you, girl." He reached behind him and delivered a ringing slap to her naked buttock. "Get dressed and come to the LV. I need you to talk to Mr. Lorient for me. He's being difficult."

He left without looking back and at last Cara let herself rub the red weal his hand had left. Huge, silent tears trickled down her cheek and into the pillow.

She made herself roll over and sit on the edge of the bed finding soreness here and an abrasion there as she moved. She needed the washroom again, wanted to scrub herself clean.

As she stood up her foot brushed against something solid, a shoe, exposed by the movement of the bed. It looked familiar. She picked it up and a stone rolled out of the toe and into the heel. She picked it out. It was about three centimeters in diameter, gritty and nondescript. She stared at it, then, for some reason her conscious brain couldn't quite fathom, she shoved it hard between the first and second fingers of her left hand. It was just too big to be comfortable, but somehow it felt . . . right.

She looked at it as cold shivers ran down her spine. Her head buzzed, and she felt as though something was squeezing all the air out of her lungs. She dropped into an untidy heap on the floor, dragging the blanket with her and sat, back against the bed, staring at the stone.

Eventually, she dragged herself upright and into the shower, scrubbing herself all over, even the sore spots—particularly the sore spots—then she dried herself and dressed in her buddysuit. Before she left the room, she dropped the stone into her tiny sleeve pocket and sealed it tight.

✦ ✦ ✦

Ben hunkered down in the shadow of the wrecked tank farm and watched the compound with the distance lens of his buddysuit visor.

Bronsen, can you sense any of them? he asked.

Wenna's in an ore carrier.

Cara?

In the dormitory riser.

Lorient?

LV as well, but not with Cara.

Damn. There was a lot of activity around the LV, at least half a squad of guards in there. He wanted to rush in, but it made more sense to try and free the others first. Besides, what might he find in there? Which Cara would be waiting? And would van Blaiden be expecting him?

Let's try and get to Wenna first. Wenna might be easier to free without raising the alarm. She also might be able to give him an insight as to what was happening with Cara.

He'd expected van Blaiden's crew to be relatively small, but it looked like he'd brought an army with him. Some of the men lounging around were obviously not military types, probably miners, but the mercs were easy to spot. Those on duty were sharply dressed in camo buddysuits with bucket half-helms, probably connected to each other with heads-up displays. They carried hefty weapons that Ben couldn't identify at this distance but which were likely to be some kind of all-purpose energy discharge armament, a Newton or a Briggs Eightex, both bad news. The off-duty ones still wore their buddysuits and stood or sat in small groups, separate from the miners. Their buckets were neatly stacked within reach as if they were rarely separated. Even off-duty they each wore a side arm.

All Ben had was his parrimer blade and his smart-dart gun, but at least both were silent and, if not immediately deadly, the smart-dart could put someone out for hours with one well-placed shot. The card was full, giving him twelve shots without reloading.

Diversion? Archie asked.

Archie, Ronan, Gupta, and Bronsen were all short-range Telepaths between Psi-5 and Psi-3, so Ben piggybacked on their abilities and joined their narrow communication net. *No. Once we start with diversions, we have to get everyone out in one go. There won't be any second chances. We wait as long as necessary until the compound clears.*

It was close to midnight before the only figures left were the ones on duty.

Now, Ben said.

Ari van Blaiden's guards were sharp, but Gupta was a veteran of twenty campaigns. He dropped the first guard where he stood with a chokehold. Bronsen took the second one down two breaths later, leaving a gap for Ben to slip through and into the river. He waded in so as not to cause a splash and swam across, his buddysuit keeping all but his head warm and dry. On the far bank he pulled himself out and listened.

Step, step, step, step, stamp, turn. Step, step, step, step, stamp, turn.

Step, step, step, step, stamp, uhh.

Ben lowered the unconscious guard to the floor.

Clear.

Four shadows ran silently over the pontoon bridge and crouched in the shelter of a groundcar rendered useless before they left. Bronsen pinpointed the ore carrier where Wenna was being held. No one tried to contact her directly in case she was being closely monitored. No sense in giving the game away.

That one? Got it. Ben worked his way past a deserted riser to the open ground where van Blaiden's pot-bellied ore carriers were lined up. There was only one guard. Ben could have hit him with a dart at twice the distance though there was little exposed flesh to aim for beneath the half-helm. He aimed for the jawline, saw him slap at the dart as if stung by an insect, and then collapse. Knees first. Onto the dusty ground.

Archie?

Archie sent in a bot to deal with the lock.

Neat. Wait there.

Ben ran to the door, hit the controls, and walked straight into a trap.

◆　◆　◆

As soon as Cara opened the door, the guard came to watchful attention. Instead of leading her down the corridor, he motioned for her to walk in front of him. Okay, she'd play it

Ari's way. The guard obviously didn't trust her, but she wasn't going to make a fuss. The guard walked her to the LV, shining in a blaze of artificial light. The door to the ops room was half open, and Cara could see several techs in there taking the matrix apart, searching for data slides they would not find.

Footsteps echoed on the ramp behind; when Cara turned to look, Wenna was being marched in by a tall, black-skinned guard.

Had she been responsible for Ari finding Wenna and Lorient?

Had faithful little field agent Cara killed hundreds of people with a few careless words? From the look Wenna gave her as she was hurried past, that same thought was in her head, too.

Stifling a sob, Cara turned back to find herself face-to-face with Craike. Before she'd had time to check her own reaction, her hand had flown down to where her side arm wasn't. A sharp laugh from a shadowed doorway to her right brought her up with a jolt. Donida McLellan was watching the interplay between Cara and Craike speculatively. She half-smiled, and Cara felt the world fall away.

There's a bank of machines; herself in a padded chair, in a movement restraint, and there's someone in the room with her. A woman, thin and dark. The woman has a name. The woman has a name. The woman has a name. Her mind whirls several times around the same thought.

Name: Donida McLellan.

Place: Sentier-4.

The machines are alive inside her head. She doesn't want to look at the woman. Pinprick eyes. Implants meshing. Stare. The woman is confusion. The darkness is inside. She tries to look past her, but the walls are too far away. There's nowhere to hide.

She must get out. Out of the chair. Out of the room.

Out.

Her world turns blood red, and she sinks into it.

"Feeling better now, dear?"

"Yes, thanks, Mrs. McLellan. Not sure what came over me."

"Deep cover can have that effect. You'll be all right once

you've put some distance between you and this mission. It will all start to seem like a bad dream."

"It already does."

"Before you let go of it completely, Mr. van Blaiden needs your help with Lorient."

"Yes, he told me."

"A small matter of a contract that needs signing. The man's being stubborn, and I can't do anything with deadheads."

Cara started to form the words: Lorient isn't a deadhead, but Mrs. McLellan had turned away already.

Something inside her was screaming: Shut up!

In the body of the LV a dozen off-duty guards lounged or stood around, some cleaning equipment, others eating from ration tins. Cara felt them watching her as she was escorted past the ops room where she could see Wenna Phipps sitting in front of the matrix screen, arms folded, eyes anywhere but the input panel. Craike loomed over her. She briefly wondered how long Phipps would last if Ari told Craike to get creative and then shuddered. Phipps might be "the enemy" in this instance, but she didn't deserve to be on the wrong side of Craike; no one did.

Ari's voice came back to her, *Leave me? I'm not so sure about that, but you could discuss it with Robert Craike. He handles severances.* The way he'd emphasized the word *severances* made Cara think uncomfortably of limb from limb and head from body.

The idea of leaving Ari seemed alien to her now. She reached across with one hand and touched the little hard lump in her sleeve pocket.

"Ah, Cara, at last." Ari stopped pacing outside the door to what had been Marta Mansoro's office and spun to face her. "Lorient's in there, but he won't sign over the colony without reassurance that his settlers will be evacuated safely. Talk to him. Explain it's in his own best interests. Tell him that thanks to you we know where all his settlers are."

"What can I offer him in terms of reassurances?"

"Absolutely anything."

"What if he wants a percentage rake-off of the mining profits?"

"Yes. That, too. Whatever he wants. Just make him believe it. He knows you."

"Yes, but he doesn't trust me, and if I offer him everything he asks for, he's quite right not to trust me. You won't give him a cut of the profits."

Ari gave her a long look.

Ah, she understood now. Ari wouldn't give him anything. Once his signature was on record, he was a dead man, but a signature made under duress was useless, so they needed not only his signature and DNA print, but also the timed and encoded medical record to go with it to prove his physical state at the time of signing.

"I understand." She really did, but she didn't like it.

"Good." Ari squeezed her arm. From anyone else it would have been a reassuring gesture, but Ari squeezed just a little bit too hard. She felt something solid dig into her flesh—the stone in her sleeve pocket.

Squaring up her shoulders, she nodded to the guard, and the door to Lorient's room clicked open for her. She took a deep breath and stepped across the threshold, face set in a tight mask of what she hoped was warm friendliness.

✦ ✦ ✦

Ari van Blaiden watched the door close behind Cara. He needed her for this one thing and then . . . A brief smile skipped across his face without quite reaching his eyes. Revenge was certainly a dish best served cold. She didn't know what was in store, but she'd soon find out.

Silently, Donida McLellan appeared at his side. How did she do that? He covered up his shock, but he thought she'd detected it. Mrs. McLellan was altogether too useful . . . but he'd really like to teach her a lesson in respect. He wondered if there had ever been a Mr. McLellan and shuddered involuntarily.

"Will she hold for a bit longer, Mrs. McLellan?"

"I've repaired the damage as well as I can under these circumstances, but I'd need weeks, not hours, to do a thorough job."

"I trust you. You've always delivered before."

"But in this case I can't work miracles. I haven't got a full picture of everything that's happened to her. I don't know how she managed to break the conditioning in the first place. That's one conflicted mind. It's holding for now, but keep a careful watch on her."

Ari still had the buzz in his groin from fucking her. She'd felt just like his old Cara. Mrs. McLellan was probably being overly cautious, but he didn't pay her to speculate and she was just doing her job.

Raised voices in the operations room drew Ari. As he arrived at the door, Wenna Phipps crashed at his feet, blood smeared across her lip and a welt across the side of her face. Ari stepped over her and looked quizzically at Robert.

"Having fun?"

"Bitch is leading me in circles. The bloody platinum records are hidden in this system somewhere, but they're well disguised."

"Perhaps you haven't offered her the right incentive," Ari said. "Mrs. McLellan, could you spare a moment please?"

Donida McLellan appeared in the doorway, took one look at Robert's face and Phipps, who was now sitting up and rubbing her jaw, and laughed. "Your way not working, Craike? You could always try cutting off her toes one by one, or maybe rape would soften her up. I'm sure you've got some strapping young men in your unit who would oblige if you couldn't get it up yourself."

"That's enough, Mrs. McLellan," Ari snapped. Yes, she really did need a lesson. If he ever found a Psi-1 who could outgun her, perhaps she'd get it. Robert would like that, and he liked to keep Robert happy. There was always a certain amount of rivalry between Robert and McLellan, but only at work. Ari would no more bed Donida McLellan than he would a praying mantis. Craike had been sharing his bed for the past year and what a revelation the man had been.

He smiled politely at McLellan and gestured toward Phipps. "Mr. Craike was only making a start while you were busy with Cara. Since you're free now, perhaps you could illustrate to Ms. Phipps exactly why she should cooperate with us."

"It would be my pleasure."

Yes, he could believe that. It really would be her pleasure. Not for the first time Ari was profoundly grateful for his youthful decision not to have an implant fitted. He'd never found it a disadvantage. Of course, he did always have a psi-tech on hand for communications. But he was safe from monsters like McLellan.

Once more he wondered about Mr. McLellan. He imaged him to be a complete deadhead, a manual worker, maybe a gardener. What would their dinner conversation be? What did you do today at work, dear? I deadheaded some roses, and you? I deadheaded some psi-techs.

Wenna Phipps began to convulse and moan on the floor. Oh, she'd started already.

The moans intensified to a shriek.

"Enough, Mrs. McLellan. I think Ms. Phipps can understand now that it's in her best interests to cooperate."

McLellan looked almost disappointed, but she backed off and the Phipps woman stilled. Ari nodded to Robert. "Give her a drink of water and a shot of analgesic and ask her about the platinum again, Robert."

"Mr. van Blaiden." Kitty Keely stood outside the door, obviously not sure whether she should come in, her way still blocked by the prone Phipps. He looked up.

"Message from Captain Tengue, sir. What would you like him to do with Benjamin?"

"Confine him for now. Make sure he's secure. Don't underestimate him." At last something was going right. Since he arrived on this bloody planet, nothing else had gone according to plan. He needed to wrap this up quickly and get airborne. Under other circumstances he'd find a more elegant solution to his problems, but quick and dirty would do if it was all he had time for. He'd get even with Crowder later for dropping him into a fubar. Hell's teeth, Crowder might even have planned this, though, for the life of him, he couldn't see why. Why would Crowder get him here in person and then warn the settlement in advance? Was this supposed to be a trap of some kind? It wasn't as if they had enough firepower to stop him or even injure him for that matter.

He saw the ensign hovering and realized she thought he was scowling at her. "Carry on, Ensign Keely."

She saluted smartly. Save him from rookies! He tried to remember why he'd thought it a good idea to bring her along. Sweet little thing, but she'd been a dull fuck, especially with Robert. Cried a lot.

"Get on with it."

"Yes, sir."

He watched her march smartly away, her back very straight. So what was Crowder up to? He'd almost certainly used Cara to lure him here in person, but why? Maybe Benjamin had answers. Whether he could get them without Mrs. McLellan's help remained to be seen. From what he knew about Benjamin's reputation, he wasn't the type to crack easily.

Chapter Thirty-six

MCLELLAN

VICTOR LORIENT FELT STUPID. BENJAMIN HAD warned him all those months ago what would happen if news of the platinum got out. He'd been too panicked about losing Danny to consider selling up the planet and moving on, and he'd lost Danny anyway. Lost Danny and lost Rena. He'd been well aware that she'd not said good-bye before taking the offered transport to safety. She could hardly bear his presence.

He'd screwed up royally, not once but three times. The first time in deciding to stay on Olyanda, the second time with Taris, and the third time in thinking he could still cut a deal with van Blaiden. As soon as he'd come face-to-face with the man, he knew he wasn't dealing with someone he could influence in any way at all. Victor's charisma had finally deserted him.

He'd been kept in a bare cell of a room and and was now expecting another interview with van Blaiden. A shock ran through him when the door opened and Cara Benjamin stepped through. What in the name of all the seven hells was she doing here? He played several scenarios through in his head, including one where the Benjamins had been planning to sell the platinum to van Blaiden all along, but none of them made sense.

He noticed a graze along her cheekbone, her slightly glassy expression, and the stiffness in her walk. She didn't want to be here any more than he did.

She sat down across the table.

"I'm authorized to negotiate, Director."

She smiled reassuringly, but it felt false. Victor wasn't reassured at all.

"On behalf of whom?" he asked.

"Ari van Blaiden speaks for Alphacorp. He has all their resources behind him. He can offer you anything you want."

His flesh began to creep. He could feel her on the edge of his mind. *Seven, thirteen, nine hundred and ninety-nine.*

"Why you?" He managed to speak even though his mind felt it was tying him in knots. "Are you working for him?"

Seven hells, he was going to have to let her in. She was trying to tell him something.

Victor, can you hear me? If you can, don't let on, but tap your index finger on the table.

He swallowed convulsively. Then . . . Tap.

"I've always been working for him," she said.

He's got to think that's true. Don't give me away. They're recording this.

Lorient took a deep breath, his chest swelling. "I want all you . . . psi-techs . . . to get off Olyanda and leave my people alone."

"You know that's not going to happen, so what can we do to sweeten the deal for you? What would you like in return for your signature on a legal contract?"

Was she . . . ? Ah, no, here came the real information, delivered in less time than it took him to blink. *Whatever you do, don't sign, but don't refuse. Stall for as long as you can. If you sign it, your value is at an end. He'll kill you.*

Victor could believe that. He'd seen it in van Blaiden's eyes. The man had no common humanity.

He thought frantically. "Where's the second ark?" he asked.

"It's safe."

He really wished he could believe that, but she said it so quickly and so glibly that it couldn't be true.

He nodded as if he believed it. "I want a guarantee that all the Ecolibrians on Olyanda will be given safe passage to a suitable planet and reunited with the second ark."

"You've got it."

Victor kept his mouth moving and his brain racing. Was she going to agree to everything he asked for, no matter how ambitious? The more she agreed to, the less likely it was to be genuine. He came up with another demand. "And I want shares in the platinum mining. Me, personally. Just ten percent. I'm not greedy."

She nodded.

He could ask for the sun and the moon, and she'd agree to it.

Ah, got it, something van Blaiden couldn't give him. That should hold him up. Victor tried not to grin in triumph as he delivered his last request. "And before I sign anything, I want to see my wife."

"Your wife?"

"You're holding her. I followed her here. I need to know she's safe."

Oh, you genius!

Cara's delighted approval flooded into his mind. Rena was already safely away from Olyanda, but Ari van Blaiden couldn't know that. How long would he waste looking for her?

✦ ✦ ✦

Cara bit back a triumphant little smile as she left Lorient seated at the table, but outside the door Ari stood stony-faced with Donida McLellan and four guards.

"Nice work," Ari said.

"Thanks." She kept her voice light. Admit to nothing until you know you're rumbled.

"Did you really think we'd buy that?"

She shrugged.

"We didn't know Director Lorient had an implant," Donida McLellan said. "He hides it well. It should be easy now."

Not as easy as she thought. What remained of Lorient's

implant was a shriveled and twisted thing. McLellan would have a difficult time getting to Lorient through it, and if she did, she might find more than she bargained for. He'd been a broadcasting Empath; he might be still.

"And as for you . . ." Ari leaned in close. "It's about time we brought our real business out into the open."

Cara felt a cold shiver run the length of her spine and settle into her bones. This was it, then. She squared her shoulders.

"I promised Robert he could be in on the kill. Nothing too quick, of course."

Two of the guards closed in. She was hopelessly outnumbered and on enemy territory. All her training told her when to fight and when not to fight, and this was a time to stand still. Wait for a better opportunity. Except, of course, this could be the kill. It might be the last opportunity she got.

"Ari, what do you mean?" Play for time. Divert his attention. "What real business?"

She lashed out sideways, took one guard on the knee-cap, spun and took the other in the throat with her elbow, but the other two were quick and efficient. One used a tangler cord from a distance while his partner stepped in and slapped a blast pack on the side of her neck. As unconsciousness began to close in, she held onto the thought that Craike had not been there. This wasn't the end.

❖ ❖ ❖

Ben sat in the body of an empty ore carrier. He didn't know what had happened to Ronan, but Archie Tatum, Bronsen, and Gupta had been savvy enough not to get caught. Van Blaiden's goons had used Wenna as bait, damn them. So much easier than trying to run him to ground in the forest. Though couldn't van Blaiden have guessed Cara would be bait enough?

Where are you? Ronan asked on a very tight band.

I'm in an ore carrier. Where are you? Ben replied.

Hiding. Close by.

Cara?

I've not seen any signs of her yet. Bronsen says he can sense that she's in the middle of the compound, but that doesn't seem likely.

Damn, that makes it a lot more complicated.

Ben felt Ronan scanning what he could see of the camp. *We've got you pinpointed,* Ronan said. *Or at least I can see an ore carrier with two guards outside it.*

* You're at least a Psi-3. Can't you get through to Cara?*

You think I haven't tried? She's shielding, or maybe unconscious.

Please don't let her be dead. *Maybe they drugged her.*

Ben felt Ronan settle down to see if he could break through to Cara. What if she was back where she belonged and didn't want to talk to them? He couldn't let himself believe that. He willed Ronan to make contact, suddenly regretting his lack of telepathic whammy.

Cara. Ronan pushed and Ben followed.

Cara!

Ronan? Ben? She sounded groggy, almost drunk.

Are you all right?

Recovering, I think. Trying to avoid a little heart-to-heart with Ari. He'll not want to see me until he knows I'm awake enough to appreciate whatever he has in store.

Where are you? Ben asked.

Dark. Somewhere—something small. Maybe a ground-car, though, no, I don't . . . Oh, fuck.

What's the matter?

Feels like I'm in a coffin.

Right. I can see where you are, Ronan said. *There's a man guarding a single ore crate. Bronsen was right. You're in the middle of the compound.*

Hold on until dark. I'm coming to get you.

Where's Ben? Cara asked.

Embarrassingly tied up in an ore carrier. I walked right into a trap.

Are you all right?

Ben flexed his shoulders, assessing damage. *I'm not injured. Just cramped.*

Get Ben first, Ronan, Cara said.

You're an easier target, Ronan said. *It'll take both of us to break Ben out.*

Guards?

One on you, two on Ben. I've got smart-darts.

Be careful, Cara warned. *They're hot. As tough and well-trained as they come.*

◆ ◆ ◆

It was the smell: antiseptic, ozone, and the gum they used for the electrodes. Victor Lorient grabbed the doorframe on the threshold of McLellan's—what? Workroom? Surgery? Torture chamber? The room held something of all three, and the stink and the sight of the chair with its restraints plunged him straight back into that nightmare he'd tried to leave behind so many years ago.

One of the mercs, a big black man with a face like a monument, shoved him from behind.

He felt his knees give way as the chair loomed, but someone picked him up bodily and shoved him into it.

He was back in the clinic, the same sticky feel of electrodes on his temples.

"Hold him down."

Was that McLellan's voice or Dr. Pargeter? Pargeter and Claire Chapel, his counselor, had both tried to persuade him to give the implant time to settle in, but he knew why they were doing it. A broadcast Empath was a valuable commodity. Valuable but dangerous. They'd never let him have a normal life. He'd be kept closely confined and brought out only when they needed him to sway a crowd or swing a vote.

Sway a crowd or swing a vote.

He was dangerous. A danger to himself and a danger to others. Dr. Pargeter obviously knew that. She wore a double damper to deal with him.

"Take it out!" he ordered her. When that didn't work, he pleaded, cajoled, reasoned, and finally—when all else failed—he began to scream his throat raw. "Take it out! Take it out!"

He felt hands holding him down and a needle in his arm. Then there was only blessed blackness.

He awoke to a voice, definitely McLellan's this time, saying, "Well, that was a waste of time. Lock him up again."

✦ ✦ ✦

Still linked, Ben felt Ronan slip through the compound, dodging from shadow to shadow, past vehicles, and stacked crates, until he was level with the guard by Cara's crate, a big man, massively broad though not fat.

Ronan pulled his smart-dart pistol and took aim. Ben could feel his indecision. He should go for a safety shot, center body, but it was likely the guard's buddysuit had armor built in. He needed to hit the man's neck, but it was a tricky shot, even in daylight, let alone in the dark.

Ronan, let me, Ben said. *Open up. Merge.*

Ben took a deep breath, leaning back against the wall so his body was supported. He felt Ronan's mind step back a pace and he flowed in. The two selves merged into one, and Ben was looking out through Ronan's eyes, holding the smart-dart with Ronan's hand. He knew just where the snout of the pistol was in relation to the man's neck and the trajectory for the smart-dart.

He brought the pistol into line and squeezed the trigger. Felt, rather than saw, the dart thunk home, but the man didn't fall. Damn! The Ronan half of the partnership knew the man was big and that he should have increased the dose.

No, it's okay. The Ben half of the partnership saw the man had gone rigid. On soft-soled boots he ran out of the shadows and caught him as he fell, easing him into the shadow of the crate.

Cara? Ben surged forward in Ronan's mind.

Enough, Ben. Ronan gently pushed him back and out, and Ben separated back into his own slumped body.

Ronan had Cara free. That was what counted.

A loud explosion shook the ore carrier. The camp's warning klaxon screamed.

The door started to slide open. Out in the compound the security lights flared to full brightness. Cara came over the threshold first, followed closely by Ronan.

Quick, here. Ben turned his back and let Ronan slice through his bonds. He had sausage fingers, half-numbed and aching with cramp from the shackles. He couldn't untie his own feet, so Ronan had to free them, too. Luckily, they were just stiff, but not as cramped as his arms.

What's going on? Cara asked.

I am. Archie Tatum sounded proud of himself. *And Gupta is.*

Ben stamped his feet to get rid of incipient pins and needles and ran through the door first with Cara and Ronan close behind. At the far end of the compound a troop of guards swarmed into action.

Move it. Ben dragged Cara forward.

The klaxon sounded again. One of the ore carriers on the landing pad erupted into a fireball. The blast knocked Ben off his feet and seared his face. He hit the ground at the same time as Ronan and saw Cara tuck herself into a protective position away from the heat. The roar of the explosion died down to be replaced by shouting and yelling as men ran all over the place. On the far side of the compound another explosion took out the engine port of a freighter. A second one ripped through a scout vessel, hurling ragged chunks of debris high into the air.

Steady, Arch! Ben said.

That wasn't me! Tatum protested.

Sorry, Gupta said. *A bit too close.*

"Well, score a couple of points for the good guys, anyway." Ronan sounded self-satisfied.

They dropped back and found shelter behind a ground-car. Around them it rained fire. In the glow the running bodies merged into the background.

"There!" Ben indicated the bolt gun in the hand of a fallen guard. It was a crude but effective weapon. "You take it, Cara."

"You trust me?"

"Of course."

He knew that his numbed hands weren't up to handling the delicate action of the trigger. Cara had no liking for the weapon, but he was confident she knew how to use it. It was vicious and unselective, offering spray-burn on its widest setting. On its finest setting it could punch an energy bolt more deadly than a projectile weapon and without the inconvenience of cartridges, but it needed precious seconds, three point two to be precise, to recharge before it was ready to fire a full bolt again.

Ben pointed to a section of the perimeter which was now unguarded. Something whistled past his ear and exploded across the river behind them. They all doubled over to run low across the compound, keeping a light telepathic contact. Around the corner of one of the cabins they came face-to-face with a guard. Ben's pace barely altered. Instead of ducking out, he ran straight ahead, and there was the soft smack of flesh on flesh as the guard went down. Ben grabbed his weapon, forcing his numb fingers round the grip, and hit the man a smart blow on the temple with it to keep him down, not too bothered if he didn't get up again.

Bent on reaching the edge of the compound, Ben wasn't interested in detail. He watched for movement of guards, lights, and men, but regarded the grounded vehicles as obstacles or potential shelter.

Cara faltered by his side.

Ben pulled her along. *Run!*

She ran.

There was one open space between them and the dark edge of the compound. The alarm had subsided, but guards were still scouring the area. The three of them paused, half hidden among a fleet of groundcars. Cara leaned against the metal shell of a parked vehicle and sucked in air. Ben swapped his gun to the other hand and flexed his fingers. Feeling was returning, but slowly.

All right? Ben turned to Ronan.

Ronan just nodded and his hand shook slightly as he grasped the smart-dart gun.

Cara?

Better once we're out of here.

Ben checked the area and nodded for her to move.

Noiselessly, they ran across the last strip between them and freedom. A bolt cracked past, so close that it sent all three of them diving for the ground. Craike came out of the darkness, straight at them, followed by at least ten armed men. Impossible odds. A bolt cracked again.

Cara reacted and dropped the nearest guard with a clean shot. As she came to her feet, she brought her gun up level and aimed it directly at Craike, but she didn't fire.

Ben came out of a roll at an awkward angle, but his talent saved him and he landed upright, perfectly balanced, with his gun on a white-suited man.

The guards dropped back. It was a standoff.

The white buddysuited man raised his arm, drawing Ben's aim. The man's palms opened wide and empty; unarmed. He pulled off his face visor and smiled.

"Ari." Cara breathed his name.

Ben heard the tone of her voice and his gut twisted, but he didn't dare turn around to look at her.

"Take it easy, sweetheart," van Blaiden said. "Tell your gorilla to put his gun down."

Ben's anger surged, but he held the gun steady.

Cara was silent. If only he knew what was going on with her.

He felt Ronan link with him, and just like he had shared his talent for targeting with Ronan, Ronan cut him in on his talent for Empathy.

Cara's feelings hit him like a rock. Ari. The man turned her knees to jelly. She wanted him more than anything in the world.

Ben's weapon never wavered from the center of van Blaiden's forehead. He itched to squeeze the trigger.

Cara swung away from Craike toward Ben. "No, Ben! Put the gun down."

"Fight it, Cara, fight it," Ronan urged. "It's the conditioning. Fight it."

Ben felt her sudden indecision. She began to swing her aim back to Craike, but her arms shook convulsively.

The window of opportunity was barely ajar. Cara's concentration was diverted for only a split-second, but it was all that Craike needed. Shit, the man was fast. He fired off two bolts with frightening precision. Ben got off one shot while in motion but knew it had gone wide.

All options reduced to one, Ben hurled himself toward Cara, feeling the first bolt slice through the air where he'd been. The second exploded above them with awesome power as he drove her down to the ground beneath him, shielding her. *I'm hit,* he thought, feeling the impact, not as pain, but as a solid, heavy force. Then his world closed in and disappeared.

Chapter Thirty-seven

TAKEN

BEN. COME ON, BEN. COME ON. CARA TRIED
to search for some sign of returning consciousness,
but there wasn't a flicker. They should be dead by now, but
they weren't. Mercifully, the impersonal efficiency of Ari's
mercs had saved them. By the time Ari and Craike had
pulled themselves together, Ben, Ronan, and Cara had been
safely immobilized and placed under guard.

They'd been thrown unceremoniously into an ore carrier.
Cara counted her wounds, grazes and bruises mostly, found
nothing life-threatening, and rolled to her knees wanting to
retch.

Ari would take his revenge. She was in no doubt about
that. It had been his plan all along. She thought about everything that had happened since Ari—or rather McLellan
had called her out of the forest, or at least the bits she could
remember. There were still McLellan-shaped holes. Hell!
She'd even had sex with Ari. _Bastard! I'll get you for that!_

Her head ached more than the rest of her. The black sickness had settled on her like a mantle. The block. She understood now. It had ensured her loyalty to Ari and though it
was broken, it had been repaired recently enough so that
residual tendrils of it still shot through her like quartz

through granite. She'd already proved she could fight it . . . she had fought it . . . but could she fight McLellan again?

"Ben!"

"Let me see him." Ronan pulled her aside gently and bent to check Ben. He had no med kit other than a couple of field dressings and emergency pain meds in his belt pouch. Ben had refused them, knowing they'd knock him out for hours, but Ronan had knocked him out anyway—a useful trick. If only it could be used at a distance. While Ben was out, Ronan did what he could, pouring energy toward Ben, stabilizing, revitalizing. There was a scorch mark across the back of Ben's shoulder where the bolt had flashed too close for comfort. The buddysuit had given some protection, but through the charred fabric Cara could see blistered and angry-red flesh. She could also sense the healing process beginning to soothe the wound. Humbly, she drew back, offering to share what psi-strength she had left with Ronan.

"Save it for yourself. I think you might need it." Ronan kept his voice low.

The doors of the ore carrier growled open slowly. Silhouetted against the light was the unmistakable figure of Victor Lorient, surrounded by guards. Ari van Blaiden stood to one side.

Lorient stumbled unceremoniously over the threshold, propelled by a firm hand. As the door began to close, Ari looked through the gloom of the cargo bay directly at Cara. "I haven't forgotten we still have unfinished business," he said.

"What did he mean by that?" Lorient asked.

Cara ignored him. Ari would take his revenge, but first he would make her sweat. She suspected that he would also wait for Ben to regain consciousness. Revenge was much sweeter when your victim had leisure to anticipate it.

Is he any better? she asked Ronan.

Let him be. He needs more time, Ronan said. *Besides, if your ex-boyfriend is as good as his word, you've got trouble brewing. If Ben's conscious, he's just going to try and protect you and he's in no fit state to take on either van Blaiden or Craike.*

You're right. She felt ashamed. She should have thought of that. *They'd kill him just to pay me back. Keep Ben unconscious if you can. Don't try and look after me. It's not your fight, and it's one you'd lose.*

They passed the remainder of the night cold, hungry, and uncomfortable.

This is it, Cara thought, as the ore carrier door opened again. She felt strangely calm, knowing that she had no more choices to make. Two mercs loomed, backlit by the early morning sun.

"You." One of them pointed to Cara and beckoned.

Ronan began to come to his feet between her and them.

Thanks, but remember what we said, she told him. *Ari van Blaiden and I have some unfinished business. Tell Ben I . . . *

You can tell him yourself when you come back, Ronan said.

Don't jolly me along. We both know what the chances are.

You'll find a way. There's no one I'd rather have on my side in a bust-up than you and Ben.

Cara couldn't look at Ben in case her shell cracked. She needed to keep her mind clear of emotion if she was going to survive.

Take care of him for me. Tell him I love him.

I think he knows that.

*Tell him I'm sorry for all the wasted time . . . *

"Hurry. Mr. van Blaiden is waiting." The taller of the two mercs, a slab-faced, dark-skinned man, noticed her hesitation, but caught nothing of her silent communication with Ronan.

Cara stepped out onto the exit ramp. What did Ari want? Revenge? Certainly. The knowledge of what she'd done with his files? Yes, though Mrs. McLellan might have extracted that information already. If she was lucky, she'd just have to face Ari alone, but if she wasn't, then McLellan and Craike would be with him.

Ari and Craike were like two halves of the same being. Ari was the brains and the personality. Craike was the brawn with an underlying streak of pure nastiness. She shuddered, aware her palms were sweaty.

✦ ✦ ✦

The guards weren't Alphacorp, but they looked like a team that worked together regularly. Did Ari have his own fleet now or were they mercenary hirelings? They marched Cara across the dusty compound, still littered with debris. They pushed her up the ramp of the LV and through the doorway into the room in which she'd met Lorient.

Cara's eyes adjusted to the change of light. Ari stood still and quiet behind a slide-out table that was doing duty as a desk.

He stepped out from behind the desk, his soft boots making no sound on the metallic floor. There was an almost overwhelming maleness about him. She would have backed away if there had been somewhere to go.

"Ah, Cara, you know, I don't suppose you'll believe me, but . . ." He laughed—one sharp sound like a dry twig snapping. "I didn't want it to be like this."

She felt him turn on the charm, playing with her emotions. If he was going to try and mess with her mind before he resorted to the heavy stuff, it would buy her some time, but she was determined not to be taken in by him again.

"Tell that to Craike."

"You let me down. I don't handle rejection too well." Ari always had a flair for the melodramatic.

"I owe you one for Donida McLellan, but I'm over you now, Ari." She was bluffing. It was still hard to resist him.

"But you still couldn't let your ape shoot me, could you?" Suddenly his voice was low and passionate. "It's not just a trick. You and I, we had such a good thing together, didn't we?"

She shuddered, whether with pleasure or revulsion was hard to tell, but she couldn't deny it. "Too good." Her voice betrayed her by breaking. She cleared her throat. "It's a pity you spoiled it."

"Your betrayal spoiled it. That hurt." He sounded as though he couldn't quite believe it himself. "It's embarrassingly corny, isn't it? I let sentiment cloud my judgment. I should have listened to Robert. If I had, you would never have come out of cryo after Felcon." He shrugged. "But I thought that with the help of Mrs. McLellan, I could have you back again. We were well-matched, you and I."

Ari was up so close that she could feel the heat from his body and smell his familiar scent.

"Cara." He pushed her up against the wall. His lips found the sensitive spot below her right ear and he kissed the side of her neck above her buddysuit collar. She felt the soft bump of adrenaline in her belly and the back of her knees began to tingle. Her response was automatic, instant and deep. She made as if to put her own arms around him and then froze. "Damn, you, Ari."

His hands lingered on her bottom and his fingers bit into her firm flesh as he pulled her pelvis tight against his. His sexuality was almost overpowering. Like a drowning swimmer she struck out for the surface. She pushed him away, knowing if she let herself go, she'd be lost. Damn McLellan's programming.

"You know, I could make you forget our differences."

"Don't you mean Mrs. McLellan could?"

He shrugged. "You'd never want for anything again, and besides, you've had time to consider the alternatives. You've still got a choice."

A choice. Ari, Craike, and Mrs. McLellan—or Ben. No contest. Ari's face was kissing close. She didn't back off. His lips found hers again, but she didn't respond. He stepped back a pace, as if surprised that she hadn't melted into his arms.

"Don't flatter yourself. It's over." She had to believe that. "So what now? Are you going to kill me?"

"Cara, I couldn't lie to you. I have never killed in cold blood. I couldn't do it."

"Maybe not personally, but you give the orders. Craike, and others like him, are your weapons. That's almost more immoral than if you'd squeezed the trigger yourself. But you've never liked to dirty your own hands, have you?"

"Robert Craike is an extremely skilled technician. The finest in his field. I only choose the best. You can't blame me for that."

"I blame you for a lot of things."

She almost saw Ari's mood swing. "I can see we're not going to get on very far like this. You've just lost your last chance to do things the easy way. Now, Robert." Ari looked to the door.

Craike entered. He was all muscle. She'd always been intimidated by him. That gave him a hold over her. Even when they'd both been, supposedly, on the same side, she'd hated the sadistic streak in his nature; and later, when she had seen him inflict pain, maim and kill, she had known instinctively, whatever his excuse or authority, that he'd done it for pleasure.

Ari backed off. "Perhaps a night with Robert might change your mind. I can assure you, he's very inventive. Maybe you'd like to take on both of us."

Craike grinned at her.

She struggled to subdue her rising panic, fighting to steady her ragged breathing. She transferred her weight onto the balls of her feet, ready to dodge if she had to, and stretched out her awareness for any telltale flicker that Craike was about to move.

"Steady." Ari motioned Craike back and turned to Cara. "For old times' sake, let's be kind to each other. Tell me what you did with my files, and I'll ask Robert to finish it quickly."

So McLellan hadn't managed to get all the information from her. Cara felt a wave of triumph. That was what all this was about.

"How about I tell you and I walk free?"

"You haven't got that kind of bargaining power."

"Haven't I? What if I've lodged copies with the files somewhere safe?" He blanched slightly. Had she scored a point? "You've got me, Ari. Let the others go. They've done nothing to hurt you."

"Wrong. Benjamin messed up Hera-3, and then he took you from me."

"You lost me long before I met Ben."

"Mr. van Blaiden." One of the mercs came in, looking worried.

"Not now."

"But Mr. van Blaiden . . ."

"I said, not now."

Outside, Cara could hear rising voices.

Ari looked to Craike. "Amuse yourself for a moment. I'll be back."

◆ ◆ ◆

"What is it?" Ari let the impatience show in his voice. He'd told them not to disturb him. "This had better be important."

Morton Tengue, captain of his mercenary guards, took responsibility. "Incoming fleet, sir."

"What?" Ari pushed past him into the ATC room and stared at the console. The young operator slid sideways to give him access to the screen, but Ari grabbed his arm and pulled him back. "Stay on it. Tell me what I'm seeing."

"Two waves of ships, sir, and—oh—there's a third."

"How many ships? Have you identified them?"

"Seven in the first wave, sixteen in the second, and three in the third. It's not possible to identify them at this range. I don't have visual yet, but the first seven are big enough to be gunships. The second wave has a mixture of sizes, troopships or cargo carriers and some smaller craft. Skiffs, I think. They're not all giving the same signature. I don't think it's a military fleet or a Monitor action, but whoever they are, they mean business."

"Third wave?"

"Likely private yachts. Whoever's in charge, I'd say. They're hanging back. The first wave is fanning out, and the second wave is coming in fast."

"How fast? How long have we got?"

"Four hours. Six at most."

Was it Crossways or—damn Crowder to hell—was it the Trust? Had he got his own black-ops fleet now? Ari had no doubt that Crowder had planned this all along. Rage rolled through him.

He turned to Captain Tengue. "Tell Ensign Keely to ready my ship for takeoff."

"Yes, sir."

"How spread out are the miners?"

"They've got five teams out prospecting. We can't get all of them back here in less than a day."

"Ignore them, then. How about your own men?"

"We can be ready to lift off in an hour, but I've got twenty men out with the prospectors. I'll not leave them behind."

"You may have to."

He recognized the look on Tengue's face. He'd seen it on the face of principled men all over the galaxy.

"I'm not paying you to get caught, Tengue."

"You're not paying me enough to leave men behind."

Ari nodded. "Suit yourself. Recall your men if you can, but in the meantime, I've got some unfinished business I need you for. After that you're on your own."

"Understood."

✦ ✦ ✦

Craike's fingers tightened on Cara's arms. "An entirely expected pleasure. I told him that the Neural Reconditioning wouldn't hold, but he wouldn't believe me. Said I was jealous. Well, we'll see about jealous, shall we? Have you got those files on you? Shall I search you to find out." He began to pat her all over.

"No."

It didn't matter now.

His hands ran over her belly and down the inside of her thighs.

"I said no!" She kicked out and caught his leg with her boot. Too bad, she'd been aiming for his groin.

He straightened up, backed her right into the wall, and smacked her hard across the mouth with the back of his hand. Her head cracked back into the wall with a bang that she felt in her skull rather than heard. Her vision started to shimmer around the edges, and her knees trembled. She pushed herself back into the wall for support.

"Enough games, we've got trouble." Ari stormed back into the room. "There's a whole bloody fleet on the scanners."

Mother Ramona's fleet. She needed delaying tactics now. "I'll tell you one thing for free, Ari. Crowder set a trap for you here."

"Garrick's fleet, I know."

"No, that was us. Crowder sent you to a plague planet. Endaemia." Cara said. "Your intel was poor."

"Endaemia? Here?" She saw the panic flash across Ari's face.

"Ready to be released. A present from Crowder. We stopped it. It's sealed. But it's still here. Be careful what you open. I could take you to where it is."

"Nice try, but no. Crowder, you say?"

"Yes, good old Crowder."

Cara read Ari's face like a book. "You've been screwed just as much as we have. Crowder wanted you here to get rid of you at the same time as he got rid of Ben. Both of you are the last ones who could blow the whistle on Hera-3. It was you, Ari, wasn't it? You and Craike and your lovely little team?" She thought on her feet, wondering how much she could use.

A young Alphacorp ensign appeared at the door. She glanced at Cara, wide-eyed, and then at Ari. What was a kid like that doing in Ari's team of mercenaries?

"Yes, Ensign Keely?" Ari snapped out.

"Sir, Captain Tengue reports incoming . . ."

"I know," he roared. "Get my ship ready!"

"Yes, sir." She fled.

Ari turned back to Cara. "Thank you for the information. You were always too truthful and too trusting. I'll even up the score with Crowder later. But there's still time for revenge. I never let a disservice go unpunished. Like a fine wine, revenge is sweeter if you allow it to mature."

"Hear me out, Ari. Crowder hasn't gone this far to let you get away again."

"I'll take my chance on that." He nodded to Craike. "I'm done with her. She's yours. I'd enjoy seeing you finish her personally."

Damn Ari to hell. Cara needed to buy time. If Craike decided to finish her quickly, she couldn't escape a clean shot from a bolt gun. She thought fast. Mercy wasn't his style. Craike's one weakness was that he enjoyed the killing process. He enjoyed inflicting pain.

He was also very good at it.

Cold sweat prickled her brow, and she fought to keep her hands from shaking. She couldn't win if everything went by the book.

She focused on Craike, waiting for him to move. "I thought you might be man enough to finish this yourself, Ari. You know my strengths and weaknesses as well as anyone, or is it only in bed where you feel you can beat me?"

Ari was silent for a few moments and then he smiled. "Robert is an expert."

Craike's tongue flickered out to lick his lips in anticipation and he moved forward, reaching for his side arm.

She couldn't wait. She launched herself at Ari, trying to keep him between her and Craike. She grabbed his neck, not a great chokehold, but good enough. Ari shoved backward hard and hurled her against the wall. She took most of the impact on her shoulder and protected her head. She turned to face Craike, praying she wouldn't find herself staring into the muzzle of his bolt gun. Ari had fallen to his knees, gasping and holding his throat, too close to Cara for a bolt. Craike would have to get her away from Ari or finish it hand-to-hand.

She was aware of a noise behind her, the guards. Craike signaled them to stand back. He wouldn't want it known that he needed rescuing. Hell, he didn't need rescuing—she did.

She buried all negative thoughts. They were as likely to get her killed as anything. Even while she was thinking that, Craike came at her, one-two. She avoided his right, but took a punch to the side of her head that set her ears ringing. He followed it with a foot to the guts that she barely rode, and though she countered with a backhand, it connected very lightly. She barely avoided a chop to her throat and twisted, off balance. His foot connected hard with her ribs. Something cracked. It should hurt like hell, but adrenaline buffered the pain.

Rolling, she went for his knees with her feet. He stepped back and hit the wall. Her hand connected with the leg of a small lightweight stool. Hurling it cost her a sharp jab under her left breast, but she didn't let that stop the long arc of the throw. Craike raised a hand to deflect it, but one leg still socked him in the mouth and up under his nose. It was enough to shock him and set his eyes watering.

It was a lucky strike. She doubled her knees under her, pushed upward favoring her left side, and thrust her right shoulder into his diaphragm, knocking him hard against the far wall. There was an audible "oof" as she drove the breath from his lungs. She dived for Craike's bolt gun and, before the two mercs could react, she grabbed it, brought it into line, and blasted a crater in the top of Craike's head at point-blank range. Then she turned it toward Ari, but her luck had run out.

A tangler cord around her knees sent her crashing to the floor and the mercs brought her down in seconds. She got off one more shot, but it went high and wide. One guard yanked her arms above her head and slapped on a pair of ferraflex wrist shackles. She screamed once as her cracked rib stabbed, but he held her firm. The other guard twisted the cord tight around her ankles. Between them, they trussed her like a spit-roast chicken.

Ari's breathing rasped. He rubbed his throat and staggered toward Craike, slumped in a bloody heap, and folded to his knees. "Robert?" The word came as a ragged gasp. Ari took Craike's chin in his hand and straightened the ruined head. "Oh, Robert." He bent over and tenderly kissed Craike's bloodied lips.

He never once kissed me on the lips like that, Cara thought. Shock ran through her. She got Craike's attraction to Ari, but she'd never realized it was reciprocated. Maybe it hadn't been in the early days, but it certainly was now. Were Ari's feelings for her ever real, or had he only been playing her for inside information on missions?

Time was frozen. Even the guards didn't intrude on Ari's grief.

Slowly he stood and turned toward her, eyes red-rimmed, mouth clamped in a tight line.

"Would you have wept like that for me, Ari?" she asked.

He clamped both fists together and used them as a hammer to smash into her unprotected diaphragm. Cara convulsed with the pain of it. All the breath went out of her, and she couldn't seem to suck more in. Her world faded to gray.

✦ ✦ ✦

"She tried to kill me, Mrs. McLellan!" Ari heard his own voice, unusually high-pitched and full of distress. It didn't sound like him. He swallowed hard and fought for control. "She killed Robert. That overrules any other disservice she might ever have done me."

He took a deep breath. Then another.

"I want her to lose something she loves . . . and then I want her to die very painfully. You've got an hour at most to prepare. Don't let me down again."

"Again? With respect, Mr. van Blaiden, I haven't let you down once. I warned you all along that I hadn't had enough time to do a proper job." She clamped her teeth together on whatever else she'd been going to say, took a breath, and started again. "Ensign Keely's readying your ship. Why don't we take Carlinni with us? I can do a much better job back on Sentier-4."

He screwed his right hand into a fist and held it firmly with his left—the only way he could stop himself from backhanding McLellan across the face.

"She kills Benjamin in an hour and then she dies. I want her compliant, but I want her to know what she's done."

"That's delicate work. An hour isn't—"

"Enough excuses. Just do it! Or Sentier-4 will need a new head of Neural Readjustment."

She paled, and he saw fear in her eyes.

"Are we clear?"

"Yes, sir, we're clear."

✦ ✦ ✦

She couldn't see either of them, but the silence that followed spoke volumes. Donida McLellan and Ari van Blaiden weren't such easy partners in crime. And make no mistake, what they'd done to her, between them, was criminal. A well of anger, dark and deep, swirled in the pit of

Cara's stomach. Whatever Donida McLellan thought she could do to her, she'd find a way to fight it.

"Put her in the chair. Strap her down." Cara heard the voice but still couldn't see McLellan. She couldn't miss the mercs, however. They hauled her upright and pressed her into a chair, strapping her wrists to the padded arms. Every movement exploded in a separate agony. Her cracked rib was on fire. Every breath hurt.

"Now then." McLellan stared into her eyes. "Let's see how you managed to beat me so soon."

Cara felt her head splitting apart as Donida McLellan bludgeoned her way into her mind, tearing out recent memories, discarding them, snatching others.

"Ah-ha!" There was triumph in her voice. "A memory stone." She patted Cara's arms, finding the small bulge in her left sleeve pocket. She quickly unsealed it, fished out the stone, smiled smugly, and popped it into her own pocket. "Now let's see how well you do."

Cara saw the stone go and felt her life slip away with it. *No. Please. Bring it back.*

But McLellan just laughed and then slipped into her mind, more subtly this time, not like a sledgehammer but like a stiletto.

There was overwhelming pressure to do nothing to harm Ari van Blaiden or by inaction allow him to be harmed.

Of course, that was a given. Ari had always been her top priority, hadn't he?

Like a stiletto.

Steadily, a picture of Ari built in her brain, from his blue, blue eyes to his shiny boots.

Like a stiletto between ...

Ari. Loyalty, admiration, respect.

Like a stiletto between the ribs!

Love!

That was a lie ... she might have loved him once, but not now. In fact, she'd never really loved him because the Ari she thought she loved was an artificial construct. She gasped at the realization, and fire shot through her left side. Ribs! Use the pain. But how? She needed the memory stone. No! She needed a memory of the memory stone.

She breathed in sharply again, and her ribs seared. She pictured clamping her left hand to the pain. Between the first and second fingers of that hand she pictured a stone, wedged in, tight enough to be uncomfortable.

She breathed in again. *Pain; hand to side; memory stone.*

Again. *Pain; hand to side; memory stone.*

As Donida McLellan ate into her brain, she breathed in time and time again. *Pain; hand to side; memory stone.*

Yes!

Chapter Thirty-eight

TERMINAL

"WILL YOU BE ALL RIGHT NOW?" MRS. MC-Lellan's face was all concern. She handed Cara a cup of water.

"I think so, thanks." She sipped the water and tried to clear her head. "You've been very patient with me. I'm sorry to be such a prima donna."

"Oh, no problems. I've seen agents far more messed up than you are. Still, you did have a tough time. I know Mr. van Blaiden was very concerned, especially about the rape. We didn't think Benjamin would go that far. Nothing in his profile suggested it."

"It's all right, honestly. I can't even remember it. You've done a great job. Still, I'd appreciate the chance to get even with Benjamin."

"I believe Mr. van Blaiden is arranging for you to do just that. For closure."

Cara grasped the arms of her chair to stand herself upright, and a pain shot through her left side. She gasped and put her hand to her ribs.

"Rib bothering you? Benjamin was rough. Here's a blast pack of analgesic."

Cara reached out with her left hand to take the shot, and stared at it, briefly puzzled that she wasn't holding anything

between her first two fingers. She shook her head and
slapped the analgesic to the side of her neck feeling the
warmth flood through her and chase away the lingering
ache from her cracked rib. "That's better. I'm ready now."

"Mr. van Blaiden is outside. He's waiting for you."

Ari! A ripple of apprehension ran through Cara as she
came down the ramp from the LV flanked by two mercs. Ari
turned his blue, blue eyes on her, but instead of seeing her
own affection reflected, she saw them cold and hard as dia-
monds. What had she done to displease him? What did she
need to do to regain his approval? He wasn't mad at her for
Benjamin, was he? It was hardly her fault.

A sudden brief memory flashed and was gone, leaving a
sweet aftertaste of walking down that ramp with Ben for
the first time and him calling her Mrs. Bemjin, teasing her
about her inability to get going again after cryo. A false
memory. Or at least, she *had* walked down the ramp with
Benjamin, but her perception was still skewed by the conditioning Mrs. McLellan had put in place to enable her to
carry out this assignment. She could never have fooled Benjamin if she hadn't believed it herself.

"It's time," Ari said. "The only way you can free yourself."

A groundcar pulled up. Two mercs prodded Ben Benjamin
and Ronan Wolfe out of the back, arms shackled behind
them. Another two mercs formed up to either side. Wolfe
looked exhausted, but Benjamin looked ill. The shoulder of
his buddysuit was charred as if from a bolt gun.

Her head spins, and she's briefly in another place.

She's running across the compound, explosions all around.
Ben and Ronan are with her. They have to get away. She
drops and twists, taking out the nearest guard with a clean
shot. She doesn't even have time to think that it's a human
being she's killed. He would have done the same to her if he'd
had the chance. As she comes to her feet, she brings her gun
up level and aims it directly at Craike.

Ben comes out of a roll at an awkward angle, but he lands
upright, perfectly balanced. He's good! Her appreciation of
Ben turns on itself as he trains his gun on a white buddy-
suited man. Ari! Ari in danger.

She waivers. Craike fires off two bolts with frightening pre-

cision. Ben leaps for her, their bodies connecting, going down in a tangle of arms and legs. His weight drives all the air out of her body, knocks her gun flying. She hears the bolt gun crack twice, smells the burning air, burning flesh. Ben goes limp on top of her.

She snapped back into the present.

Between them, the four guards forced Ben and Ronan to their knees about two meters apart.

"Kill them, Cara. Benjamin first." Ari nodded and stepped back. The guard on her left handed her his knife. It was meant for business, a slim eighteen-centimeter blade, carbon black, frictionless. The handle was molded to fit his hand, but even though her hand was smaller, it felt well balanced with a nice heft to it. A good killing knife.

You can do this. Donida McLellan was in her head. *You need to do this. You need closure. Up close and personal. Knife across the throat. The bastard will never grin at you again as he's inside your body, taking what's yours.*

"Ben?"

"Hey, Cara. How are you?" His voice was low, easy. He looked at her eyes, not at the knife. He wasn't grinning now, but there was something in his eyes. Concern, maybe.

She sees him smiling down at her. They are in bed and her body is still singing. He leans over and blows a raspberry on her belly button. She pulls his head down into her breasts, but they aren't big enough to suffocate him in, so they both dissolve into easy laughter. What would the psi-techs think of their commander if they saw him now, hair loose, completely relaxed? They'd probably think that he was a very nice guy. She used to think that nice was a mediocre adjective, but Ben doesn't have a mean bone in his body.

She puzzled, searching for the reason she had to hate him. She remembered their first time.

She's sleeping with him to worm her way into his affections. She's lying in a bed in a room in the visitor center on Mirrimar-14. She's thinking of Ari, and she mustn't or she won't be able to go through with this.

Benjamin reaches across to pull the sheet up, his hand brushing against her breast. She flinches before she can stop herself.

"Did I hurt you?" His voice is full of concern.

"No. You were wonderful."

She tries to make him feel good, but she's not sure he's buying it.

It wasn't good sex, but it wasn't rape. In fact, didn't she instigate it? She faltered and turned to look at Ari, standing about twenty meters away as if he didn't trust her with a knife in her hand. Mrs. McLellan was standing beside him. Where was Craike?

Craike with a crater blown in his head. The stink of burned flesh and singed hair. Ari kissing Craike's bloody lips.

She took a deep breath and felt a sharp stab in her ribs. She put her left hand up to the sudden pain and felt a discomfort between her first and second fingers. That was a bloody silly place to wedge a stone. She looked down. There was no stone there, just a memory of one.

Oh, fuck! She breathed out and looked at Ben again. She could see the pain lines etched into his face from the burn on his shoulder, but Ronan must have done a good job because he was awake, upright, and holding his pain in.

"I'm fine, now," she murmured, not daring to risk mind-to-mind contact with Ben. Donida McLellan was too close. "How are you?"

"I've been better." Despite everything, his eyes held a smile that was just for her. "But I'll hold together for a while longer."

She raised the knife, holding it lightly in her right hand. "I'm supposed to use this."

"I know. Do it quickly if you're going to."

"I killed Craike. He's not going to let me live."

Finish him! Donida McLellan was in her mind again. She felt her grip on the knife tighten, and she took a pace forward involuntarily.

Ben's eyes narrowed.

A tiny explosion of dust at her feet drew her attention. A sapper bot, barely three centimeters long erupted from the pounded earth, crossed the short distance between her and Ben, and disappeared behind him. She didn't dare let her eyes follow it.

Kill him. Take the knife, cross over, stand behind him.

Left hand under chin, swipe the blade across his throat in one clean movement. Watch the blood spray over the ground. Let him fall forward, choking out his life. Feel immense satisfaction. Justice at last. Right the wrongs. Do it!*

Cara felt her right foot take a step forward all by itself. She glanced back to where Ari and Donida McLellan stood together. McLellan had one hand out. Ari was supporting her. Supporting her! Getting inside Cara's head and staying there was obviously taking its toll.

McLellan wasn't invincible.

A light switched on in Cara's head. McLellan had taught her some hard lessons, but she'd always been a good student.

See how the abused learns to abuse! She wasn't sure whether she sent that thought at McLellan or whether it was purely for herself. She turned back to Ben. Locked eyes with him, felt energy flow, felt Ronan in the mix. She expanded to take in Ronan's strength as well and then seized McLellan's last thought and turned it back toward her.

She's in a corridor and there's a door with a small clear panel in it.

Place: Sentier-4.

She peers through the window and sees a bank of machines; a padded chair with a movement restraint and there's someone standing beside it. A woman, thin and dark.

Name: Donida McLellan.

She takes the woman, grasps her by the shoulders, turns her around, and stares into her eyes. The woman stares back, supremely confident. Then her confidence wavers. Cara hisses, "It was you who raped me, you bastard. You and Ari van Blaiden. You. Will. Pay. Both of you."

She forces the woman backward into the chair. She stares her down. Implants meshing. She gives her nowhere to hide. See how you like it, Mrs. McLellan! You've taken your last victim. She goes deep into the woman's head, finds the source of her power, the core of her implant and . . . switches it off.

She backs away, leaving the woman in the chair, head lolling to one side, a thin trickle of drool coming from one corner of her slack mouth. She turns and runs toward the light; running blindly, stumbling forward.

Someone catches her.

Ben.

McLellan dropped to her knees, scrabbling at Ari's arm. He stepped back, shaking her off like a street beggar, his face a mask of surprise and revulsion. She didn't even look human anymore.

Cara was free of McLellan at last. Reality crystallized. She'd been on the run. There had never been a deep-cover mission. They'd needed her information, and Ari had been playing games for his own amusement. Maybe for revenge. Who could tell what went on inside Ari's head. The man was a menace. A dangerous menace.

And unless she did something about it right now, they'd never be able to touch him for all his crimes. He'd have his mercs kill Ben and Ronan, kill her and probably Lorient as well, and he'd waltz home to Alphacorp with a platinum planet in the bag. Fireproof. Unless . . .

She had the knife. Ari was twenty or thirty paces away at a dead run, preoccupied with an insensate McLellan. Of the half dozen guards, only two were close enough to give her any trouble physically, though they might all be dead shots. She had to try . . .

An echo of: *protect Ari at all costs,* flicked through her brain, and she squashed it.

She turned.

Don't. Ben was inside her head.

This is the only chance.

I know. Ben powered up from his knees, his hands freed now by Archie's bot. He barreled into her, snatching the knife from her grip and throwing it underhand in one smooth move.

As she crashed to the floor, Ben's arms around her protectively, the world turned upside down and she saw Ari frozen for an instant with a look of surprise on his handsome, cruel face, the hilt of the knife protruding from his right eye. Then his knees buckled, and he collapsed to the ground, twitched horribly, and lay still.

She heard shouting and an explosion rocked the compound. Ben pulled her head in close to his chest and another heavy weight landed on the other side of her. Ronan.

A second explosion and a third. Then the sound of craft screaming overhead, people running, utter confusion. The three of them huddled together while the world went mad.

She didn't know how long it was before the dust cleared and Ronan rolled sideways. Ben took a moment or two longer before he relinquished his hold on her. By the time they'd pulled themselves together and Cara had managed to stand upright, cursing her rib, the first of the ships from Crossways was already down on the landing pad and van Blaiden's mercs had surrendered. Ari himself was tumbled like a discarded toy among the debris while Donida McLellan still scrabbled at his corpse pathetically, fingers hooked into talons, eyes locked in a thousand-meter stare.

Two black-suited soldiers picked up the shrieking McLellan between them and carried her away. Cara stared at Ari and the knife horrifically protruding from his skull. She felt her gorge rising and turned quickly to Ben, standing quietly behind her, his face gray with exhaustion and pain.

"How do you feel?" Ben asked.

"About Ari? Ask me this time next year. Anyway, I should be asking you that. How's the shoulder?"

"Holding for now."

She heard the tension in his voice and knew he was lying, but he didn't give her time to be solicitous. They walked toward where Mother Ramona and a man she presumed was Norton Garrick stood by their cruiser, attended by a small squad of personal guards. Behind them, Gen and Max emerged from the *Solar Wind*, hand in hand, grinning and waving.

"Where are Wenna and Lorient?" Cara asked.

"Ronan's gone to free them. Van Blaiden had them both dumped back in the ore carrier," Ben said. "Lorient was supposed to contemplate the benefits of signing the contract."

"He didn't sign?"

"Said you told him not to."

"I did?" She shook her head. "I can't have been as far gone as I thought, not all of the time anyway."

"You've always been a lot stronger than you give yourself credit for."

"I'm not sure about that. I feel as though I've been holding onto the edge of sanity with my fingernails."

"You held on, and you didn't let go, and I love you for it, Mrs. Bemjin."

"Oh . . ." She stopped in mid-stride.

"What is it?"

"I'm not."

"What?"

"Mrs. Bemjin."

"Does it matter?"

She relaxed and smiled.

Then they were shaking hands with Mother Ramona and Garrick. She was hugging Gen and Max. Everyone was asking questions at once and trying to answer them at the same time. Archie Tatum was walking across the compound toward them, still lugging a crate of bots and . . . it was all too much. Cara's side hurt like fury and her knees felt wobbly. She still wasn't sure if she was going to throw up, and all she really wanted to do was lie down and close her eyes.

She grabbed Ben's hand. "Can we get out of here?"

He squeezed her fingers and nodded toward the *Solar Wind*, still standing with her ramp down. "Look at that." He grinned. "Gen didn't break my shiny new toy."

"Are you sure? Should we go and check?"

"Let's do that."

She forgot to let go of his hand as they walked toward the *Solar Wind*. Together.

S. Andrew Swann
The Apotheosis Trilogy

It's been nearly two hundred years since the collapse of the
Confederacy, the last government to claim humanity's colonies. So when signals come in revealing lost human colonies that could shift the power balance, the race is on
between the Caliphate ships and a small team of scientists
and mercenaries. But what awaits them all is a threat far
beyond the scope of any human government.

PROPHETS
978-0-7564-0541-0

HERETICS
978-0-7564-0613-4

MESSIAH
978-0-7564-0657-8

To Order Call: 1-800-788-6262
www.dawbooks.com

CJ Cherryh

The Foreigner Novels

"Serious space opera at its very best by one of the leading SF writers in the field today." —*Publishers Weekly*

"Her world building, aliens, and suspense rank among the strongest in the whole SF field. May those strengths be sustained indefinitely, or at least until the end of *Foreigner*." —*Booklist*

To Order Call: 1-800-788-6262

www.dawbooks.com

CJ Cherryh
Complete Classic Novels in Omnibus Editions

To Order Call: 1-800-788-6262
www.dawbooks.com

Gini Koch
The Alien *Novels*

"Gini Koch's Kitty Katt series is a great example of the lighter side of science fiction. Told with clever wit and non-stop pacing, this series follows the exploits of the country's top alien exterminators in the American Centaurion Diplomatic Corps. It blends diplomacy, action, and sense of humor into a memorable reading experience." —*Kirkus*

"Amusing and interesting...a hilarious romp in the vein of 'Men in Black' or 'Ghostbusters'." —*VOYA*

To Order Call: 1-800-788-6262
www.dawbooks.com

Tanya Huff
The *Confederation* Novels

"As a heroine, Kerr shines. She is cut from the same mold as Ellen Ripley of the Aliens films. Like her heroine, Huff delivers the goods." —*SF Weekly*

A CONFEDERATION OF VALOR
Omnibus Edition
(*Valor's Choice, The Better Part of Valor*)
978-0-7564-0399-7

THE HEART OF VALOR
978-0-7564-0481-9

VALOR'S TRIAL
978-0-7564-0557-1

THE TRUTH OF VALOR
978-0-7564-0684-4

To Order Call: 1-800-788-6262
www.dawbooks.com